E. H. Alger

Website: https://ehalger.weebly.com
Twitter: @MySaldana
Instagram: Benapearl

A catalogue record for this book is available from the National Library of Australia

National Library of Australia Prepublication Record
Author: Alger, E.H., author.
Title: Winterhued / E.H. Alger.

ISBN: 9780648172505 (paperback)

Subjects: Fantasy | Australian
Princesses--Fiction.
Fantasy fiction.
Genre: Speculative fiction.

WINDSHIP

WINDSHIP PRESS

Bena, Victoria, Australia
https://windshippress.weebly.com

Winterhued

E. H. ALGER

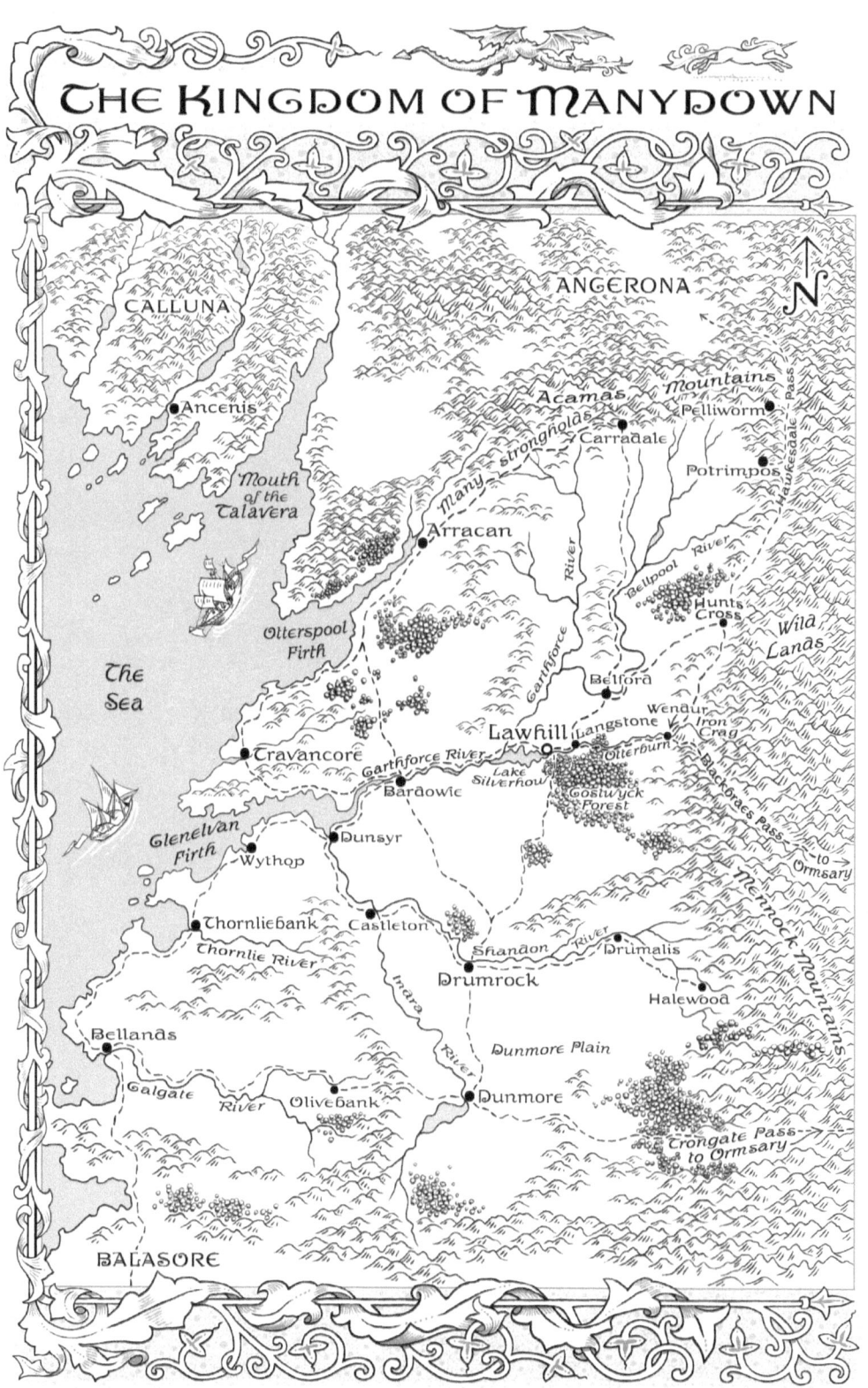

THE KINGDOM OF MANYDOWN

CALLUNA

ANGERONA

N

Ancenis

Acamas Mountains
Pelliworm

Many strongholds
Carradale

Potrimpos

Mouth
of the
Talavera

Arracan

Garthforce River

Bellpool River

Hunts
Cross

Wild
Lands

Otterspool
Firth

Belfora

The
Sea

Wendur
Iron
Crag

Lawhill Langstone

Travancore

Garthforce River

Bardowie

Lake
Silverhow

Otterburn

Costuyck
Forest

Blackbraes Pass

to
Ormsary

Glenelvan
Firth

Dunsyr

Wythop

Mennock Mountains

Thornliebank

Castleton

Drumalis

Shandon River

Thornlie River

Drumrock

Halewood

Bellanas

Dunmore Plain

Galgate River

Olivebank

Dunmore

Trongate Pass
to Ormsary

BALASORE

Dedication

To Cecilia Dart-Thornton for her unfailing inspiration
and encouragement, and to my sister Carolyn , the book's
first reader and champion.

ONTENTS

Map vii

Dramatis Personae xi

Prologue 1

Chapter One 1

Chapter Two 25

Chapter Three 51

Chapter Four 75

Chapter Five 101

Chapter Six 123

Chapter Seven 149

Chapter Eight 181

Chapter Nine 213

Chapter Ten 241

Chapter Eleven 267

Chapter Twelve 297

Chapter Thirteen 323

Chapter Fourteen 349

Chapter Fifteen 383

Chapter Sixteen 413

Chapter Seventeen 441

DRAMATIS PERSONAE

WITHIN CASTLE LAWHILL

The Royal Family & the princess's ladies-in-waiting

King GERS, *son of King Caradoc and grandson of King Bragdo*

Princess WINTERHUED, *only child of King Gers and heir to the throne*

Lady NOMIA, Countess of Dunsyre, *cousin to Winterhued and married to Sir Auchencairn*

Lady BRENN, *Winterhued's second cousin and her youngest Lady-in-Waiting*

Lady ULIDIA, Marchioness of Thornliebank, *senior Lady-in-Waiting, wife of Sir Garthwray*

Lady AMINTA, *Lady-in-Waiting, daughter of Sir Garthwray and Lady Ulidia, twice widowed and presently betrothed to the Earl of Bellands*

Lady BENICIA, *Lady-in-Waiting, oldest daughter of the Duke of Drumrock, betrothed to Sir Criffel*

Lady MANICIA, *Lady-in-Waiting, youngest daughter of the Duke of Drumrock*

Lady PERA, *Lady-in-Waiting, daughter of Lord Ladstock*

Councillors, courtiers, knights & nobles

Sir AUCHENCAIRN, Earl of Dunsyre, Constable of the Realm, Knight of the Four Winds, King's Champion, *married to Lady Nomia, Winterhued's cousin*

Lord HIGHMOOR, Chancellor of the Realm

Sir GARTHWRAY, Marquess of Thornliebank, Butler of the Realm, *married to Lady Ulidia*

Lord LADSTOCK, Chamberlain of the Realm

Sir GUNFORD, Captain of the Royal Guard

Sir AUDNY, Duke of Travancore

Sir PARCHIM, Marquess of Potrimpos, *last descendant of the Neaths of Potrimpos*

The Duke of DRUMROCK, *the King's best friend and father of Benicia and Manicia*

Lord TEMPLEMORE, *former suitor to Winterhued*

Sir CRIFFEL, Earl of Dunmore, *former suitor to Winterhued, betrothed to Lady Benicia*

Lord PRIWALL, Ambassador *(from Balasore, Manydown's peaceful southern neighbour)*

Sir STOREGRUND, Constable *(of Castle Lawhill)*

Sir ALMENDRAL, Marquess of Carradale, *visiting from the north, a member of the Carigerne family, son of the Duke of Arracan and married to Lady Fennia*

Sir DECHMONT, *nephew of the Duke of Drumrock and knight of Sir Auchencairn's brave company*

Sir WYNFORD & Sir HOWTH, *knights of Sir Auchencairn's brave company*

Sir SOUKAR, *knight of good family but little significance*

Squires, servants & underlings

ANCAIOS ('Stench'), *from a family of latrine cleaners (or gong-farmers)*

EUDORA, *scullery maid of Callunian descent, promoted by Winterhued to chamber maid*

DECCAN of Wythop, *squire to Sir Soukar, and soon to be a knight; promised to Lady Brenn*

JERSBEK, *a squire; colleague of Deccan and liegeman of Winterhued*

KYNANCE, *a young squire*

ORLA, *chamber maid to Winterhued*

GARSTON, *man-at-arms, servant to Sir Criffel*

ESTO, *man-at-arms, servant to Sir Criffel*

MASHONA, *Lady Brenn's maid-servant who had accompanied her from Drumalis*

ELSEWHERE IN MANYDOWN

A knight unnamed, sometimes called 'The Knight of the Unicorn'

NAL of Pengworm, *the knight's squire, son of a baker*

The Duke of ARRACAN, *powerful lord in the north, head of the Carigerne family*

Lady FENNIA, Marchioness of Carradale, *former lady-in-waiting and friend to Winterhued, married to Sir Almendral*

Sir DARTFORD, Earl of Drumalis, *former suitor to Winterhued, father of Lady Brenn*

Lady LITA, Countess of Drumalis, *Winterhued's cousin, mother of Lady Brenn and married to Sir Dartford*

Mistress MAYHILL, *innkeeper in the village of Wendur*

ZINITA and TAMARIS, *young girls living in Wendur*

Sir ADDERLEY ('The Adder'), *leader of a gang of outlaws terrorising travellers in and about the Forest of Gostwyck*

Sir RATHDOWN RAVENHILL, Commander *(of Manydown's army)*

Sir PINMORE, *a lieutenant in Manydown's army*

Lord ROSEBERY, Sir LYNTON and Sir HOLLINWOOD, *captains in Manydown's army*

SINDIA, *a camp follower travelling with the army*

PROLOGUE

Winterhued was as cold as death. Her tears froze as they fell, whirling in the bitter wind like shards of glass. She stood atop a vertiginous rock at the edge of the world, a place where nothing was remembered and tales were never told, and gazed through her tears at the mountain range that stretched to her right and to her left, further than eyes could see. Upon its precipitous flanks, half a league below her feet, an ocean of clouds broke like waves against a cliff.

Winterhued did not know why she stood alone at the verge of the world. She did not know why her tears flowed and her heart ached. She could not recall whether she'd been here for a moment or for an eternity, but she knew that time meant nothing in this place. Beneath the beat of the sun and the slow blink of the moon, pounded by the *immense ocean of air that ebbs and flows like sea-tides above the world, these iron escarpments endured, unheeding and unseen.*

She turned from the edge. Reeling, weightless before the wind, she drifted through a waste of snow and tumbled rock, scored by crevices. The wind hunted her, moaning across gale-bitten bluffs and wailing down deep clefts where ice hung in ragged veils.

But, beside herself, not a living thing shrank from its gelid touch, for only bones of the long-dead lay upon these folded heights. Huge bones, hollow and bleached; they cracked and crunched beneath her feet. She climbed over and around them; ascending a high point she looked out across more bones, half swallowed by snow, piled in gullies and scattered across distant ridges. Thighbones and ribs poked gaunt fingers at the sky.

Winterhued sobbed; her grief hurt like a wound. 'Yet I know not why,' she whispered. Still the merciless wind pushed her on.

The lowering sun dazzled her eyes. It cast a blade of light across a vale between two crags and turned the pool of water in its centre to molten gold. Winterhued stumbled to a halt, shading her eyes with shaking hands.

''Tis a pool of tears,' she breathed, 'and I am dreaming. But this is no dream.'

Beside the pool were more bones. These were not bleached and scattered, but black with blood and held together by vestiges of sinew. They rose above the trampled ground like a ruined edifice, vast and tenuous. Shreds of flesh, clinging to splintered ribs, flapped in the wind. Out over the spattered rocks sagged the remnants of wings, fused to the ground by old blood. At one end of a shattered spine, a lean head the size of a dray turned an empty eye socket to the sky. Its muzzle, snarled back from teeth like bloody scythes, was half-sunken in the pool as if it tried to slake an impossible thirst.

The wind wailed over the pass, crumpling the pool's surface. And from high above, resonating on the wind's breath, came a cry

– a desolate, animal cry. It was a cry from a throat that had never cried and it made the immovable mountains shudder.

Winterhued fell to her knees, her hands over her head. But she could not shut out that terrible cry or the sound of the wings as they came thudding down through the air above her like the world's heartbeat, gusting like a gale and knocking her into the snow. She lay blindly, face down, gripped by numbing terror, waiting for talons…

CHAPTER 1

A t the edge of all that was known, a mountain reared its peak into
the sharp winds and driven snow of late winter. Beyond its flanks
lay the Wild Lands where no man trod, but before it, undulating for
many peaceful leagues between the mountain and the sea, lay the prosperous land of Manydown. Dwellers in that land had a name for the
mountain – they called it Iron Crag – but they seldom ventured into its
dark and tangled woods and they did not like to think of the drear
spirits that haunted its wind-blasted heights.

Yet scarce three day's ride from uncanny Iron Crag, over the settled
land to the west, where fields lay fallow under puddles of half-thawed
snow and beasts lowed companionably in warm byres, stood a great,
grey castle by a wide, silver lake.

Like a beast the castle crouched, its staunch feet planted below the
still waters, its mighty battlements shouldering the wide sky. A town

of spires and steep, tiled roofs huddled against its enduring flanks. Cold under cloud were its stones and warm in the sunlight. The seasons and the years passed over its bulk like cloud shadows on a windy day.

Through many a season and many a year, Princess Winterhued, heir to Manydown's throne, had walked the long galleries and climbed the narrow stairs in great Castle Lawhill by the lake. Every morning she had woken in her chamber where lake-light danced on the ceiling.

'I'm growing old,' she sighed one late winter's morn, yawning as she sat in her linen-draped bathtub with soapsuds up to her chin and the steam curling. There was no lake-light this day, only the glow of fire and lamp, for beyond the frost-painted window panes dawn's first gleam barely penetrated the fog that lay heavy upon the waters.

'Nay, ma'am,' puffed her lady-in-waiting, old Ulidia, as she soaped the princess's back. 'While most of us are busy at that, m'lady doth never grow old, and certain it is, there's not a body in the land wouldn't call her the most beautiful in it.'

'Fibber,' said the princess. She flicked some suds at Ulidia, which clung and hung from the old woman's chin like a little beard.

But indeed, most would have called Winterhued beautiful. Her eyes were great and dark, her skin was clear and fair and her long black hair, tied now into an ample knot, was plenteous. Most famously, the princess possessed a slight smile that was known the length and breadth of Manydown and was talked about in lands beyond. It was a smile that had inspired poets and painters and it seemed to hold the secret of the world.

As well as her smile and her hair and her eyes, any person fortunate enough to have seen her this morning disrobed for her bath could well have delighted in her form: so slender still, yet shapely. And all who knew her every morning and every day, even if discomfited sometimes by her quick temper, most often took joy in her compassion and her wisdom, though they may have wondered why she seldom laughed.

Yet it is unlikely that any of them, even faithful Ulidia, suspected that sometimes, alone in her chamber, the princess wept.

But now she smiled to see Ulidia wipe away her beard of soapsuds.

'Wait till my lady hath seen as many years as myself,' said the old woman as she trotted over to the fire to spread linen towels to warm before the flames; 'then she may talk of 'old'. Why, this very morn when my maid woke me, I rubbed my face and felt the bristles poking from my chin and thought "ah, the silly wench hath woken my husband instead of me".'

The princess laughed aloud, surprised at Ulidia's jest. But the old woman looked up in confusion from where she bent over at the hearth. 'Begging m'lady's pardon,' she said, 'but it seemeth to me no laughing matter when a woman sprouteth whiskers from her chin.'

'Ah, Ulidia,' said the princess, disappointed to see that the old woman had not, after all, grown a sense of humour, 'thou hast my permission to laugh at me when I sprout some of my own.' She yawned again, twice, three times.

'So sleepy?' said Ulidia straightening from her task. ''Tis not like m'lady.'

'Nay, it is not,' agreed the princess; 'but of late I lie wakeful half the night.'

'Wakeful?' gasped Ulidia, tottering back towards the bathtub, 'Why hath my lady not told her old Ulidia? I could make for her a draught…'

'Canst thou make a draught to prevent dreams? For that is why I do not sleep. I am afraid to, for when I do I fall straight into a terrible dream.' The princess's voice sank low. 'It is always the same dream and it fills me with fear.'

'Oh my dear! Wherefore should my lady suffer nightmares when she doth live safe and sound with the love of the king and all her…' Ulidia paused; her ears had detected a faint knock at the door.

It opened and a pale face looked in, eyes barely raised above the floor. The rest of a thin girl followed after, half carrying, half dragging a brimming wooden bucket, steam rising from its contents into the morning air. Once inside the door she shut it behind her and bobbed an awkward curtsey.

'Thou tookst thy time,' grumbled Ulidia, glaring at her with eyes like black beads. 'Bring the bucket to the tub, then go.'

A wan thing the girl looked, dressed in a gown of grey serge covered with an apron. A few strands of brown hair escaped from beneath her linen cap. She glanced up once, quickly, and her eyes were blue.

Lugging the bucket towards the tub, she lowered her head once more for she was aware of her position: to be seen by no one and to see nothing herself beside the task before her.

'Get a move on!' snapped Ulidia, but her impatience only caused the girl to stumble so that hot water spilled down her apron and poured into her shoes. She dropped the bucket and more water sloshed out to form a puddle on the floor's rush matting. The unfortunate girl stared at the puddle and a moan escaped her lips.

'Poor child. To carry it all this way...' began the princess sympathetically, but Ulidia threw up her hands. 'Who on earth,' she shrieked, 'sent such a tardy drudge as thee to m'lady's chamber? Fie on thee, stupid child! Don't stand there wringing thy foolish hands, dripping water hither and yon. Pick up the bucket... nay, nay, give it here! Now get on... I never heard tell of a body kept from work by a wet apron. What art thou at? Fie! Leave that... take that other bucket... nay, nay, that one thou daft thing! Th'art fortunate there be water enough left in this or I'd send thee straight off for some more. Now, away with thee!' Ulidia waved her hands at the girl as if at an insect. 'And do not return,' she snapped as she herded the servant out the door, 'to empty the bath until the princess be gone from here.' The sound of the door shutting almost covered her closing remark. 'Clod-footed and empty headed,' she muttered, 'like all of thy race.'

'Ulidia,' said Winterhued, a note of warning in her voice. Suds ran from her as she stood up in the bathtub.

'Well, anyone can see she be Callunian,' said the old woman; 'look at those washy eyes.' She tested the heat of the water in the partly emptied bucket, picked it up and got herself up on a stool beside the tub. Even then she had to reach up to tip the clean water over the princess's shoulders. 'Slow and stupid and strange they be,' she puffed, 'and conniving; they won't ever look a person straight in the eyes. Keep to their own ways they do and the tales I've heard tell of their secret gatherings and goings-on...'

'Ulidia, thou art too old for this task,' said the princess, stepping from the tub. 'I shall have the Lady Aminta assist me; she is younger and stronger and will not bore me with thoughtless remarks...'

'Aminta!' gasped Ulidia, struggling down from the stool. 'Aminta loveth no-one but herself...'

'...and with groundless rumours spread by scaremongers, liars and cowards,' finished the princess. 'Where is my towel, old object? And thou dost call Callunians slow.'

'My lady,' moaned Ulidia as she trotted over to fetch the towels, 'do not send me away... would Aminta lift a bucket? Nay, she'd fill the chamber with scuddles and drudges, spilling water on the floor and leering at my lady. And could she dress my lady? Do her hair...? Oh my lady, Aminta knoweth not her highness as the silly old woman Ulidia knoweth her.'

'The silly old Ulidia doth deceive herself,' said Winterhued, pulling the towel from the old woman, 'for she hath just proven that she knoweth me not at all. Leave it, I shall dry myself. Hast thou fetched my gown? Thinkst thou I have all day to idle here listening to thy nonsense?'

Ulidia hurried into the wardrobe, a small room between the chamber and the garderobe, where Winterhued's gowns hung on rods and her cloaks and undergarments lay folded within scented chests. At the doorway she stepped over a little tabby cat where it lay sprawled after overheating itself in front of the fire.

'Aminta... never Aminta,' she could be heard moaning as she knelt to pull garments from a chest. (Which was strange considering that Aminta was Ulidia's only daughter.) She was silent for a moment before calling out bravely: 'How can my lady think my words nonsense?'

She came back through the door, tripping over the cat on her way. 'What of His Highness, my lady's father?' She tottered towards the princess, her arms laden with garments. '*He* hath little to say for Callunians and he is the king. The king, my lady! And look,' she said, regaining her balance and indicating the damp floor, 'here be the proof... a watery puddle to match her water-puddle eyes. A clumsy, stupid, strange thing like all...'

'And thou, Ulidia,' interrupted the princess, 'art mean and dull-witted like so many Manydownians. What proof is that? Hath no Manydownian ever spilled a bucket of water? Not that gown,' she said, plucking the garment from Ulidia's pile and dropping it on the floor. 'Fetch the dark blue damask.' She pulled the undergarments from Ulidia's arms and began to dress herself.

Ulidia gathered up the unwanted gown and trotted back to the wardrobe. Tears brimmed in her little black eyes. The cat scampered out of her way and jumped onto the bed.

'Dull witted,' mumbled Ulidia from the wardrobe, her voice a whimper amongst the slitherings and rustlings of silk and damask. 'Dull witted sayeth my lady, but my old wits are not so dull that I do not remember why my lady looketh fondly upon Callunians.' She paused for a moment. 'Yet I also recall that, betwixt all the wailing and weeping that went on, she did name that particular Callunian "dullard" and "dolt".'

Winterhued looked sharply at Ulidia as the old woman came back through the door. 'That was long ago,' she said. 'I was but a child. Ulidia, do not weep; I do not want Aminta.' She laughed humorlessly. 'Manydownian or Callunian, all men are fools.'

Ulidia sniffed. 'How can my lady say such a thing?' she said. 'Men are our lords and masters.' Pushing aside the cat, she draped the princess's gown over the bed then returned across the room. 'Yet mayhap there be some sooth in it,' she said, knees cracking as she squatted down at the princess's feet to hold open an underskirt, 'for where was the husband, I ask you, who should have been nigh to feast his eyes upon my lady as she rose shining from her bath?'

The princess stepped into the underskirt. 'I need no husband,' she said, 'and certainly no lord, or master.'

'Mayhap not my lady, but I'm sure all of us lesser women do,' said Ulidia as she pulled up the garment and tied it at the princess's back. It was of satin that gleamed like the sky at dusk.

''Tis they that need you,' said Winterhued, 'Where, for instance, would Sir Garthwray be without his Lady Ulidia?'

The old woman gave a gasping laugh, ridiculously pleased. 'Doth my lady then forgive her old Ulidia?' she asked as she went to fetch the gown.

'As always, my dear,' said Winterhued, stooping to put on her shoes, 'yet it grieveth me that, despite gathering years aplenty, thou hast never gathered much in the way of wisdom.'

'The gathering of years is easy,' puffed Ulidia as she returned with the heavy gown. 'I cannot mislay years, try as I might, whereas if ever I happen upon a thought, straight away do I mislay it.'

Ulidia helped her mistress into the gown of midnight damask. She pulled tight the laces at the back and tied them.

'It must be pleasant,' said the princess, 'to possess a mind untroubled by thought.' She smoothed the skirts that fell full below the high waistline and lengthened behind to form a train.

'Well, I have got by,' said Ulidia. 'My old father (bless his memory) was always wont to say that a woman's thoughts are worth less than dust swept out the door.'

Winterhued looked sadly at the old woman as she fastened a jeweled belt about the gown's high waist. 'Alas, Ulidia,' she sighed, 'that is the sort of arrant nonsense that dribbles endlessly from the mouths of men. My father for one.'

'My lady!' protested Ulidia. 'He is the king, m'lady...'

'Even the brains of kings,' said Winterhued, 'may shrink and grow sluggish from lack of use. Our king groweth more addle-pated by the minute. Oh, why so anxious? Methinks thou remembrest too well the reign of my grandsire. He would have had thine ears off just for hearing such a thing, but my father...'

The princess broke off with a stifled cry and spun round as something thudded and scraped against the window.

'Oh,' she gasped, one hand pressed to her heart, ''tis but a raven.'

The bird, a ragged shadow through the rimed glass, slipped again on the icy window ledge and flapped its wings, etching thin streaks in the hoarfrost. It gave up the struggle to stay on the ledge and, with another thud of wings against the thick panes, launched itself out into the grey dawn.

The princess stared at the window for a moment.
'Why so fearful?' she breathed.

Along a cold passage in the thickness of the castle walls shuffled the blue-eyed scullery maid with her empty bucket. She'd been lucky today; a few of the chamber girls having been laid low with chills, she'd been promoted from her usual work scrubbing pots and pans in the kitchens. Up hours before dawn, she'd lit and attended fires, swept stairs and antechambers and lugged water down cold passageways and up steep stairwells. 'Keep thyself clean, keep thyself tidy, keep out of the way, don't speak unless th'art spoken to, and make sure to keep them eyes downcast,' wretchedly red-nosed Orla had instructed her. 'And don't get lost; ask the other servants if thou canst not find thy way.' She'd done all that, though she hadn't always managed to keep her eyes downcast, for there was much to see. Why, until today she'd rarely been out of the kitchens, let alone walking the corridors of the inner bailey... and stepping within the princess's bedchamber! But she didn't want to think of that.

The scullery maid's sodden gown clung about her knocking knees and she left a damp trail on the flagstones behind her as water squelched from her shoes. She wiped her right sleeve across her face where angry tears trickled, and sniffed.

It would be a while before the princess vacated her chamber, what with all the dressing and hair-dressing and the like, and the drudge decided she had enough time to warm herself and maybe dry her skirt and apron in the bakehouse before she returned to dispose of the bath-water. And if she could make the baker feel sorry enough for her she might even be able to cadge from him a hunk of still-warm bread. She sobbed aloud and her empty stomach complained at the very thought.

The passage was barely illuminated by its few deep arrow loops and at this early hour quite deserted. Most of Castle Lawhill's more fortunate inhabitants were still tucked up in their warm beds, or eating a hearty breakfast before a roaring fire. Shivering violently, muttering and sniffing and half blinded by tears, the girl tripped on the hem of her gown and stumbled against the wall. She flung out her hands to save herself, dropping the bucket. It banged and scraped down the rough stone, rolled under her feet and over she went, falling to the flagstones in a tangled heap. After a flailing struggle she sat up, a wail of despair on her lips. But immediately she clamped a hand to her mouth.

She was sitting near a door to the outer bailey. It was slightly ajar, admitting a seepage of grey light and the sound of voices; booming men's voices half muffled by the clinging fog. Then came a clamour of baying hounds and a clatter of horses' hoofs as iron shoes struck sparks from the bailey flagstones.

The wretched scullion sat sprawled on the floor, snivelling, shaking and sucking at her grazed hand, until the last sound of jingling harness and jovial voices had faded. Then, tugging at her gown, she got clumsily to her knees, hitched up her skirts and staggered to her feet.

'Good morrow, Eudora,' said a voice. 'Ye chose a happy place for your rest; I was myself heading to this very spot to take my ease, the floor here being so warm and soft.'

'Arrgh, Stench,' growled the startled girl, hastily dropping her gown and taking a step back, 'hie thee hence, thou filthy worm!'

'But I have a gift for you, lovely maid.'

A dark-haired youth emerged from the gloom of the passage into the light from the door. He was garbed as a peasant in a thigh length tunic of homespun, belted at the waist. His elbows were patched, and so too were the knees of his coarse leggings. But though the girl had called him filthy, he looked somewhat cleaner than she did. He regarded Eudora with a tentative smile and held out a cloth-wrapped bundle before him on an open palm. She hissed through her teeth and fumbled for her bucket.

'I do not want anything thou hast touched, gong-boy,' she snapped. 'What is it?'

'A sugar-cake,' said the lad called Stench.

'Thou didst steal it,' said the girl. She half picked up the bucket, but it slipped from her cold-numbed hand and bounced and rolled to the lad's feet. Retrieving it, he stepped towards her.

'Nay, sweet damsel,' he said. 'The cook gave it me for cleaning his privy.'

Eudora took the bucket with a grimace, as if it had become a dirty thing, but then made a grab for the sugar-cake, shoving it into the pouch at her waist.

'Tis easy for thee to clean privies,' she said, smirking at her own cleverness, 'for thou liv'st in one.'

The boy shrugged. 'I have heard that before,' he said. 'Yet… lo, at least now the maid's tears have dried and she looks not so vexed as she…'

'Corpse-Eyes and Jake-Stink! Corpse-Eyes and Jake-Stink!' came a gleeful, high-pitched yell as a kitchen boy scampered past, a bag of salt in his arms. 'When be the wedding day, lovers?'

'Gangrel puppy,' growled Stench, looking down the passage as the laughter faded. 'Take no notice of names, 'Dora.' He began to turn back towards her. 'Ye have pretty eyes, like blue fl…'

His kind words were cut off as Eudora's heavy bucket hit him in the side of the head. He staggered sideways and abruptly sat down on the flagstones.

'Do not speak to me again!' she rasped. 'Ever, thou loathsome maggot.'

She stomped off, but then, as if she'd forgotten something, turned and came back. She glared at Stench as he sat rubbing the bump on his head. 'I saw the princess this morning,' she said. 'I shall have a word. They shouldn't allow thee within castle walls, stinking gong-boy, jake-boy.'

He sat, a hand to his head and one eye squinting with the pain, and watched her turn on her heel and squelch away, banging her bucket angrily against the wall.

'Fie, idiot," he muttered. "Should have given the cake to Ma after all.'

'Lovely,' said Ulidia as she fastened a jewelled collar round the princess's slender neck. Winterhued inspected herself for a moment in the mirror, touching the collar's pendant of an enamelled unicorn with a ruby eye and a diamond horn. Her hair had been plaited and coiled, then hidden beneath a headdress of gilded netting upon which sat a bejewelled coronet. Ulidia stepped back to admire her handiwork but Winterhued pulled a face at her in the mirror and rose to her feet with a soft susurration of satin and damask. She smoothed her skirts as she crossed the room.

'Take care m'lady or the wind may change course,' said Ulidia, as she always did, hastening towards the door.

'Aye, as it's done many times,' replied the princess, pulling another face at Ulidia as the old woman swung wide the door for her, 'and lo! Behold the sad result.'

Her face composed again, Winterhued stepped into the small ante-chamber. 'Good morrow Lady Aminta, Ladies Benicia and Manicia.

Wake up Lady Pera. How dost thou fare this morning cousin Brenn?'
She did not wait for an answer, but strode across the chamber as her
ladies jumped to their feet, two of them yawning and the youngest of
them rubbing sleepy eyes.

This day had Gers, King of Manydown, risen betimes to ride with
hounds in the sharp dawn, but not very long after his daughter was
away to her work. The low, wintry sun glanced in through a traceried
window to alight briefly upon her gown of midnight blue and her snow-
white skin, then caught a swirl of velvets and brocades as her chattering
ladies-in-waiting hurried at her heels. The wall hangings lifted uneasily
with the swiftness of their passing.

All through the morning, ensconced in an oak-panelled chamber,
the princess discussed matters of household and matters of state with
the chamberlain and the chancellor; she read petitions, studied lists
and set the royal seal upon acts and statutes, warrants and grants. When
the king and his men returned, red-faced and loud with boasts of the
hunt, the princess met her father with a sheaf of parchments and he,
with hardly a glance thereon, dipped quill in inkpot and spattered his
name below the chancery clerk's careful hand. Then, while he ate his
fill and dozed by the fire, the Lady Manicia knelt to help the princess
into her wooden-soled overshoes and the Lady Aminta wrapped a cloak
about the princess's shoulders and Winterhued stepped forth into the
winter cold to inspect storerooms and armouries and walk an echoing
outer bailey to review the royal guard.

When King Gers was well thawed, well fed, well rested and garbed
in his ermine robe, he strode the long galleries like a moon dragging
a tide of courtiers. With his daughter and his favourite hound at his
heels he entered the loftiest hall, the King's Hall, where folk both high
and low crowded and whispered. The hall was brave with banners and
its vaulted stone roof, almost lost in smoky gloom, was painted all

over with gold sunbursts and horned silver horses. The princess stood beside her father's throne on its high dais with the favoured hound at her feet and, one step below her, the kind-faced, grey-haired chancellor.

The common folk of Manydown, and the noble, had come from near and far for an audience with the king; knights, dignitaries and burghers, merchants, farmers and beggars. They had come to present petitions, to air grievances, to plead, to thank, to beg. With her hand on the king's arm, the princess leant to advise him: 'ask this,' 'answer thus'... and so he did, for he had no inclination to overtax his brain. But sometimes he interrupted proceedings with a peevish quibble for it had lately come to annoy him that his daughter presumed to instruct him. Stultified by a burgher's long-winded grievance, he yawned, then caught the chancellor's eye. 'Need to get her married off, eh Highmoor?' he grumbled. 'Find a man that'll keep her in her place.' It was just habit speaking; he'd attempted that track too often not to know that its ruts were deep, miry and impassable. Another track, untrammelled and interesting, had opened before him and now it led him delightfully away from dull matters of state. His eyes roamed about the hall seeking out handsome women. Ah, there were the two daughters of his friend, Drumrock; pretty plums both, ripe for the plucking...

'Methinks my lord's mind is wandering,' interrupted Winterhued. 'The good burgher doth wait for an answer.'

The king scowled. 'Wandering?' said he indignantly. 'When doth my mind ever wander? Nay, I have more important matters to think of; matters that will affect the future of the realm!' He waved his hand dismissively. 'Answer the fellow as thou wilt.'

Shortly after the last petitioner had been heard, King Gers and his daughter parted company in a passage outside the hall. A shaft of sunlight slanted in through a small mullioned window and lit the top of his head like a halo.

'Ye know I try only to be your highness' devoted and dutiful daughter,' said Winterhued earnestly.

'Do I?' asked the king, turning to stump away down the passage, his hound and his sycophants at his heels. The princess bit her lip as she watched him go. He was on his way to his couch to rest before facing eighteen courses of supper; the princess was due in the council chamber where learned men with black gowns and long faces awaited her. But just for a moment, she paused, leant on the deep sill and seemed to look out through the thick, distorting glass of the little window. Past the great thickness of the castle's impregnable hide the view was narrow; the top of a tree, tossing leafless black boughs, a rectangle of grey lake, whipped into wavelets, a small carrack loaded deep and scudding under shortened sail towards the town's docks. Stark in the pale sky a single rook, wings flapping but making no progress, turned suddenly to vanish down the wind.

But the princess did not see the rook with his ragged wings; inward she looked and felt those other wings that plucked at her nerves, taut as the strings of a lute. Since the dreams had begun they had been ever present, fanning the margins of her mind with unexplained dread. Yet they were not her only fear. 'The king holdeth my destiny in his hands,' she whispered; 'and he hath turned against me.'

She left the window, smiling at the three ladies-in-waiting who accompanied her yet. As she passed them, she patted the chestnut hair of Lady Brenn, the youngest, who had a bundle of embroidery over one arm and some threaded needles poking out of her bodice and the cuff of her left sleeve. Then she was away again, moving swiftly to outpace the fear in her mind, and little Lady Brenn had to run to keep up. Down a cold gallery they went, then up a newel stair, along a wall-walk, down an outside stair, and after a brief stop to put on overshoes, across a windy courtyard where, in the fading light, a big bay gelding ran snorting circles round a small stable-boy. In they went through a stone-arched doorway, up another spiral stair to another long gallery, and at last under a low wooden lintel into firelight and candlelight. The ladies-in-waiting sat down in an antechamber and took out their needles and thread while the princess set to with the learned men around the council table; issuing proclamations, drafting reforms, examining bills of complaint, appointing commissioners, bestowing endowments, granting licenses and stifling yawns.

'...and furthermore,' intoned the grey voice of sanctimonious Lord Ladstock, Chamberlain of Manydown, 'I suggest respectfully before your highness that we do make submission unto the duke to hereby agree that he and all his successors, at this time and in the future, taking into account all previous missives concerning the oak trees and with due regard for...'

'Ah forsooth man!' snapped Sir Garthwray, Marquess of Thornliebank, Butler of the Realm and husband of old Ulidia. 'I say drat the duke! What matters his forty-seven oak trees and his neighbour's swine?' Despite his fierce voice Sir Garthwray was as frayed as an old garment, with scarcely a hair left on his head. 'How long, I ask you,' he bellowed, 'must we have our brains numbed by his dreary disputations? Of more pressing import is the matter of profits arising from the piepowder court...'

'Aye. The profits,' agreed the chancellor, Lord Highmoor; 'they must betimes be levied and accounts rendered unto the exchequer. And what of the fines taken, eh? And how have the fees and dues been calculated?'

'Sirs!' cried the dull, grey chamberlain. 'In faith, we durst not set aside so blithely this matter of the duke's, for I deem...'

'Ladstock,' interrupted Sir Auchencairn, Earl of Dunsyre, Knight of the Four Winds, King's Champion, and Constable of the Realm, 'as the duke's oaks will stand for a good deal longer than the duke, no doubt the matter will soon resolve itself.' Auchencairn looked amused and easeful. His great fists lay relaxed on the table before him. He was a huge man, with iron-coloured hair and a head as round as a cheese. His shoulders were adrape with chains of office and his knight's insignia of enameled gold and pearl gleamed against his broad chest. 'I wish,' he continued, 'to address a matter concerning our soldiers at Belford and in the northern garrisons. Though they have meat aplenty, they have made demand for more.'

'More?' spluttered Garthwray. 'Slothful, swilling idlers are they; prey to their bellies! Forsooth... they need some strife to try them hard!'

The princess, ignoring the butler's outburst, spoke quietly: 'Our soldiers consume too much flesh; it maketh them sluggish and dull-witted. Why not supply each garrison with seed and tools to grow their own...?'

'Vegetables?' interrupted Auchencairn with a laugh. 'There will be rioting, mutiny, desertion!'

'Because they might have wholesome food to eat? As things stand, we all know what a drain they are on the lands about them and that they have little to do...'

'They're soldiers, m'lady,' interrupted Ladstock, 'not farmers. And soldiers need meat. Or their courage will flee and their man-parts shrivel.'

Auchenairn guffawed and the princess laughed, though she knew Ladstock was not jesting.

Kindly faced Lord Highmoor coughed. 'Ha hum,' he said softly, "tis a marvelous time in which we live, that we may talk of turning our soldiers into farmers.'

Winterhued turned to him. 'Peaceful days make idle soldiers, dear chancellor,' she said. 'But think on this: caring for crops could result in fewer incidences of dicing, drinking and disturbing of the peace.'

'I wonder,' said Auchencairn, suddenly earnest, 'how our soldiers *can* be idle while outlaws yet plague the east road. I say we tell Ravenhill that until his men have driven every last two-legged pig from Gostwyck Forest, they'll not get a taste of the four-legged sort.'

Sir Garthwray snorted. 'In that case they'll never eat pork again,' said he.

"Tis no laughing matter,' said Auchencairn, leaning forward. 'With the northern threat decreased, "The Adder" and his villainous band in Gostwyck should be our most pressing concern. But time and again hath that fool, Ravenhill, proven himself unequal to the task.'

'Ravenhill is my father's friend...' began the princess, but Auchencairn cut in. 'A toadying milksop,' he growled. 'M'lady, let me once again take some men east this spring. I know I can catch the bloodsucker this time; I have a strategy...'

'Better than the last one?' asked the chamberlain. Auchencairn shot him a look through narrowed eyes and the princess held up her hands. 'The Adder,' she said, 'is a problem that cannot be solved at a council table. I shall consider thy proposal, Sir Auchencairn, if thou shalt consider mine. And gentlemen, we'll not reach an agreement today, but can I ask you all do the same?'

The councillors gave their ayes and their nods but Sir Garthwray, as always, had the last word on the matter. 'Hang Ravenhill and hang the soldiers,' he grunted, 'then we'll have no need to feed them!'

The princess looked at the angry little man and suddenly recalled how Ulidia had mistaken herself for her husband. She bent her head to hide a smile.

'Well then,' said the chamberlain, coughing dryly and rustling through a sheaf of papers, 'leaving the soldiers to grow turnips or hang themselves, I must, yet again, bring to your notice more grievances from the sheriffs. Herein,' he declared, waving a parchment before his face, 'we find that, despite the king's ordinance, daily is deceit done by wool merchants who put under their good fleeces stones and dirt and... unwholesome stuff...'

'Forsooth!' spat Garthwray. 'Why do the sheriffs come bleating unto the council with their complaints? I say flog the scoundrels! What do they think their wages are for?'

'Flog the sheriffs, Garthwray?' said Lord Highmoor with a faint smile. 'Somewhat severe, eh?' Without waiting for a reply he turned to the chamberlain. 'But I'm puzzled Ladstock, why do the sheriffs attend thee? Surely Auchencairn is the man...'

'Ha!' grunted Auchencairn, 'if any durst come asking me to do their work for them they'll be flying out the door with my boot-print on their backsides!'

'Auchen...!'

'But old Ladstock here,' continued Auchencairn, talking over High-moor's protest and patting the chamberlain's thin back with a huge hand, 'old Ladstock has whiners and complainers jammed into his ante-chamber, spilling out the door and half way to the keep, for they know he'll give 'em a nice soft ear to chew on.'

'Auchencairn,' said the princess quietly.

'Apologies, m'lady,' said Auchencairn. A slight sneer of disdain twisted his mouth as he turned to regard Ladstock. 'Yet look ye upon the poor man; he hasn't slept for years. His knees are worn through with praying and his shoulders bent with the toil of bearing up the kingdom.' He gave the chamberlain a thump on the aforementioned shoulders.

'Tush, sir,' wheezed Ladstock, 'I do but serve the king as best I can.'

'And I'm sure the king,' said Winterhued, 'shall be eternally grateful. But mayhap, Lord Ladstock, some of thy precious hours might be saved if thou didst but remind the sheriffs that the enforcement of the king's ordinance on merchants within their bailiwicks is their business and not a matter with which to trouble the council.'

She stifled a yawn. Desperate for sleep, she could scarcely keep her mind on the matters in hand. Her eyes wandered to the window and the dwindling day where a raven winged his way down the dreary wind... and immediately felt them, those other wings that ever shadowed her... they were there, whenever she paused, whenever she allowed her thoughts to drift. They washed at the verges of her mind like twilit waves upon a strand, leaving at their ebb a scum of fear. 'Something terrible cometh this way,' ran her panicked thoughts, 'but what is it?' Beneath the oak table the princess wrung her hands. Her heart beat in her ears and for a time she did not hear the earnest voices as they ground on, wearing down the sullen time as smatterings of rain rattled the windowpanes and the slim height of the candles diminished to a fat sprawl of wax.

'...But certes,' said the chamberlain, 'this doth naught to address the problem of weights and measures and how the standards are to be enforced. Why, just two days ago as thou knowest, the fishmongers formed riotous assembly and marched through the streets waving knives and dead fish...'

'Ah,' sighed Winterhued, and most of the faces round the table turned towards her.

'Madam?' enquired the chamberlain, but the princess had collected her thoughts and smiled, having just noticed Highmoor nodding so far his head was almost on the table.

'What?' said he, waking abruptly as his nose made contact with the polished wood.

'Weights and measures, chancellor,' said Auchencairn loudly.

'Ahh! Fie sir, I'm not deaf yet! Weights and measures? Weights and measures? Wearying her highness, as ever, with thy weights and meas...'

'I am not wearied, dear Lord Highmoor,' interrupted the princess. 'Every matter, small or large, pertaining to this realm is to me of abiding interest and, after all, weights and measures are no small matter. But I think for now the weights must wait, for it is time for supper.'

Leaving no room for protests, Winterhued was on her feet and had crossed the chamber so swiftly there was barely time for a startled clerk to throw open the door for her. She gathered her attendants as they bundled up their paraphernalia of needles and fabric, and swept out under the low lintel and away down the long, night-draped gallery. Swift before her, her shadow leapt along the floor then bounded up beside the portal to meet her as the servant boy with the flaring torch scurried past to fling wide the door. Spilling fitful gusts of orange light he led the way into the draughty pit of the stairwell and the princess followed him, fleeing from black wings that beat louder than her heart.

CHAPTER 2

Night came down upon the castle by the lake. As more torches and candles and fires were lit to shut out the darkling sky, the second largest hall (called the Queen's Hall, though it was many years since there had been a queen of Manydown) was arrayed for the feast and the bright throngs took their places at the long tables. The chancellor was there, and the other learned councillors; dukes were there, and duchesses, marquesses and marchionesses, earls and countesses, all of them accompanied by their squires, their servants, their hounds and their lapdogs (but not, of course, their children).

To a shout of trumpets the king, in purple and ermine, entered a step or two before his daughter, who was clad now in royal blue embroidered with silver curlicues. The king's eyes sparkled and he beamed upon his subjects, for eating was his great pleasure. The servants brought forth the fare, the boards were laden till they groaned, minstrels struck up in the gallery and the business of the evening began.

'Look around thee, daughter,' said the king from sheer habit, as he sucked his fingers and mopped gravy from his chin. 'Canst thou not see a husband here? Over yonder,' he said, pointing languidly with a pheasant bone, 'the Duke of Travancore... young, but a match for thee with his long shanks...'

'Yet his face is longer than his shanks, for methinks he never learnt to smile.'

'Thou dost desire a smile? Well, look there, the Marquess of Potrimpos... a passing jolly man.'

'And what a splendid sight his three teeth do make when he doth laugh.'

The king tossed the bone to his favourite hound and reached for a partridge cooked in malmsey. 'So,' said he, "tis teeth now. Well, look thou at that mouth; no man hath more teeth than Lord Templemore.'

'Yea, verily,' answered the princess with a sigh (for this had all been said many times); 'he hath need of them all to chew through the mounds of flesh his great belly doth crave.'

'There's naught wrong with a great belly,' said the king, patting his own, 'yet if a lean man wouldst please thee...'

'Father, forbear! Ye shall list every unwed man in this hall, full belly or empty head...'

'Empty head? If thou lookst to find a man with aught in his head I shall never see a grandson. Besides, thy mother, thy dear, patient mother, was content to take as husband a man with naught in his head.'

'Nay,' objected the princess politely, though she knew that this was but her father's jest for, since childhood, the flattery and guile of courtiers and councillors had convinced him that he was the cleverest fellow in all the land.

Bored, he turned from her. The great carnivorous Duke of Drumrock sat at his left and now the two of them, with meat-juices dribbling down their chins, began loudly to discuss the relative merits of flesh. 'Quail, sir?' she heard the king say. 'Only merit in quail is the killing of 'em. My falcon can bring me half a dozen in less time than it takes me to get off m'horse. But to eat? Pah... food for faeries! All those choking little bones for a morsel of meat! Nay, I like to set to, and I need more than a morsel to sate me! Give me a juicy haunch of venison! Or a succulent side of beef!'

Princess Winterhued reached for a handful of almonds and ate them one by one. The fires in the hearths leapt high, the torches flared and, high aloft, bright banners moved lazily in the up-draughts, casting benign shadows across the gilded hammerbeam roof. Along the tables flames flickered atop a slouching army of candles, their light gleaming on ebbing mounds of food. The princess smiled, for the faces all about her were jovial and above the incessant hubbub of happy voices the musicians were playing her favourite bass-dance. The music rose like a glad shout, like a banner, like an heraldic unicorn rearing rampant across a red field.

Hidden beneath the hem of her gown, Winterhued's feet danced a pattern on the floor and she idly wondered whether she missed the suitors. Once, on a night such as this, there would have been half a dozen or more, come from near and far to ogle the prize and, if they were fortunate enough, to kneel at her feet or — oh, favoured few — to dance with her. She would have bestowed a charitable smile or two upon each posturing prince and narcissistic noble, each lumpish lord and blushing boy, and provided an attentive ear for their honeyed flatteries, their loquacious praises, their monosyllabic mutterings or their embarrassed stutterings. But in the end all she had had for each and every one of them were a few gentle words, just enough to send even the most ardent back to his home, dusty kneed and without hope.

She patted the king's favourite hound who had come to rest a lean, greying muzzle upon her lap. 'Good Gunda,' she murmured, gently pulling the hound's ears, 'good, faithful girl.'

Looking about her at the merry throng, she remembered the royal progress she had made with her father last spring across the length and breadth of Manydown, how the people had met them with great welcome, the children with flowers, the townsfolk with gifts and praises. 'I am not lonely,' she murmured to the hound. 'I love and am loved. I am content.' The hound licked her hand.

Some way down the table, past gowns of tawny velvet and russet damask, past robes of blue brocade shot with gold, and crimson satin sewn with pearls, past headdresses like horns, like hearts, like steeples, sat the princess's second-cousin: her youngest lady-in-waiting. Lady Brenn's eyes kept wanting to close as she stared dazedly at her half-consumed cup of wine and tried valiantly to attend to the round-faced squire seated beside her. He, with his stiff, brown hair and excitedly glowing cheeks, barely three months away from his knighting, prattled about his new horse, his new plate armour, his new sword, his new mace and his new poleaxe. 'What think ye of that?' he would ask her every few minutes, never waiting for a reply. The girl's head had nodded so far that her nose was close to disappearing into her wine cup.

'By my spurs! How can ye be drowsy?' exclaimed young Deccan of Wythop as Brenn woke with a start. 'Why, ye do but sit all the day by the fire with your needles and thread, whilst I, I'm off with m'lord at break of day for a stag or two, then home and straight into the lists to knock a few churls into the mud.'

''Tis but a week and three days since I came up to court,' said the girl, 'and in my home we went to our beds when the night came down for my father was loath to waste candles.' She looked round sleepily at the dazzle of light the length and breadth of the hall, and at the glittering lords and ladies who, having eaten their fill, strolled now from table to table to chat with friends and show off their gorgeous raiment.

Oh, how different it all was to the quiet manor house in which she had been raised, and not just in the quantity of candles consumed. What peacocks these courtiers were! The women glided gracefully about, sweeping the flagstones with their voluminous trains and trailing diaphanous veils of gauze from their towering headdresses. Some of them wore their bodices so low and their breasts pushed up so high that they could have balanced wine goblets in front of their noses. As for the men, they strutted and swaggered about, their buttocks and legs encased in tightly fitting hose. Their jackets, worn over high-collared doublets, had pleats running in a 'V' shape from wide shoulders down to narrow waists, and were so short that Brenn hardly knew where to look. And yet the sleeves on these same jackets were long enough to brush the flagstones. All of the men wore their hair long, and slim daggers hung at their hips. Jewels trimmed their caps and precious stones glinted upon their fingers. Some of the men had pointed toes on their shoes that were so extreme they would have tripped over them if the ends had not been fastened to garters beneath their knees. Most astonishing of all – an outstanding specimen was this minute being paraded before her – were the brazenly padded and protruding codpieces (she'd heard giggling Lady Benicia call them 'brag-bags') worn by many of the younger men. Brenn looked down at the table and put her hands over her bewildered eyes. But in her present state not even a courtly congregation of codpieces could suffice to keep her conscious.

'By my spurs, ye be dull company this eve!' exclaimed Deccan. 'Ye had best get off to bed.'

'Nay, for when abed I do not sleep.' Brenn tried to stifle a yawn. 'Since I have been here my nights have been troubled by a fearful dream. It hath kept me wakeful.'

'I never dream,' said Deccan. 'Meseemeth I must then keep you from sleep with a little entertaining converse... did I tell you of the

tourney this autumn past? I deem ye have never seen such a thing in
rustic little Halewood, but certes…'

'I come from Drumalis, not Halewood.'

'Drumalis, Halewood? Almost the same place. Both small and rustic
and no-one hath heard of either.'

'Drumalis is not small, nor rustic,' managed Brenn though her
words were slurred and her eyelids drooped. 'They say the church
steeple is as fine as…'

'But have ye seen a tourney there? Of course not. Certes, how it
would have made your heart glad last autumn to see the bright pavilions
and the trappings of the horses and the best knights in the land galloping
and walloping and smiting each other down to the earth on every side!
I wish ye had been here to witness such marvellous deeds of arms. See
there, Sir Dechmont, surrounded as ever by lovestruck ladies.' Deccan
pointed enthusiastically into the crowd. ''Twas he who proved most
worshipful by winning the autumn prize – such a handsome man and
an exceeding good knight…'

'Oh… aye, good night,' mumbled the girl. Her head subsided
towards the horizontal; unless she was wakened shortly she would
fall into her half-eaten apple tart. Fortunately the round-faced squire
happened to glance towards the head of the table.

'Look,' he said urgently, 'your lady ariseth!' He stood up.

'Oh,' gasped the girl, scrambling to her feet and tipping the remains
of her wine over the tart. Still asleep she confusedly tried to mop at the
wine with her napkin, all the while apologizing.

'Leave that,' said the lad; 'go to your lady; she doth look for you.'

The princess had indeed risen to her feet. And with a great scraping
of bench-legs on the flagstones, so had everyone else in the hall
excepting, of course, the king.

'Father,' said she, 'I am off to my bed.'

'So soon?' snorted the king. 'Where is thy staunchness, eh? In good sooth thou art not like thy sire; why, thou eatest scant enough to save a sparrow from starving and tumblest into thy bed as soon as the sun hath sunk.'

Winterhued stooped to kiss his greasy, bejewelled hand. Along the table her ladies had put down half eaten cakes and fruit, dabbed at faces with napkins and murmured goodnights to neighbours and lovers. Hurriedly they had come from their places to hover at the princess's back.

Lady Ulidia was there, and her daughter Aminta, a little taller than both her parents and as bossy as her mother. The princess smiled to see Aminta; the woman strutted proud as a peacock as her wedding (her third) to the handsome and much younger Earl of Bellands, was but two weeks away. The sisters Benicia and Manicia, daughters of the carnivorous Duke of Drumrock, hovered behind her. Benicia was beautiful, buxom and bright, with a tongue that babbled like a brook. Manicia was her sister's quiet shadow.

The Lady Pera arrived, her eyes downcast and syrup smeared on her chin. Eleven days ago she had been the youngest of Winterhued's attendants, now she'd progressed to being the second youngest. The daughter of Lord Ladstock, she was an earnest, quiet girl who produced the most beautiful needlework Winterhued had ever seen.

Lady Brenn, flushed and breathless, was the last to reach the princess's side. The youngest lady-in-waiting's needlework left much to be desired and yet the princess found her little cousin exceedingly promising. The girl daydreamed constantly, her needle would remain poised in the air for long moments as she gazed from a window or, as they crossed the castle, she would stop to look upon the scenery or lose herself in some tapestry legend and then have to run to catch up. *If I had not been the king's daughter,* thought Winterhued, *that might have been me.*

The princess gave Brenn an encouraging smile, then turned and for a few minutes walked along beside the table to bid goodnight to her friends. She exchanged pleasantries with a duchess or two, the old chancellor sleepily paid his respects and the Ambassador to Balasore, Manydown's southern neighbour, kissed her hand and murmured something unintelligible. Beside the mountainous Sir Auchencairn stood his thin wife, Nomia, Countess of Dunsyre, the princess's first cousin. A glance round at her husband had her brushing the crumbs from his clothes and straightening his chain with its enamelled insignia of a mounted knight at full gallop. He extricated himself from her attentions with a: 'Leave off thy bothering Nomi dear,' and bestowed upon the princess a broad smile; a wide flash of white teeth that crumpled his cheeks into good-humoured creases. She smiled back, for no one seeing that smile could help but return it.

'Lord Ladstock,' said Auchencairn, 'hath requested... nay, demanded, that I make apology to your grace for uttering in her presence that... fearsome word, "backside". Ah, fie on me,' he said, clapping a hand to his mouth; 'I've said it again.'

The princess smiled as Nomia frowned and poked her husband's arm. Behind her she heard her lady-in-waiting Benicia hiccup and giggle.

'Verily sir,' replied Winterhued, shaking her head sadly, 'thou art a rude knave and it is high time thou didst heed my poor cousin's instructions in the courtly graces.'

'In vain have I tried,' said Nomia, 'but alas; fine courtly ways are an ill fit for his thick, country head.' As she uttered each of the last three words she clipped him lightly over the ear, standing his thick, country hair on end.

'Well, dear Winterhued,' said Auchencairn, stooping to kiss her hand, still with his hair poking up comically, 'herewith I do beg your highness' pardon for my churlish ways... and beg for your highness' yeasay to my request.'

'Thou art forgiven,' replied the princess. 'And though I can ill afford to spare thee, thou hast my leave to go hunt the outlaw.'

Her cousin huffed impatiently as she patted her husband's hair flat. 'That "Adder" villain is all he hath had in his head this past year,' she grumbled.

'Aye, well the sooner he's dead,' said Auchencairn, 'the sooner he's out of my head. My thanks, dear lady,' he said, clasping Winterhued's hand; 'we shall hook the brute this time.'

'Good night, good knight,' said Winterhued, as she so often had. Yet as she took her hand from his warm grasp and turned away, her heart felt so suddenly heavy that she almost spun about to order him to stay.

But several more courtiers had stepped forward to convey their goodnights and to make use of the princess's well-kissed hand and so she walked on, acknowledging them all with smiles and pleasant words. Then abruptly she paused, suppressing a gasp of surprise because before her, straightening from a low bow, was a man she had not seen for five or six years. He was the Marquess of Carradale, a lean man of middle height and greying hair, with an aquiline nose and mirthful eyes, blue as a glimpse of the lake on a cloudless day.

'I am amazed sir,' said the princess, somewhat breathlessly. 'A dire circumstance it must be to have dragged thee to court from thy remote acres! I need not ask, I suppose, if my dear friend, thy wife, hath also bestirred herself?' He shook his head. 'Alas! I thought not.'

'I am sorry for our neglect,' said the marquess, 'yet I have but a little business I must perforce attend to; a day or two, no more.' He took her hand and kissed it, looking at her intently. 'Is it well with m'lady?' he asked and the princess just smiled her answer and pressed his hand fondly. 'As ever,' he said, 'she is fair as the waxing moon risen in a midnight sky spangled o'er with countless stars.'

'And, as ever,' answered she, 'thou art as full of dross as a gong-farmer's barrow.'

'Ahh, compliment indeed,' he murmured, bowing slightly, and she graciously inclined her head.

'The day hath been long,' said she. 'I trust I shall see thee on the morrow for I would dearly like news of thee and thine. I have almost finished the writing of a missive to thy wife; thou canst deliver it thyself.'

'Verily, on the morrow then… whensoever, wheresoever, my lady doth wish.'

Winterhued shook her head and smiled slightly as the marquess bowed. Then she turned and walked from the hall with beating heart, looking neither to right nor left, her six ladies-in-waiting hurrying after her.

There was little need for the page who scurried before them bearing a lantern, for this part of the castle was well lit. But it was cold as a dungeon, and as they made their brisk way along a passage within the bailey wall their teeth chattered and they hugged themselves against the chill. Between painted cloth hangings flames in sconces flared and hissed and sent thin curls of smoke up to blacken the whitewashed ceiling. At the door to her apartments in the southeastern tower, where two guards stood to attention, the princess dismissed all but the youngest of her ladies-in-waiting.

'Thou dost look weary, old thing,' she said, embracing Ulidia and sending the old woman off to the bed she still shared with her fraying husband, Sir Garthwray. The Ladies Aminta and Pera also went straight away to their beds but the pretty sisters Benicia and Manicia returned to the fires, the feasting and the flirting. Plump Benicia giggled and hiccupped. Her boldly revealed cleavage was deep enough to secrete half a dozen love letters.

Her quieter sister looked at her sideways, slyly. 'Benicia!' she hissed. 'Who was that?'

'Who was what?' asked Benicia, still giggling.

'She… m'lady… talking to a Callunian!'

'What Callunian?' Benicia tripped on the edge of a flagstone and her sister grabbed at her arm.

'Shh!' hissed Manicia, giving her a shake. 'That man… he had blue eyes…'

'Oh him,' said Benicia, instantly losing interest. 'Dull as ditchwater. But didst thou see mine own sweet Potrimpos... oh, his beautiful hair! He is such heaven!'

Manicia pushed Benicia away from her with a gasp of repugnance. 'Of course I saw him... "Sir Brag-bag" was drooling all over thee. But thou dost like him only because he dotes disgustingly upon thee. Why, Bee, I never do notice his hair. And I don't notice... well, further down, even though he flaunts himself shamelessly. All I can see is that he hath but three teeth in his head!'

Benicia stopped and turned to face her sister. 'How cruel thou art! Thou dost only say that because he never sees thee... little mousy thing...'

Manicia emitted a strangled squeak and took a step towards her sister, but Benicia dodged and ran past her. 'Besides,' she giggled, 'he is vastly more handsome and entertaining than that long-faced dolt Travancore that thou dost think so highly of.'

'I do not!' Manicia sneered. 'And even if I did, Bee, thou hast led him on so, that now he is fallen sore in love with thee.'

'With me?' Benicia laughed as she cupped her ample breasts in her hands and bounced them up and down. 'Dost thou not mean with these? He stares at them and can scarcely say a word!'

Manicia snorted. 'I saw him trembling as he spoke to thee!'

'And didst thou see the sweat on his brow?'

'And his eyelid twitching.'

Benicia shrieked with laughter but Manicia just curled her lip. Suddenly she pushed her sister away and backed towards the wall. Benicia turned, and she too backed up against the wall. They both curtseyed low as the king approached them, a crowd of servants at his heels. Surprisingly, he stopped before the two girls and with narrowed eyes looked the both of them up and down. His lips curled into an unpleasant smile. 'Lovely,' he said and then he nodded, his several chins wobbling, and went his way.

Benicia looked round-eyed at her sister.

'Mayhap he doth look for a new wife,' said Manicia quietly.

Her sister emitted a muffled screech. 'How disgusting!' she breathed, then clamped a hand over her mouth and giggled.

'Not so disgusting to be Queen of Manydown,' whispered Manicia.

'But... Winterhued is to be Queen,' said Benicia.

Dismissing the topic with a shrug, Manicia grabbed her sister's arm and towed her towards the Queen's Hall. Though quite why she wanted to return thither was a mystery, even to herself, for it was unlikely that she'd find more to do there than watch Benicia flirt.

Along the passage behind them the king, despite his claim to staunchness, shuffled bloat-bellied off to his big soft bed. His friends Drumrock and Ravenhill, and those grubs Gunford and Ladstock, had been whispering in his ear of late and he had much to think about. He didn't care about disappointing his daughter. She was, after all, only a woman and so damned willful it'd be justice...

But King Gers never mulled over any subject overmuch or for too long, so by the time he climbed into his bed within its heavy hangings of woven dreams and tales of heroes his thoughts had all fled and sleep came quickly, troubled only by indigestion.

At the top of the second stage of the winding tower stair a torch burned brightly in its bracket beside a studded wooden door. Winterhued opened the door and stepped into the antechamber between the stair and her bedroom. As the chamber was lit only by the embers of a dying fire, she left the door unshut. She had barely taken three steps into the room when the inner door to the bedchamber opened and a servant-girl came quickly through, turning to close it behind her.

'Leave the door ajar,' commanded the princess. The girl jumped and spun around, wide-eyed. She immediately lowered her glance and ducked into a curtsey.

'Oh, my lady...' she gasped. 'I weren't expecting... I brought firewood, y'ladyship, and tended the fire.' She waved a grubby hand in the direction of the princess's bedchamber. Winterhued recognized the wan, blue-eyed scullion who had spilled the bathwater that morning. Though her apron was now dry, it was smeared with ash and speckled with sawdust. She stared fixedly at the floor.

'Where is Orla?' asked the princess.

'She be poorly, m'lady. She took a chill, m'lady. I was sent in her place.'

'A chill? I am sorry to hear that. Lady Brenn, fetch my cloak and bring to me two of the oranges from the bowl by the window seat. What is thy name?' She asked this last question of the scullion who fidgeted nervously and found much of interest on the floor as Brenn went by her into the bedchamber.

'Eudora, your highness,' said Eudora, bobbing another curtsey and chancing a quick upwards glance.

'Well Eudora, I am sorry thou tookst a scolding this morning. Lady Ulidia can be sharp at times. My thanks, Lady Brenn,' she said, taking the proffered oranges from Brenn. 'A little gift for thee, Eudora. I hope it may make up for this morning's unpleasantness.'

She put one of the oranges into the servant's grubby hand and the girl stared at it, tentatively turning it over, open-mouthed.

'I do not suppose thou hast tasted an orange,' said the princess. 'These came from Balasore, with the ambassador. This other,' she said as she handed the second orange to Eudora, 'thou shalt deliver to Orla, and with it my wishes for her swift recovery.'

'Oh my lady,' whispered Eudora.

'Mayhap it will put some colour into thy cheeks,' said Winterhued, looking kindly upon the girl, 'to match thy pretty eyes. Thou hast very pretty eyes, Eudora: the colour of forget-me-nots.'

The servant-girl glanced up at the princess in dull surprise. She bobbed another curtsey. 'Oh m'lady,' she breathed, 'I do thank m'lady.'

Winterhued nodded and the girl understood that she had been dismissed. After yet another curtsey she backed across the room and fled into the stairwell. Brenn looked regretfully after the oranges as the princess took the cloak from her lady-in-waiting's arms. She pushed Brenn gently towards the inner door where firelight spilled across the threshold.

'Wait for me,' she said, 'in the warmth. Sleep. The moon is full this night and I am fain to look upon it and have some time with my thoughts.'

'The moon, m'lady?' said the girl. 'But it is so cold.'

'I'll not be long,' said the princess, and Brenn found herself propelled into the room with the door closed behind her.

She walked towards the delicious warmth of the fire before which a pile of cushions lay beckoning. About her the rose-gold light glowed on wainscoted walls and floor-to-ceiling tapestries of forest-green enchased with flowers and mythical beasts. Flickering flames danced mirrored in the panes of the deep-set mullioned window above its cushioned seats all piled with books, a lute and a shawm. On the canopied bed, beneath the half drawn hangings and over the blossom-embroidered counterpane, stretched the tabby cat, blinking green eyes contentedly, her mouth opening in a miaow of welcome. Brenn sighed and sank sleepily into the cushions.

Winterhued took the torch by the outer door from its sconce and climbed the stair to the narrow walk betwixt the slate roof and the stone parapet. Leaving the torch in the stairwell she stood in the dark atop her own tower, under clouds that blanketed the stars and moon. She found, to her surprise, that it was warmer without than within, for the north wind had died and a breeze had sprung up from the south, bringing with it the scent of early blossom. But she was still grateful for her cloak and pulled it close about her as she waited for her eyes to grow accustomed to the dark. The night was quiet but for the distant sound of merrymaking from the hall, two sentries exchanging words on a wall-walk somewhere and the soft call of an owl. To the north, beyond the castle's bulk, came the faint hum of the town and from far below, where the tower buried its buttressed feet in the lakebed, came the ceaseless hiss and slide of wavelets on the shingled shore.

In the lighted chamber below, Brenn clutched a cushion to her breast and stared into the fire. She wondered who the man was that had startled her mistress and why his appearance at court had so discomfited Winterhued that she must needs venture into the cold night to gaze at the moon. Was he the one? For Lady Brenn harboured a notion that, once upon a time, the princess's heart had been broken by a man unknown; a man whose name began with a 'D'. This idea had come to her but five days ago when she had glimpsed the book that the princess carried about in her reticule, a little volume bound in silver with, etched on the cover, the letters 'W' and 'D' entwined.

'Ohh,' she sighed, sinking down before the fire and hugging the cushion tightly, 'I must discover his name.' But then she fell backwards, flinging away the cushion with a little noise of disgust. 'But he's so dull,' she whispered, lying on her back, spread-eagled before the fire. 'Neither handsome, nor heroic, and so old… and with those eyes… he must surely be… Callu…'

Her voice faded and her eyes closed. The cat jumped from the bed, stretched in a leisurely manner and strolled across to the fire to climb onto Brenn's prone form. Purring happily, she curled up and went to sleep on her new bed.

At the bottom of the stairs Eudora had passed the guards without so much as a glance in their direction. She kept to the darkest shadows as she skirted the inner bailey, sometimes casting a look towards the feast-hall that still brimmed with light and revelry, but never towards the ancient keep that stood gloomy and deserted up on its mound. Rather than leave the inner bailey through the King's Gate and risk snide comments from the guards stationed there, she darted beneath a low door and entered a poorly lit wall passage that would take her through to the outer bailey. Now and then other servants hurried past, wheeling barrows and lugging buckets, carrying bed linen, candles and bundles of wood, but she walked with her eyes downcast and spoke to no one.

In the outer bailey she passed the kitchens and the bakehouse, where the main business of the day was over. A small army of scullions, of which she would normally have been part, scrubbed away at a mountain of pots and pans, or got down on worn knees to scour the flagstones. She passed the buttery, the pantry and the well, where a queue of lackeys chattered as they waited to draw up the water needed for their tasks. She passed the great stables where lanterns burned and the stable-lads were hard at work; cleaning bits and polishing leather, carrying tubs of feed and water and armfuls of hay, brushing and currying glossy hides. The warm smell of hay and grain, of hot bran-mash and dung, assailed her nostrils as she drew nigh the big main door. A few horses within stamped and snorted. She heard a loud, splintering thud as an iron-shod hoof hit a stall-partition, then, with a spray of sparks on the cobbles, a huge grey courser sprang through the main stable door, towing one of the stable boys behind it. A bald-headed man appeared in the doorway and watched as the boy toiled to control the stallion. Though he was a tall boy, and strong, he had a job to keep the horse's hoofs near the ground.

'Walk 'im till 'e calms,' ordered the man. 'Don't know what the devil's got into 'im tonight.'

He turned and went back into the stables leaving the boy to struggle with the plunging horse. Its hide was dark with sweat and its eyes rolled. Eudora took a wide detour round it, keeping well out of reach of those heavily shod hoofs.

Beyond the stables stood the forge, its fires banked and glowing, and beside the forge the King's Menagerie, vast and high-roofed, its tall doors always bolted. Eudora had never seen any of the mysterious creatures that lived within, but she had heard their strange voices and smelled their peculiar smells. Once, that pest Stench had told her that the animals in there were all dying of broken hearts. She was still proud of her answer: 'Dumb beasts have no souls therefore they can't have feelings. Besides, what wouldst thou know, maggot? Thou art the last thing in the world the king would allow anywhere nigh his valuables!'

The menagerie animals seemed restless this night. But they did not raise their voices. As she hurried past one of the smaller doors that stood slightly ajar, Eudora saw a gleam of lamplight within and heard the creatures shuffle and scrape, scratch and thump; she heard a soft little wail and a sad moan.

But then those small sounds were drowned out as all the hounds in the kennels on the other side of the bailey began to bay, followed straight after by men's voices, cursing and growling at the hounds. Eudora put her hands over her ears and began to run.

Winterhued stood atop the north side of her tower under the black sky, looking down over the castle where it sprawled in darkness below. A few patches of yellow light fought the night; lighted windows gleamed here and there, three torches sputtered where upper wall-walks entered towers and, beyond the black bulk of the feast-hall roof, the light from its tall windows fell across the flagstones of the inner bailey.

All of a sudden the clouds parted and it seemed that the castle sprang up from the darkness, stark in the fall of moonlight; a vast overgrowth of crenellated towers and gabled halls, of machicolated galleries and arrow-slitted walls. In the centre of the inner bailey, blanched in the light, hunched the ancient keep with its windows like vacant eyes. Far away in the outer bailey all the hounds in the kennels gave voice to the moon.

Winterhued shivered and pulled her cloak tight. She walked around the top of the tower, running a hand along the cold stone as she went. On the southern side she leant between the wind-smoothed merlons and looked out over the lake to the low line of silvered hills that rimmed the sky.

'I wish thou hadst not come,' said the princess to the air, to the marquess, wherever he may have been, 'with thine eyes and thy smile so... like his. Alas,' she breathed, 'thou hast woken memories best left unwoken.'

Over the far-flung distances beyond her gaze lay lands seldom mentioned and almost unimagined, and yet, she thought, mortals such as we walked there and drew warmth from the same sun and turned lovelorn faces to the same moon.

'Oh moon,' she whispered, 'when thou dost turn round the world, remember me to him. I *know* that he liveth yet, but oh... I would I knew that he was hale... and happy.'

But immediately she pushed herself angrily from the parapet. 'Why do thoughts of him hurt me yet?' she gasped. 'He was a churl... he ran away on his dolt's quest and hath sent no word! Moon,' she hissed, 'if thou dost see him tell him he is naught but a thief... and a liar.'

Clouds drifted across the moon's face and the princess subsided against the cold stone. 'Tell him to come home,' she whispered as a tear spilt and ran down her cheek.

After a time she stood up again. 'I am not lonely,' she said; 'I am not... wearied to distraction.' She hit the stone with the flat of her hand. 'Why may a man ride away and drink his fill of the world, while a woman must stay behind, imprisoned within walls?'

Yet standing there, sad and angry and alone, she heard, rising up through the dark, the faint voices of country folk singing as they wended their way homewards from the town. And she saw, across the lake, the tiny lights of scattered farms and villages twinkling a welcome.

She leant out again over the lake and it seemed to her that she had but to reach out to embrace the whole realm where it spread beneath her under its blanket of night. She felt every thaw-swollen stream that leapt down from the blue hills and purple moors, every spilling river that coursed through thick-growing woods and wide meadows, and she sensed spring that rose even now in the dipping dales to clothe the bare trees and scatter flowers on the hills.

'I have my land, my good land,' she said. 'I *will* be content.'

Eudora slowed her running as she felt the oranges in her pouch bounce against her hip. She stopped for a moment to unfasten the pouch and pat the lovely round shapes, a slight, incredulous smile lighting her sallow face. But then her hands found something else at the bottom of the pouch... something tiny. She squeezed it between thumb and forefinger, then her face crumpled and she broke again into a breathless run.

Punctuating the walls near the northeastern end of the bailey, not far from the huge gatehouse, stood a squat, square tower that served as a dwelling place for many of the castle menials. Eudora dived in through its door and bounced off the ample breasts of a large woman who was on her way out. 'Careful, lovey,' said the woman, but Eudora pushed past without a word and stumbled up the stairway that climbed the tower within its own narrow turret. In the wooden-floored chamber two storeys above were twelve beds and a dying fire in the middle of a wide hearth. The scullion stood breathing heavily and looked about her. She could see by the fire's light that four women were already abed, the blankets pulled up over their heads. One snored softly.

Eudora fed a log to the fire, lit her stub of candle and went to sit on the low pallet that lifted her straw-filled mattress above the floor-boards. She took the oranges from her pouch and contemplated them with wonder. She kissed one of them, then, with a quick glance over her shoulder, hid them both in the small chest of clothes by her bed. After another furtive look about the chamber, she fished around in her pouch and withdrew a tiny silver chain upon which hung a small moonstone. Hunched around it and holding her candle close, she gazed at the trinket.

'Such a tiny thing,' she breathed; 'she'll never notice 'tis gone.' But then she moaned and clutched the moonstone tight. 'I'll return it... if I have another chance to tend m'lady's fire... I shall toss it down amongst the cushions... she might think she dropped it herself...'

In Castle Lawhill's southeastern tower, within the fire-lit glow of Princess Winterhued's bedchamber, Lady Brenn slept deeply. A blackened log settled in the hearth with a sigh. The little cat woke with huge, black eyes and stared at the window. She flattened her ears, bared her small, needle teeth and spat. Then she got down from her bed and crept across the chamber, tail bristling and belly close to the floor. Brenn slept on as the fire spread its friendly warmth.

Up on the tower battlements Winterhued straightened and into her mind came a thought of warm counterpanes and pillows. Then the moon again broke free of cloud and as its white light sharpened the night a sound at her back, softly susurrant, stood her hairs on end.

She swung to face the north but there was naught to see beside a fall of moonlight on stone and an empty sky. The sound faded and the princess, with a puzzled frown, began to edge sideways towards the

glow of torchlight in the stairwell. Her hand, as she ran it along the battlements, trembled. Then she stopped, fear crawling up her spine, for
the sound had welled up again and it was a terrible sound. It swelled
louder and louder, a shrill reverberation, a clamorous whirring, until it
shivered the air and curdled the sky.

The princess flung up her hands for suddenly the night was full
of birds. They rushed past her, skimming by her face, catching in her
clothing; she felt the scrape of their wings and the scratch of their talons
and heard the high keening of their fear. Dropping to her knees with
her hands clasped over her head, she crouched for long minutes on the
cold stone until the dark, shrilling, fluttering crowds of them had all
fled away into the south. She stayed huddled, and with a low whimper
put her hands over her ears. For far away a terrible scream tore at the
night, high, thin and filled with desolation.

Three days ride to the east, high on the haunted slopes of lonely
Iron Crag, a creature the colour of moonlight ran across moonlit snow.
She had felt the wind change direction and as she came down the rocky
slopes her step was light. She shook her head, she leapt and spun; she
tossed snow to the moon. The sound of her going awakened sleeping
things in the earth with thoughts of spring.

She propped, she stopped, the swirling snow settled at her feet.
Very still she stood and the vapour of her breath thinned, drifted and
vanished.

For a few moments the moon was blackened by dark clouds of
birds flying over from the north, from the west. The night was swamped
by their small voices, laden with the beating of their small wings.

But beyond the birds there was something else.

The creature stood motionless but for the heartbeats that, almost
imperceptibly, rocked her whole body. She knew that somewhere
above the ground and under the moon something moved, something

akin to herself but completely unlike, something unfettered, ancient as the earth.

The birds passed away into the south but the creature remained, silent, scarcely breathing until, as though to match the beating of her heart, the very air began to thud and shake. The tremor faded and passed, it was but a whisper, an echo of something far away. Yet with it came a reek of decay, and the carrion stench of torn flesh.

Winterhued sank to her knees before the hearth, her heart still racing. Beside her, Brenn lay sleeping, curled in a nest of cushions, her hair spread like tumbled autumn leaves and her breathing deep and even. The fire burned low, casting a lambent light over her bedchamber and all the dear, familiar things within.

'Fool, fool,' she breathed, 'how often have I heard that cry? 'Tis but the wretched red ape in my father's menagerie. Poor, hapless creature, crying for his family and his lost land. And the other? Why, 'twas but birds flying over; small, harmless birds just returned from their wintering. Alas... what drear things torment my mind of late! If I could but cast them forth and be myself again...'

She spread her hands to the fire's warmth, but they betrayed her unstill heart with their trembling and the knuckles of one were grazed from her hurried flight down the winding stair.

'Puss... Thistle,' she whispered and turned to scan the chamber, but the little cat was nowhere to be seen. She got to her feet and tiptoed round the room looking here and there, peering beneath the bed, behind chairs and chests, opening closets and lifting the curtains and hangings. At last, down on her hands and knees for a second search of the chamber, she spied a small shape crouched in the deep shadow beneath the furthest end of her bed.

'Thistle, come to me,' breathed the princess but the little tabby, backed against the wall and half buried in the bed-hangings, would not move.

The princess got to her feet and stood frowning for a moment. Reaching up to search for the pins holding the coronet and headdress to her head, she fumblingly removed them, then released her hair from its plaits and coils. She shook her head thankfully and her hair fell about her face and cascaded down her back like strands of night.

'So weary...' she whispered, rubbing her hands over her eyes. After a while she walked back to feed some wood to the fire and poke at it, sending sparks spurting up under the big stone hood of the hearth. She needed Brenn to unlace her gown, but the girl slept deeply and looked too peaceful to wake. Sinking down upon the cushions, she gazed into the flames where her sleepy eyes saw a demon face with a tongue of fire and a spired city burning to red embers and crumbling grey ash.

She was riding through a forest on her mare... or was it her old pony? She could not see for it was dark in the forest and the leaves were all black. She heard her father coming behind her but she could not turn and it was so very lonely in there. The tears began to roll down her face. 'Why didst thou send him away?' she sobbed and her father answered: 'He was putting dead dogs and dung under his good fleeces.' Before she could ask him how he knew this, she spied beside the path a fat man cutting down a tree. 'Thou canst not do that,' she cried, 'for it is the duke's oak tree and he needs it to calculate the profits.' The fat man turned to her with a lustful leer and his mouth was black and toothless. Blood dripped from his axe. 'This,' said her father in a big voice, 'is thy husband; thou shalt wed him on the morrow.' Her father was bellowing as he passed her but he was small and naked and went on all fours to eat acorns. She turned back to the fat man but he had flown into the treetops, leaving his sword plunged deep in the pale hide of a dead horse. Its gaunt flanks bared rows of blue-shadowed ribs and its head was a staring skull with a long, gleaming horn issuing from its forehead. She began to sob again but she did not know why for it would have died anyway. The fat man, her betrothed, was above her, flying. She tried to see him but he was always just out of sight. She glimpsed his long, black robes fluttering and his grey hair. 'I cannot marry him, father,' she gasped, 'for that is the chancellor and he is too old.' 'But if not me,' shouted the chancellor, 'then who shall levy the profits?' He raised his voice above the wing-beats but they were stronger, they thudded and thumped like a giant's heartbeat as the air turned blood-coloured and vibrated with fear. Out of the corner of her eye she saw them, wings of torn skin, wings that had flapped for aeons across dread lands of dearth and decay. She put her small, white hands up into the blood-black sky and waited for talons...

And woke, crumpled in soft cushions beside a dying fire, with tears on her face and a cry in her throat. She saw the girl with the chestnut hair gazing at her with round eyes and she gave a little laugh and struggled to sit up.

'Oh... I was dreaming,' she gasped, but then she saw that the girl, who sat with her knees clasped under her chin, had tears coursing down her face and her shoulders shook with sobbing.

'Alas child, what ails thee?' said the princess. She stretched out her arms and Brenn came crawling and slithering over the cushions, half tangled in her gown, to curl against Winterhued like a frightened puppy. The princess stroked her hair as the girl sobbed, feeling her own heart still hammering and the tears still wet upon her own cheeks. As Brenn's sobbing subsided the princess murmured in her ear: 'What is it, little cousin? Tell me.'

Brenn suddenly pulled away from Winterhued's arms as though she had just realized who it was that comforted her so closely. She turned, round-eyed, tear-blotched and confused. 'Oh, my lady... m'lady is still dressed. I thought it was morning and I had slept all night...' She began to cry again. 'I thought I was at home,' she sobbed.

'Poor Brenn,' breathed the princess. 'Didst thou dream of thy home?'

She took the girl's hand and Brenn looked up at her through brimming eyes and barely whispered her answer. 'I dreamt, but not of home... a terrible dream that I've dreamt before. They make me so afraid... the wings. They are so big and have no feathers. They are...' She put her free hand behind her head as if trying to protect it and her voice shook with remembered horror. 'I cannot see, for I cannot turn my head and I am so afraid.'

Winterhued gripped Brenn's hand and stared at the girl. 'That is my dream,' she said.

It was then that the air above the tower began to thump and gust. It came rolling down the chimney in such a burst that the sinking embers exploded into flame. The girl gave a muffled shriek and the princess leapt to her feet and spun to face the window. She saw a huge tongue of flame rush, roaring and curling, towards the lake. She heard slate tiles and leading slide and crash onto the shingles below, and stone torn from its mortar as battlements toppled and fell. She heard fear: screams and cries of beasts and men. She heard the girl behind her whimper, face down in the cushions, and she heard the little cat under the bed mewl softly, terribly.

'Oh,' gasped Winterhued. She stood for but a moment, the remnants of flames beyond the glass panes dancing in her eyes, before resolutely wiping damp hands on her gown and striding for the window. With just a quick glance out, she pulled the heavy shutters to and fastened them. Then she made for the door. As she opened it she turned back to the frightened girl who watched her, huge-eyed, from the cushions.

'I will return as soon as I may,' she said. 'Stay here. Keep away from the window. Go to the chamber below if... if the need arises. Do not be afraid.' She stepped into the antechamber and turned. 'Look after Thistle,' she said and closed the door.

CHAPTER 3

As the sun peered up over the edge of the world the creature that was the colour of moonlight stood atop Iron Crag and looked down upon a sea of golden cloud. The shining air was still and the morning bright as birdsong but the creature felt, more clearly than usual, that odd, empty place within her.

She turned to face south, where the jagged tips of a mountain range rose above the clouds like a chain of islands, and then she turned again. Far to the west, almost beyond sight, the clouds thinned to show the greening land below. An ugly, black smudge stained the distant horizon and above it a raptor soared, catching the sun's first rays on wide, wide wings. Too wide.

The creature stood frozen, then she ran about the summit in an agitated circle and came back to stare. She turned to leave, then spun and stared. She circled, but swung round to gaze again to the west. Her shadowed tracks in the snow crossed over and over until she was no longer on the mountaintop but moving through the trees. Melted snow dripped from the branches as she followed the chatter of running water downhill towards a lake. She knew the snow there would be untrodden, the water smooth as a mirror, and the silence as deep as the mountain's roots.

But she halted some way from the lakeshore, her eyes bright with alarm. Within her breast her heart jolted and every part of her being urged her to flee, yet she stayed, motionless, the clouds of her breath thinning till only the barest wisp of vapour drifted through the droplet-hung branches.

There were hoof prints across the dimpled snow on the far side of the lake, there were ripples crossing the water towards her, gleaming silver circles; the silence was broken by the snort of a horse, the jingle of harness.

A knight had ridden his white war-horse down to the lake's edge. The horse drank noisily, snuffling and snorting. His tangled mane fell down across his eyes and floated on the water.

The knight looked round to watch another horse emerge from the trees and shuffle through the snow towards the lake. He was a big, red gelding with a flaxen mane and a wide splash of white from brow to muzzle. A thin youth, his parchment face pinched with cold, perched atop the gelding's broad back like a bundle of sticks.

The red horse lowered his head delicately, his pursed lips sucking at the air well before they touched the water. The white stallion, having drunk his fill, raised his head and stared across the lake, water dripping from his whiskery muzzle. There came a slithering and a thump as a tree lost its snowy load and the knight glanced up, gazing across the lake towards the point upon which his horse's attention was fixed so intently. The frosty breath of horse and man hung on the air.

The knight was a lean, strong man, not so young as once he was. There were one or two threads of grey through his long, dark hair and his face looked gaunt and weary. But his mouth had a slight curve to it, as though a wry smile might be its customary expression, and the eyes he turned upon the trees and the lake were as blue as shadows on snow.

The horse he sat was old; a tall, broadly built fellow with scarcely enough flesh to cover his large bones. His coat was white with age, flecked all over with remnants of the steel-grey he once had been. His head was big and honest and his dark eyes undimmed.

But the moonlight beast saw little of this. She was like a maid who has spied two huge spiders. She stood, full of terror and revulsion, her skin crawling, but she would not turn to flee unless the things scuttled towards her.

The knight, who had seen nothing amongst the trees, dismounted. 'Thou art quiet, lad,' he said to his shivering squire. He pulled off his leather and steel gauntlets and tossed them onto the saddle.

Stepping over to the chestnut, he fetched down two flasks from where they hung upon the horse's harness. The boy perched on the gelding's back showed a few snag-teeth in a grimace and pulled his cloak tighter. 'Toocoddadork,' he muttered through juddering jaws.

'What a blessing then is the cold,' said the knight, stooping to fill the flasks with lake water. Clumsy with the cold, he re-attached them to the saddle then reached up, pretending to wipe his dripping hands on the boy's tousled hair. The lad growled and ducked away and the knight smiled. He dried his hands on his cloak instead and pulled his gauntlets back on. Swinging easily into the saddle he gathered up the reins and murmured words to his horse.

The watching creature waited motionless behind the snowy trees, as first the grey horse then the chestnut, began to move. With a clicking of their old joints they turned away from the lake.

The harness creaked, and the knight's two swords clanked together. The moonlight beast shrank from the ugly sound and turned her head towards her mountain. She would drift away up the slope and leave those deadly things to scurry where they would.

But then a flash of red at the corner of her eye brought her head round. She saw again the grey horse and the chestnut clanking slowly away from the lake, she saw harness of dull leather and armour of dull steel. But the knight's shield was red. Not russet like the red horse but a deep scarlet red, like blood. And across the red reared a great white beast. A beast with a flowing mane. A hoofed beast. A beast that flaunted, thrusting from its forehead, a single, spiraled horn.

Across the lake came a heavy flap of wings as a raven took to the air. Faint and far away sounded the wind and the melted snow chattered on.

The creature stood motionless for a long moment. Then, without understanding why, she took one look back towards her home and set off silently through the trees. She was not moving uphill. Instead she walked round the lake and followed the knight with the unicorn shield away from the mountain.

A terrible morn had come at last to Lawhill-by-the-Lake and discovered much of the town ablaze. But the castle stood. Through a thick haze of smoke its flanks glowed golden where the sun shafted down from a break in the clouds.

Deep within its fastness Princess Winterhued leant against a mildewed hanging with her head down and the heels of both hands pressed to her eyes. She felt ill. It was gloomy and cold in the basement of the old Watchtower, and filled with the odour of mould. Worse, another stench wafted in occasionally that most likely issued from the neighboring latrine pit. A fire, doing little to dispel the chill, sputtered and struggled on the hearth under a hooded lintel, but the chimney shaft must have been blocked higher up for much of its smoke hung in oily coils about the chamber.

In through the single arrow-loop seeped weak, yellowish light and yet more stink and it was this smell that was sickening the princess. It was akin to meats over-roasting in the kitchens. But there was no roasting today for the half-timbered kitchens, built up against the stone of the outer bailey, had been reduced to charcoal. Winterhued did not want to think too hard on the cause of that stink of cooked flesh.

The chancellor began to cough again and the hound beneath the king's chair whimpered.

'This is a dismal place,' said the princess, looking up with a sigh. 'Surely there is somewhere more wholesome...'

'More wholesome, your highness? More wholesome?' croaked Sir Gunford, Captain of the Royal Guard. 'I dare say there is, I dare say, but my lady, this is the stoutest tower, the stoutest... the plinth being exceeding thick here and the vaulting above us staunch. Only the keep is built stronger... and we cannot venture thither, your highness, we cannot venture thither.'

The princess glanced over at him, her lip curling at the tremor in his voice. Above the polished splendour of his half-armour, his eyes were glassy and sweat trickled down his stubbled face. His ash-coloured hair poked from his head at unlikely angles as though he had just climbed from his bed.

'Stoutest tower?' rejoined the princess. Starting up restlessly, tired, grief-filled and angry, she began to pace the room. 'I cannot see,' she said, 'any use in staying cooped up in the stoutest tower, snug and sweet-smelling as it is, while the town burns and our people die. I think we should go to the King's Hall. There we may...'

'My most sovereign lord and lady crowded with the rabble?' said Sir Gunford, his voice rising. 'With but a few slate tiles between your highnesses and... that?' He gestured vaguely at the arrow slit.

'Of more importance, what of our breakfast?' said the king through a mouthful of cold pheasant.

Winterhued frowned at him wearily. Neither she nor his councillors had been able to impress upon him the dire nature of their situation. Yet she answered him patiently enough. 'The kitchens, my lord, are burned, so for now my lord must needs forego a full breakfast and eat as though he were in a field of battle. For though the castle is well stocked and plenished we little know the number of mouths we must feed now that many of the townsfolk take shelter within our walls, and neither can we tell for how long we are like to be held thus under siege.'

'Siege? Forsooth!' said the king, spitting driblets of pheasant. 'This is nonsense! From all that's been seen and told, 'tis but a bird out there. How is it that a single bird can set a thousand lily knees a' knocking and lay siege to a castle full of men that merrily kill birds every day?' Old Gers got to his feet, waving his pheasant bone. His hound rose too, on lean, trembling legs, then sank again to her haunches. 'Where are our guards, our knights, our bowmen?' spluttered the king. 'Why, at the first strife in their coddled lives, do they scurry away to hide in the walls like insects? Let them take up arms and go slay the wretched thing! Where is our man Auchencairn? He won't be skulking in the dark like a craven cockroach; let him gather some men and venture forth: kill the stinking bird and then we can all get on with our hunting, our dining, and our dallying…'

The king's voice wavered and he subsided into his chair, dropping the pheasant bone on the flagstones. For a moment the princess thought he had started to sob, but he just yawned hugely and reached for more pheasant. '…and our planning,' he concluded, casting a sly look at his daughter. The hound beneath his chair finished crunching the dropped bone then nervously cleaned the flagstones with her tongue.

'Sir Auchencairn,' rasped the chancellor between bouts of coughing, 'hath done as your highness would have him do. Ever dauntless he did bestir three brave knights and the best of your highness' guard,' he glanced disdainfully at Sir Gunford, 'and forth they went at daybreak, keen and armed to the teeth.'

'But neither he nor his men have been seen since,' said the princess. 'Oh, my poor cousin Nomia,' she murmured, pressing a hand to her aching forehead, 'She must be frantic.'

She turned to look at the king. She was still dressed in the gown she had worn the evening before and her hair hung loose, its dark fall shadowing her face. 'Father,' she said, 'what your highness sayeth doth seem good sense, but this beast appeareth too mighty for us. Though we are many, what chance have we when pitted against a creature so puissant it can burn houses with a single breath and topple walls with a wing-beat? All our strengths seem feeble and our strategies doomed. Half of the guards have perished already, and the messengers and pursuivants that were sent forth to seek the aid of our army were likely carried off, or fried and devoured where they perished.'

In a corner of the chamber Benicia and Manicia, the only of her ladies-in-waiting to have come to attend her in all the chaos, clung to each other. They sat amongst a pile of blankets upon one of the five pallets that had been brought downstairs sometime in the night and which had afforded members of that small party a few snatched moments of sleep. Benicia had just woken. She rubbed her heavy eyes then, remembering, she whimpered and tears began to course down her face. She buried her disheveled head against Manicia's breast. Manicia, wide-awake, patted her sister's shoulder, a tiny smile upon her lips. Winterhued turned distractedly to the two girls and Manicia pulled her sister to her feet.

'Lady Manicia,' she said, 'I have a task for ye twain... for thee in truth Manicia, and as I have been so wearied by thy sister's constant weeping and, lo, it begins anew, thou canst take her along with thee.'

Benicia looked up with a sob. Her pretty face was discoloured and soggy. Manicia pushed her away and bobbed a half curtsey. 'Your highness,' she said. She could not prevent an expression of sly triumph from stealing across her face.

'Go ye, if ye can... carefully, keep to the lower wall-walks... go ye to the chambers of Sir Garthwray in the Bellhouse Tower,' said the princess, 'and see if ye may discover how fareth my Lady Ulidia and her husband.' She glanced towards the arrow slit. 'I am told the tower is broken, yet... yet they should be safe in the lower levels... I wonder she hath not found me...'

'How are we to find anyone amongst the havoc?' blurted Benicia, clinging again to her sister's arm. 'I do not want to go up there again.

I saw dead folk...' Her voice caught and she sobbed loudly. '...there was a woman... she...'

'Benicia, be quiet,' hissed Manicia, elbowing her sister and stepping forward. 'Verily, my lady,' she said quietly, "twas terrible out there. We had such a time finding your highness. The lower walks were full of people... castle folk, lords and lackeys both, and folk from the town. They sat and lay crowded on the flagstones... some were burnt and some dead. They wailed and cried and screamed...'

'Aye, I have seen how they suffer,' said Winterhued quietly. 'Yet, brave Manicia, methinks thou shalt find a little order restored now, for while ye slept...' She broke off and turned as she heard a scuffle of footsteps in the stairwell. 'At last, here is Travancore. What news, Sir Audny?'

Sir Audny, the young Duke of Travancore, had come bounding, long-legged, down the last of the steep stairs, his sword scraping and banging on the steps behind him. The booted feet of two soldiers appeared above him but he held up his hand and they came no further. He turned and bowed.

'Your highnesses, Lord Chancellor...' He spoke in a breathless voice, barely louder than a whisper, as he glanced past the princess towards the king. But Gers gave no indication that he'd heard a thing; with a sidelong leer at Drumrock's daughters, he leant down to feed pheasant giblets to his hound. The hound licked his face wetly.

'Ah... as my lady ordered...' said the tall young duke, 'we... the constable and I... have gathered and brought the people into the King's Hall and... ah, persuaded many of the gentry into the cellars beneath.' Travancore's breath was short and a sheen of sweat glistened on his long face. He looked exhausted. Even so, as he talked his gaze would stray now and then towards Benicia, as iron to a magnet. Benicia, with her reddened eyes and blotched cheeks, was looking far from her best, but as it was not her face that Sir Audny gazed upon this was hardly a disadvantage to her.

'Ah... um... there... um, we have begun to feed them,' he continued, still in that low, hoarse voice, 'and... ah, tend the wounded...'

'What are their numbers?' asked Winterhued.

'We counted over six hundred souls; the final number will be closer to eight...' The duke's voice caught and he bent his head, trying to suppress a fit of coughing. Like Sir Gunford, he was clad in a gleaming steel breastplate and Winterhued wondered briefly why the men had put on their armour and how they thought it might avail them.

'Begging pardon m'lady,' he said hoarsely, wiping his mouth with the back of his hand. 'Your highness was wise... the King's Hall is strong and its roof being steeply pitched and spiked with steel the... ah... creature seemeth loth to light upon it. The walls too are built thick and the windows narrow.'

'But it can be only a temporary sanctuary,' said the princess. 'I think we must shortly decide...'

The duke interrupted her with a nervously raised hand. 'My lady, begging your grace's pardon,' he breathed, 'but I... I believe it is safer to speak as quietly as we may. If the... ah... the thing heareth aught of humankind it is more likely to come a-hunting.'

'Ahh,' sighed the princess and gazed at him a moment, watching a trickle of sweat make its way through the stubble on his jaw. 'I think we must soon decide,' she continued in a low voice, 'whether to stay or leave. Removing eight hundred souls from the castle will be difficult... and besides, what safety is there outside the shelter of its walls? But if we stay the lords must stop eating so much; the stores must straight away be tallied and the victuals rationed.'

King Gers twisted in his seat. 'Eh? Rationed? Nonsense!' he growled. 'There's enough in the castle stores to last for years! Ration my vittals and ye'll rue the day! More wood on this fire! If ye make it burn it'll cease its damnable smoking. And if ye'd all cease your jabbering and go up and do what needs to be done, why then, we'd have no more call to sit starving on our backsides in this dank pit!' He glanced again at the princess's two ladies-in-waiting. 'We could all get on with more important matters, eh ladies?' he said.

Winterhued watched the king bend once more over his pheasant carcass and hoped that the wink she'd seen him make had been caused by smoke in his eyes. Dread needled her as she turned to one of the guards beside the door. Wordlessly she pointed at the fire, and the fellow propped his halberd against the doorframe and scurried to the task.

'A fire, too, is... um, dangerous,' hissed Travancore anxiously, 'It doth betray our whereabouts...'

'Aye, that was my advice,' said Sir Gunford, taking two steps forward. Winterhued looked at him and he took two steps back.

'Fie, Sir Audney!' she said quietly. 'How may the creature find the smoke from our small fire? Lawhill burns, the Queen's Hall, the kitchens, lie in smouldering ruins. Why, the air is thick with smoke from a hundred fires! Thou, and Gunford here... ye would have us all dig ourselves into holes and hide there 'til we freeze or starve!' She stopped as she saw a look of distress cross the young duke's weary countenance. 'Oh, Sir Audny, forgive me. Thou hast done well, and I value thy diligence. Yet,' she said, 'we shall have our fire.'

He bowed slightly, anxiously. 'I thank my lady and I... I am sorry if I seem over cautious. Yet,' he glanced up, the whites of his eyes flashing, 'I have been up... up there...'

'Tell me,' interrupted the princess, 'how stand the castle walls between here and the Bellhouse Tower?'

'Ah... the battlements are broken in places, but the walls are sound and the walks within... um, passable, my lady. The King's Gate standeth strong.'

Winterhued turned to her two ladies in waiting. Manicia watched the duke with a sneer. 'Manicia,' said the princess, 'thy way should be easier now. I must know how fareth my Lady Ulidia, and see if thou canst discover aught of Aminta and Pera.' She pointed to the guard who had just taken up his post after seeing to the fire. 'Thou,' she ordered, 'go with these ladies.'

Sir Audny had been looking steadily more alarmed as the princess spoke. Without thinking he moved to block the door. 'Nay, my ladies,' he said, looking at Benicia and forgetting to whisper, "tis perilous without! Why would your highness send these ladies? Let this man go,' he said, indicating the guard, 'or send one of my men to the task.'

'Sir Audny,' said Winterhued quietly, 'girls are not as stupid as thou mightest believe; they will not rush wailing about the battlements.' She fixed Manicia in her gaze. 'They will go quietly, keeping to the lower walks. They will take care at the gatehouse, climbing to the chamber above and *not* crossing the open gateway. They will keep away from doors, windows and arrow loops and they will not look outside. It is but a short distance. Now, away with thee, Manicia. Do thy best.'

Manicia, her smug look restored, shrugged away her sister's clutching hand and bobbed a curtsey. 'I'll not fail m'lady,' she said, backing towards the door. Benicia sketched a curtsey too and made a grab for Manicia's arm. 'Craven girl,' admonished Manicia as she ducked around Sir Audny and towed her sister away up the narrow stair. The guard bowed and was quickly at their heels. There was a scuffle of booted feet in the stairwell as the duke's soldiers pinned themselves against the wall to let the trio pass.

'Take heart, Benicia,' called Winterhued.

'Good girls, those,' said the king. 'Drumrock's buxom lasses.' He had finished the pheasant and was now tucking into some cold beef.

His toady, Sir Gunford, leant against a wall hanging and grinned at Gers. His forehead glistened as brightly as his armour. Loud, pompous and a bully to his men, he had always treated Winterhued with fawning condescension and she felt a little satisfaction now to see him dissolve like a lump of mud in the rain.

The tall young duke still stood with one hand on the doorway, gazing up the stairs.

'Verily, Sir Audny,' said Winterhued, 'thou dost waste thy time with the Lady Benicia. Knowest thou she hath been promised to the Earl of Dunmore?'

The duke's cheeks flushed. 'Oh... aye, m'lady, aye,' he stammered, 'I... I am not...'

'Promises can be broken,' said the king, 'for the right man, eh Audny?' He winked and chuckled. 'Nice ripe lasses, those; well bred.'

Winterhued pretended she hadn't heard him. 'Tidings, Sir Audny,' she said. 'Firstly... Sir Auchencairn?'

'Naught my lady,' he answered, 'not since... ah... he took three knights: Sir Howth, Sir Wynford and... ah, um... Drumrock's nephew...'

'Sir Dechmont?'

'Aye, Dechmont, as well as ten pikemen and five bowmen. They... ah... they crossed the bailey and entered the keep, m'lady.'

'The keep.'

'Aye, m'lady.'

Winterhued ran a hand across her face and closed her eyes. 'How fareth the castle?' she asked.

'Ahh... within the inner bailey...' The duke thought aloud, staring at the flagstones at his feet, 'the turrets on this tower and the Bellhouse are toppled...'

'That accounts for the blocked chimney,' croaked the chancellor.

'...yet the towers themselves stand strong. The great halls, thou dost know of. The keep...'

Winterhued glanced at him. 'Aye, I have seen the keep,' she said.

'Most of the chambers... the king's apartments, audience chamber... damaged, some afire. The library, the clerks' and stewards' chambers... all burnt to the ground. Yet the King's Tower, the East Tower, thine own tower, m'lady, and most of the walls between stand unbroken, staunch.'

'And the outer bailey?'

'Kitchens and bakehouse burnt... and the granary... but the cellars, buttery, pantry – all the old parts, built solid – so too the prison, the armoury, the menagerie, the mews... not a stone shifted, not a slate dislodged.'

'The stables?' asked the princess, half knowing the answer. She folded her arms and stared at the floor.

'Great and Little Stables both burnt. But there are a score or more of horses running about in the bailey, so some of them got away. I was told two stable lads braved the fire to release them. The... the creature doth eschew the beasts. It appeareth that only the meat of human-kind is to its taste.'

Winterhued smiled grimly. 'It is a just beast then,' she said. She wished so much to ask about her own beloved black mare, but how could she when the world burned and her people died?

'What of my grey courser?' asked the king indistinctly, rising to his feet with a clatter of chair legs on the flags. His mouth was full of meat and he peered bulge-cheeked at Sir Audny. 'And my hounds, my hounds,' he muttered, then swallowed hard, 'what of my good hounds?'

'The kennels too are burnt, sire,' said the duke gently, 'yet some of the hounds were got out and now they make a healthy racket in the basement of the Constable's Gate. As for my liege's courser, I cannot say... but two or three of those in the bailey are grey...'

The king sank back into his chair and put his head in his hands. 'My horses, my fine horses... my good, faithful hounds,' he breathed and, as his attendant hound rested her head on his lap and whined softly, the king began to sob. Winterhued watched her father but made no move to comfort him.

'Continue, Sir Audny,' she said; 'we are barely half way round the bailey.'

'Ah... um, the forge is burnt, also the slaughterhouse. The Garrison Hall and soldiers' quarters are smoking ruins, so too the Retainers' Hall, the lodging house and the hay store. The fuel store too. The roof of the outer bailey chapel is gone. The menials' tower and part of the castle walls to the northeast have fallen into the ditch. The Constable's Gate standeth whole and strong, but...'

'But?' asked Winterhued when the duke hesitated.

'Outside, m'lady... outside the gate... hundreds of townsfolk, trying to get within the walls as the town burned... they were trapped, m'lady.' His voice had sunk so low that she could barely hear him. 'We think the, the... thing did swoop down and blast the drawbridge with flames as they crossed. They fell into the stream below or piled up, dying, against the outer portcullis.'

'The portcullis? Why was it lowered?'

The chancellor looked up, his eyes bloodshot and watering. The king had ceased his sobbing but sat slumped like a sack in his chair.

"Twas no-one's fault,' replied the duke. 'The windlass had failed, dropping the 'cullis until it jammed about an arm's span above the roadway. They were working on it when the... ah... the creature came last night and... it was abandoned. Those from the town that managed to gain refuge here crawled beneath it with scant trouble, but when... ah... a great mob of mazed and burning townsfolk...' The duke searched for the words, gave up and shook his head.

Winterhued stared at the fire. It still burned sluggishly; a coil of grey smoke oozed round the lintel and drifted up the blackened wall. 'They'd surely have fared better if they'd run away from Lawhill,' she said. 'And... as I hear thy reports of toppled towers and a destroyed granary, I deem that we too must think of leaving.'

'Cravens all,' muttered the king, still slumped in his seat.

'It will be nigh impossible to get the people out,' said the duke. 'Mayhap your highnesses, under cover of dark...'

'We stay or leave,' interrupted the princess, 'with our people.'

'The Constable's Gate is blocked with the dead,' said the duke; 'even if we clear it, the drawbridge is burnt and the town beyond... who knows if it is passable? We are surrounded by water, but for the ditch and the broken wall atop it, and they are treacherous and exposed. The posterns admit but one person at a time and lead nowhere and the Watergate hath not a boat yet afloat. We cannot swim across the lake, m'lady.'

Winterhued ran a hand over her tired eyes. 'There is a chance,' she said, 'that at least one of our messengers hath escaped the creature and is even now on his way to alert our army. I shall wait seven days. Meanwhile, our supplies must be tallied and rationed; with the granary burnt I fear we shall be hard pressed to feed eight hundred for more than a se'nnight. And we will do our utmost to destroy the creature ourselves; bowmen shall be stationed atop every tower...' Winterhued turned her face away. 'Oh,' she breathed, 'I would I knew what hath betid Sir Auchencairn.' She looked back at Sir Audney. 'Hast thou seen the creature?' she asked.

'I... I... nay...' stammered the duke. 'I... I did see a vast... darkness that came stooping to block the light at a window, but the wind of its passing shattered the glass and... ah... knocked me down. We have boarded up and shuttered all the windows now and there are few that would brave...'

The princess interrupted him. 'Hast thou spoken to any who *have* seen it?'

'Nay, my lady. Ah... 'tis clear there is... ah... something about this beast that preventeth men from looking upon it, for when it approacheth even the bravest knights fall down upon the earth, their innards turned to water. Any who *have* set eyes upon it have also perished, my lady.'

'Nay, that cannot be. Sir Audny, go thou, find and bring before his highness, myself and the council (which, at present, consisteth solely of our dear chancellor here) some person who hath had sight of this thing. I would know what it is we deal with. The word hath been avoided and hedged around, but I deem we will find this creature to be a dragon.'

The king snorted. 'Nonsense,' he said, 'there are no dragons. Never have been.' Sir Gunford sneered knowingly and chuckled his agreement.

'No dragons, father?' said the princess, looking over at him with a small, strange smile. 'Now go, Sir Audny,' she said, then changed her mind. 'Nay, thou art busy enough.' She turned. 'Sir Gunford, thou hast had little to occupy thee these past few hours... thou shalt find our witness.'

Sir Gunford's bulbous eyes widened. 'I am here to guard the person of our most gracious sovereign lord, your ladyship,' he said, looking toward the king as though he expected the said sovereign lord to countermand his daughter. But the king was absorbed in stroking his hound's ears and feeding her a piece of pheasant.

'There is a chamber full of soldiers directly above us, sir,' said Winterhued. 'If thou dost desist from taking all of them to protect thee on thy quest, I deem our gracious sovereign shall be just as safe as he would be with thee at his side.'

Sir Gunford made a slimy obeisance. 'Ever my lady's obedient servant,' said he in his unctuous manner and backed, still bowing, towards the stairway. But sweat rolled on his face, and fear gleamed in his eyes.

'Gunford,' said Winterhued as he reached the stairs, 'if thou dost see our Lord Chamberlain or Sir Garthwray, send them hither. We are in need of their good counsel.'

'Highness,' he answered, bowed again and was gone, away up the stairs to gather the strongest dozen of his stoutly armed lads.

Unlike Gunford, Sir Audny was anxious to be away. As soon as he had ascertained that he was no longer needed, he took his leave and his soldiers from the stairs. The princess watched him go, then turned back to the chamber. 'Get some sleep, chancellor,' she said. 'You also, father. There is little we can do at present but wait. And hope that at least one of our messengers is even now on the road to Belford and our army.'

She paced to the fire, but now that all was quiet she could feel the arrow loop at her back. It had been tugging at her ever since she had last stepped up to it and peered out. That had been some hours since, as dawn's first light had seeped through the drifting smoke.

The chancellor coughed as he curled up on his pallet. Winterhued went to cover him with a rug, and then returned to the fire to stare at the flames. Sliding her hands beneath her hair, she ran them over the nape of her neck, and then pulled her shoulder blades together as though she could feel eyes on her back.

At last, she turned to face the opening. It narrowed as it pierced the huge thickness of the buttressed wall and all she could see at its far end was a slit of weak daylight. With a shudder she stepped towards it.

The loop was high in the wall; if she had not been so tall she would have had to stand on tiptoes to see through it. She looked out from the low chamber just above the level of the bailey flagstones. The view was narrow. To the left a few timbers smouldered where once a wall of the clerks' chambers had stood. Directly before her was the inner bailey well, and beyond that the keep.

Five hundred years ago the keep had been the heart of Castle Lawhill; in fact there had been little else besides a gatehouse and an encircling wall that followed the outline of the present inner bailey. The keep had been built atop a rocky outcrop at the end of the peninsula that jutted into Lake Silverhow. It was a great square edifice with massively thick walls and tiny windows. Within, beyond a forebuilding with a murder hole and a drawbridge, were the garrison quarters and constable's chamber, on the floor above, a galleried hall without a fireplace and a great chamber with a fireplace but no chimney, and above that a chapel and two cold, uncomfortable chambers. At the very base of the keep, partially hewn from the rock, were the storerooms, a well and a terrible prison.

Over the long years, as the rest of the castle grew around it, the keep's importance had dwindled. No one lived there now; no one had lived there for three hundred years. It was a treasury, a strong room, a storehouse and, with its grim face and vacant eyes, it troubled castle children in their nightmares.

Winterhued had been an almost fearless child, but her young companions had so delighted in telling direful tales of that ancient edifice that the little princess had grown, for a time, mortally afraid of the keep.

Of course, being but a pile of stone, it had ceased to frighten her long ago. Yet as she looked at it now her heart quaked and she could not help the moan that escaped her lips. Night after night as a child she had seen the keep, turgid with horror, in her dreams. Now she saw it again, just as she had seen it then, but this was no longer a dream.

The battlements were broken, scorched and blackened. The lead from the roof had melted and poured down the walls leaving trails like dark candle wax. Dirty smoke oozed from the glassless windows. Expelled from the battlements, pushed through the windows and piled on the rocks at the keep's base were bloody carcasses, half stripped of their meat, some charred and burnt, some still clad in ragged clothing. Blood smeared the walls, dribbled down the rocks.

As a little child she had seen it thus in presageful dreams, and had known that something monstrous dwelt within. And this very morning (it seemed long ago but was barely six hours), Auchencairn had told her that the creature had taken the keep as its lair.

About the skirts of Iron Crag, still deep within the leafless forest, rode the knight and his squire. The road they took was little used; pitted, puddled and overhung by dripping boughs. Streams chattered down all of its furrows. The two horses, grey destrier and chestnut rounsey, were spangled in pale sunlight as they splashed their way through slush and dibbled snow.

On either side the trees crowded thick and silent, black trunks rising from snow-mounded roots to spread in an entanglement of bare branches. Amongst the trunks loomed the dark shapes of a few hardy evergreens and here and there an eager tree anticipated winter's end with a fuzz of pale green. The sun climbed as high as it could on winter's last day, then began its roll westward round the curve of the world.

'Why are we 'ere? Where do we go? Why do we go?' whined skinny Nal for the twentieth time. He clutched the pommel of his saddle and shifted his scant weight as though his seat bones pained him.

The knight, who had already answered twenty times (though not, it must be said, in any detail), regarded the boy for a moment. The grey stallion, ridden easily on a loose rein, jogged a few strides, his long mane floating up at each stride. He tilted his head to glance behind him, the white of his eye gleaming.

'It was thy choice to accompany me,' said the knight, still looking at the boy as he leaned to stroke his horse's neck. 'Thou couldst have remained happy-ever-after baking bread in Pengwern.'

'Bakin' bread? Bakin' bread?' said the boy, annoyed. 'Why do ye 'arp on about bread? I never baked bread.'

The knight looked down at the road with a smile. 'Thou wast a baker, lad,' he said, 'like thy father.'

'My father were a knight, a knight, sir. He fought at...'

'Thy father was a foot-soldier turned baker and thou couldst scarcely wait to leave him. Yet now thou complainest about thy service with me every waking moment. What didst thou expect?'

The boy sneered. 'All them sods sayin' ye were best knight in the world, "of great renown" they said. And there's me thinkin' my life would be full of 'igh deeds and... and danger and such like.'

'Thou hast a yearning to slay ogres?' asked the knight, his smile widening, 'rescue damsels in distress, kill dragons?'

'That's what knights do, isn't it? Not freeze and starve as they trudge through an endless sodding wilderness for...'

'I've met an ogre or two in my time, Nal,' interrupted the knight, 'but dragons... they're difficult to find these days.'

'But there are damsels!' said Nal, perking up. 'Why don't we turn about and go back to... what was the name o' that town? With the big tournament.' The red horse jogged to catch up with the grey and the boy hung on to the pommel and bounced. 'That there Lady Whatsit,' he said, 'she liked you exceedin' well; I could tell. Daft woman failed to see ye were a madman, but never mind that... we could 'ave gone to live with 'er, eaten barrow-loads of meat, slept till noon in a feather bed...'

'That may not have pleased her husband,' said the knight. He stroked his uneasy horse's neck.

'Methought she were a widow,' said the boy. 'Where were 'er 'usband then?'

'Thou dost prate too much,' sighed the knight, looking tiredly at the boy.

'No I don't… where were 'er 'usband?'

'Ailing, she said. She was sad. Methinks she loved him. Now, some peace, Nal.' He turned in his saddle to look back at the road, frowning.

The boy ignored him. 'If we'd tarried a bit, 'e may 'ave died. We could go back now: 'e'll be dead and ye can wed 'er… why, she's comely enough for you, surely. And then we could live comfortable instead of wanderin' about frozen with our bellies grumblin'.'

'Thou couldst bake her bread – that would please her.'

Nal made an angry noise in his throat. He thumped his heels into the chestnut's ribs and the horse flung up his head and bounded stiff-legged along the road for two or three strides. The boy's head jerked back; but for the saddle's high cantle, he would have fallen straight off over the horse's rump. He yanked at the reins and the curb-bit made the animal stop abruptly, head seesawing, mouth open.

The knight pushed his stallion over to the chestnut and pulled the reins from Nal's hands. 'Nal,' he said calmly, 'if thou canst not learn that there is a mouth on the end of these reins, thou shalt get off and walk.'

The boy made a face. 'Aye. Ye would,' he whined, 'ye would do that, for ye do ever think 'ighly on these ancient nags before ever ye think on me. Fie on you. I wish I were 'ome… and don't say naught about bakin' bread!'

The knight dropped the reins onto the chestnut's neck. The gelding shook his head then turned to snuffle noses with the knight's horse.

'Lad,' said the knight, putting a hand on the boy's shoulder and giving him a gentle shake, 'I do think well of thee… but I would think more of thee if thou couldst learn to use thine ears more and thy mouth less. And as for wishing thyself home, thou wast never happy there…'

'"Twas better than stumblin' about in a trackless wilderness.'

'Trackless?' said the knight, picking up his reins and urging his horse forward. 'Look down, lad. What dost thou travel upon?'

'A bony old nag,' answered Nal, sniggering at his own jest.

The chestnut gelding had started walking after the knight; he rarely took instruction from the boy on his back. Behind the grey, he splashed his way over a lively rill that rushed down over its rocky bed from the forested heights above.

'May's well be trackless,' said Nal. 'Not a woodcutter's cot nor a charcoal burner's 'ovel for weeks and what are we supposed to live on when that morsel o' mouldy bread and stinkin' dried beans are gone, eh? And what o' the 'orses? The shoes on my jade are thin as gold leaf in a miser's prayer book. One o' them 'ind ones comes off and 'e'll be lame in five minutes on them white feet of 'is. So, what 'appens then, eh? We ride through this dismal forest wi' the snow dripping on our 'eads till the 'orses tumble down, then we totter on a bit till we drop. "And so it came to pass",' intoned the boy, putting on a pompous, story-telling voice, '"the most famous, the most clever, the most admirable knight in all the 'ole wide world perished from 'unger and cold, all alone, apart from his trusty squire, in the middle of a sodding forest".'

'"Trusty squire",' said the knight with a smile, 'some hours ago we left this road and journeyed through a forest that was indeed trackless, to water the horses at a small lake.'

'Did we?'

'Mayhap thou slept; I do recall the blessed silence. Dost thou not remember a lake?'

'Oh... aye, ye dripped freezin' water on me 'ead.'

'Didst thou not wonder how I found that lake?'

'Why should I?' muttered Nal sulkily. 'Stands to reason that, as ye know everything, ye must know the whereabouts of every sodding lake in the world.'

The knight shook his head. 'I don't,' he said, 'and besides, we had
no need of a lake with snow-melt all about us. But I wished to see it.
I've been there before.'

'Certes,' said the boy sourly, 'If a *sane* man 'ad seen such a dreary
place once, 'e'd never go nigh it again.'

The knight ignored him and pointed down the road. 'There, lad.
Look.'

Their way had taken them steadily downwards for several hours.
Before them now the road dropped away, running like a stream. At the
bottom, sloping away from the road was a clearing where woodcutters
had been at work in years past. Between the stumps a few saplings
raised wispy, winter-bare limbs above clumps of yellow grass that poked
through the thawing snow.

'We shall see something from there, Nal,' said the knight.

The horses slithered down the road on their haunches, accoutrements clashing. 'Leave the horse alone,' said the knight, glancing round
at his squire. 'Drop the reins and let him find his own way.'

Nal sneered resentfully at his back. 'Never leaves findin' fault, does
'e?' he mumbled under his breath.

'That is because,' said the knight without turning, 'the lad doth
never learn, for he hath not listened to a word I've said to him this
past year.'

The horses finished their sliding descent and turned onto the
clearing. The red horse dropped his head to tug hungrily at the tough
grass. Looking round at the boy, the knight gestured before them.
'Manydown,' he said with a strange smile.

Framed between the trees on either side of the clearing a view had
opened out from the mountainside. Two darkly forested spurs sloped
down on either side of a narrow valley perhaps eight hundred feet
below the road. A stream glinted silver as it carried melted snow in
deeply etched curves along the valley floor. Several hardy sheep grazed
on tussock grass within low stone walls amongst bracken and hawthorn.
Beyond the mountain spurs, the stream ran out into a wider valley,

gleaming emerald in the soft sunlight. And at the centre of this broad vale a dozen cottages and a spired church clustered in the midst of a patchwork of strip-fields, ploughed and fallow. Meandering through the fields, past a vineyard and a walled orchard, a cart track led out to a small castle that sat above its reflection in a moat. The track continued on, following the stream along the verdant valley floor, passing in and out of woodland until it disappeared into hazy distance.

The knight sat silently, frowning slightly as he gazed over Manydown through eyes bluer than the sky. A breeze from the valley, bearing a faint scent of ploughed soil and habitation, lifted his dark hair.

'I smell food down there,' said Nal, wiping his nose on the back of his hand; 'trencher-loads of roast beef, dribblin' with juices.'

The knight sighed. 'We won't be down ere nightfall, lad,' he said, 'so forget your meat for the while. Besides, I think we may not go into Manydown... we shall go round the foot of the mountain and take the road to the north.'

Nal turned to face him with his mouth hanging open. 'Not go?' he wailed. 'Noooo!'

But at that very moment, the chestnut gelding flung his head into the air, grass trailing from his mouth, and spun about. The knight's horse too, jumped, sidled, and stood staring back the way they had come. Three ravens took to the air with a crack of wings. Nal picked himself up out of a puddle with a muttered curse.

The knight sat his horse as it pranced back a few steps, murmuring words as he felt the stallion's heart beating through the saddle. He reached for the pommel of his long sword and loosened it in its sheath as he gazed back along the road.

The forest was grey, silent, still. Lengthening shadows reached out across the clearing.

Nal grasped his dangling reins and moved in close to the solid bulk of the big red horse. 'What is it, sir?' he asked in a small voice.

'I do not know,' said the knight quietly. ''Tis passing strange. The forest is so silent. There are no birds... only ravens, carrion birds.

The horses have grown ever more restless all the day. Something…
is abroad.'

But turning towards Nal, he saw the fear in the boy's eyes. 'Never
mind, lad,' he said with a wry smile, 'we're in no danger. We've nought
to tempt robbers and scarce enough meat on our bones to feed a
wolf-cub. So get back on thy horse… we've a way to go before nightfall.'

CHAPTER 4

The Duke of Drumrock's two daughters hurried along the passage within the wall that divided Castle Lawhill's baileys. They held hands over their mouths against the smoke that curled aside as they passed. The passage they trod was the lower walkway, used by servants and soldiers. It was narrow and plain, the whitewashed walls rising to a pointed arch so low that a tall man walking there would be forced to stoop. Frequent arrow loops squinted out through the thick walls into the outer bailey, and on the other side of the passage an occasional barred door led into the inner ward.

The girls had been stopped by four of Travancore's soldiers upon entering the passage. 'We are about the princess's business,' Manicia had said imperiously, but the effect was spoiled as she burst into a crimson-faced fit of coughing.

The sisters' accompanying guard nodded to the officer in charge. 'Aye. Princess Winterhued's orders,' he said gloomily, but 'women interfering in men's business,' said his look. Travancore's men backed against the walls and bowed to the ladies as they started off again down the passage. Manicia, her lip curling into a dainty sneer, had not failed to notice how their heads all turned together, like little mechanical men, as Benicia's cleavage passed before them.

Since then the passage had been deserted. The guard, a broad fellow with a heavy walk and a phlegmy cough, took the lead now. Manicia scowled at his back and shrugged off Benicia's clinging hands. Her lip still curled, she turned to examine her sister's red eyes and blotchy face, her pearl headdress all awry and her peach velvet gown, so becoming at the feast last night, torn at the hem and smeared with ash.

Manicia's sneer transformed itself into a smirk. 'Beautiful Benicia,' she sniggered.

'Manny, not so fast,' gasped Benicia. 'My shoe is falling off.'

Manicia would have ignored her, but the guard stopped and half turned, forcing her to halt. She waited impatiently as Benicia, breathing noisily, hopped for a moment on one foot, still clinging to Manicia's arm, to pull her shoe back on. Her breasts jostled like jellies, threatening to escape over the top of her gown's low bodice.

'Unmannered knave!' snapped Manicia and the guard dragged his eyes away from the lovely sight, mumbling an apology. 'Keep thine impudent mouth shut and get thyself moving.' As he set off again she yanked her sister forward. 'I should have left thee with our father,' she hissed, though it was plain that she gained some satisfaction from observing the enfeebled state of her sister.

It was just last night (though it seemed much longer), well after the princess had retired to her chamber, that Manicia had sat silently, watching Benicia hiccup, giggle and flirt shamelessly with the gummy Marquess of Potrimpos. All of a sudden had come a great commotion and the sisters had looked up to see the roof of the Queen's Hall explode into fire.

Though they had survived unscathed, running, pushing and shoving amongst the terror-stricken mob as flaming crossbeams and gobs of molten lead rained down about them, Benicia had looked thereafter upon the burnt and the dying and been so filled with fear and pity that she could scarcely stand. Manicia, barely affected, had dragged her sister hither and thither until they had found their father, his face still greasy with meat, complaining selfishly beneath their burning apartments. But instead of leaving Benicia with him she had towed her sister off in search of Winterhued. After all, to wait upon the princess was what the two of them had been brought up to court to do.

And Manicia had looked scornfully at her sister and decided that she herself would be unafraid and strong.

The trio entered the tower on the east side of the King's Gate, crossed the empty guardroom at its base and climbed the stairs to the floor above. Most of the rooms within the gate's flanking towers were occupied by Sir Auchencairn, Lady Nomia and their household whenever they came up to court from their own lands in Dunsyre. But, separate from these apartments, a passage ran along the northern side of the gate, giving access to the crenellated wall-walk that looked down over the outer bailey.

At the top of the stairs the guard turned left into the passage, but Manicia went right, stepping through an arched opening out onto the wall-walk. Benicia gasped, cowering at the top of the stairwell. 'Your ladyship!' protested the guard. But Manicia put her hands on the cold stone, stuck her head between the merlons and looked out over the castle's outer bailey.

Disappointingly, she could see very little.

The air was filled with smoke. The castle walls to left and right and the solid bulk of the closest towers faded into the dirty yellow haze. The blackened beams of the kitchen and bakehouse smoked and smouldered, and mounds of ash and wreckage had buried the ovens. A frightening pall of silence lay over the castle, yet harsh in the stillness she could hear horses somewhere in the bailey, running to and fro, pausing, then running on.

Manicia looked down and stared for a long moment at an ashy heap at the foot of the gatehouse. It took her some time to realise that she was looking at burnt bones. Her eyes wandered dispassionately about the mess, seeing three or four hands like clutches of scorched twigs, scraps of singed cloth, a shrivelled leather shoe on the end of a charred shin-bone.

There appeared to be at least five corpses down there, tangled together. 'Lackeys, most likely,' murmured Manicia under her breath. She continued to stare, with the same curiosity she felt when, bored with some dull sermon in the chapel, she would gaze at the wall-painting of the martyr flayed alive.

The seconds slowed and crawled past and Manicia seemed glued to the wall. 'Your ladyship,' said the man-at arms.

'Manny,' whimpered Benicia, 'what dost thou see?' Manicia pushed herself away from the wall, turned and swayed. 'Manicia!' cried Benicia, scurrying towards her, 'art thou ill?'

'Don't make a racket,' said Manicia shortly, pushing away her sister's comforting hands. ''Tis but the smoke.'

She straightened, but stood for a moment with her head down and one hand outstretched to the wall for support. Then suddenly she pushed past her sister and the guard and walked quickly into the passage.

In the chamber above the gate she passed the windlass and slapped at it angrily as she passed. The top of its massive, spiked and studded portcullis jutted up into the chamber through a slot in the floor, suspended between the windlass and the wall by ropes that passed through triple-sheaved pulleys. Unseen beneath them the lower part of the portcullis hung like bared fangs above the gate passage. On the other side of the chamber, sunk down through the floor were three murder-holes.

The sound of voices slowed Manicia but even so, as she walked out of the windlass chamber, she almost ran into Nomia, Countess of Dunsyre, who stepped backwards out of her apartments into the passage. The tall woman was followed by three servants who struggled under the weight of a huge, rolled tapestry.

'Down to the basement,' she said, pointing to the floor at her feet. 'The floor is damp, so lay it across the chests.'

The servants passed her, bending the tapestry carefully as it went round the doorframe, along the short passage and down into the newel stair within the wall of the gatehouse's west tower. More servants followed behind, lugging heavy, wooden chests.

'Alas, Lady Nomia,' burst out Benicia, 'how fare ye?' Her eyes brimmed with tears.

The countess turned to the girls. Her calm face was pale and there were shadows beneath her eyes like bruises. 'Benicia, Manicia,' said she, 'what do ye here?'

Manicia elbowed her sister aside. 'At the princess's orders, I am to find Lady Ulidia and bring her to the King's Hall... which is perhaps where ye should be yourself, madam.'

Lady Nomia smiled slightly. 'The day is dire when Winterhued must ask aught of such an unkind child as thee, Manicia.'

'I do my duty,' said Manicia, her cheeks hot, 'which is more than most!'

'Ahh,' murmured the countess, still smiling. Her bleak eyes held Manicia for a moment, then moved to her sister. 'I thank thee, Benicia, for thy concern. Thou mayest inform the princess that when I have got our chattels out of harm's way, I shall go where I have been told to go, and there await tidings of my husband.'

Without another word she stepped back into her apartments as, unseen at her back, Benicia bobbed a curtsey and the guard bowed.

'Oh Manny,' said Benicia, catching at Manicia's hand as they started towards the newel stair, 'she did not mean that. 'Tis but anxiety over her missing husband...'

Her voice trailed off breathlessly as she scrambled down the steep stair after her sister. From just ahead of them, round the bend of the stair, came muttered curses and the thud of wood against stone as the countess's servants manoeuvred the heavy chests downstairs.

'She's so brave,' continued Benicia. 'Methinks, if 'twas I...'

'Brave?' interrupted Manicia. 'What wouldst thou know? She is doubtless rejoicing her husband's demise. I would be if I were wed to such a huge lump of old cheese. I know not how she could bear him.'

Benicia's astonishment stopped her on the steps so that the guard coming behind had to do his utmost to avoid colliding with her. Unaware of the hapless man as he struggled to regain balance, she scurried down the stairs into the guardroom. The servants with the chests had continued on down to the basement; Manicia was already half way across the room. The three guards stationed there scrambled to their feet, one concealing the loaf of bread and flask that they'd been sharing, the others opening surprised mouths to reveal lumps of chewed bread sticking to whatever teeth they possessed.

Benicia caught up with Manicia as she entered the wall-passage running west from the King's Gate. 'How canst thou say such a thing?' she gasped. 'Sir Auchencairn is clever and important and... and... he hath always been nice to us!'

Manicia turned a scornful look upon her sister. 'Nice!' she hissed. 'Thou dost think all men are nice if they but look at thee.'

'Manny! What hath come over thee? Lady Nomia was right; thou art unkind.'

'Naught hath come over me. Thou hast spent all thy life with me, but never noticed anyone but thyself. Fie! Thou dost call me unkind but I could name half-a-score who would say the same of thee!'

The two girls continued bickering as they scurried along the wall-passage towards the Bellhouse Tower. The guard, who'd paused for a word or two with his colleagues and a bite of bread, was startled to find himself left far behind. He swallowed down the dry morsel and broke into a laborious run to catch up.

'Who? Who? Tell me, Manicia,' insisted Benicia. 'Who... besides stupid Travancore? See? Thou canst think of no one else!'

'Thy betrothed, Dunmore,' said Manicia triumphantly. 'Art thou not unkind to him?'

'Dunmore? He could have naught to say as he scarcely knoweth me!'

'Well then, here's one who doth. Thou mayest ask him thyself.'

Making himself useful for once, Sir Parchim, Marquess of Potrimpos, had just appeared, making his way along the passage towards them. Accompanied by a few retainers, he was likely on his way to the King's Hall.

'Ask *him* if thou art unkind,' said Manicia. She noticed that her sister had almost returned to her usual, bright self. 'Tell him to be truthful, Bee,' she said, 'and thou too, for what is the use in dissembling when we are all of us shortly to die?'

'No, Manny! The castle is strong, surely, and the soldiers shall...'

'Soldiers?' snorted Manicia. 'What use are soldiers against a creature emerged from the pits of Hell? It will fry and devour them, then break open the castle and pick us all out like worms from a rotting log. It will find thee very tasty, plump girl.' She poked at her sister with each word, then gave her a shove. 'Go, ask thy lover if thou art tasty.'

Manicia's shove almost pushed Benicia into the marquess's arms. He held her off with his left hand, as his right was bound in a bloodied cloth, and looked at her tear-blotched face with an expression that was more frightened than fond. For a man who had a jest for every occasion, he looked serious enough.

'Oh Benicia... Lady Benicia,' he said in a voice that was pitched somewhat higher than normal, 'grateful I am to see you hale. Ah... you also, Lady Manicia,' he added with a brief glance in her direction.

The marquess was a handsome man when his mouth was closed. But he opened it again to say: 'What do ye here?' revealing a glimpse of rotted teeth.

'The princess's business is no business of yours,' said Manicia. She crooked a finger at the puffing guard and the two of them edged past

Benicia, Potrimpos and his band of retainers. Benicia failed to notice her sister's exit through the arch into the base of the Bellhouse Tower.

'Oh Potty,' she sighed, 'I am so glad to find thee living. But... thy poor hand!'

'My poor head too,' said the marquess, turning so that she could see the bloody mess of matted hair on the back of his head.

Benicia gasped and reached up to touch, not the wound, but the pale gold hair of which she was so enamoured. Thick and uncurled, it hung to just below shoulder-length and, even though it was at present uncombed and dirty, she felt her usual desire to stroke it. But the marquess caught her hand and pushed it away.

'Nay Lady,' he squeaked. 'Do ye not know who hath come up to court? He had words with me! I told him there was naught... but I must not speak with you. I have been told to go to the King's Hall. Go ye with your sister.' To Benicia's astonishment he physically pushed her away.

'But she hath gone... I know not whither...'

Potrimpos pointed over her shoulder. 'Bellhouse Tower,' he said and hurried away without a backwards glance.

Benicia's face crumpled as the marquess and his retinue disappeared down the gloomy passage. All alone, she sniffed loudly, scrubbed at her eyes with both hands and looked around hopelessly.

She had no idea where her sister had gone. Though she knew that they'd been sent to find Lady Ulidia, she hadn't listened to the princess's instructions and had not an inkling where ill-tempered Ulidia spent the few hours of each day in which she was not waiting upon the princess. And though Benicia had, since the sisters' arrival at court six months ago, followed Winterhued around the castle scores upon scores of times, her mind had always been occupied with other things, and she'd been too busy chatting and giggling to take much notice of her surroundings. To add to her confusion, they'd made most of this day's journey at ground level, which she'd never done because only the lackeys and soldiers went there.

A few sobs shook Benicia's shoulders as she bent her faltering steps towards the low arch at the base of the Bellhouse Tower. She entered another empty guardroom, a five-doored chamber full of drifting smoke.

The doorway closest to the one by which she had entered led to a newel stair giving access to the apartments above. Benicia gave no thought to trying the stairs because one thing she did know was that Potrimpos lived in this tower and it seemed unlikely to her that he'd share it with the horrid Ulidia and her ancient husband. The next portal along was a larger one that led to the walls of the outer bailey, but obviously Manicia had not gone that way because its iron-barred door was locked. Directly in front of her another door led to the Watergate that guarded the castle's small wharf. Benicia did not know this, but as her vague sense of direction told her that the lake lay that way, she took the only remaining door and hurried south, into the western wall of the inner bailey.

'Unkind Manny,' she whimpered, 'where art thou? Oh, what did she tell us? Why do I not remember?'

She sobbed and trembled, only half with the cold. Her stomach felt hollow; the fear in its pit and the nauseating stink that pervaded the castle had prevented her from eating so much as a morsel all day.

The passage was long and empty, with not a sign of Manicia. But passing an arrow loop in the western wall she caught a glimpse of shimmering silver. She stopped for a heartbeat, then crossed to the loop and peered out.

She looked down over a small lakeside garden – she recognised it as the princess's favourite place on a sunny day – and, beyond the garden, low battlements that shielded the stairs leading from the Watergate to the dock. Through drifting smoke the lake's surface danced to a long breath of wind. A vessel drifted, mastless, rudderless, trailing a plume of smoke as flames chewed at its bulwarks. Sodden objects floated here and there on the lake and a mass of them bumped and ground against the castle's wharf. She saw hair trailing in the water, and a bluish hand.

Benicia pulled herself away and began to run, clumsy with despair, along the passage. Her knees wobbled and shook.

Suddenly the wall to her left was no longer there and she stopped with a gasp. She remembered her sister's words, that the creature would pick them out from the castle like worms. And there before her was a hugely gaping, jagged hole, seeming proof that before this creature's might the castle had no more strength than a rotten log. There had once been buildings erected against the bailey walls here, fine dwellings and chambers that now lay in smouldering heaps.

With a shock, Benicia realised that she was looking straight at the Queen's Hall, where just last night had been feasting amongst music, light and laughter. One wall, the wall with the huge and beautiful windows that had glowed like multicoloured gems, had collapsed completely. The magnificent painted roof was gone, burnt to cinders, and all the bright hangings, the intricately carved screen, the musicians gallery, the dais, the long tables, all consumed by flames and their charred remnants buried beneath drifting ash.

With growing horror, Benicia's eyes focused on the hole in the wall before her. There were four wide stairs leading up to it from the bailey. She remembered now: it had been a doorway that she'd passed through many times whilst trailing the princess, and there, behind her, were the stairs that led up inside the wall to the passage above, and to the main entrance to the Queen's Hall.

The iron-hinged door was gone, the very stone archway was gone, ripped away and scattered across the bailey as though it had been built of nothing stronger than worm-riddled timber.

Benicia looked down and saw at her feet the long grooves and scrapings that gouged the floor, and she saw smears of dried blood across the cold flagstones. Fear squeezed the breath from her lungs as, in her mind's eye, she saw prey hooked and dragged through the ragged gap by impossible talons.

She raised her head, shuddering, her breath coming in gasps, and looked out past the broken hall, across the inner bailey to the keep, hunching dark through the smoke.

Even as she looked, the keep changed shape. It burgeoned upwards as though it were sprouting a hump, then it sighed, with a vast noise like wind fanning a forest fire. A round object fell, or was tossed, from the ramparts. It bounced once off the buttressed wall, then hit the bailey flags with a splash and a dull crunch. It seemed to have hair... long hair.

Benicia stepped backwards, tripped on her skirts and fell with a thump against the wall behind her. She tried to rise, but her knees were water. She began to crawl, tangled in her skirts, her heart beating in her ears. She fell, she scrambled, she cried soundlessly; it mattered not to her where she went as long as it was away.

Upon entering the Bellhouse Tower Manicia had, of course, gone straight to the stairs. In the months since she'd arrived in Lawhill she had made it her business to discover as much as she could about the castle's inhabitants and was well aware that the Marquess of Potrimpos lived at the top of the tower (his apartments surely burning or severely damaged, she thought with satisfaction), and that Lady Ulidia and Sir Garthwray occupied the first and second floors.

She climbed up, spiralling steeply into the smoky gloom, the guard at her heels. About half way to the first floor a slit through the thick walls let in a trickle of grey light.

'Rap at the door,' she said to the guard as they came to a narrow landing and a timber door. She brushed at her grey velvet gown and pushed a strand of hair in under her headdress as he stepped up to the door and tapped at it with the shaft of his halberd. When there came no sound from within, Manicia, without a word, continued her climb upwards.

'Mayhap the old woman is dead,' she murmured hopefully. A few steps further on she heard footsteps and halted just in time, for the four descending were coming so fast they were barely able to stop.

Ulidia's daughter, the Lady Aminta, jumped with fright when she saw Manicia and almost sat down on the stairs. She put out a hand to the curving wall to steady herself.

'What dost thou here?' she said shrilly. She was red-faced and agitated. Though she had halted two steps above, being a short woman, her head was not much higher than Manicia's. Behind her stood a ladies-maid, then the skirts and apron of a serving girl, then the feet of a guard, high up on the bend of the stairs.

'The princess sent me,' began Manicia, her heart beating too hard. How irritating it was that this small woman, and her even smaller mother, should intimidate her so. 'M'lady is anxious to...'

'If she wisheth to know of my mother,' interrupted Aminta, almost shouting in a strange, high-pitched voice, 'thou hast wasted thy journey for a message was sent not fifteen minutes ago and Sir Parchim followed soon after! So thou canst turn about and go hence for I'm sure thy sullen face is the last thing my mother hath need to see.' Suddenly she started to sob. 'Why can no one tell us what is amiss?" she wailed. "Why is there no one to help us? Why do a few low soldiers tell us we must go to the King's Hall? What is it that hath brought such fire and chaos?'

The maid behind her put out a comforting hand to her mistress's shoulder, but Aminta was weeping in earnest now, the tears coursing down her face. Without giving the startled Manicia space to answer, she went on, her shrill words interspersed with wails and sobs. 'Why do they send a stupid girl who knoweth naught and can be of no help to anyone? Oh, if my betrothed were here, yet he is far away in Bellands and not journeying up till our wedding... oh, wedding, wedding! How canst there be a wedding now? My father is up there, lying lifeless... dead as a doornail, and my mother soon to follow for though Sir Parchim told us he'd quenched the flames, the man is an idiot and I'm sure the ceiling is afire. But thinkst thou I could get the stubborn woman to leave?'

'Your father, Sir Garthwray... dead?' Manicia managed to push her way into the torrent of words and weeping. 'How is he dead?'

But Aminta seemed not to hear her. 'How may we inter him?' she wailed. 'He should lie at Thornliebank, where all our family rest. Oh, my brother would know what is to be done, but he is at Thornliebank... by heaven, he is marquess now and he knoweth not!'

A change had come across Manicia's face and she began to smile, very slightly. Why had she ever been frightened of this craven woman?

'Of course he knoweth not!' she retorted. 'Why do ye not calm yourself and think, lady?' Aminta's tirade had stopped and now she stared at Manicia. 'Ye do call me a stupid child, but it is you who doth act thus, instead of behaving like the twice-married matron ye are! Go ye to the King's Hall, but I advise you, do not pester the princess, for she hath no time for women who weep and wail.'

The Lady Aminta had ceased all her weeping and wailing. 'Fie! Order me about? How dare thee?' she shrilled. 'Ill-tempered, bad-mannered chit of a girl!'

'I am the daughter of a *duke*, madam,' said Manicia, stressing the word duke for Aminta's father had been but a marquess, 'and *I* am not a coward. I but do as I am instructed and I have been told to get you to the King's Hall. So get ye thither madam and I shall send your mother along shortly.'

'Send my mother?' shrieked Aminta. 'Why, thou insolent chit...' Her tears dried upon her hot cheeks.

'Come ma'am,' said the ladies-maid, gently putting an arm around Aminta's shoulders. 'Let us to the King's Hall.'

Aminta huffed angrily, but let herself be led past Manicia and away.

'Duke's daughter?' Manicia heard her say. 'The chit... I am twice, nigh three times, a countess. How dare she? I'll have words with her father!' Her voice faded as she wound her way downstairs.

Manicia laughed. 'How wonderful,' she said. She glanced at the guard who stared politely at the wall, but no, she could hardly share her delight with a common dullard. So she turned and danced up the stairs.

At the next door she didn't bother to knock. She could hear sobbing from within (Ulidia... weeping? She could scarcely believe it), so she just opened the door and entered.

She saw Sir Garthwray straight away, laid out upon the bed. He was not burned; there seemed not a mark on him. Below his nightgown his feet poked out, knobbed and blue-veined, and above it his wispy, bald head, white as paper.

'Manicia! What dost thou? Marching in without a by-your-leave?'

No, it hadn't been Ulidia crying. Manicia pulled her eyes from Sir Garthwray and saw the old woman sitting at the end of the bed, her little black eyes glittering and her voice as sharp as ever. Manicia's nerve almost failed her.

'The princess sent me,' she said, staring back at Ulidia. She saw that the ancient woman clutched a cloak about her shoulders hardly voluminous enough to hide a nightgown well nigh as old as its wearer. Her hair (Manicia had never before seen her hair) was thin and grey and very long. It was tied back untidily from her face, which looked a paler shade of grey.

'And I did knock,' lied Manicia, 'but ye heard me not.' She went on talking, not looking at Ulidia, but searching for the source of the sobbing. 'It is fearfully smoky in here. Methinks ye should go to the princess before ye do burn to death.'

'The fire is quenched,' said Ulidia. 'Potrimpos' men saw to it before they left.'

But Manicia's eyes pricked and watered with the smoke as she looked about the chamber. It was sparsely furnished, with not a single hanging upon its curved, whitewashed walls. Stark and threadbare like those who dwelt within it, thought Manicia. Sitting beneath a narrow window she spied dull Lady Pera, her face tear-ravaged and her black hair falling loose and stringy about her shoulders. She appeared half frozen and both her hands were bandaged. Manicia might have guessed it would be Pera weeping, as the girl seemed always to be lurking somewhere about Ulidia as though she actually liked the woman.

'Hath her highness ordered my attendance?' asked Ulidia.

'Nay,' answered Manicia, 'yet I think ye should go to her as she is sorely anxious...'

'Nay,' echoed Ulidia. 'If there hath been no order I'll stay here with my husband. There are things that must be done, but I know not how or when. I did send for the friars but no friars came and neither hath the messenger returned. There should be prayers said and a dirge sung and bells rung; my husband left five sovereigns for the friars to pray and sing for him on his deathbed. And the other executors must be sent for and then there is the matter of where he is to lie; it was to be in the chapel at Thornliebank, but I know not how we may accomplish that when there seemeth no one to help us.'

Manicia was disgusted to see that Ulidia stroked her husband's feet as she rambled tediously on.

'I sit here and I sit here,' continued the old woman, 'yet no one cometh. So, Manicia, thou must needs return to the princess and tell her of my plight. But take Pera with thee. No my dear,' she said as Pera made a noise of protest, 'I do not need thee here and thy hands must be seen to properly.'

Pera had risen to her feet. She stumbled across the chamber and into Ulidia's arms.

'There, there my dear,' said Ulidia, patting the girl's back. 'Go with Manicia. 'Tis not good for one so young to keep lengthy company with the dead.'

Pera burst into tears again. 'Poor Sir Garthwray,' she sobbed. 'He was more a father to me than mine own father hath been.'

'I know, my dear,' said Ulidia, gently turning Pera so that both of them were looking at the wizened old man, 'but there he lies, come to his end as all we must. Though he was not a peaceful man, nor a handsome, he was a good enough husband to me. Never wed for love, Pera. A love match seldom turns out to be a happy one. Why, I was wed at thy age; no more than five and ten years and thought myself the most wretched creature alive, saddled with a bad-tempered boy who could barely sit a horse and thought a sword a wall-decoration. All my dreams of chivalry dashed. Yet I grew fond of him as the years flew by and I cannot but say that we became content each with the other.'

Ulidia's romantic recollections were interrupted as something fell above them with a loud thud and, here and there, smoke spurted between the planking of the ceiling.

'We must make haste; that fire burneth yet,' said Manicia urgently. 'Lady Ulidia, methinks ye must needs accompany me as well. I pray you, do not protest. Know ye that no one will come to quench the fire or sing dirges for your husband. Mayhap it hath escaped your notice that chaos hath fallen upon all of us. The princess keepeth counsel in a dungeon; she is yet clad in the gown she wore last night, her head is bare and her hair falleth loose.' Manicia saw she was right in calculating that this news would be more horrifying to Ulidia than any report of death and destruction. 'She hath lost two counsellors, for it seemeth certain that Sir Auchencairn is perished also, as he went out at dawn to kill the dragon and hath not been seen since.'

'Do not talk nonsense!' snapped Ulidia, but her voice held an unaccustomed tremor. Pera stared at Manicia, wide-eyed.

'I talk no nonsense, my lady,' said Manicia. "Tis a dragon that hath come; I heard the princess say so myself. It hath destroyed half the castle, brought death to hundreds, and even now crouches atop the keep awaiting prey.'

'That cannot be true. 'Tis a child's tale,' said Ulidia. 'But thou sayest the princess's hair is loose?' Manicia nodded. 'It seemeth I must go to her then, though why didst thou not attend to it thyself, thou dim-witted lump of a girl? Thou knowest how to dress hair.'

'I had other things to do,' said Manicia angrily. 'Put on your clothes, m'lady, make haste. I shall wait without; when ye are ready we shall go to the King's Hall and find some men there to carry Sir Garthwray thither.'

Manicia got away from the old woman as fast as she could and banged the door loudly behind her. 'She's far worse than any dragon,' she muttered, "and more stupid.'

The guard, who'd been sitting on the steps patiently getting on with his phlegmy cough, climbed to his feet.

'Fie! I didn't find out how he died,' Manicia said, to the fellow's puzzlement. 'I must wait for the Lady Ulidia,' she said sharply, upon noticing his existence. 'I do not wish to look upon thee, so descend ten steps and wait there.'

He bobbed a slight bow and took himself down two steps, then stopped and looked back at her. 'Begging pardon, y'ladyship,' said he, 'but be it Sir Garthwray's death ye do wish to know of?'

Manicia stared at him as though he'd broken wind. 'What business is it of thine?'

'No business, y'ladyship, howbeit I can tell you of it if ye so wish.'

'Thou?' she snorted. 'How wouldst thou know?'

The insolent fellow tapped the side of his nose. 'Y'ladyship might be surprised,' said he, 'to know how quick us lowly folk come to know aught. 'Twas an apoplexy, y'ladyship, what took the old lord off. Flew into such a rage, he did – so I did hear – when none came to quench the fire, that he fell down, and shortly after departed this life. That's the truth of it, y'ladyship.'

With a sly look, the fellow gave another bow and shuffled down-stairs away from Manicia's sight.

The duke's daughter was not, however, allowed to wait in peace. As the servants had all gone and Pera's burnt hands were painful, Manicia soon found herself back in the chamber and engaged in a task she'd never imagined performing, even in her nightmares: dressing Lady Ulidia.

In the King's Hall the blue-eyed scullery maid lay huddled in a blanket, with but some rough sacking between her and the cold flagstones. Eudora had just woken from sleep and she stared unblinking at nothing in particular. She thought about the dream she'd been having, because it seemed better than remembering why she was here, lying on the hard floor.

She'd been back in her village, playing hopscotch with the other village children. Sun spangled the street and dust rose in little puffs from the children's bare feet as they skipped and hopped. She held onto the dream for a moment longer as though it were something good, but then remembered that if she had indeed been in her village, playing with those children, it would not have been long before they began to call her names and throw things at her.

No, it was better to be here, no matter what fell terror had come a-calling, because this was where Winterhued was. Though Eudora had only met the princess yesterday, she had decided she loved her more than anyone else in the world. Why, the princess had told her she had pretty eyes and had given her an orange. And an orange for Orla.

Orla must surely be dead now, and both oranges burnt to cinders.

Eudora had still been sitting fully dressed upon her bed and sunk in miserable thought, when the terror had come with a noise to freeze the blood. She'd heard cries and shouts and felt the squat tower rock to its very foundations. Without thinking, she'd been on her feet and running for the stairs. As she crossed the floor, a foul gust had come ripping down the chimney and blown the fire across the chamber. One log flared up and she'd seen the rush matting on the floor ignite in bright flame. She'd not returned to wake or help a single soul for she'd been on her hands and knees, gagging in the unthinkable stench.

On the stairs, crawling downwards in almost pitch darkness, Eudora had felt knees thumping into her back, feet pushing down her head, frantic hands tearing at her hair as more of the tower's inhabitants scrambled and clambered over the top of her. She'd heard their gasps and curses. Though knocked flat several times she had struggled on amidst the trampling crowd till she'd burst from the door at the foot of the stairs, gasping for breath. A piece of falling masonry had grazed her shoulder making her stagger and cry out, then she'd felt a helping hand on her arm, pushing her forward. 'Run,' shouted a voice in her ear. 'Make for the inner bailey!'

She'd heard the tower fall, heard cries and a long roar of flame, she'd felt horror at her back, but she hadn't looked round. Falling three or four times, she'd floundered back to her feet, tripping and tearing her skirts. She'd grazed her knees and lost a shoe. Passing the menagerie and the stables she'd heard animals screaming and the frantic thudding of the horses' hooves against the stall walls. She was dimly aware of other people running beside her, chasing their black shadows in the horrible, flickering light. At last, amidst a press of bodies, she'd squashed through a narrow door into the shelter of the bailey wall.

There they'd huddled in panting, gasping darkness until someone came with a torch and she'd seen their round eyes and the sweat glistening on their bloodless faces. They were mostly menials from the collapsed tower, with a few stable lads and soldiers amongst them. Their voices rasped and shook.

'Mercy on us... what dread mischief is this?' ''Tis not possible, whatever it be.' 'Did anyone see? I couldn't look.' ''Twas the very devil.' 'Well, it did stink most foully.' 'How could any creature...? Didst thou see? The whole tower...' 'Aye, all afire and knocked into the ditch like 'twere made of twigs.' ''Tis a punishment come from God.' 'Aye, punishment for the godless amongst us, not namin' names.' 'But what were it? Why hath it come? How many hath it took? How many sorrows must we wretches bear?'

Eudora, crouching in shadow, unclenched her right hand. Her nails had cut into her palm until it bled. Looped still in her hand, where it had been when she'd first leapt up from her bed, lay the moonstone pendant on its thin silver chain.

Dropping it furtively into her pouch, she slid down the wall until she was sitting on the floor. She tucked the end of her torn skirts around her shoeless, frozen foot and put her head in her hands.

For the rest of the long night, the menials were herded about inside the walls of the inner bailey. Soldiers and lords came and went, ordering them here, then ordering them there; all looking as confused and fearful as the servants. Eventually they were told to stay at one end of the King's Hall, given a meagre amount of food and bedding and promised better soon.

Eudora had spoken not a word. Images of her colleagues waking in terror filled her head. She saw them engulfed in flames as the tower collapsed around them. None of the women asleep in the chamber had been her friends, in fact she was certain that they had ofttimes sneered at her behind her back but, she told herself, it would surely have been possible to turn back and wake them before she had saved herself.

'But I am not myself saved for certain,' she murmured. 'That dread thing hath not departed. Every one of us may perish... even Winterhued.'

Eventually the girl had fallen asleep, to wake some hours later from a dream of a dusty village street in sunshine.

She rolled onto her back and stared up at the high banners that moved faintly in the draught beneath the massively vaulted ceiling. Beyond the banners the ceiling's gold sunbursts and silver horses were lost in darkness.

Throughout the day the tall, narrow windows had been covered up and now there was only one that still admitted light. It was turning blue as the day outside darkened. No fire had been lit in either of the huge hearths and it was so cold that the hall seemed carved of ice.

Eudora, shivering violently, raised herself on one elbow and looked about her. Most of the folk in the hall were refugees from the town; the castle servants had kept themselves apart at one end, huddled together for warmth. Their numbers seemed few. The lords and ladies, thought Eudora, might have to do a bit of fetching and carrying for themselves.

Then she recalled that, hours earlier, some of the women had gone off to help tend the burnt and the dying. Eudora had been afraid to go.

Close by in the gathering gloom two women spoke in hushed tones, but most sat or lay in silence; they had all been instructed in person by some great, skinny duke, whose name Eudora could not remember, to 'prithee keep yourselves quieter than church-mice.'

The two women were speaking to a youth who crouched before them. One of them pointed towards Eudora and the youth rose and looked straight at her. She sank down and pulled the blanket over her head, but she was too late. The boy came, leaping nimbly over two or three prone bodies, to kneel beside her and tug at her blanket.

'Dora!' whispered the boy they called Stench. 'I've been asking all over for you. I was sore worried to see your tower fallen, but... certes, I'm glad to find you living! Dora, I can get you out of the castle...'

'Go away,' said Eudora.

'Nay, I will not, for I can take you to safety. 'Tis perilous here, Dora.'

'Stop calling me Dora.'

'Why? 'Tis nicer than Corpse-Eyes.'

Eudora hit out at the lad, but he grinned and ducked out of her way. He looked, it must be said, disreputable and wild. His dark hair was a tangle, his usually neat clothes were dirty and looked damp, as if he'd been swimming in them, and there was an appearance of singeing about his person. And for once, he lived up to his name.

'Urrgh, thou dost stink,' said Eudora, wrinkling her nose, 'like pig dung.'

'What a good nose ye have,' said Stench. 'Nay, listen Dora. I was in the town... last night. I heard it above; it was crushing the buildings with but its weight. 'Tis a vast and monstrous thing!' The boy whispered louder and louder in his excitement. 'In the streets I saw horses, pigs, dogs, chickens, all running hither and thither, but it was not them it hunted. It skewered men and women on talons long as... as roasting spits. I saw them lifted skywards... I heard it snuffling and sniffing... so I've got this, Dora, I've got this!'

From beneath one arm he pulled a loosely rolled oilskin and from its folds a cloak, damp and filthy. He half spread it before her. A foul dust rose from it and bits of half-dried dung fell from its folds. Though Eudora was accustomed to bad smells, its pungent aroma of farmyard and rotted grain had her reeling backwards.

'Urrgh, thou art disgusting,' she hissed. 'Get thee hence, worm!'

'Ye do not understand,' said the boy. 'This can save us! Listen...'

''Tis thou that dost not understand,' snapped Eudora. 'I want thee gone, rot-worm!'

'Dora, listen, I pray you, listen!' He waited a moment, looking at her earnestly, and when she did not speak, went on: 'I reckoned the creature's sight seemed poor, and on hearing all that snuffling, thought mayhap it uses but its nose for hunting. So I got myself this here cloak,' he said, bundling the malodorous garment into the oilskin and stuffing it under his arm with an apologetic look. 'I know 'tis a horrid item, but it did the trick. In my parents' house I soaked it in a tub of our cow and pig's dung, with a half bag of rotted barley, then when my cloak had dried a bit, I put it over me and I walked – right beneath the creature, Dora, right beneath it – as it straddled the coopers' street! I could hear it sniffing; I could feel the heat of its breath, but I just walked down that street, even as the dwellings either side of me burst into flame, and the creature let me be! It couldn't smell me so it let me be! Well Dora, what think ye? Will ye come with me? If ye be brave and don't mind a short swim, I can get you away from here!'

'What do I think?' breathed Eudora. 'I think thou'rt a madman. I'll not put that stinking thing over my head and I'll not go *swimming* anywhere with thee, gong-boy!'

The lad looked at her for a moment. She seemed a sad, slight figure under her clutched blanket, her face pinched and blue with the cold. But she was pretty in her thin way and she had something about her that made him want to try one last time. 'Dora, I pray you,' he pleaded, 'this hall is a perilous place; ye've all been herded in here like beasts to the slaughter. Aye, it looketh a solid pile, all stone and slate, but there's plenty in it that'll burn and besides, I've seen how easily this creature doth break open roofs. I do not believe it is stupid; it knoweth ye and all these,' he swept his arm about the hall, 'be in here. It may be that its appetite is sated for now, but sooner or later it *shall* come a-feeding, Eudora, and I would rather it did not feed upon you.'

'So thou knowest better,' said the girl sarcastically, 'than that great, tall duke... and the constable, and the king, and the princess?'

'Nay, but meseems they have not seen this beast. I have, and I know how vast it is, how puissant, how terrible. I think it is as old and strong as a mountain.'

'And I think what thou sayest hath as much worth as what thou digst with thy shovel. Why would I put the words of a dung-worm before those of a fine duke, or Princess Winterhued?'

The boy sighed. 'Ah well, I did try,' he said, 'but as ye seem determined to stay in this chill slaughterhouse, at least I have something for you.'

He'd been holding a blanket when he first arrived, which he'd put on the floor. He unfolded it now and spread it over her. 'They gave it to me when I came in here,' he said, 'but I'll not be needing it; I've got my fine cloak.'

He got to his feet. 'Farewell Dora. I pray ye, keep safe.'

'Tarry,' said Eudora suddenly, 'I have a gift for thee. Come close. Put out thy hand.'

Stench looked surprised but did as he was told. The girl fished under the blankets, then furtively brought out her closed right fist.

'I'll drop it in thy hand,' she whispered. 'Close thy fingers and don't look at it till thou art out of the hall. It be a beauteous thing; no doubt the finest gift that ever shall be given thee, but understand that on the giving thou shalt nevermore come nigh me. And thou must promise not to tell a soul who gave it thee. Dost thou promise?'

'Aye, I promise.'

'And promise never to come nigh me again?'

'I promise that too.'

'Hand on thy heart.'

'I promise not to tell a soul and I promise not to come nigh you,' said Stench, with one hand on his heart and the other held, somewhat tentatively, palm up towards her.

Eudora put her hand over his and he was surprised to feel a slight, slippery coolness drop into his palm. He closed his fingers over it as instructed and got to his feet.

'I like you yet, Eudora,' he said, 'if ever ye do change your mind.'

'But I hate thee,' answered the girl, 'and that will never change.'

Stench gave her a little half-bow and turned on his heel. Halfway across the hall he looked back at her, but she was buried beneath her blankets.

Though she was the lowliest of servants, he couldn't blame her for not wanting to be seen with the son of a gong-farmer. For that was a job for worms and he was but the latest in a long line of worms. Stench's grandfather had been a gong-farmer, and his great-grandfather and so on back many generations, and one day all too soon, if Castle Lawhill and at least some of its inhabitants survived, Stench himself would take up the family shovel. He was not eager for that day when he, like the king, would be followed about all day by a band of devoted courtiers, because in his case they would be buzzing black flies.

Still, he felt sad looking at the girl with the blue eyes, huddled all alone in the gloom, for she had turned away the one who cared for her and now she was friendless.

He walked on a few steps then stopped, looked down at his hand and opened his fingers. He saw the moonstone on its slim chain and his heart skipped a beat. Instantly he knew to whom it belonged. Eudora had, of course, never learnt to read; to her the coiled metal in which the stone was set was mere decoration. But Stench (the beneficiary of a secret and improbable education) saw straight away that the gleaming stone was sweetly enclosed in a curling, silver 'W'.

'Alas, Dora,' he whispered. He knew that she had a habit of taking things that didn't belong to her. Pushing the necklet deep into the pouch at his belt, he continued on across the hall.

'Somehow,' he murmured, 'I shall return this to the princess.'

CHAPTER 5

Night crept into the basement of the Watchtower. A servant lit candles and the darkness fled from the flickering light into the far reaches of the chamber. Inky shadows lingered under table, chair and truckle bed.

Hearing several pairs of boots come thudding down the narrow stair, Princess Winterhued looked wearily up from her scant evening meal. Her plate was surrounded by parchments covered in figures; since the Duke of Travancore had handed her a hastily written list, two hours past, she and the chamberlain had been hard at work, calculating, apportioning and meting out the castle's remaining supplies.

Sir Gunford, Captain of the Royal Guard, was the first to enter, his red face beaded with sweat and his breath short. She saw his eyes alight upon her briefly then go darting round the chamber in search of the king. Smiling slightly, she waited for his attention to return to her, for she knew that her father was lying belly-up on one of the narrow beds, snoring with his mouth agape.

The captain bowed. 'Your highness,' he said obsequiously, 'I have done as your highness ordered. I have found a man who hath seen the creature. 'Twas no easy task, ma'am, no easy task, as those who have been anigh the beast and survived – and they seem few indeed, all too few – did feel such an oppression of fear come upon them that they scarce could move, let alone lift their eyes to behold the beast. Yet I found one, ma'am, indeed I found one... but I am afraid he is a lowly seafaring fellow and hardly fit to stand before your highnesses.'

He glanced over at the king as he said this, but old Gers made it quite plain that he cared not a jot who stood before him, or behind him, or on top of him for that matter.

'I admire seafaring fellows,' said the princess. 'Bring him forth, Gunford.'

She pushed aside her plate, and taking the topmost parchment from the table, got to her feet. As she handed the sheet to the guard at the door, with orders to deliver it to Travancore, the chamberlain (who had joined the basement party at midday) looked up from where he'd been leaning beside the hearth, talking quietly to the Balasorean ambassador. The old chancellor, slumped in a chair beside him, peered towards the door through watery eyes.

They watched a young man enter the chamber, escorted by one of Gunford's men. His hair, bleached yellow by the sun and wind, flopped forwards as he bowed low. Straightening, he gazed up at the princess and saw her, tall and flawless in her blue gown, with her unbound raven tresses tumbling to her waist. She looked at the berry-brown sailor and smiled the smile that had inspired poets, and he glanced away as though she dazzled his eyes like sunlight on water. He bowed again, awkwardly, then stood with his eyes downcast; a lean, wiry fellow in shabby, singed clothes and borrowed shoes.

'This is the man, your highness,' said Sir Gunford. 'He swam to the Watergate from his burning ship.'

'The king, the council, and I do thank thee, good man,' said Winterhued, 'for thine attendance upon us. I trust thou hast been fed and given some place to sleep?'

'Aye, your highness, I have, thanking your highness,' he said croakily, bowing slightly every time he said the word 'highness'.

'That is well,' said the princess. 'So... thou hast seen the creature.'

'Aye, that I have, your highness,' he answered, 'though not for long, for I became as a child afraid of monsters in the dark, and fell upon my face. But before that mine eyes beheld it trailing fire as it went above the three masts of my ship so that they blazed up like dry twigs.' The fellow was warming to his task, though he still avoided looking at the princess. 'Its very passing sucked up the air then sent it rushing back like a gale at sea so that the sails and stays came raining in a blast and set the deck to burn as well.'

'It flew above thy ship. It has wings then,' said the chamberlain. 'Is it a bird?'

'Nay, m'lord,' answered the sailor, 'I think not; its wings seemed more a bat's than a bird's. Though I must say I could scarce see them in the raging night. But what I can say for certain is that they seemed the wings of a dead thing for they blasted forth a stink so bad that I got up on my shanks and jumped over the bulwarks in my attempt to escape it... which was as well for my raiment was ablaze.'

'So,' said the princess, 'it hath wings like a bat's and it stinks. Hast aught else for us?'

'I did not see a head, your highness, but belike it doth possess one, for meseems that is from whence its fire doth issue. I did see a tail; 'twas like a lizard's but long as a street. Of its body, it seemed scaly, and all bones and black shadow... and wounds.'

'Wounds?' questioned the chamberlain.

'Aye, m'lord, the creature seemed covered in jagged... holes, is all I can say. But I have to add, in all truth, the night was dark and the fire did dazzle mine eyes.'

'What was its whole size?' asked Winterhued.

'As big as the town it seemed, your highness, though I can only say in all honesty that it was a deal bigger than my ship. And that's about all I can say, for the night was too dark, the beast too swift, the fire too bright and myself too afraid.'

'Thou hast been helpful,' said the princess. 'Prithee accept our thanks. Beyond doubt, thou art a man of courage.'

The sailor flushed beneath his tan. He bowed thrice and took a few steps backwards in the direction of the door. 'One more question,' said Winterhued; 'prithee tell us the name thou wouldst give this creature.'

The man bobbed another bow. "I have to say, your highness, that I'm no authority on creatures, but I've sailed o'er many seas to many lands and seen wondrous and varied sights. Yet I cannot say as I've ever seen the like of this beast. Most nigh would be the great scaly lizards in the southern lands, but I cannot say I've ever seen one with wings. But I've heard tales, many tales, from all over, and I've seen carvings and paintings and pictures in books, of made-up creatures, creatures from stories and myths: unicorns, wyverns, griffins and the like… and dragons. And that's the name I'd give this beast, your highness. I'm not a man of learning, but I've seen a deal of the world and no one has ever called me a fool – at least not to my face – but that, your highness, is the name I'd be giving this creature: dragon.'

The king's snores grew louder, almost drowning out the moan of the old chancellor and Lord Ladstock's uneasy cough. Winterhued did but nod to herself and laugh softly.

With a few more clumsy bows the mariner left, his feet unsure and his eyes gazing at thin air. In less than the space of one day the fellow had seen two things to make his heart stop, but it was the smile of the princess, though he had glimpsed it for but a moment, that had pierced him to the quick. Even as he stumbled from the chamber a poem had begun to form itself in his mind, in which he likened the majesty of a wild, moonlit ocean to the beauty of his princess.

Quite unaware that she'd just transformed a good sailor into a bad poet, Winterhued turned back to the chamber to see her father, woken by a particularly loud snore, struggle into a sitting position. His hound, lying beneath his pallet, got to her feet with a clatter of claws on the flagstones.

'What?' said the king, then coughed twice and yawned hugely. 'Where's my supper?'

The princess took her plate over to him. 'Have mine, my lord,' she said; 'I am not hungry.'

'Huh, I'm not eating this,' he huffed, stuffing a slice of her apple and walnut tart into his mouth. 'Food for women,' he mumbled around his mouthful. 'Why are we still here? Haven't they killed the wretched thing yet?'

'The "wretched thing" is a dragon, my lord,' said the princess.

'Stuff and nonsense!' spluttered King Gers.

'We have, just now, heard a description of the creature, my lord,' replied the princess calmly. ''Tis clear it can be naught but a dragon.'

'Stuff and nonsense,' repeated the king. 'A dragon is a beast from tales; silly tales to frighten children.'

'My lord, I do recall you once telling me that there were scores of dragons living in the world.'

Gers looked at his daughter blankly. 'Nonsense,' he said. 'If such a thing befell, thou must have been a very little child, and I telling thee a fairytale.'

The princess's hair brushed the king's shoulder as she leaned to speak in his ear. 'It doth pain me, my lord,' she said, 'that that which altered the life of your only child and caused her to weep and wail for half a year hath left no trace in your memory.'

The king looked astonished. 'Ladstock,' he said, upon seeing that that gentleman was closest to him, 'she accuseth me of causing her to weep for a year by telling her, when she was but an infant, a fairytale of dragons!'

The princess turned away with a shake of her head. 'Father, put this from your mind.'

'Of course I shall,' replied the king, putting more tart into his mouth. 'I never think too hard upon the fancies of women. Any effort in that cause doth make my head ache.'

Winterhued found the Balasorean ambassador at her elbow. He was a pale, plump man, shorter than herself, with glossy black hair cut straight just above his shoulders. He was still neat in his dark velvets, but his damp brow was furrowed and he chewed at his lower lip.

'Your highnesses,' he said, bowing towards both of them.

'What is it, Lord Priwall?' asked the princess.

'My situation groweth intolerable, your highnesses,' said the ambassador. 'It is imperative that I return to Balasore. Surely there must be a way to get to one of the ships in the town docks and slip away under cover of darkness...'

The princess looked at him in some amazement. 'The ships in the docks are all burned to the waterline, sir,' she said, 'but if ye so choose, ye may swim out to one of the two ships that float adrift upon the lake, climb aboard and attempt to quench the fire that slowly consumes the vessel. If it then proves seaworthy ye may set sail, or row if there are no sails, for Balasore. Or, failing that, ye may venture into the outer bailey, catch one of the horses that runs to and fro there and ride it – bareback, as the saddles are destroyed – over the broken wall (as the gate is blocked), down into the perilously steep ditch, past the burning town and away south to Balasore. If, sir, ye could manage either of those feats without being cooked and consumed by our watchful gaoler, ye would certainly earn my undying admiration.'

'Ha ha. Go to it, ambassador,' chuckled the king mirthlessly. 'Undying admiration eh? That's surely worth the attempt!' Gers snorted, wiped his nose with the back of his hand and took a gulp from his goblet. 'Nay sir, patience; 'tis only a matter of time before the beast's slaughtered. 'Tis but a dumb thing after all; we're the ones with the brains, eh?' The king tapped his thick skull. 'Meanwhile, eat, drink and be comfortable, sir. We have an exceeding good mead here, come all the way from your own Balasore... why, methinks ye did bring it yourself! Where's a goblet for the ambassador? Partake of a drop or two of that, sir, and ye'll find the time slides by more tolerably. Meanwhile, ye be the man I wish to speak to. Sit down.'

Gers patted the bed next to him, which made the Balasorean so confused that he spilt his mead. The king's hound, also confused, jumped up onto the bed.

'Come sir,' said the king, pushing the hound off; 'no need for ceremony in a dungeon.'

The princess walked towards the fire, wearily rubbing her eyes. She smiled at the chancellor as he looked up at her and reached for her hand to touch it lightly with his lips. For a while she stood at his back with a hand on his shoulder and her mind empty, watching the flames. Beneath her fingers Highmoor's bones felt as thin as a bird's. A log in the fire burned through and subsided with a sigh as the princess gradually became aware of her father's converse.

To her astonishment he was questioning the ambassador about a tale that that lord had enthusiastically recounted at a banquet in his honour soon after his arrival in Lawhill. He had told of a knight of great renown who had ridden some while ago into Balasore. The knight had come up from the south with a reputation that travelled before him and had duly defeated all comers at Balasore's greatest tournament.

Lord Priwall answered the king distractedly; he had more pressing matters on his mind and looked bewildered that he was being questioned on a subject so inconsequential. He mopped at his brow and gulped down his mead.

'Nay, your highness,' he said, 'I do not remember the knight's name. I think I never knew it. He revealed little about himself. And no, I do not recall to whence he was bound upon leaving Balasore... mayhap back south.'

'Nay, nay,' said the king impatiently, 'I'm sure ye said that the man was northward bound... east to Ormsary, ye said, then north.'

'Aye, your highness,' said Priwall wearily, 'methinks your highness may be correct. I had forgotten my own words.' The ambassador emptied his goblet.

'Thought so,' said the king. 'Certes, he'll be here any day then! More mead for the ambassador.'

Winterhued, who had been staring at her father open-mouthed, could contain herself no longer. 'My lord!' she exclaimed. 'Surely my lord doth jest? This fellow was in Balasore, how long... six months... nine months ago? How likely is it that he would happen to ride up to Lawhill now? And even if he did, how could one puny knight slay such a monstrous beast?'

'Puny? The best knight in the world?' questioned her father. 'If this thing be a dragon, as thou dost insist, child... certes, thou hast had thy nose stuck to a book half thy life, so thou must know that all the old tales say that dragons are slain by knights.'

'They are tales, father.'

'So are dragons,' rejoined the king. 'No more argument; I shall send forth a messenger to find this fellow, with a promise that, if he doth deliver us, he shall be rewarded with thy hand... and, potentially, my kingdom. I see thee ready to protest as ever, but daughter, thou shalt *not* refuse the man who doth deliver us!'

'But this is nonsense, my lord!' cried Winterhued. 'Why send some unfortunate forth to risk life on such a foolish errand? What chance is there that this knight could be found? The fellow may be a thousand leagues away! And even if he were outside our very gates, he would go to his certain death were he to undertake this task. He is just one man, father. He may be skilled at galloping up and down the lists in his armour, knocking other men into the mud, but I doubt he'd be happy to take on our dragon and thus part with life so easily.'

'For such a prize...' began the king.

'I am no prize, and as for the realm, I am dismayed that my lord doth think, even for a moment, of giving it away to a man he hath never met.'

The king chortled unpleasantly as if he'd just remembered a rude joke. 'Dear, dear daughter,' said he, 'if I do not, ha ha ha, manage to magic-up a son and heir...' He glanced towards Ladstock and gave that lord a wink. 'If not, ha ha, Manydown shall, lawfully and properly, be thine, daughter. But, as I've oft times told thee, a realm needs a man, a kingdom needs a king.' Winterhued opened her mouth to speak, but Gers held up a hand. 'Hear me out. Of course the man thou dost wed cannot be king in name, but he will do a king's work for without a man to lead, without a strong *prince*, a realm is weak and vulnerable.' The king slurped another mouthful of mead and smiled triumphantly. 'And if thou hast aught to say on the matter, I don't wish to hear it.'

Winterhued frowned, watching mead drip from her father's chin. She turned to Lord Ladstock but the man averted his gaze and smirked at the floor. With a slight shrug of her shoulders, she returned to the fire to take up her position behind the chancellor's chair, and that good old friend took her hand and patted it encouragingly.

Lord Ladstock, emboldened by the king's conspiratorial wink, coughed. 'My sovereign lord,' he began and coughed again. 'Begging my sovereign lord's pardon, but... but we are all of us vulnerable at this time and I feel it my duty to suggest that getting down upon our knees and... and... praying will do no harm.'

As the king did not immediately jump down his throat at the suggestion, the chamberlain continued a little more confidently. 'I have heard that which some of the people are saying, your highness. They say that this beast has come as a punishment from God; punishment for our Godless existence. Methinks it would be all to the good if the king were to say a prayer... perhaps a visit to the chapel...'

King Gers snarled and the chamberlain flinched.

'Thou knowest I will not pray to the god that murdered my wife,' growled the king. 'If it had not been for your god and his damned church, I would have a wife yet, my daughter a mother and a brother or three: a male heir for Manydown, by heaven!' The king's voice had risen to a shout. 'I say any god who can't be bothered to look after a visitor to his house, doth not deserve the worshipping! I will not pray, Ladstock, so save thy breath.'

The chamberlain's face gleamed palely above his black robes. His nostrils flared. "Tis not my breath,' he said, 'and not my words, my liege. The king's subjects themselves do say that this... visitation, is a punishment to... to their king for abandoning God.'

Gers emitted a furious snort, but it was Winterhued who answered in a quiet, equable voice. 'Wouldst thou not say, Lord Ladstock, that it is an unjust punishment indeed when the king lives and hundreds of good church-goers have perished?' Without waiting for a response she went on, still in that same pleasant tone: 'Know thou, sir, that whatsoever the outcome of this misadventure, this land is, and shall continue to be, ruled by a secular government. What short memories the people of Manydown have. Why, it is not so long ago that my great grandfather, and his father, and his father before him, ruled Manydown with a "good" churchman ever at the king's shoulder, and fear and dread lay upon the land.'

'Your highness!' protested the chamberlain. 'I was not advocating that we bring back the torture of heretics. My intention was merely to suggest that it would not hurt if we were to bend our knees in the chapel for five minutes.'

Winterhued looked steadily at the chamberlain for a moment as he bent his obsequious head and wrung his pious hands. He was an able member of her council but she had always been aware that, behind his sanctimony, he could be conniving and cruel. His own daughter, unhappy Lady Pera, was deeply afraid of him. And now Winterhued was certain that he was one of the men who had lately been whispering against her into the king's ear. Her father's ridiculous wink had made that abundantly clear.

'I shall go to the chapel, Lord Ladstock,' said Winterhued, 'if only to see that my orders were carried out and that Sir Garthwray hath been carried thither and laid there in state. I shall give what comfort I may to my dear Ulidia, and say a prayer for us all. Then I shall go to the infirmary to visit the wounded and to the King's Hall to talk to the people and see my poor cousin. I shall organise another search party if poor Lady Benicia hath not yet been found. And then I shall go to bed...' she glanced at Sir Gunford, 'in my own apartments.'

'Doth your highness think that wise?' asked Gunford with a sneer.

'My tower hath not yet fallen or burned, but if it doth do either of those, I give thee my word sir, that I shall bow to thy superior wisdom and straight away return hither.'

Winterhued knew that the sweaty sycophant cared not a whit whither she went or what she did, as long as it did not hinder his plans to keep King Gers, and himself, safe. She was also aware that he was another of the men who had been conspiring to turn the king against her.

Returning his sneer with one of her own, she turned dismissively from him. Then she kissed her father, who had almost forgotten his anger due to the arrival of two servants bearing platters of ling and salted eel, took her leave of the Balasorean ambassador and of the chancellor and the chamberlain and, with a lantern-bearing guard going before her, swept from the chamber.

But on the second stair she paused and looked back at the king. 'Father,' she said, 'I beg Your Grace not to send forth a messenger to search for a nameless knight. 'Twould be a foolish and a wasted journey.'

'Child,' answered King Gers through a mouthful of eel, 'thou art stubborn and thou art clever, but I am stubborner and I am cleverer. My mind is set on this.'

Brenn, Winterhued's youngest lady-in-waiting, stood tip-toe upon the latrine seat and peered out through the slit in the curved stone wall of the garderobe. As the shutters in the bedchamber were still closed tight, this narrow opening had been her only view out to the world for a night and a day.

All she could see now, as daylight faded, was the same hapless ship aground in the lake's shallows, its fires sunk to glowing embers and reflected like the undulations of a crimson serpent across the twilit waters. The vessel's masts had gone overboard some time before and now, even as the girl watched, a cloud of steam arose as the fire reached the waterline.

'Brave ship,' murmured Brenn; 'strong wast thou built and stalwart thy timbers.' Since her arrival in Lawhill, Brenn had discovered that she was fond of ships. Instead of getting on with dull needlework she had often found herself dreaming of distant lands as she watched them beat down across the lake under wind-hardened canvas, eager for the wide river and the far sea. But never again would this ship spread her flaxen wings to the world's winds.

Brenn shivered and climbed down from the wooden seat. She picked up her dwindling candle from the floor and crossed the wardrobe, where the princess's gowns hung on racks. Brenn had spent some time in here during the long, lonely, fearful day gazing, in anxious pleasure, at beauty; at damasks, silks and velvets, at exquisite embroideries, rich trimmings and gem inlays. Even now she could not resist running a hand across the marvellous fabrics as she passed.

Having been without a fire all the day, the bedchamber was as cold as the smaller rooms and full of darkness. The girl extracted another candle from the bundle that had been provided by the servant who had brought her, hours ago, a cold meal. She lit it, then blew out the stub and squashed the new candle down into the melted wax in her candlestick. She crossed the chamber to light two of the eight cressets that were mounted against the walls. Black smoke curled up as the oil flamed. Then she snuffed out the candle and placed it on a low table.

Huge shadows jumped about the walls as she moved to the princess's bed and, with another pang of guilt, climbed onto the blossom-embroidered counterpane and wrapped herself in a thick blanket. She had slept several times during the day and found that the dream of wings no longer troubled her. Yet, awake, her heart leapt at every noise and her whole being seemed weighed down by dread.

But at least the princess's cat, curled up in a rug on the bed, appeared more settled. She stretched and rolled onto her back, showing off her plump belly. Blinking her green eyes, she started a rumbling purr as she kneaded the air, her paws flexing and curling. Brenn was unfamiliar with cats. She would have liked to bury her face in the soft fur of the cat's stomach as she had once seen Winterhued do, but was unwilling to brave those fearsome claws, sharp as curved pins. "I thrive upon danger," the princess had said, laughing. Brenn had noticed that, beneath her long sleeves, Winterhued's hands were criss-crossed with thin red scratches.

Brenn tentatively rubbed the top of the cat's round head, where the tabby stripes merged to form a little black cap. 'Thou art the most fortunate cat in all the world, little Thistle,' she said. 'In my home cats must work. They hunt for mice and rats in the kitchens and the stables and are never allowed within. I thought 'twas only witches that kept cats before I came here... but the princess is never a witch! She is the most beautiful, cleverest and kindest lady in the world! I wish she would come back.'

Brenn's stomach complained noisily. 'I wish someone... anyone, would bring some food,' she added.

As if a lurking fairy had immediately granted her wish, there came a knock upon the door and a voice called out, 'Lady Brenn, be not alarmed. 'Tis I... I have brought victuals for you.' Before she could decide who 'I' was, the voice went on: ''Tis your friend Deccan... Deccan of Wythop,' he added, as though she might know many Deccans.

Despite an overwhelming gladness that someone had come at last, Brenn pulled a face as she climbed down off the bed, taking the blanket with her. The cat had scuttled off to hide somewhere and Brenn admired her good sense. But she had seen no one but a servant all day and Deccan's company was better than none at all. And he would surely have more news to impart than the surly girl who had merely told her: 'The princess be still in council. I was told to tell m'lady that she is to remain here.' When Brenn had questioned her, she had mumbled something about the kitchens burning down and lots of folk a'dying and then some tale of a dragon come to live in the keep. 'That's nonsense,' Brenn had said, whereupon the girl became even more sullen. Brenn wondered what had become of her own lady's maid; a lass that had travelled with her from Drumalis and was as daft as a rabbit. Though she was not overly fond of the maid, the girl's unwonted absence only heightened Brenn's anxiety.

'Ye may enter,' she called out to Deccan, after she had carefully pushed aside the princess's lute and several books and sat herself primly at the cushioned window seat, tucking the blanket about her knees.

She could not help but laugh when the young squire entered. She had expected him to be accompanied by a servant bearing the food, but instead he staggered in sideways, pushing the door open with his shoulder and struggling beneath a tray upon which were balanced several dishes, a jug and a small lantern.

'I thought ye were in training to be a knight, not a serving drudge,' she said.

The lad's cheeks flushed. 'I am no drudge!' he exclaimed. 'All squires serve their lords, so it is no lowly thing to carry meat, lady. Here... ye may have your food. There's some for a cat as well.' He put the tray on the floor just inside the door, picked up his lantern and turned to leave.

'I pray ye come back, Deccan,' said Brenn. 'I am sorry. I was... surprised to see you. I am grateful though. And so is the cat.'

Deccan had paused in the doorway and now he came back into the chamber, still frowning as he picked up the tray. 'I offered to bring this. I've been enquiring after you all the day.' He looked at her sideways as he put the tray on the seat next to her. 'I heard a servant saying that orders had come from the princess to bring victuals hither... and I knew then where ye were. I knew then that ye were not perished.' His cheeks were still pink. He shivered and hugged himself. 'Arrgh, by my spurs, 'tis cold as a Callunian's eyes in here.'

'There are blankets,' said Brenn, making a start on a barely-warm vegetable pottage. 'Wrap yourself, then tell me all that hath happened. I have been alone in this chamber forever; sometimes I feared I was the only person left alive in the world.'

Deccan was not listening. 'By my spurs! Never did I think I'd be in here,' he said, looking about him in awe at the princess's chamber. 'No one will believe me when I tell them.'

'Ye had better not tell them then,' said Brenn, through a mouthful of pottage; 'especially as ye should not be in here... with me. 'Tis not right and proper.'

''Tis not right and proper there be a demon on the roof, 'tis not right and proper Sir Auchencairn is likely dead, 'tis not right and proper the Queen's Hall is burned to the ground, 'tis not right and proper that so many servants are perished that the lords must see to themselves. I do not think anyone would concern themselves over...'

'Demon?' interrupted Brenn. 'Sir Auchencairn dead? The Queen's Hall burned? Sit down,' she said, indicating the seat opposite her. 'I have heard naught of these tidings, except the kitchens burned and some servants... and... and a dragon, but I did not believe...'

'Aye, that's what they're saying... a dragon,' said the boy, then abruptly changed the subject. 'Do ye always stumble about in the dark down in Drumalis?' He took the candle from his lantern and lit the other six cressets, having a good look at everything in the room as he did so. Then he lit four candles on the hanging candlebeam in the centre of the room, and finally the big candle on its iron tripod by the door. Warm golden light spread gleaming upon the wainscoting and the tapestries, transforming the room into a sunny forest glade spangled with flowers.

At last the boy sat down at the window seat, facing her. The space between the seats was narrow and their knees almost touched. His were large and knobbed and clad in wrinkled russet hose, but at least (and for this Brenn felt absurdly grateful) he wasn't a 'brag bag' man.

'Well then,' said Deccan, and forthwith launched into an account of the happenings of the night before. Brenn pushed herself as far back on her seat as she could manage. But after a moment she had forgotten about the proximity of his knees. She had even forgotten to eat and she gazed at him round eyed, with her mouth slightly open. It was not long though before her usual annoyance with Deccan returned. In her short acquaintance with him she had noticed how he liked to embroider a tale and now, if she were to believe every word, it would seem that he and 'his lord', the mightily courageous Sir Soukar, had rescued every damsel in the hall from certain death. 'What think ye of that?' he asked her for the sixth time, not expecting an answer.

'I think naught of that,' said Brenn. 'Why did ye and your lord, brave and fearless as ye be, not leave the damsels' rescue to lesser fellows and go slay the creature? Ye have had enough practice, surely, and such a deed would have been of far more use to us all.'

He stared at her for a moment, his lip curling slightly. Brenn stared back, wondering if she should tell him that he had a flake of dried snot dangling from one nostril. Though her parents and his had spoken together and it seemed likely that a betrothal was imminent, she knew at that moment that marriage to a spotty-faced braggart was not something that she remotely desired. He shivered violently and she found herself pitying him. 'Go get a blanket from the chest by the bed,' she said.

He ignored her instruction. 'By my spurs, how can ye say such a thing?' he exclaimed, his teeth chattering. 'Ye know naught; shut up in this pretty chamber all the day, ye know naught of the danger and death that is everywhere about us. And though I cannot admit to having seen this... this thing with mine own eyes, I have seen the dying and felt their terror, and I know that no mortal man, however brave and fearless, could slay this creature. I assure you that if I thought such a feat could be accomplished, why then, by my spurs, I would be the first to try!'

'Here,' said Brenn, pushing her own blanket at the boy and getting to her feet. By the time she had returned with another for herself, Deccan had wrapped himself against the cold and was tucking into her food. She sat down again and began to question him, mainly as to the health and whereabouts of her few acquaintances at court.

'The Duke of Drumrock's daughters?' he mumbled, his cheeks bulging. 'Lady Benicia... she's the one with...' He cupped his hands some distance out from his chest and instantly looked embarrassed. 'Pardon, Lady Brenn,' he muttered. 'Nay... I've not seen her, but I saw her sister, whatever her name is, not half an hour hence. She stood with her father in the hall and complained bitterly over something. I saw too the Lady Aminta; she wept still at her father's passing. Ye knew not about Sir Garthwray?' he asked upon noticing Brenn's surprised expression. 'Nay, I suppose ye did not...'

He went on, answering her questions unsatisfactorily and eating her meal. She ate a little more herself, enough to sate her hunger, and watched as he shovelled the rest of the food down his gullet. His face was quite round and his nose was short and snub and she found herself disliking him more with each passing minute. He seemed barely interested and hardly had a word to spare on anything that did not directly concern himself.

All of a sudden, she stopped him. "Do not eat that,' she said. 'It is for the cat.' He half choked and spat out his mouthful of chopped meat. His reaction inspired her. "'Tis rat,' she said, half turning to hide a little smile, 'minced rat, Thistle's favourite.'

'Urrgh,' groaned Deccan. 'Why did ye not warn me?'

'Why should I have need to warn you?' said Brenn. 'Ye've just consumed my supper! How was I to know that when ye'd finished that off, ye'd make a start on the cat's? I've a good mind to send you off to fetch another tray.'

Deccan's cheeks flushed. 'By my spurs,' he said, 'I am sorry. I had no thought... I am thus with food. My mother could tell you... she's ofttimes complained of it... when there is food before me, I eat it.'

'One day ye shall have a belly the size of Lord Templemore's,' said Brenn.

'By my spurs,' exclaimed Deccan, 'I'd be happy to have his belly if I also had his wealth!'

'But ye're already wealthy. Is that not why my father is so keen to see us wed? Ye shall get my breeding and I shall get your money.'

Deccan looked at her with a slight, embarrassed smile on his face. 'Ye speak very straight, my lady,' he said.

'Why should I not when it is the truth? It is true, I suppose... ye *are* very rich?'

'My family hath prospered, it is true. But we're not as wealthy as Lord Templemore.'

'Yet he is only a lord, without great lands,' said Brenn, puzzled, 'so how is it he hath such wealth?' As soon as the words left her lips she regretted them for ever since her first meeting with Deccan, he had constantly reminded her of how little she knew about anybody.

'I am amazed, Lady Brenn, that ye be so ignorant when it doth come to the nobility of Manydown,' said the lad, employing the pompous tone he always used when instructing her. 'Though Templemore's estate is small, 'tis exceeding prosperous and besides, he doth take a great deal of rent from commercial properties in Lawhill and in the great port of Dunsyre and in my own town of Wythop on the firth.'

Brenn, reminded of what an authority Deccan was on people with peerages, changed the subject. 'Deccan,' she said, 'a man arrived at court... yesterday methinks, though it doth seem a hundred years ago. The princess spoke with him; he seemed her good friend. He... he hath blue eyes.'

'That is the Marquess of Carradale," said the squire without hesitation, 'from the marcher lands in the north. Seldom seen at court, which is no wonder. Hardly a penny to his name, like all those northern lords, and all of them mad as spring rabbits. His father is the great Duke of

Arracan, in his dotage now, but once powerful enough to stand up to old King Caradoc himself. Ye do know, I hope, that Caradoc was King Gers' father?'

Brenn huffed indignantly. 'How would I not know who King Caradoc was when he cut off my grandfather's head? I am not as ill-informed as ye do think,' she said. 'In fact, I could recite to you all the kings and queens of Manydown back five hundred years or more.'

Deccan laughed. 'Any child could do that,' he said, still in his pompous voice. 'Anyway, that great duke, the most powerful lord in the north, was fool enough to take for his wife a woman who'd washed up on his shores after fleeing in a leaky boat from Calluna, which doth account for the marquess's blue eyes.' He laughed again. 'By my spurs, what bad timing, eh? To show his face at court for the first time in years, right at the same moment that another visitor doth come a'calling.'

Brenn felt an urge to kick Deccan, but instead she asked him: 'What is his name... the marquess?'

'The family name is Carigerne.'

'What is his given name?'

Surprisingly, Deccan was unsure. ''Tis Dal something,' he said. 'Dal... Dalmenal methinks.'

Brenn's heart leapt. Then it must be he: the unknown lover whose name began with a 'D'; the man whose initial, entwined closely with Winterhued's, was etched in silver upon the cover of the little book that she carried with her always.

Yet Brenn felt disappointed. What sort of lover was he, to have married the princess's friend and ridden into the north, seldom to be seen again? And he hardly looked the sort of man for whom a beautiful princess should harbour an ardent and never-ending love.

'Nay, I was wrong,' said Deccan. 'I've remembered... 'tis Almendral.'

'Are ye sure?'

''Perfectly. 'Tis Almendral. Why do ye ask? Are ye in love with him?'

Brenn snorted. 'Of course not, lackwit! He is as old as my father. But Deccan, as ye be so clever with the names of every nobleman in the land, who, besides yourself,' she gave a laugh, 'doth possess a name beginning with the letter "D"?' The squire looked at Brenn as though he suspected she'd taken leave of her senses. 'I know 'tis a strange question, but answer it anyway... to make up for eating my food.'

Deccan scratched his head, rumpling his stiff, brown hair. It was cut short some way above his shoulders, and framed his round face like the ears of a wiry-haired spaniel.

'Certes, how strange,' he said. 'I cannot think of anyone. I had never guessed at how rare a thing is mine own initial. But wait... there is your own father, Sir Dartford... and he is Earl of Drumalis, so has two "D's" to his name.'

'Nay, never my father,' said Brenn, feeling sick at the idea. 'Keep thinking.'

'I can think of titles only... Sir Auchencairn is the Earl of Dunsyre...'

'Oh... poor Sir Auchencairn,' said Brenn quietly.

'Aye. An exceeding good knight: strong and dauntless. 'Twill be a great loss if he is fallen. Ah... here's another: I had forgotten Sir Dechmont who accompanied Sir Auchencairn and is also missing; he is a great knight too.'

'He's very young, is he not?'

'Nay, he must be all of twenty years...'

'Too young.'

Deccan shrugged. 'There's the Earl of Dunmore,' he continued. 'He arrived in court yesterday; another with unlucky timing! He doth look a dull sort of fellow; more the mien of a clerk than a knight. And there's the Duke of Drumrock...'

Brenn interrupted him with a half-stifled snort. She imagined lovelorn Winterhued secretly pining for Benicia's father, a big, balding man with meat-greases smeared on his face and dribbled on his raiment, and so rotund he could no longer sit on a horse. If she had been less tired and anxious she may not have found this image funny, but now she was helpless to hold back the laughter. She laughed until the tears rolled down her face and she was doubled up, sobbing.

Deccan stared at her in confusion. 'Lady Brenn,' he asked anxiously, 'are ye unwell?'

The girl drew a shuddering breath and croaked: 'I... I'm laughing.' She gave another stifled cackle and leaned forward, her shoulders shaking with mirth.

'What said I that so amused you?'

'Naught,' sobbed Brenn, choking. 'Ye said... ye said naught. Besides, 'tis... 'tis not... 'tis not even funny!' But those words served only to set her laughing harder than ever.

The boy looked at her with a vexed frown. He got to his feet and poured her some wine from the jug he had brought, but she waved it away, mopping as she did so at the tears that streamed down her face.

'I shall be on my way,' Deccan said awkwardly, 'or they'll be wondering what hath become of me.'

'Before ye go... put the... put the... put the... rat meat on the floor! By the bed!' Brenn doubled over and cried with laughter.

The boy did as he was told, then put a new candle inside his lantern, even though the old one was but half burned. Frowning, he lit it with the old candle, as all the while Brenn kept up her helpless giggling.

'It's not rat, is it?' he asked, sullen and bewildered. The girl said naught, but pulled the blanket up over her face and shook.

'Good night, Lady Brenn,' he said and bowed stiffly but, still racked with mirth, she saw him not. 'I do not see that ye can have aught to laugh at,' he added as he crossed the room; 'if our army cometh not soon, we shall all of us perish.'

She heard the door close behind him and uncovered her flushed and tear-streaked face. 'I'm sorry, Deccan,' she whispered, her laughter all fled. 'Come back... I don't want to be alone.'

She stood up with the blanket still wrapped about her, and shuffled towards the bed, stopping half way to cast her eyes about the chamber. Locating a snuffer on the table, she proceeded to extinguish six of the cressets and all of the candles; her stern Drumalis upbringing was so ingrained that she scarcely thought about what she was doing. The little cat had emerged from beneath the bed upon Deccan's exit and, having polished off her chopped meat, sat cleaning her whiskers with a neat paw. Brenn scooped her up awkwardly and dropped her upon the bed, and the two of them curled up beneath a blanket upon the flowered counterpane.

Thistle purred as the girl stared up at the shadowy ceiling. The stone corbels supporting the ceiling joists were carved and painted as clusters of leaves, fruit and flowers. Dark ivy banded the heavy beams, gold leaf gleaming between each painted leaf and tendril. The timbers between the joists were patterned with leaves in various shades of green; she saw oak, chestnut, alder and elm. Her eyes wandered on across the ceiling and she noticed, despite the gloom, that the leaves patterning the next section changed colour to gold and russet and brown. But suddenly the leaves spangled as tears welled in her eyes. She covered her face and heard the silence pressing in, thicker than the castle walls; she felt the cat's small, breathing warmth beside her and knew that beyond that was only cold: cold, dead stone... cold, dead corpses.

For a long, horrible moment she listened to huge wings thumping through the air above the tower, until she realised it was her own heart, hammering in her ears like a kettledrum.

The cat had stopped purring. Brenn sobbed once, quietly, then lay in wide-eyed silence as tears rolled down her cheeks.

CHAPTER 6

A few shreds of azure still banded the western sky as the knight and his squire rode down a steep dip in the road. All day they had traversed the lower slopes of Iron Crag as the road rose, fell, twisted and turned about every crease and fold in the mountain's flanks. Its peak loomed into the south-eastern sky now: almost behind them. The knight led the way across an ancient stone bridge, then turned aside to halt on the mossy banks of the stream that rushed beneath it, clear and icy down from the mountain's heights. The horses dipped their heads to drink. Moss-draped trees lined the banks and beyond them were more trees, bending and whispering away into the gathering gloom.

Beside the road, within an overgrown clearing, was a roofless, tumbledown stone hut. The knight dismounted and led his horse over to the broken walls. He unhooked his helm, his shield and his two swords from the saddle, then unbuckled the girth and the surcingle, the breast-plate and the crupper. Lifting the heavy saddle from the stallion's back, he propped it on its pommel against the lichened stone. He rubbed the damp coat where the saddle had been and the horse stretched out his neck, closed his eyes and sighed.

The chestnut horse had followed the grey and stood patiently, the squire still sitting hunched in the saddle, staring vacantly at naught. The knight looked round at him.

'Dost thou plan to sit up there all the night?'

'Huh,' grunted the boy, 'this place is grand. Why don't we stay 'ere forever? This 'ouse doth match you perfectly.'

'Get off and unsaddle the horse,' said the knight equably. 'And if thou dost hope to stay warm this night, thou canst help me gather wood for the fire.' He slipped the bridle over the grey's ears and the horse walked off to graze on the tough winter grass.

Without another glance at the boy, the knight set off around the edges of the clearing, stooping to pick up whatever wood he could find. He was clad in half-armour: steel cuirass, with pauldrons and vambraces on shoulders and arms, over a quilted black arming-doublet that had a collar and skirt of chain mail. On his long legs he wore black thigh-boots of worn leather. He was a tall, strongly made man; broad shouldered, hard-muscled and lean. He moved a little stiffly, troubled, in the cold and damp, by an old wound.

'Are there robbers in this place? Outlaws?' asked the boy, his eyes glinting in the twilight as he glanced over his shoulder.

The knight straightened. 'If there were, they'd be sorely disap-pointed in us. Nay, lad, the only folk that use this road are woodcutters, charcoal burners and bark peelers, and they possess naught that would tempt robbers. Besides, their visits are infrequent and never this early in the year.' He dropped an armful of timber by the hut wall and turned to search for more.

'Wolves then?' asked the boy. 'There's somethin' bad about... ye said so yourself.'

'Nal, bestir thyself,' said the knight without turning. The boy obeyed at last, slithering awkwardly from the saddle. About fourteen or fifteen years old, he was short for his age and as thin as a thatch-reed. He was clad in a grimy, quilted jack over a brown woollen jacket, brown hose and short boots, and his head was bare for he had lost every hat he'd ever owned. Muttering under his breath, he fumbled at his saddle's girth straps.

The pieces of the knight's armour that he was not presently wearing were wrapped in oiled linen and attached, in bags, to the chestnut's saddle. The squire should have removed these first, as well as the bundle that contained the bedrolls, cooking pot and the rest of the knight's meagre belongings. But, as usual he did not, and after much heaving and tugging, managed to drag the whole heavy lot with a crash and a clatter onto the ground. But this time, although he'd unbuckled the crupper, he'd failed to remember the leather breastplate, which skewed around the horse's neck but remained firmly buckled to the saddle. The gelding, with the weight off his back, moved off to join his companion, dragging the saddle and baggage beside him along the muddy ground. Wincing, the knight continued his wood gathering, leaving the cursing boy to sort out the mess.

When, a short time later, he looked up, it was to see the lad angrily kicking at the stationary saddle while the horse wandered away, treading and tripping on his trailing reins. Without a word, the knight tossed down his bundle of wood beside the hut and walked over to remove the red gelding's bridle, giving the horse an affectionate pat and a few kind words. On his way back, he lifted the saddle that Nal had been feebly tugging at, carried it to the hut and propped it next to his own.

'Did ye kill someone?' asked the boy suddenly.

'What?' said the knight, looking round at Nal with a frown. 'Speak sense, boy.'

'Well, ye did say ye came from this place... Many... Many... whatsit.'

'Manydown.'

'Aye, Manydown. There must 'ave been a reason ye left and a reason ye be afeared to return.'

'I've killed men, but none in Manydown,' said the knight, retrieving his tinderbox from a saddlebag. 'I'm not afraid to return.'

He made a pile of the kindling he'd collected and struck a spark, steel upon flint, into the box. A thin curl of smoke arose as he held the smouldering tinder to the kindling. He had to work at it for a while, kneeling to blow gently at the first struggling flames, for the kindling was damp. As fire blossomed at last around the steaming wood, he sat back on his heels and turned to regard the boy. Nal slouched against the broken doorframe with two twigs in his hand: his sole contribution towards the firewood.

'I left Manydown,' said the knight, 'because I am the seventh son of a marcher lord. There was no inheritance for me.' He smiled. 'I began with naught, and have, with great skill, managed to keep it all.'

'I pray you, don't teach me *that* skill,' said the boy.

'Thou needst not worry as I have been unable to teach thee anything.'

Nal sat down by the fire and poked at it with his two twigs. Beyond the flickering orange light, darkness gathered. 'I don't need your teachin',' he said sullenly. 'All o' me skills I learnt from me pa.'

'So he taught thee to trip over thy feet, ride into low branches and fall off thy horse,' replied the knight, feeding some larger pieces of wood to the fire.

'Fall off?' spluttered the boy. 'When did I last fall off?'

'This day.'

Nal was silent for a moment, and then said: 'Ye never do believe me. I told you I didn't fall; I jumped off.'

'And landed on thy head.'

'Nay! On me 'ands.'

'Then thy head. Very adroit. Did thy father also teach thee that feat?'

The boy looked up at the knight with an ill humoured scowl. 'Ye do try always to make a fool o' me.'

'Never, Nal,' said the knight with a smile. 'That would be a waste of my time, as thou dost do it so well by thyself.'

Nal threw his bits of half-burnt twig at the man, who ducked and laughed, then got to his feet. 'Never mind, thou hast a simple task for now,' he said. 'Stay here by the fire and keep it alight.' The boy shot him a black look, but promptly picked up a soggy piece of wood and dropped it into the middle of the flames. The wood hissed, the fire sputtered and the knight sighed. "I've told thee before," he said resignedly; "when the wood's damp, lay it at the fire's edge to dry somewhat, then feed it in slowly.'

The squire wordlessly did as he was told, managing to push the damp wood to one side with a stick. He wrapped his skinny arms about his skinny legs and rocked upon his heels, sulking. Smoke curled up through the firelight and vanished into darkness. The looming slopes above, and the thick forest all about, lay black and silent.

The knight got out the cooking pot and walked down to the stream. He filled the pot and returned, picking up more firewood on his way, then set the pot upon the fire to boil. Unbuckling a bag from the boy's saddle, he brought their last meagre supply of food to the fireside. He drew a knife from his belt and, on a flat stone, cut up three small onions, four split and misshapen carrots, and a parsnip. Taking a handful of dried beans from a pouch, he dropped them into the water with a little salt. 'I'm not eatin' that muck again,' mumbled Nal. 'I only eat bread and meat, like a man.'

The knight, cleaning his knife, ignored the boy. He laid out the oiled groundsheet and bedrolls by the fire then, giving the pot a stir, moved it away from the flames so that the boiling water subsided to a simmer. 'Stir it sometimes,' he said, handing the boy the stick he'd just used, 'and when the moon rises, add the vegetables.'

Finding a wooden-backed brush in the baggage, the knight walked over to the horses that grazed untethered and un-hobbled at the clearing's edge. They stood almost beyond the reach of the firelight, barely illuminated by the flames' faint flickering. Above them a million stars pricked pinholes in an indigo sky.

Beginning with the grey stallion, the knight ran the brush over the sway back and bony ribs, scrubbing at dried sweat and splashes of mud. He stopped to pull a handful of moulted winter coat from the brush's bristles and the long white hairs floated to the earth like late snow. The horse turned his head and rested his chin on the knight's shoulder and the knight smiled crookedly and gently ran his hand over the horse's closed eye.

'What has made thee uneasy this day, eh Hougomont?' he murmured. He looked westward, across the horse's back towards the dark trees and the heavy silence. 'So close...' he sighed, his head sinking down until his dark hair fell across the horse's white fur. He felt so weary he could almost have fallen asleep right there and then, propped up by his horse.

But he pushed himself upright, moved round to the horse's off-side and finished the job. Walking over to the red gelding, he set to with the brush. 'Good lad, Dunboyne,' he said and the horse sighed and leaned into the strokes, stretching out his neck, pursing his lips and rolling his eyes blissfully when the brush found an itchy spot below his withers. The knight completed his work and knelt to clean the brush on a boulder of granite.

As he did so the moon rose above the mountain's low spur in the east and cast its light across the clearing. The man looked up and gazed at it for a while as it hung glowing above the trees. It was waning, but only a day from full, and looked like a huge gold coin. The knight turned away with a shake of his head and got to his feet. 'Gers liveth yet, so I cannot go west,' he said. 'North... I *shall* go north.'

He returned to the fire to discover, to his surprise, that it was still alight and that the vegetables had been added to the simmering soup. But the boy would not look up and sat hunched and sulky. He had a blanket over his head, which made him look like an old peasant woman.

'I am sorry Nal,' said the man. 'Forgive me.' Nal shrugged, grunted and stared at the flames.

The knight sat down by the fire and as soon as the vegetables had cooked, doled equal amounts of the thin soup into battered pewter bowls. He took out half a loaf of hard bread, cut some mould off the crust, divided the bread and put the pieces straight into the soup. 'Well done, Nal,' he said, handing a bowl to the boy.

'What's well done?' muttered Nal.

'The fire burneth bright, and the soup is neither burnt nor boiled away.'

'Is that supposed to be praise? If it is, that's a skill ye don't possess.' The boy took a sip from his bowl. 'And ye can't cook neither.'

'If thou canst not eat such slop..?' said the knight, stretching out a hopeful hand towards the boy's bowl. He'd already eaten his soggy hunk of bread and most of his soup.

Nal scowled and turned away, clutching his bowl tightly as he stuffed the bread into his mouth. The man finished his meagre meal and stirred the fire. 'On the morrow,' he said, 'we shall come at last into the village of Wendur, and I promise thou shalt eat thy fill, even if I must chop wood for it.'

'Chop wood,' said the boy disgustedly, 'Why? Ye've money.'

'Twelve copper coins from Ormsary,' said the knight. 'They won't go far after a blacksmith's been paid.'

Nal grunted. He put down his empty bowl and pulled the blanket tighter around his head.

'Art thou afraid of the moon?' asked the knight, smiling his wry smile.

'Everyone knoweth ye go mad if ye sleep in the moonlight,' said the boy.

'But thou'rt not asleep.' The boy shot him a look, but didn't answer. 'I've been sleeping in the moonlight for years.'

'No need to say nowt then, is there?' said Nal with a sneer. 'Ye be perfect proof of it.'

The knight regarded the boy for a moment, then asked: 'Hast thou forgiven me?'

'Nay. But I know ye're just after me 'elp with your armour.'

'Aye, I am that, or I shall have an uncomfortable night. But I'd like thy forgiveness as well.'

Without a word, the boy wriggled his way over to the knight and got on with the job of unbuckling the man's armour. As he still clutched the blanket tightly round his head with one hand, the unbuckling of buckles and the untying of points was made somewhat difficult. 'If there is aught left after we've paid for the blacksmith and food,' said the knight, 'we shall buy thee a hat for the moonlight. And nail this one to thy head so thou dost not lose it.'

He looked at the sorry, sulking boy, remembering how he'd taken him on as squire almost out of pity. Pengwern, where the lad had been born, had just made an uneasy peace with its neighbour after a bloody war in which its population of young men had been well nigh decimated. The knight, and the fine lad who'd been his squire at the time, had gained some glory fighting as mercenaries in that war. After knighting young Lasbek, he'd given him his blessings and half their earnings, as well as a handsome bay stallion and a good suit of armour, and sent the young man home. He'd then searched high and low for a replacement, but a boy of gentle birth had proved difficult to come by. But there was Nal, a baker's son, who'd been trailing round behind him for days in the sure belief he followed the greatest hero the world had ever known. 'Take 'im and good luck to you, sir,' the baker had said. 'I've got two other lads a deal more useful to me than that lout. I've not been able to beat a morsel of sense into 'im, and I warn you sir, unless ye've the patience of a saint, ye'll be knockin' the lad on the 'ead and leavin' 'im in a ditch before the week's out.'

'What's a marchin' lord?' asked Nal suddenly, tugging at the buckle that attached the knight's right pauldron to his backplate.

'I've no idea,' answered the knight.

'But ye said you're the seventh son o' one of 'em.'

'A marcher lord,' corrected the man. 'The marches of Manydown lie along her north-western border. Over that border lieth Angerona, a wretched land ruled by a succession of warmongers. Though there hath been peace of a sort for many years, 'twas not always so. For hundreds of years the marches were lands of raids, plundering and bloodshed. Castles were built on every hilltop and every farm had a pele tower and an armoury. My father is, or was – I know not if he yet lives – a powerful lord with vast tracts of land, but it is not rich land; the folk scratch a meagre living from its thin soil. 'Tis beautiful though.' The knight's voice grew soft. 'The mists drift ever across the purple moors, and the grey waters of Otterspool Firth lie smooth and still as glass. I would like to see it again.'

'Thin soil and meagre folk sound dull,' said Nal, helping the knight out of the last of his armour: the close-fitting breastplate and backplate cuirass.

''Tis thy brain that's dull,' said the knight, standing up in his rusty doublet and flexing his arms and shoulders.

'Thought ye were after forgiveness,' scowled the boy. 'Ye'll not get it now.'

The knight hardly seemed to hear him. Deep in thought, he wrapped his armour in oiled cloth and wrapped himself in his threadbare cloak then walked down to the stream to wash the cooking pot and the bowls. He came back and sat down by the fire, shivering.

'Who'll keep first watch?' asked Nal.

'No need for watches,' said the knight.

'No need? But ye said yourself… ye said that somethin'd made the birds leave the mountain.'

'Aye, so I did. But I'm tired. If that something wishes to come and eat me in the night, well and good; it'll save me the trouble of getting up in the morning. But keep watch if thou dost wish to.' The man pulled his bedroll closer to the fire and climbed into it, throwing his cloak over the blanket. Sparks shot into the air as the boy pushed a flaming branch further into the fire.

'Tell me about Manydown,' said Nal.

'Manydown,' murmured the knight, his eyes shining in the firelight, 'is a land of plenty. In Manydown people laugh and sing, the meadows are green and the crops abundant. Artists and men of learning prosper. In great castles the light of a thousand candles gleams upon velvet gowns and wondrous tapestries. Music is played, feasts are consumed, feather-beds are slept in, and one may take a hot bath...'

'And we're not goin' there. Fie!' said the boy disgustedly. 'We're goin' north, ye say. To that Anger place. Wretched, ye said.'

'Angerona, aye.' The knight rolled onto his back and stared up at the sky. 'I travelled there when first I left Manydown. A mountainous, storm-swept land where grey castles crouch in endless rain above hungry villages. The lords and nobles that dwell in those castles are brutes who believe that mercifulness is a vice. Their swords are ever in their hands. They hoard their gold and live well enough, but their serfs starve.'

'Why do we go there then?' asked Nal in a small voice.

'We shall but pass through on our way to the west; northwest first to gloomy Farsund, where the rain never ceases, then by boat across the great Talavera into Calluna, or at least, what was once Calluna before that land was overrun by the warmongering Angeronish and subjected to a hundred years of oppression. 'Tis still a fine place though, of green meadows below snow-capped heights, of handsome towns beside deep fjords. My mother came from Calluna. We shall find a ship there, in Ancenis, to take us south.'

'A ship! On the sea?' said the boy, glancing round at the knight with a little more enthusiasm.

'Aye lad, on the sea.'

'I've never seen the sea. What's it like?'

'The first time I saw it,' said the knight, his voice low, ''twas slate-grey and storm tossed. Gulls circled above foam-flecked waves and their aching cry came drifting on the wind. It seemed the very edge of the world. But men say there may be islands, vast lands perhaps, far beyond the western horizon. No one will take us west, but 'twill be good to sail south. A lovely thing to behold is a fine ship running before the wind with her sails bellied, and dolphins leaping beside her amongst the white-capped waves.'

'Will the south be... be...' Nal yawned hugely, 'warmer than this place?'

'That doth depend on how far south the ship will take us.'

'And what's in the south?' The boy had lain himself down, and his voice came muffled from within the wrappings of his moon-shield blanket.

'Far, far south...' murmured the knight, 'are towering, sand-coloured fortresses straddling rocky crags above deserts of heat... black-shadowed gates spewing forth armies... hedgehog ranks of spears glinting and wavering through heat-shimmer and dust and great silver lakes that are not there.'

The knight lay wide-awake, gazing up at the sky. Stars dusted the heavens and a cloud drifted across the moon.

'To the east, to the west, to north and south, have I travelled, lad,' he murmured, 'over leagues and leagues of the wide earth. And every-where have I seen at work the greed of men. Greed that subjects lands to strife and oppression, that sees poor folk starving to the clash of steel and the thunder of armies on the march. Greed that makes rivers run red; that builds forests of gallows and mountains of corpses. I have seen greed turning the night sky red as villages burn, and the black smoke of greed blotting out the moon. I saw, lad, because I was there... with my bloodied sword...'

He rolled onto his side and looked at the boy, who had started to snore softly.

'I am tired of it, Nal,' he sighed; 'I want to go home. Yet here I am, at the edge of the land wherein dwelleth my heart, and I must ride by.'

He propped himself on one elbow to feed more wood to the fire, then lay down again and looked up at the sky. The moon came out from behind cloud and its light silvered the fine, strong bones of his face. He pulled his cloak and blanket up around his ears and closed his eyes.

Beautiful, buxom Benicia was dreaming of Potrimpos; she stroked his beauteous hair and kissed his comely lips but, like a churl, he pushed her into the lake. The black water closed over her head and spread its bitter cold through to her very marrow. It filled her mouth and ran down her throat. Gasping for air, she woke with a jolt to find herself lying huddled in a tight ball. She seemed to have frozen during the night into an immovable lump of ice. Painful stone pressed against her hip and shoulder. She wondered if she'd fallen from her bed, but surely then she'd be lying on the deep carpet that she loved to feel against her bare feet when she rose in the morning. And, as ever, there would be a crackling fire in the hearth to spread its warmth.

She tried to open her eyes but they seemed swollen and glued shut. Putting her freezing hands up to her face, she rubbed and poked at her eyes until she felt sure they were open. But she saw only blackness: deep impenetrable blackness that pressed into her skull.

In a panic she attempted to scramble to her feet, but her head thumped into something hard and she cried out with the pain. As she subsided again to the cold floor, memories began to return; horrible memories of consuming flames, of wounds and death, of stink and smoke, of the cruelty of her sister, the shattered door, the scored stone, the bloody corpses and the keep.

She knew not where she was, but she remembered crawling into this dark corner hours ago.

'I am a worm in a rotting log,' she whispered into the darkness. Her throat was hoarse and dry. She curled into a ball again, crying, though her tears were all spent. Her breath came in gasps and she shook: from the cold, from hunger, from fright.

Her eyes were still wide open so she saw the light of flames that spread flickering along the floor. She cringed back and put her hands up to blot it out, whimpering. She heard shuffling and the scraping of talons along the flagstones.

'Here she is, my lord,' said a man's voice. 'Are ye still living, m'lady?'

A hand was held out to her and she took it. It was as warm as the sun. The man helped her to stand. Light was all around and she could see now that she'd been hiding under a wooden bench in a deserted guardroom. She looked at her saviour. He was a young soldier with yellow hair and a handsome face and he had his warm hand beneath her elbow to steady her. His other hand held high a flaming torch, and it must have been his sword that had scraped along the flagstones as he bent to search for her.

'Ye do seem to be all in one piece,' he said with an encouraging smile. He took off his woollen cloak and wrapped it about her shoulders. 'We've been a-searching all over for you m'lady. Your father hath been fearful, and the princess. So too hath my lord here.' He nodded towards the door.

Benicia looked round with the beginnings of a glad smile on her face. But it was not Potrimpos who had come to rescue her. Amazed, she beheld in the doorway her betrothed, Sir Criffel, Earl of Dunmore, accompanied by two more soldiers with torches. Her smile vanished as the earl looked her up and down. She became aware of how wretched she must look, with her face swollen and dirty, her headdress gone and her hair all undone, and her peach velvet gown torn and besmirched. She was still shivering so violently with the cold that she could scarcely stand, yet in the bright torchlight and with three strong soldiers standing close by, some of her fears had fled.

'Fie!' said the earl in his hard, thin voice. 'What do I find here?'

Benicia remembered her manners and bobbed a clumsy curtsey. Her knees almost gave way and the yellow-haired man caught her elbow again to steady her. 'Sir,' she croaked. She coughed and tried again. 'Sir Criffel... I did not know ye had come up to court.'

'Oh, that was made perfectly plain to me yester eve,' he said coldly.
'I saw you, madam, with the Marquess of Potrimpos. I chose to arrive
unannounced, yesterday, two hours after noon. I could perhaps have
chosen a more fortunate week for my visit, however, now that I am here
I must make the best of it.' His nose was wrinkled as though scenting
a particularly bad smell and it was such a short, snub nose that Benicia
could see right into his nostrils. 'Now madam,' he continued, 'would ye
be so kind as to explain to me why I have been obliged to spend half
the night engaged in the irksome, the *dangerous*, task of searching for
you, only to find *my future wife* looking like a dirty drudge?'

Benicia felt her mouth trembling and tears prick at her eyes, but
she didn't wish to weep in front of this loathsome man. She'd known
for years that she was one day to wed him, but had always pushed that
unpleasant knowledge to the back of her mind.

'I was lost,' she whispered, pathetically.

'Lost?' Sir Criffel laughed. 'How long have ye dwelt at Lawhill?
Come madam,' he said, gripping her arm, 'allow me to escort you to
your father before ye disgrace yourself further.'

Benicia whimpered and tugged her arm free. 'I can walk without
your assistance,' she said.

'Very well,' he said impassively. 'Don't dally.'

He strode away from the guardroom down a narrow wall passage,
with one of the soldiers hurrying in front of him to light the way.
Benicia tottered after him as best she could on feet that were so cold
they had lost all feeling. Enfeebled by hunger, she tripped on the torn
hem of her gown and almost fell, but a strong arm come about her
waist to hold her up. She glanced round at the soldier with gratitude
and he smiled at her. She saw now that he was one of the earl's own
retainers for over his brigandine he wore a green livery jacket that bore
the Dunmore badge of a fetterlock.

'Take heart, madam,' he said quietly. 'Be strong.' His hair glowed
golden in the torchlight and she did feel stronger.

'I saw it,' she whispered to him; 'the dread beast.'

'Ahh,' he sighed, looking at her with admiration. 'Your ladyship hath been through much.' He lowered his voice even more. 'Take no heed of Mistress Criffel. He barks a good deal but seldom bites.' Benicia's eyes widened and the soldier shrugged slightly. 'That is what all of his men call him,' he whispered, putting a finger to his lips. The girl gave a breathless little laugh and shot a look in the direction of the earl. That gentleman, suddenly aware of the whispered voices behind him, spun on his heel and glared at his betrothed with narrowed eyes.

'Garston,' he snapped, 'go thee in front.'

'Very well, my lord,' said Benicia's friend nonchalantly and strolled past the earl. His torch appeared to pass carelessly close to Dunmore's face but the earl, scarcely noticing, continued to look hard at Benicia. 'Keep up,' he said as he turned and walked on.

The daughter of the Duke of Drumrock did keep up. She wiped her dirty face with a dirtier hand, she sniffed twice, then she held up her head and walked steadily, despite her lumpish feet, down the passage behind her future husband.

In her state of exhaustion it seemed a long walk. They passed through tower after tower (though if she'd kept tally, she'd have counted no more than three). The wall passage was low, narrow and unlit. Before their torches the darkness gave way, only to close in behind them as thick as treacle. Regularly, to their right, deeply recessed arrow loops appeared out of the blackness, and everywhere was the acrid smell of charred wreckage.

They turned a corner through a guardroom at the base of a tower. This one was not deserted, and the three guards stationed there stood to attention and stared at Benicia. She shuffled past them, with a vague thought that she might know this place but with no idea that only two floors above, Lady Brenn, the tears drying on her cheeks, lay asleep upon the princess's bed.

Benicia regarded the earl's narrow back and wondered how he wore his fur-lined cloak after he had seen her shivering. Well, let him keep his smelly cloak; she was much happier wearing the cloak of a common soldier. She pulled it close around her and whispered his name, 'Garston,' very softly. He had lovely hair: long, thick and bright, she thought, looking past the earl at the soldier's back.

She glanced at Sir Criffel's hair; it was thin and black and lank, and though she could only see the back of it, she knew it was receding rapidly from his forehead. It was strange that he had so little hair on the top of his head when on the rest of his body – the parts she could see anyway (and the parts she couldn't see didn't bear thinking about) – he was the hairiest man she had ever seen. Though he was clean-shaven, the whole of the lower half of his face was blue with potential hair; there was hair on his neck and curling up from under his collar, and the backs of his white hands and fingers were thick with black hair.

She stared at his legs as he strutted along before her like a scrawny cockerel. They were sure to be hairy too, and they looked remarkably thin and shapeless in their wrinkled grey hose. *Oh dragon*, she suddenly thought, *come and eat this man. Or eat me instead, for my life shall not be worth the living when I am made his wife*. She felt surprisingly happy at this idea, for she had just realised that the death a dragon might bring her was as naught compared to the horrors that could await her if she lived.

They had come up to a doorway in the left hand wall of the passage, lit on either side by torches in brackets and guarded by a soldier who leant half asleep upon his pike. He stood up straight as Garston and the other soldier in the lead turned and passed through the portal. As Dunmore followed, he looked over his shoulder to make sure that Benicia kept close behind him. ''Tis well it be too dark to see you clearly, madam,' he said coldly, 'else I would be ashamed to accompany you.' Benicia stumbled after him down some worn stairs. *Come hither dragon*, she thought.

They crossed a storeroom, or it may have been an archive with its stacked rows of iron-hinged boxes, and came through a second doorway. Benicia looked about her in confusion, as in all her time in Lawhill she felt certain that she had never seen this place. She stood in a long, wide hall at the end of one of three rows of massive round columns that supported a stone ceiling of groined vaulting. To her left stretched a succession of gigantic barrels, hulking out of the darkness, while along the blind arcade of the wall to her right were set four torches; hardly enough to light such a large space. It came to her that she must be in the undercroft of the King's Hall, used as the castle's cellars. The air was cold and a musty smell assailed her nostrils.

Then she saw the people, sitting bundled in furs on the stone seats of the arcade, or lying on pallets under mounds of blankets and furs. Most had some of their belongings in boxes or chests beside them, many were accompanied by their hounds and lap-dogs, and a few at the far end of the hall had had their servants rig up curtains around their beds for a scant bit of privacy. Some spoke quietly together, several snored, one sobbed.

Benicia stared in wonderment and smiled a little. *Mistress Criffel may be ashamed of me,* she thought, *but I am no worse than these! Here are all the mighty lords and ladies of Manydown, hiding beneath the earth like frightened rabbits.*

The yellow-haired soldier, who didn't look at all like a frightened rabbit, chanced a glance round at his lord's betrothed, and she looked at him. But so, unfortunately, did the earl. 'Garston, thou mayst go,' he snapped. 'Thou also, Esto. Why must I be plagued with caitiffs and miscreants such as you? The twain of you, go find the Duke of Travancore and offer him your services for the rest of this night, with my compliments. Garston, pray tell him that thou art mightily skilled in the slaying of fearsome beasts, and hopefully he will set thee single-handedly to the task.'

Benicia looked at Garston with alarm, but discovered to her surprise that the man was grinning at the earl, and even more surprisingly, that the earl's mouth had a wry twist to it that may have been a smile. Garston and Esto bowed to Dunmore, and then the yellow-haired man made a quick obeisance in her direction. 'Madam,' he said, then had straightened and was gone. Benicia didn't dare watch him go.

If I never see him again, what care I? she thought, staring at her feet; *I am a duke's daughter and he is a servant.*

But she looked up to find that the Earl of Dunmore was staring at her with eyes that glittered blackly in the torchlight. 'When ye are my wife, madam,' he said, 'I see I shall have to watch you like a hawk.' Benicia looked away from his unpleasant smile. *Oh dragon,* she thought, *come and devour this man.* But instead of the dragon, it was her sister who came.

Manicia trotted towards them accompanied by a serving girl bearing a tray of victuals. Benicia's jaw dropped when she saw her sister, for not only was Manicia wearing an apron over her grey velvet gown, but she carried a brimming jug in one hand and bore several folded blankets in the other. She had managed to remain neat and clean and comely. She'd hitched up one side of her gown and pinned it in an elegant fashion so that the silvery silk of her underskirt showed. Not a wisp of her hair escaped from beneath her headdress. And over it all she wore an air of smug busyness.

She stopped abruptly when she saw Benicia. Sending the servant to attend to a group of noble refugees, she walked on towards her sister and future brother-in-law. She bobbed a curtsey to the earl but barely glanced at Benicia.

'Oh Sir Criffel,' she exclaimed in a responsibly hushed tone as he bowed his head to her, 'ye have found my hapless sister. Well done, sir! I thought that I had left her safe with the Marquess of Potrimpos; I thought mayhap they had eloped together! But then when he appeared and there was no sign of her, I was sorely distressed. But I've had not a moment, sir, to search for her myself. As ye do know, sir, servants are in short supply and there is much to be done. Dear old Lady Ulidia is distraught and doth ask for me constantly, also Lady Aminta. Lady Pera hath burnt her poor hands and I must dress them.' Benicia's mouth had fallen open as she heard her sister's deceit. 'Just this moment,' continued Manicia, 'have I brought food for the Wychwoods and ale I have here for Sir Soukar and blankets for the Gladbrooks. Then there are the wounded to be seen to.'

Benicia pulled Garston's cloak about her and looked away. She was well aware of Manicia's loathing for Lady Ulidia and knew that she felt naught for Pera but despite. She also knew that in the whole of her seventeen years, her sister had never lifted a finger to help anyone, except for Benicia herself. Manicia had been Benicia's shadow since they were little children and Manicia had done everything that her older sister asked of her, even at the risk of dire punishment. Now, to Benicia's bewilderment and sorrow, her sister had proven a lying traitor.

Her father too, who constantly told her that she was his dearest lass and how loath he was to lose her, had betrayed her. It mattered not how many times she told him that she hated the Earl of Dunmore, 'But it's all arranged,' was always his reply. 'Besides, I like the fellow,' he'd say. 'Not much of a horseman and can't hold his drink, but he's lord of the richest and finest lands with the fattest cattle in all of Manydown, and he's my neighbour, so thou shan't ever be far from thine old pa.'

At eighteen years of age, and with the earl at almost a score and ten, Benicia would have been wed by now if it had not been for the intervention of Princess Winterhued. That dear lady, sensing Benicia's dread of her impending nuptials, had told the earl that she needed Benicia at her side. Of course she did not, but Dunmore, and even her father the great Duke of Drumrock, could hardly gainsay the princess of the realm.

Benicia listened absently to her betrothed as he praised her sister. 'Your benevolence and industry in the face of adversity are to be admired, my lady,' he said. 'Ye could indeed stand as an example to all.' Benicia knew that he looked at her as he said this, but she ignored him and asked Manicia: 'Where is our father?'

'He doth sleep,' answered Manicia. 'And let me tell thee, if it be thine intent to wake him, I shall refuse to take thee to him.'

'Manny!' exclaimed Benicia. 'Thou knowest Father would wish to see that I am safe.'

'As ever, thou dost think only of thyself, Bee,' snapped Manicia. 'Our unhappy father hath much more need of sleep than he hath to look upon thy splotched countenance.'

'I say fie, madam,' added Sir Criffel, 'for after having put the duke to so irksome a worry, ye would now deprive him of his sleep.'

Without waiting for him to finish, Benicia spun about and tottered off down the hall, determined to search amongst every soul present until she found her father. She had hardly gone ten steps though, before she almost collided with Princess Winterhued who, in the midst of taking leave of her cousin Nomia, stepped backward straight into Benicia's hurried path.

'Benicia!' exclaimed the princess. 'How glad I am to see thee!' She held Benicia's shoulders and inspected the girl. Her hair fell across her shoulders and down her back like a drift of black silk, and her smile was as lovely as the rising sun. 'Is it thou, Sir Criffel,' she asked, turning to him, 'to whom I must give thanks for my dear girl's safe return?' The earl who, some years ago, had been Winterhued's least successful suitor, bowed deeply and his sallow cheeks flushed puce.

'Now, my dear,' said Winterhued, looking back at Benicia, 'thy father will be glad beyond measure to know that his darling is safe. He was asleep when last I saw him, but come, let us wake him! Then we must get thee fed, washed and rested. Poor child, thou swayest upon thy feet.'

The princess turned to farewell her cousin Nomia who stood beside a pallet-bed holding a little white dog close beneath her chin. She tilted her head so that her cheek lay against its silken coat. 'Sleep if thou canst, my dear,' said the princess quietly, 'I do hope and pray we have news by the morrow.'

Putting an arm about Benicia's waist, Winterhued gently propelled the girl forward. Benicia, who felt so tired that she could barely manage each step, glanced gratefully up at her. 'I thank your highness for delivering me from that unpleasant man,' she whispered, 'and make promise that henceforth I shall not vex m'lady with weeping... for I am no longer afraid.'

Winterhued stooped as she walked to lightly kiss the girl.

The Earl of Dunmore and Lady Manicia watched them go, Manicia clutching her blankets tightly. Some of the ale in her jug tipped out and splashed onto the floor. The earl's face was still flushed and sweat stood on his brow. 'Well, well,' he said.

The boy called Stench walked along a poorly lit passage somewhere between the King's Hall and the Watchtower. Some time ago he'd picked up a wooden bucket and tried to look purposeful in order to blend in with the occasional servant who happened along, bearing food, firewood or bedding.

But the bucket swung now from the crook of his arm, forgotten, and he wandered along vacantly, hardly aware of where he was. A smile played upon his lips and his dark eyes shone.

He was no longer walking a gloomy servants' passage carrying a bucket and a manure-stinking cloak; he was no longer clad in his threadbare peasant's garb. In his mind he wore a shining suit of armour and a crimson cloak, and he knelt before Princess Winterhued as she tapped him lightly on the shoulders with a gleaming sword. 'Arise, Sir Ancaios,' she said, smiling her beautiful smile, and the multitudes within the hall raised their voices in one almighty cheer. 'Thou hast slain the dreaded dragon,' said the princess, her voice ringing high and clear right up to where the bright banners floated and the golden sunbursts and silver unicorns gleamed upon the painted vaulting, 'and as thy just reward the king hath granted thee the richest dukedom in the land.' Stench saw his parents and his sister standing together in a place of honour beside the king. They were scrubbed clean and rosy-cheeked and clothed all in velvet and brocade, and they joined the throng in another glad acclamation. His mother wept with joy. As he looked down upon the crowd, he caught sight of Eudora, jostled amongst a press of bodies. She was still clad in her dirty drudge's apron, and she gazed longingly at him, her blue eyes brimming with remorseful tears. The boy bowed stiffly to her and bestowed upon her a distant smile. He *would* rescue her, he decided, but he would keep her waiting... just for a few days.

'What dost thou here, gong-farmer's boy?' rumbled a harsh voice.

Stench, jolted from his reverie, found himself come to a halt like an idiot. Even worse, he was still bent over in a half-bow. He removed the haughty smile from his face, straightened and swung round to find the constable of the castle, Sir Storegrund, with a torch-bearing soldier at his back, glaring at him. 'I thought I told thee,' said the constable, 'to get thyself to the King's Hall and stay there.'

'I... I was ordered to fetch water, sir,' lied the boy, holding up the bucket.

The constable looked at him through narrowed eyes. He was a fat old man with a bald head and a voice like gravel. 'Who sent thee?' he growled.

'The... the Duke of Drumrock,' answered the boy, compounding the lie.

'Well, where dost thou think thou art going, to fetch the duke's water?'

'To the well, sir.'

'What well?'

The boy didn't answer, but waved his bucket in the general direction of the inner bailey.

'Dost thou think, daft lout,' said the constable, 'that we would be sending the servants *outside* to fetch water? Someone once told me that thou wast a clever lad, but I have never seen sign of it. We are using the well in the basement of the East Tower.' He jabbed a thumb back in the direction that the boy had come. 'Go fetch the duke's water, then hie thee back to the King's Hall and stay there.'

'Aye, sir, I'll do that,' said Stench, lying yet again. He bobbed his head in a suitably subservient manner and set off back the way he had come. After a while he stole a glance over his shoulder and seeing that the passage appeared empty once more, stopped, leant against the wall for a few moments, then resumed his original course. He crept along carefully, listening for footsteps, though he had no idea what he'd do if the constable returned that way.

Actually, he had very little idea what he was doing anyway. He was possibly the only person who could quite easily leave the castle – he'd done so already – but here he still was, creeping about like a thief, hiding in dark corners and telling lies.

He could have gone with his parents and his sister some hours ago. They'd packed a few belongings and deserted their house on the edge of town to attempt an escape down the south road towards Drumrock. They had no intention of ending up in a dragon's belly, they'd said. 'Don't be a fool, lad. Come with us; we'll make our way south and look for employment somewhere safe. Though half of Lawhill will be on the road with the same idea, there's always work for gong-farmers.'

But no, what the boy wanted was to stay and help greatly in some way, and most of all to help Princess Winterhued who was more wondrous to him than the heavens, yet as dear as his own mother. *If I could become a hero to her... and to the king and everyone,* ran Stench's thoughts, *I would surely rise above my birth and need never lift a shovel again.*

'But how?' muttered the boy, and then answered himself in a whisper: 'If I could but slay the dragon...'

Stench had come to a halt outside the guardroom in the east tower of the King's Gate. He put his bucket down and listened for a moment but, as he had expected, the room was unoccupied. He stood a while longer, knitting his brows, full of indecision. 'But how may a turd-shoveller achieve such a thing,' he breathed, 'when even the mighty Sir Auchencairn...?'

The boy's frown faded. Abandoning the bucket, he crossed the guardroom in a few swift and silent steps, passing the stairs up which the constable had surely gone. As the nearest torch flickered in a bracket some way down the passage outside, the room was drowned in shadow. He had to hold out a hand before him to avoid colliding with the wall. Lightly touching the stone with his fingertips, he turned to his right and felt along the wall until he came to the postern that led out into the gate passage. The door was unbolted and he carefully eased it open.

'Sir Auchencairn,' he whispered. 'My first worthy deed: find him.'

He halted in the doorway to unfold his reeking cloak and drape it over his head and shoulders, and then stepped outside. The gate passage lay in inky shadow but at each end, beyond the lowering fangs of the portcullises, white moonlight bathed the baileys.

Stench could see a few horses in the outer bailey. Hoofs clattering, they walked with necks lowered and muzzles close to the ground, hungrily searching for any stray blades of grass that may have poked up through the stones. A big grey, shining silver in the moonlight, came right up beneath the outer portcullis. He stretched out his neck, snuffling and snorting softly at a heap of ash and debris lying at the entrance to the gate passage, then snorted again, loudly this time, spun on his heels and took off across the bailey. The other horses threw up their heads and plunged after him, slipping and sliding in their panic. Sparks flew from their iron-shod hooves.

Stench watched them go, then closed the door behind him and crept quietly along the passage in the opposite direction: towards the inner bailey.

Long he stood at the edge of the moonlight, staring out at the keep. It gazed sightlessly back at him from windows like gouged sockets. The night was as still as a corpse; the noise of his own heart as it thumped in his ears smote dumb any other faint sound there may have been. But his heart had been thus in the street of the coopers until his cloak lent him the courage to venture forth. And then, though he had walked right beneath the fell creature's belly, it had let him be.

Yet still he hesitated.

It was a long, moonlit way from the gatehouse to the keep, across half the bailey. The flagstones were strewn with wrack and wreckage.

A choked path climbed from the bailey up a grassy motte, wretched with carrion, to a wooden stair that looked half-burned and perilous. Beneath the portcullis at the first floor entrance, the broken door hung from one iron hinge and above it loomed the drear walls, drenched in moonlight and as silent as a charnel house.

It hath deserted its lair, thought Stench, *Mayhap it hath gone a' hunting.*

Yet he could not venture out into that merciless light. He moved his cloak aside and, glancing up at the sky, saw that he had but a moment to wait before a cloud swallowed the moon.

As the night turned black, he pulled his cloak about him and stepped out from the shelter of the gatehouse. But he did not take the fraught path to the motte and the burnt stairs; instead he turned to the left. With a few crouching strides he crossed to the inner bailey well and climbed onto its low coaming. Almost invisible in the dark, the chain hung at its full extent from the windlass. Stench leant across the black hole of the well and, groping in the dark, took hold of the chain. Chary of the slightest clinking, he gave it a trial tug, and then slowly lowered himself until the chain took his whole weight. He heard the bucket far below splash and clatter against its chain. It hit the well's stone sides with a hollow clunk.

Behind him, above him, all around him it seemed, came a long sigh, deadly as a forest fire, and a scraping, a slithering, as of a ship hauled across a shingled shore. The boy's heart came into his mouth. *I was wrong,* he thought, *the beast is at home.*

He waited not a moment longer, but as fast as he could he slithered, slid, jerked and skidded his way down the rattling chain. Into pitch-blackness he went, and vanished completely from the night.

CHAPTER 7

Thistle meowed thrice: quick, happy meows. Brenn had half woken as the little warm creature beside her climbed from beneath the blankets and jumped to the floor with a soft thump. Tail straight as a flagpole, the cat trotted towards the door, as from the antechamber came the sound of brisk steps. Brenn sat up, throwing off the blankets and scrambling from the bed just as the door opened and Winterhued stepped into the room. With her black hair and her moonlight skin it seemed as though she brought some of the night with her. Brenn dropped into a curtsey, but the princess didn't see her for she had bent to scoop up the little cat.

'Brr, 'tis icy in here,' she said. 'We must have a fire.' She turned, still holding the cat, crossed the antechamber and spoke down the stairwell.

While she was gone Brenn frantically folded the blankets and smoothed the creases from the counterpane. She heard footsteps on the stairs and the low voice of a man, enquiring. 'Send the girl Eudora hither to light a fire,' she heard the princess say.

Brenn rearranged her gown, tidied her hair and tried to compose herself as the princess returned, but all of a sudden felt tears, unbidden, flow down her cheeks.

'My poor girl,' said Winterhued; 'I have been neglectful and left thee alone all the day. Hast thou been afraid?'

'Nay, m'lady,' said Brenn, wiping her face with the back of her hand. 'I... I did not mean to weep.' She sniffed and looked up at the princess with an embarrassed smile.

'Hast thou eaten?' asked Winterhued, her eyes full of care.

'Aye, m'lady. Twice they brought me food. I fed the cat. Deccan came. He told me... he told me it was a dragon.'

'Aye, it doth seem we have tumbled into a fairytale... except that most fairytales have happy endings, and who knoweth how this may end?' Brenn was suddenly frightened to see Winterhued's eyes brim with tears.

'My lady doth weep also,' she said, her voice shaking and tears springing once more to her own eyes. 'Are we all then to perish?'

'I do not know, little cousin,' said the princess. She put the cat onto the bed, turned and held out her arms. Brenn went to her and felt the princess enfold her, and the tears she shed now were tears of relief to be no longer alone.

'I weep,' said Winterhued, 'because I can do so little to help my people. All day long have I examined strategies and options, but I am clueless and helpless. I have visited the injured and the dying, but I can neither heal nor ease their hurts. I cannot bring solace to those that grieve.'

Brenn drew a shuddering breath. 'Who is dead?' she asked. 'Deccan said Sir Auchencairn.'

'Aye,' answered Winterhued, speaking in such a low, hushed voice that Brenn could scarcely hear her. 'Methinks dear, brave Auchencairn hath perished, even as he attempted to deliver us from this terror. Old Sir Garthwray is gone from us also, as well as the Marquess of Castleton and his mother, and a few others that thou, my dearest, wouldst never have met.' The princess held the girl tighter and rocked her gently as she spoke. 'Many were injured,' she whispered, 'some sorely, as the Queen's Hall burned, yet we of the castle's inner bailey appear to have... escaped lightly, for I fear that many, many servants and soldiers, and hundreds of townsfolk, have perished.' Brenn could feel the princess's heart beating.

'What will happen to us?' she asked.

'I must trust that we shall be saved,' said Winterhued. 'Some of our messengers surely got away and Manydown's standing army is but two day's ride to the northeast. Though our castle bowmen have been unable to inflict injury upon the creature, surely so many men, armed with two hundred crossbows, eight hundred longbows...'

She held Brenn from her and looked down into the girl's wide eyes. 'Poor little cousin,' she said, 'thou must wish thou hadst never come up to court.'

'No, m'lady,' said Brenn, with a shake of her head. 'Even with this... I never want to go home.'

'Why do we stand shivering in the cold?' asked the princess. She steered the girl towards the window seat, gathering as she went the blankets Brenn had folded. Wrapping themselves, they sat down side by side, and Thistle trotted over to join them, wriggling her way beneath the coverings on the princess's lap. Winterhued put an arm around Brenn and the girl nestled up to her, her tears and fears all fled away.

'So, thou wishest never to go home,' said the princess. 'But Drumalis is such a pretty place, and what of thy parents? Dost thou not miss them?'

Brenn turned to look at the princess. 'I think m'lady doth know my parents,' was her only reply.

'Though thy mother is my first cousin,' said Winterhued, 'I scarcely know her. I knew thy father though.' The princess met Brenn's gaze, and something in her look made the girl feel quite satisfied. Brenn's father had always bragged to his wife that if he'd so desired, he could have married Winterhued and been 'king' of Manydown.

'M'lady doth not like him,' said the girl. 'Well, neither do I. 'Too many daughters' is all he doth say. He hath no dowry for me. My sisters all wed, and I alone left with my mother who doth naught but weep when she is not scolding. Now they say I am to marry Deccan, for his parents will take me without a dowry. But I think... I do not want to.'

'Thou dost not like Deccan?'

'He doth brag and brag about naught. "By my spurs!" he says, then: "what think ye of that?" as if he expects me to swoon at his every deed. Yet I suppose there must be worse men that one could marry.'

'Never marry if marriage is likely to end in weeping all day... like thine unhappy mother.'

'I think I have no say in the matter.'

'Of course thou hast a say! Thou art my cousin, and thou canst do with thy life whatsoever thou dost wish.'

Brenn laughed. She sat unspeaking for a moment, and then asked, rather tentatively: 'Why hath m'lady never married?'

A silence ensued and, certain she had displeased Winterhued, Brenn felt her heart beat a little faster. But finally the princess spoke, and she was not at all angry.

'If fortune, and my father, do favour me,' she said, 'I shall one day be Manydown's lawful queen. In that position I can bring about change... mayhap make this land a better place. My mind is clear on how I may achieve this; I have pondered these things all my life. But the king and a few of his cronies,' she looked at Brenn and a little smile curled up the corners of her mouth, 'like to talk of their "fear for this land" when a "weak woman" sitteth upon the throne. Of all the suitors that bent their knees before me, the ones that the king loved best were the loud, strutting, forceful men, for it was his dearest wish that I marry a man who would rule me and thus rule this land. But that is just what I have always feared: that upon marrying me, my husband would demand to be, if not in name then in deed, king of Manydown.'

'Not every man would wish that, surely,' Brenn said aloud, though her thoughts ran more along the lines of 'not the man whose name begins with a 'D'.'

'But perhaps any man who bowed and scraped and meekly said "aye" to my every whim, I would soon despise,' said Winterhued with a soft laugh.

'I think,' said Brenn, 'that all men admire m'lady and know that she is cleverer than they, and will make a wise and just queen.'

The princess laughed again. 'Well, if that be true,' she said, 'it may explain why all my suitors have run away. I suspect men are afraid of clever women... or perhaps they are merely bored. It was thy father himself, little cousin, who once said to me: "there is naught more tedious than an educated woman".'

Brenn curled her lip, looking suddenly quite like her father. 'Aye, that is my father,' she said. 'Five daughters: we were all taught to read, but there was never a book in the house. I am so ignorant, m'lady! I see the ambassador from Balasore and I hardly know if Balasore be north, south, east or west!'

'Dost thou wish to learn?'

'Oh, aye, m'lady!' breathed the girl. 'I want to learn everything that can be learned, I want to keep it all in my head, to mull over it, sort through it, until I have discovered for myself the precepts by which one should live.' Brenn, remembering herself, glanced up at the princess. Her cheeks glowed. 'Mayhap I am not clever enough to do that,' she said.

'I think thou art clever, Brenn,' said the princess, hugging the girl closer. 'And if thou dost desire to learn, I shall find for thee a tutor, and put at thy disposal whatever books may be found. Our castle at

Olivebank has a small, but fine collection.' Winterhued's voice trembled. 'Oh, Brenn... Lawhill's wondrous library... hundreds of precious books! So many that a score of lifetimes would hardly have sufficed to read them all. And now they are naught but heaps of ash, blowing away on the... Ouch!' she suddenly exclaimed.

'M'lady?' said Brenn, looking at the princess with startled eyes.

Winterhued laughed. "Tis but the cat, kneading me with her claws. I shall throw thee off, wicked creature,' she warned the purring mound beneath the blanket on her lap.

'Methinks it strange that m'lady keepeth a cat,' said Brenn. 'My mother doth keep a lapdog but our cats live in the stables. The people of Drumalis say that only witches keep cats.'

'Brenn, that is nonsense! Witches!' cried the princess. 'Oh, 'tis the usual story: men fear clever women, they call them witches and want them dead. And of course clever women like to keep cats, for they are such fine friends.' Winterhued laughed and displayed the scratch-marks on her hand. Then she shivered and thrust the hand back beneath the blankets. 'Where is Eudora?' she asked. 'Are we never to have our fire?"

'Mayhap she is dead.'

'Nay, I spoke to her in the hall not an hour hence.'

'Why didst my lady ask for her? She is such a dirty, sullen drudge.'

'Brenn, that is unkind. She is a poor, sad lass. I feel pity for her and would help her if I could. Callunians... Callunians, thou knowest, do not have an easy time.'

'I do not know any. My father doth hate them and will have none on his lands. But he hateth everyone. He is angry every moment because old King Caradoc cut off my grandfather's head so that he could give most of our lands to the Duke of Drumrock.'

'Whose son is my father's best friend... so there is a wrong that cannot soon be redressed.'

'Don't redress it,' said Brenn quietly. 'Never give aught to my father; he is miserly and cruel. Ask the folk who work our land.'

The princess turned to look at Brenn intently. 'We are alike in more than just our dreams,' she said.

Brenn's eyes went wide. 'Aye, m'lady, I have wondered at that all the day. M'lady and I, we both dreamt of... and then...'

'That is no mystery. My grandmother was Andorinha...'

'My great-grandmother. She came from Balasore.'

'Aye, and her mother was an Ormsarian princess... but thou knowest that. Though mayhap thou didst not know that she had the "sight". Some of her descendants... some of the women in our family see things before they come to pass.'

Brenn gasped. 'I shall dream horrible dreams again? That will come to pass?'

'Only time may answer that,' said the princess. 'Thou mayest never have a prophetic dream again, or, if thou dost, it may be a pleasant one.'

'Hast m'lady had others...?'

'Aye... but many years ago I dreamt of my wedding, which doth prove that I cannot believe them all. I have also ofttimes dreamt of the king falling into the Otterburn and as I leap in after him, I spy the chancellor hanging upside down like an old black fruitbat in a tree.'

Brenn laughed, but somewhat distractedly as her mind had become so full of thoughts.

'And two or three nights past,' continued the princess, 'I dreamt that the moon fell from the sky and lay amongst the pebbles by the lake. It was so tiny and I saw it too late as I ran by, so could not help catching it with my toe and kicking it into the lake. It sank... and that was the end of the moon.'

Suddenly, she fished the cat from under the blankets and put her onto Brenn's lap. 'I possess a piece of moon,' she said, getting to her feet. 'I shall show it to you.' She crossed the room and knelt to open a wooden chest at the foot of her bed. Taking out three jewellery caskets, she opened the only one without a lock and began to pull pieces from it, laying them upon her lap. 'Compared to my rubies and diamonds, this is worth naught,' she said, 'yet it is one of my favourite things in all the world.'

Eudora had been lying wide-awake on her pallet in the King's Hall when she'd been approached by a guard. 'Clean thyself, slattern,' he'd said. 'Cover thy hair. Where's thine other shoe? Thou shalt need to fetch kindling, a tinderbox and a basket. Firewood thou'lt find in the under-chamber. Lord knows why the princess asked for a dirty foreigner,' he grunted, 'when any of us could have done the job straight away and a deal more handsomely too.'

Shivering in the bitter cold, and after begging the loan of two matching shoes from her neighbour, Eudora did as she was told. Clutching a candle, and her basket, kindling and tinderbox, she passed the leering guards in the basement of the princess's tower and climbed the first flight of stairs to the under-chamber. She piled as much wood as she could carry into her basket, then struggled up the stairs and across the antechamber to knock at the princess's door.

'Come in, Eudora,' came the princess's voice. The girl opened the door and straight away saw Winterhued kneeling by the wooden chest, with her jewellery caskets about her and glittering trinkets spread across her skirts and spilling onto the floor.

Eudora froze and the blood drained from her face. But then her heart started up again, thudding in her ears, her hands began to shake and she could feel crimson spreading across her cheeks. The princess and some other blanket-swathed person had barely glanced in her direction, so plucking up her courage she managed to enter the room and shuffle across to the fireplace.

With her back to the princess to hide her trembling hands, the scullion struggled to get the fire lit, burning herself twice in the process. She heard Winterhued open another casket to pull out gold chains and strings of pearls and rubies. Eudora felt certain that the princess must notice her ears; poking from beneath her cap, they surely glowed like beacons of guilt.

'It is not here,' she heard Winterhued say at last. 'I do not know how I could have lost it. Why, I'd sooner throw all of my diamonds into the lake than lose my moonstone.'

Eudora coughed and stood up, wiping her hands on her apron. She turned towards the princess and saw her scooping up her jewellery and dropping it in a tangle back into the caskets.

'M'lady,' said the maid. Her voice sounded thin and strange, and the words that came into her mouth seemed to arrive there of their own accord. 'I think it my duty,' she said, 'to inform m'lady that I have seen that boy Stench lurking about nigh here. That... that thing m'lady hath lost... 'tis likely the dirty boy hath thieved it.'

Winterhued frowned silently at Eudora and Eudora stared at the floor. *Fool!* she thought to herself, *she was talking of 'lost' and I blurt 'thieving'. They'll search him and he'll tell them where he got it. Then it'll be his word against mine, and though he's a dirty gong boy, at least he's got eyes like a proper Manydownian.*

It took a while for the princess's voice to penetrate the turmoil in Eudora's head. 'No, no,' Winterhued was saying, 'It's not been stolen; after all, the casket was full of baubles of far greater value. No, 'tis mine own carelessness: I have mislaid it, and it will be found by and by. Besides, in this terrible time, 'tis a paltry matter.'

The princess had got to her feet and was walking towards Eudora. 'That is a lovely fire,' she said. 'I thank thee Eudora.'

The girl's cheeks and ears still burned and she wrung her hands together to disguise their trembling. She could not look up, but she was aware of the woman's tall presence drawing nigh and heard the swish of her gown across the floor. Bobbing an ungainly curtsey, she took a backward step towards the door before remembering her fire-lighting stuff. She knelt to scoop the tinderbox and extinguished candle into her basket, desiring only to remain upon her hands and knees and crawl from the chamber like a maggot.

'What are those things upon thy feet, Eudora?' asked Winterhued. 'Thou couldst sit down inside one of them and row thyself across the lake.'

'I lost my shoe when... the tower fell, m'lady,' mumbled Eudora, getting clumsily to her feet. 'These I borrowed.'

'I have forgotten who dealeth with the servants' shoes, but tell whoever it is that giveth thee orders that when thou dost come to tend Princess Winterhued in the morn, dragon or no dragon, she shall expect to see her chambermaid wearing well-fitting shoon and a warm, clean gown.'

'I thank your highness,' whispered Eudora, curtseying again and backing towards the door.

'And Eudora, do not call the lad Stench. That is cruel. His name is Ancaios.'

The girl backed through the door and pulled it shut behind her. She turned hurriedly and one of the large shoes flew from her foot and went tumbling across the antechamber. Shaking like a leaf in a gale, she stumbled after it.

Her heart still pounded in her ears.

I am her chambermaid, she thought incredulously; *she called me her chambermaid! But... I took... I stole from her.* Eudora's heart sank like a stone. *She will find out... she will know. As she knoweth everything.*

The shoe back upon her foot, she clumped through the door and groped her way down the steep, dark stair. Fastened to the curving wall beside the under-chamber door was a welcome torch, and as she paused beneath it to catch her breath, a thought made its way into the confusion of her mind. 'Aye, the princess doth indeed know everything,' she muttered, 'for she knoweth even the name of a dung-worm like Stench.' Eudora could not even remember that name now.

She started down the stairs again, then stopped. 'But before yesterday she did not know my name,' she said. 'So how is it she knoweth the name of a gong boy?'

'Come to the fire, lass,' said Winterhued, stirring the flames with a poker.

'Hmm,' answered Brenn.

'The poor girl seemed terrified,' said the princess, 'as though, like the fell beast in the keep, I was about to breath fire upon her.'

'Oh... pardon? M'lady?' said Brenn. Her mind had been elsewhere and she'd hardly noticed the servant's departure.

'Come hither, Brenn. Don't sleep there; come to the fire.'

Brenn dislodged the cat from her lap and got to her feet. 'I've been trying to remember my dreams. I have one where I can fly, though it is a great effort. I am flying away from my father and mother, so part of it at least hath come to pass.'

'I think all of us have dreams of flying. Alas, mine have never come true.' The princess, her eyelids heavy, sank down upon the cushions before the hearth. Brenn sat beside her and held out her hands towards the growing flames.

'We should not sleep here,' murmured the princess. 'There is a truckle bed beneath the big bed that we can pull out for thee; Lady Ulidia hath slept upon it oft times and assures me it is comfortable.'

'Aye m'lady, I thank m'lady,' said Brenn, a little shy again. 'Doth m'lady wish now to be unlaced?'

'Aye,' sighed Winterhued as she got to her feet.

'My favourite dream,' said Brenn, untying the lacings of the princess's gown, 'one that I have ofttimes dreamt, is of a little white horse, as beautiful as the moon. Sometimes she danceth on a mountaintop and sometimes in a meadow, and she hath a horn... a single horn in the middle of her forehead.'

Winterhued was wide awake. 'Thou hast dreamt of a unicorn,' she breathed, turning to look at Brenn. 'Lace me up again, then fetch our cloaks. We are taking a walk.'

The night was fraught with cold. Not a breath of wind stirred the bare branches as the creature the colour of moonlight splashed through the stream and stepped into the clearing. Only the water chuckled and chattered as it rushed away down the flanks of Iron Crag into the night-hushed land of Manydown.

Walking in the nimbus of her own breath, the little beast shone like the stars that frosted the sky above.

Watching her, as in a trance, the old grey stallion and the red gelding stood as still as stone upon the sleeping earth while the moon cast indigo shadows from their gaunt bones. Unblinking they gazed, as the reflection of the moon-bright creature danced across their night-dark eyes.

They watched her walk to the prone forms upon the ground beside the broken hut and the dying fire; they saw a shudder run through her as she looked at the knight as he lay sleeping, the sharp planes of his face pale against the spreading pool of his hair. They saw her lower her head and arch her neck until the murderous tip of her single horn almost touched his breast. Reflections from the fire's embers ran down its spirals like spilt blood down an assassin's sword.

The stream whispered on and the stars wheeled in their courses above.

The grey stallion neighed, softly, anxiously, and took a step forward. The knight stirred in his sleep and the other huddled shape on the ground began to emit a gurgling snore.

The horned beast lifted her head, as if waking from a nightmare. She took three steps back and then turned to look at the knight's shield where it lay propped against his saddle. The shape thereon was naught more than a layer of flaking paint, yet it made her heart race.

For another long moment she stood tense, quivering. Thoughts, memories, that had not entered her mind for thrice three thousand years rose within her like a tide.

Once there had been another such as she: another creature white as moonlight with, issuing from her forehead, a single, spiralled horn. An image came to her of the fawns that ran with their dams upon her mountain each spring; budding new lives that knew little more than that the big, warm bulk beside them would provide protection from all the world's perils. She had been like the fawns once: with a dam that had succoured and protected her. But that seemingly omnipotent being had been unable to protect herself as well, and had perished with the head of an iron spear buried deep within her breast. Her blood had spread in a pool upon the cold earth.

The horned one looked back at the sleeping knight. It had been such a man that had slain her dam ten thousand years ago or more. This one was subtly different, but still a mindless brute like all men. Yet life burned within him and she knew that, just as she could not deliberately crush the lowliest insect that scuttled on the forest path, neither could she take this creature's life.

She knew this as surely as she knew that the great rock upon which she stood circled the sun and that the sun was but one in an eternity of stars.

For the horned creature was one of the old, old beings, and possessed a vast knowledge of all things. For centuries had that knowledge lain within her like a subterranean lake, silent and undisturbed, and she had lived like the deer, aware only of the moment: of thirst and hunger, of night and day, of cold and warmth, of the warning cry of a bird, of tracks in the snow, of an ominous scent in the wind.

For an aeon had her eyes beheld the swirl of bright leaves, the flurry of snow, the first flush of green on bare branches, and the drowsy, dappled light of summer. She had run beneath clouds and through mists, sought shelter from storms and the wind's bite, with never a thought as to what she was or how she had come to be.

Without a question in her mind had she seen countless arrow-heads of geese winging their way south, measureless clouds of finches rising from the meadows at her approach, unnumbered mobs of rooks clacking their wintry cry from bare branches, untold generations of glossy ravens hopping from rock to rock, their heads cocked towards her and their eyes agleam. Unwittingly had she crushed their dead bones into dust beneath her feet.

With hardly a thought in her head had she witnessed snow falling and thawing, wildflowers springing up to spangle, so briefly, the high meadows, grey-green lichen growing, spreading, then crumbling to dust on the splitting rocks, and saplings rising and swelling, stretching limbs to the sky, only to wane, rot, break, and then lie mouldering on the forest floor.

Without reason had she heard the ceaseless murmur of the land and the song of all the birds of every spring, seen a millennia of pink dawns and purple evenings, walked in never-ending moonlight and beheld the eternity of the heavens all dusted with stars. She had lived unthinking as the very rocks grew old and the mountain wore down, washed and blown away by winds and rain and time.

All these things had the horned beast witnessed and known, but she had not thought upon them, for thinking made her feel as hollow as the sky. *I am the last,* she thought now, as she gazed at the painted shape upon the knight's shield. *I have always known that I am the last.*

Moonlight poured down like sorrow upon the little being as she turned and walked from the clearing. The old grey stallion's joints clicked as he moved to follow her, and the red gelding came after, his shoulder pressed against the stallion's flank. Their gleaming eyes were fixed upon the horned one and the moonshine made patterns with their bones.

At the stream the little creature halted and swung round to regard the horses. They stood pressed together, and the clouds of their breath mingled palely in the moonlight. Their coats were shaggy and coarse, their hooves as broad as boulders and they were as honest and true as the earth.

The horned one stretched out her perfect neck. She touched their muzzles with her own and blew gently into their nostrils. Then, with hardly a splash, she crossed the stream and vanished into the night.

The knight awoke and rolled onto his side. He propped himself on an elbow and looked across the fire at Nal. The boy was bundled tightly within his blanket; all that emerged was the burbling rattle of his breathing. The knight sat up, scooping hair back from his face, and leaned across to push a half-burned log further into the fire. As a few sparks swirled into the icy air, he pulled his blanket and his meagre cloak round his shoulders and shivered.

The fire seemed the last warm light at the edge of the world. Beyond the clearing at his back the mountain dropped down into lands of fence and field, where fires burned upon hearths and lamplight shone at windows. Before him, looming blackly above the walls of the abandoned hut, rose Iron Crag's northernmost spur, and beyond that lay a land where firelight and lamplight never glowed. For hundreds, perhaps thousands of leagues to the east and northeast stretched the Wild Lands where no man dwelt. And if any had ever set foot in that tangled desolation, he had not returned to tell the tale.

The knight glanced round at the clearing. But for the light of the fire darkness would soon envelop them for, up from the west, crept a mass of clouds, devouring the stars as it came. Something caught the man's attention and he got to his knees to stare intently at the horses. They still stood beside the stream gazing into the forest, the grey two steps ahead of the red. Moonlight limned them with silver.

Nal's stertorous breathing climaxed in a snort and he woke with a start. He sat up, staring about him in alarm.

'Look Nal. Look at the horses,' said the knight softly.

'Wha..? Eh… where… wha' was that?' muttered the boy.

'Thou wast snoring, lad. Thou didst wake thyself.'

'What? Nay, I never snore. I weren't asleep.'

'Of course not. Thou wast keeping watch. Look at the horses, Nal.
How fine they are.' The knight had a slight, puzzled smile on his face.

At that moment, in eerie unison, the horses turned to look at him.
Their eyes, lambent in the moonlight, seemed filled with wisdom. Their
shadowed coats glowed with a luminosity like phosphorescence on
the sea.

'Destriers for a mighty emperor… or the king and queen of
Faery,' said the knight in a quiet voice. 'Look, Nal, they seem horses
from legend.'

Nal carefully draped his blanket round his head like a shawl, and
then glanced at the horses. He turned back, his brows askew, to eye the
knight. 'Well, that be sure proof about sleepin' in moonlight,' he said.
'Ye've gone mad. Them's but the same old jades wi' nowt but a bit o'
moonshine on 'em. An' I'll never know why ye don't 'obble 'em; they'll
run off one night, and what sort o' knight will ye be then, traipsin'
about on your own shanks?'

'They'll not run off,' said the knight, unaware that his horses had
almost done so not five minutes since. He watched them as they turned
back into the clearing and began to graze.

'I'm 'appy to find nowt's eaten us yet,' he said quietly, imitating
the boy's manner of speech. He fed more wood to the fire, pulled his
blanket close and lay down.

'If owt came, I'd eat it first,' said Nal unconvincingly. 'My innards
are so empty they 'urt.'

'Aye, lad, I know,' replied the knight. 'But we'll be passing through
Wendur on the morrow and there, I promise thee, thou shalt eat.'

''Ow far is it?' asked the boy, lying back down on his bedroll
and shivering.

'Not far. It lies at the end, or the beginning, of this pass: at the very
edge of Manydown. Wendur is as far into Manydown as we shall go.'

'Why? Why are we avoidin' Manydown, when 'tis plain that's where ye wish to go?'

'I'd rather sleep than talk,' said the knight.

'Ye're unfair. Ye drag me into misery, but won't tell me nowt.'

The knight sighed. 'In few, there are two reasons why I shan't stay long in Manydown,' said he, and then fell silent. The horses cropped the grass noisily as the moon disappeared behind the clouds.

'Well?' mumbled Nal sleepily. ''Ave ye gone to sleep?'

'The first is... of no great importance,' said the knight at last, 'but I'll tell thee anyway for methinks thou shalt not fail to notice it when we come into Wendur.' He laughed quietly and lapsed into another brief silence.

'On the morrow,' he began again, 'thou shalt meet the people of Wendur. They think themselves brave because they dwell where most Manydownians would fear to: beside Iron Crag and close to the Wild Lands to the east, and whatever wraiths and ghouls they imagine inhabit those regions. Thou mightest then be surprised lad, to see how some of these bold folk look askance at me as if I were one of those ghouls, to be feared and mistrusted.'

'Why? What'd ye do to 'em?'

'Naught, lad. They shall mistrust me simply because my mother was born in Calluna. Even if I were to inform them that my father is a Many-downian duke, it would scarcely make a difference.'

'How will they know? About your ma?'

'Because of the colour of my eyes. All 'purebred' Manydownians have brown or hazel eyes.'

'What colour are yours, then?'

'Somewhere in the middle of grey and blue.'

'Uh. What colour are mine?'

'Pink, last time I looked.'

'Nay, they're never pink!'

'Hazel then... greenish hazel.'

'Is that alright?'

The knight laughed. 'Is that all that dost concern thee?' he asked.

'What else would concern me?'

'Dost thou think it fair that men and women are regarded as untrustworthy... evil even, because of the colour of their eyes?'

"Ow would I know?' said Nal. 'Maybe you Calloo... Calluvians are evil. I've met but one, so I wouldn't know.'

'But Pengwern was full of folk with blue eyes. Were they all evil?'

'But they weren't Calluvian.'

The knight laughed again and said nothing. The horses had ceased tearing at the grass and the silence pressed in as heavily as the darkness.

'So even women won't like you in Manydown,' said the boy suddenly. 'Good, that'll make a change. But ye said two reasons. What's t'other?'

'Why dost thou not sleep?'

'I'm too 'ungry.'

'I'm hungry too,' said the knight. He lay staring up into the black nothingness of the clouded sky. 'Many years ago,' he said; 'two hundred or more, this pass was the major highway between Ormsary and Manydown. But wayfarers have always feared Iron Crag; feared what may dwell on and beyond its flanks. They say this place is haunted. So Trongate Pass was opened to the south and now few men come this way. But I love Iron Crag. In summer or winter that little lake below its southernmost spur is the stillest place in the world, the reflections upon its surface perfect, its peace profound. And it holds for me the remembrance of a kiss.'

'A kiss?' said Nal sourly, his voice like a rusty gate. 'Ye must 'ave 'ad 'undreds o' them. Lady must 'a been a goddess...'

'Aye, she was,' replied the knight, and his quiet voice smiled. 'Peerless.'

'And she's the second reason?'

'Nay, not her: her father. Now lad, go to sleep.'

'Ye're afraid o' one ol' man?'

The boy received no answer. Though the moon no longer shed its dangerous light, Nal pulled his blanket tighter round his head and huddled into his bedroll. The fire's warmth gave a little comfort, but the boy's back and his feet were frozen, and his stomach griped unceasingly. Sleep had deserted him. He lay with his eyes wide open, listening to the knight's even breathing, and knew that the man slept unafraid.

But the silence around him was vast and ominous, the blackness of the night deep enough to drown in. Beside him gaped the door of the ruined hut and above that the mountain loomed unseen like fear itself. He remembered what the knight had said about wayfarers being afraid of Iron Crag and after a while several small scuffling sounds convinced him that a band of wraiths had come creeping out of the dark door. With tattered black rags rustling, they crouched above him now, their fleshless mouths a-grin and bloody swords naked in their skeletal hands. Nal's heart beat hard but he suppressed the urge to leap up shouting, for the knight always became annoyed when he did that. 'There's no one there,' he said to himself over and over, but still he lay too frightened to move, his heart hammering and his eyes staring sightlessly into his blanket.

Shadows leaped up the curved walls of the stairwell as Brenn scurried downstairs after the princess. She'd already stumbled once and, flinging out a hand to save herself, had grazed her knuckles on the stone. Holding up her lantern, she hitched her skirts higher so that she could watch her feet. Before her the princess, who had seemed half asleep just moments ago, moved down the stairs as lithe as a cat. A ring of iron keys jangled from the crook of her elbow.

She stopped beneath the torch outside the under-chamber and pushed the door open. Brenn followed her across a dark room, bare but for a stack of firewood piled against the wall. Winterhued put her

own lantern on the floor to search through her keys. She glanced round
at Brenn and smiled.

'Poor lass,' she said, 'thou dost sleep on thy feet. But stay upright for
a little longer my dear, for I wish to show thee something... something
that will bring thee wide awake.'

She opened the door into the main chamber, picked up her lantern
and entered. Brenn shuffled after her and stopped inside the door to
gaze around in bewilderment at the crowded room. The light from the
two lanterns fell across mounds of beautiful objects; it gleamed upon
many-branched candelabra of gold and silver, it illuminated huge rolled
tapestries draped over heavy oaken chests, it glittered upon gold and
enamelled caskets and a magnificent salt-cellar, intricately ornamented.

Within the lanterns' pools of light gleamed a matching set of ebony
footstools that stood on carved lion's feet with ivory claws; beside the
stools rose a pile of exquisitely embroidered cushions, and behind the
cushions stood a mahogany frame bearing a side-saddle of blue velvet,
complete with trappings of velvet and embossed leather, all fastened
with buckles of gold. Just visible beyond the lanterns' light were more
objects, stacked against the chamber walls and heaped up in the middle
of the floor.

Winterhued smiled at Brenn's astonishment. 'This is not why I've
kept thee from thy bed,' she said. 'These are valueless trinkets compared
to that which thou shalt see.' She crossed to the chamber wall and,
pushing aside a tapestry that hung there, revealed a low wooden door
with hinges shaped like spreading ivy.

'All those things,' she said dismissively, fishing through her keys, 'I
have instead of a husband. These lower chambers were to be his, but
I could say 'yay' to no man, so the suitors kept coming. From within
Manydown and from all the lands about they came; some came twice,
or thrice, or more, and every time they came a-wooing, they bore gifts
which they hoped might aid them.'

She turned the key with a click. The small door, no bigger than the
door to a broom cupboard, opened with a groan from its seldom-used

hinges. 'So now,' she continued, 'instead of one unwanted object, in the shape of a husband, I have a whole chamber full. Though, in sooth, not all of the gifts came from suitors. Some are from towns and villages; many are from foreign lands. That silk thou dost admire,' (Brenn had stopped to run her fingertips over a bolt of fabric that shone like the lake's surface on a still day), 'came from Ilala to the southeast, beyond Ormsary.' The silk had sheens of olive and topaz that changed as Brenn moved. 'How it doth suit thee!' exclaimed Winterhued. 'I shall have it made up for thee: a gown for thy wedding day.'

'My wedding day?' Brenn glanced around at the princess, her cheeks glowing in the lantern light. 'Haply that will not be soon.'

'The silk will keep. Thou hast plenty of time to find someone worthy of it.'

'Worthy of this? Not Deccan then.'

'Mayhap not,' said the princess with a smile. 'Yet I am glad to have found a use for one of my gifts. Now come, my dear,' she said, pushing the door wide and picking up her lantern. 'We have a little further to go and then... oh, thou shalt see a wonder!'

Brenn crossed to the door, half expecting to see this 'wonder' inside the cupboard. Her eyes grew wide as she looked past the princess's shoulder and found herself staring instead into a narrow passage.

With a tilt of her head Winterhued indicated that Brenn should step in first. But the girl hesitated; it was so very dark within.

'Be not afraid,' said the princess; 'there is no danger here, only the dark... and we have our lanterns.'

Brenn stepped through the door and stopped; though she held her lantern before her, the darkness seemed as solid as a wall. Winterhued came in behind her, stooping beneath the low lintel, and then turned to tug the hanging back across the opening. The door closed with a gasp from its hinges and a click from the lock. Putting a hand on Brenn's shoulder, Winterhued urged the girl forwards.

'Fare forth, my dear,' she said. 'We shall come anon upon some stairs, so watch thy step.'

Brenn set out, holding her lantern in her right hand and feeling along the wall with her left. She had many questions, but the passage was so close that there seemed insufficient air with which to breathe and talk at the same time. The princess's hand was still upon her shoulder. The passage curved round to the left and suddenly there were the stairs before her, slanting steeply into the darkness.

Down they went, in silence but for the scrape of their feet, the sibilance of their breath and the swish of their gowns against the stone walls. The stairs eventually ended but for a while the walls drew in so close that Winterhued, already stooped, was compelled to turn half sideways. 'Certes!' she gasped. 'I shouldn't like to come down here if I were a tall man, and big in the shoulders. Yet I know one such who came through here many times.' She laughed breathlessly. 'I have not been here in years.'

'Where is "here"?' asked Brenn.

'"Here" is secret! Verily, this is a secret passage! Lawhill is full of them; they were built into the fabric five hundred years ago. This one is the least secret of them, but there are others...'

'Secret passages!' interrupted Brenn. 'Whither do they go?'

'Here, there and everywhere,' said Winterhued laughing again. 'I discovered most of them while I was yet a child. Some had been utterly forgotten; even my father and the castle constable knew of only four. (They still do!) There is but one other person in all of Lawhill who knoweth them as well as I; probably better than I.'

'Whither goeth this one?'

'We have just walked beneath the wall 'twixt the inner and outer baileys. Above us and to our left lie the burnt kitchens. This passage goeth all the way down to the Constable's Gate, but we leave it at yonder stairway.'

Even as she spoke, Brenn's lantern revealed a gap in the wall on the left side of the passage and, as she reached it, a flight of uneven steps leading steeply upwards.

'I must precede thee now,' said Winterhued, edging past Brenn to swiftly climb the stairs. By the time the girl had caught up she had stopped before a small door of rivetted iron to search through her keys.

'This looks to be the door to a strongroom... or a dungeon,' said Brenn.

'Aye,' said the princess, inserting a big iron key into the door's big iron lock. 'Something exceeding precious is kept here. 'Tis worth more than my diamonds... more than the crown jewels.'

There was a drop from the threshold down to the floor below. Tall Winterhued ducked under the low opening and jumped down easily, then turned to help Brenn. As soon as her feet touched the flagstones below Brenn realised where they were, for a myriad of tiny noises reached her ears: rustlings, sighings, chatterings and flutterings, and a myriad of pungent smells assailed her nostrils.

'The King's Menagerie,' she breathed. 'I have never been within this place.'

'Few have,' said Winterhued quietly, turning to push the heavy door shut behind her. Unlike the door through which they had entered the passage, this one was not concealed, but it was high above the floor and so small that anyone would have taken it for the door to a hatch or a cupboard.

Brenn patted down her skirts and looked around. They stood in a dimly lit corridor with bare stone walls on either side. At one end was a big iron door and at the other an alcove within which a guard sat snoring. His head lolled forward onto his steel-clad chest and a string of spittle dribbled from his mouth. He still gripped his tall halberd, but it had sagged forward until it touched the opposite wall, blocking their passage.

'Guard,' said the princess, stopping in front of him. The man sprang to his feet, jerking his halberd upright so that it clanged against the top of the alcove. He stared at Winterhued in bewilderment, drool dangling from his chin.

The princess looked back at him coolly; she was a little taller than him and her frown was ominous. He stammered a few incomprehensible words, looking all the while as though he wished only to fall lifeless to the floor. Brenn had to turn away from his embarrassment.

'Thou hast been stationed here every night for the past ten years, I think,' said Winterhued, and the fellow nodded dumbly. ''Tis surely the dullest and most pointless post in all of Lawhill, so sleep on, with my blessing.' The princess fished an embroidered handkerchief from her reticule. 'Wipe thy chin,' she said, handing it to him and walking away. As Brenn went to follow she glanced again at the man and saw him staring at the handkerchief, as confused and dazed as if the princess had just hit him over the head with a plank of wood.

Behind Winterhued, Brenn turned a corner and saw that now, to either side of them, rose high, narrow cages of bare stone, fronted by iron bars. Torches placed at intervals along the corridor scattered fitful yellow light amongst the shadows. Winterhued barely glanced to either side as she walked, and Brenn scurried to keep up. She got little more than the merest glimpse of flea-bitten monkeys and apes huddled in the dark, of the gleam of their sad eyes as they watched her pass. She saw strange four-legged beings with mangy, balding hides, snuffling in a bit of straw; she saw a creature that looked like a horse with stripes across its back like shadows in a forest. It glanced at her with dark, reproachful eyes and turned away. She saw a great, gaunt cat with a threadbare mane and a bloody sore on its elbow; she saw a tattered eagle hunched upon an iron bar. It glared at her with an eye so fierce that she flinched and ran from it.

She caught up with Winterhued at a junction of corridors and to her dismay saw, in every direction, rows of iron bars disappearing into the gloom. Another guard stood to attention. He had seen the princess coming but still looked stunned that she should have appeared before him: a dreamlike apparition at midnight, with her moonlight beauty and her night-dark drift of hair flowing down across her shoulders and halfway to the floor.

She said not a word, but brought forth her keys and pointed to the high, armoured door at his back. He held her lantern while she turned the key in the lock, and passed it back to her as she pushed the silent door ajar. Brenn followed her in and waited while she shut the door firmly between them and the guard.

The two of them crossed a large, sweet-smelling chamber stacked with bales of straw and clover-hay. Along one wall stood barrels brimming with chaff, oats and rolled barley. The princess turned her keys in the lock of a second heavy door, its timbers reinforced with crossed strips of iron, and they entered a smaller room; cold, clean and bare, but for three wooden buckets upturned beside the door. Their lanterns provided the only light, though far above them a square skylight, heavily barred, showed a patch of night sky and a sprinkling of stars. This chamber was surely the very centre of the menagerie.

Brenn looked round for Winterhued and found her leaning with her back against the closed door and a hand across her face. She glanced up at Brenn and tears shone in her eyes.

'This is the most terrible place in all of Manydown,' she said, and her low voice shook. 'One day, please fortune, I shall raze it to the ground, but for now I can do naught. The king will not hear me; he is boastful of this hell. He showeth his "collection" to ambassadors and the like, and 'tis unfortunate that most of them appear impressed rather than sickened by the sight of those wretched, dying beasts.'

She wiped at the tears with the back of her hand and put her lantern down on the clean-swept floor. 'To this chamber however,' she added in little more than a whisper; 'no ambassador or dignitary hath *ever* been brought.'

She looked at the girl as if she knew not what to say. 'I will go no further...' she breathed. 'Brenn... little cousin... thou art yet a maid.'

Though this seemed a statement, Brenn thought it might have been a question. 'A maid?' she responded, puzzled.

'Thou hast not lain with a man.'

Brenn felt her cheeks flush. 'Oh... no,' she stammered. 'Never, my lady.'

'I had to be certain,' said Winterhued with a small smile. 'As I am that thou hast followed my wishes and eaten no flesh since thine arrival.'

'Aye, my lady; I've been glad not to.'

Winterhued looked past Brenn and pointed. 'Go,' she said. 'Look thou upon thy dream.'

Brenn, confusion upon her face, turned and walked in the direction that the princess had indicated. Holding up her lantern she crossed the bare flagstones and suddenly saw that in the far left corner of the chamber was a short, dead-ended passage. She entered the passage and saw to the right more iron bars.

A creature stood beyond the bars. It looked at Brenn and her heart stood still.

It seemed at first glance to be a horse, but a horse made of light, as if a star had fallen from the sky. The yellow glow from her lantern seemed barely to touch its luminescent flanks.

It looked at her with its night-sky eyes and for a moment she felt as though she stood on the edge of the world, and that if it withdrew from her its dark gaze she would fall into an abyss.

Then it shook its head and she remembered to draw breath. Its tangled mane and forelock, hanging almost to the floor, rippled like a moonlit stream. It turned away its perfect head and she saw the great spiralled horn, as full of light as a diamond, and half as long as she was tall.

'Oh... 'tis a unicorn,' sighed Brenn. 'Like my dream.' Suddenly her knees buckled and she sank down to the cold floor. Tears ran down her face.

'Aye, a unicorn,' came Winterhued's voice from where she still leant against the door. 'He liveth yet. How doth he appear?'

'Oh... he is beautiful... beyond all belief, he is beautiful,' breathed Brenn.

'Aye: beautiful, but how fareth he? Is he thin? Doth he suffer?'

Brenn blinked back her tears. The creature had stepped closer so that his glinting horn protruded from between the iron bars. His lucent eyes were upon her again. She flinched from that fathomless gaze and looked down at the floor, her heart hammering in her ears. For a moment she knelt, drawing breath, then she wiped both hands across her tear-streaked face and lifted up her eyes to behold once more the creature of dreams.

He shone with such power and was so perfect in his beauty that it was a terror and a wonder to look upon him. He made her heart leap and race. But yes, he was thin. Every rib stood out, his hips were spare, his shoulders gaunt, and his neck, under its weight of mane, was roped with muscle but fleshless.

'Aye, my lady,' whispered Brenn, 'he's exceeding thin.'

The unicorn lowered his head to the level of her own. His eyes were as deep as time. Through flickering nostrils he made a little noise that wrung Brenn's heart and she began to sob again; whether it was desperate sadness she felt, or an exultant joy, she could not have said.

The princess listened to the girl weeping and let her be. She sat down upon a bucket, put her head in her hands and shed a few tears herself.

After a time, Brenn wiped her face and looked up. The unicorn still gazed at her. 'I thought ye were a mythical creature,' she breathed.

''Tis possible he is the last,' came the princess's quiet voice. 'Though it may have been better if he had died rather than suffer, for so many years, this joyless existence. But he did not die; mayhap he cannot. Unicorns live for so long that the years that pass us are to them as a drop in the wide seas. Yet one day he will have his freedom... and as unicorns are the wisest creatures in all the world, I am sure that this he knoweth.'

'How is it he is here?' whispered the girl. 'Why doth no one know? Why is he a secret? How could...'

'Shh, not all at once, my darling. The unicorn is a secret because, as I did tell thee, he is worth more than the crown jewels... oh, much,

much more. For many years the king hath been afeared that if this creature's existence here were known, Lawhill would be besieged by thieves
and robbers; that armies would march upon us from Angerona, from
Balasore, from Ormsary and Ilala. And I think he is right in this.'

'Verily, I do see why all rulers would desire him for their own, for
he is the most perfectly beautiful being in all the world.'

Winterhued gave a low, sad laugh. 'Alas, no,' she said, 'they would
not covet him for his beauty. They would kill him, for he is worth far
more cut into a thousand pieces. All the gold in Manydown would
scarcely suffice to purchase his hide, and his horn would fetch twice
that. A strand from his mane or tail would be likely to fetch thy weight
in gold. But most coveted of all is the carbuncle, the ruby, to be found
in his skull at the base of the horn. It is the most precious, the most
rare stone in the world.'

'Why..?' whispered Brenn, 'Why would anyone desire these... these
dead parts when the living being is so... so...?'

'Because, my dear, it is written that each part of the unicorn can
cure illness and annul poison. A single hair may mend a sadness, the
smallest square of hide cure a colic, a little pinch of powdered horn
the plague; indeed every affliction may be remedied by a particle of
unicorn. I have read that a few hairs from his forelock, placed within
the deadliest wound, will cleanse any purulence and heal with miracu-
lous speed. Verily, that is what men of learning have, for hundreds of
years, been saying in their treatises. But I think they could not know,
for they also discuss the existence or non-existence of unicorns, thereby
making it clear that they have never seen one.

'My father could put the theory to the test, as he hath had every
hair the creature ever shed carefully collected. But he doth hoard his
collection like the most miserable of misers and keepeth it all to himself
in case he should ever fall ill – and he is never ill.'

'Is that not proof,' said Brenn tentatively, 'that he *doth* use them?'

'He would have told me...' said the princess, and then she laughed.
She was silent for a moment and then she laughed again.

'Did... did my lady,' asked Brenn, 'never think... to try?'

'Look at him, Brenn, and tell me... dost thou think he is here on this earth for our benefit? Have we the right to use any part of him for aught, even the preservation of our own wretched lives?'

Brenn still knelt before the unicorn. She looked up into his anthracite eyes and breathed: 'No, never. He is more than all of us.'

She noticed that around his neck, almost buried beneath the profusion of his mane, was a collar of tarnished gold. 'How could anyone bear to keep him captive in this cold, lightless place?' she whispered. 'How came he hither? And from whence?'

'That is a long story,' said Winterhued, rising and pulling her cloak around her, 'and can only be told in comfort before a fire.'

'A little longer, m'lady, please...' said the girl, 'I do not want to leave.'

'Oh my darling girl, if I leave thee here thou shalt soon be naught but a statue of ice.'

'May I see him again?'

'Perhaps thou wouldst like care for him?'

'Verily?'

'Aye. Twice every day a maid doth come to feed and water him and clean his stable. He cannot abide men or flesh-eaters; the sole viewing the king may have of his prized possession is through a tiny spy-hole. But the fine lass who hath fed and cared for him these past five years hath met a lad and wisheth to marry. I had thought to replace her with Eudora, but if thou...'

'Eudora! I beg my lady, do not let that lowly drudge be his keeper. She is dirty and stupid. She is not worthy!'

Winterhued was silent for a moment, and then she said: 'Thou hast not touched the unicorn. Step forward now and touch him.'

'Never; I would not dare...'

'But he wanteth thee to touch him. I cannot see him, yet I know that he standeth unmoving at the bars, watching thee. Am I not right? If the bars were not in his way he would come to thee.'

Brenn got to her feet, her eyes upon the creature. Her heart sounded loud in her ears. It was as the princess said: the unicorn stood motionless as moonlit marble, and as close to the iron bars as he could without touching them. And still he watched her.

She stretched forth her trembling hand and felt his warm breath brush her fingers. It was the lightest whisper, but its effect was of a tempest charged with lightning. She knew that she stood yet upon the hard flags, but felt as though a gale tried to pluck her from the earth. Still she stretched forth her hand, and with the tips of two fingers, touched the silken muzzle... touched life itself.

There was nothing else.

The tumult faded from her ears and it seemed that she was borne up on wings of light until the world looked small and far below. It lay like a book before her and she could read every truth upon its open pages. How wondrous, and how simple were those words!

The stars sang like glass and she felt, cool upon her cheek, the wind that moves forever across the heavens. Yet all the while she stood upon stone in a bare chamber and touched with gentle fingers the exquisite head of the unicorn: the fine bones, the gossamer coat, the satiny abundance of forelock.

Leaning forward until her face pressed against the iron bars, she kissed the great beast, and he closed his eyes and sighed. 'Thank you,' she whispered and then, with her feet on the ground and simple truth in her mind, she turned and walked away.

Winterhued held the girl tightly. 'How strange,' said Brenn, and she looked up at the princess with tears shining in her eyes. 'Everything hath changed. I love everyone... everything. I love spiders and deadly serpents. I love all living things. I love my father... I truly love him. I love Eudora too, and I am sorry I said those things about her. I even love Deccan; if he so wisheth, I shall marry him.'

The princess smiled. 'Hush, dearest. Thou mayst love every man in Manydown, but thou needst not marry them all. These feelings shall fade and tomorrow thou shalt despise fools again, yet I know that henceforth, little cousin, thou shalt be just and clear-sighted, and value all life.' She turned Brenn round to face the door, and picked up her lantern and keys. 'Come now fearless one, my omniscient angel; we shall return to our fire where I shall tell thee a tale.'

As they left the chamber, Brenn stopped and touched Winterhued's arm. 'My lady brought me hither to show me my dream,' she said, 'but though that is indeed a unicorn, it is not the unicorn that danceth within my dreams.'

CHAPTER 8

Cloud had long since swallowed up the moon and now Castle Lawhill crouched as still as a riven mountain within the gulf of night. A breeze blowing up from the south whispered across the lake and sent bitter plumes of smoke eddying and swirling. It set drifts of blackened ships' timbers grinding against the shingles and it set the corpses bobbing on the wavelets and jostling for space as they were cast up on the shore. But naught else moved. Darkness and fear draped the castle walls like molten lead and lay in a viscous spill upon the smouldering town below.

Yet somewhere beneath those castle walls, along a passage even more lightless and silent than the night, hurried Princess Winterhued and her youngest lady-in-waiting. They held their lanterns high, tiny pricks of yellow light in the massy darkness. The girl walked in front, with Winterhued's hand on her shoulder, and their light footfalls and the swishing of their skirts were the only sounds that they made. A little, wondering smile touched the girl's mouth and her eyes shone.

Not so very far from Winterhued and Brenn, though separated by impenetrable rock, huddled the lad called Stench. Shivering, he waited for daybreak in the gelid darkness of a forgotten passage, somewhere deep underground between the shaft of the inner-bailey well and the keep. The blackness and silence pressed in so thickly and were so absolute that he wondered for a time if he'd been struck blind and deaf, but no, he could hear his own breathing, slow and steady. He'd dozed a few times and woken confused. Now he was unsure if he still faced the well from whence he'd crawled some hours ago (or maybe it was only minutes?) If he did, surely he must soon see the first seepage of light as it crept down the well-shaft before dawn.

Time passed, or perhaps it didn't. The boy wished he'd kept the blanket he'd given Eudora. He had only his stinking cloak to wrap himself in, and now that he was likely to need it again, he worried that it was losing its potence. He curled himself into a ball and pulled the garment about him.

'Dawn will never come,' he croaked, through chattering teeth. 'The world hath ended and been cast into eternal night and I am the only speck of life left.' His stomach had begun to give him ample proof that he hadn't gone deaf. 'Sooth, but I'm hungry!' he moaned.

Somewhere above Stench and a little to the southeast, the scullery maid Eudora sat in the King's Hall wearing a clean gown of grey fustian and shoes that almost fit her. She'd been afraid to lie down in her new gown in case it became creased or dirty, so she had squatted until pins and needles pricked her legs unbearably. Then she'd staggered up and, dragging her bedding to a pillar, had sat with her back against the cold stone, her skirts carefully smoothed. The two blankets she clutched around her shoulders, but she still shivered miserably. Hunger nagged at her; it had been hours since she'd eaten and that had been almost nothing. They'd first handed her a lump of greasy pig on a plate and she'd handed it straight back, gagging; since a little child, she'd never been able to abide the thought of chewing on flesh. All they could give her instead had been a hunk of hard bread.

A flame flickered in a cresset down by the gallery screen. It cast a faint light across the sleeping bodies that lay huddled in blankets upon straw-stuffed mattresses. All about her she heard the noises of slumber; some folk tossed in their comfortless beds, some snored, some muttered as they slept.

She tilted back her head and gazed into the darkness. The massive column she leant against towered up like a tree into the night sky, but it wasn't sky up there: it was stone vaulting, roofed with slate. The tall windows between the columns were narrow and had been hastily boarded up, but the protection the roof and walls offered seemed flimsy, she suddenly thought, compared to the mighty horror that lurked without. Stench may have been right: mayhap this grand hall would turn out to be nothing more than a well-stocked larder.

Except for her shivering, Eudora sat motionless. But her mind ran back and forth, and to and fro. Should she have left with Stench? She despised him. In the eyes of the world he was as low as a maggot, and he forever hovered about her like a dirty fly, waiting to drag her down into his dung-pit. And now, unbelievably, she'd been given a chance to rise! Chambermaid to the princess: the kindest, loveliest princess in the world! But what use was that if they were all, Winterhued included, to be naught but meat for a ravening monster? And if they were not eaten, and life within the castle was to continue as it always had, how long would it be before she was found out as a thief? She thought of the princess sitting on the floor in the pool of her blue gown with her dark tresses looped over her shoulders and cascading to the flagstones, and frowning as she surveyed the overturned caskets and the tumbled jewellery.

Eudora moaned. What had possessed her to take that small stone on its silver chain? And how could she now make amends for her moment of mindlessness? Her *two* moments, for she'd made matters worse by giving the thing to Stench. She'd done that spitefully, without thinking at all. Why, she could have dropped the trinket on the floor in the princess's chamber and no one would have been the wiser. But how was she to know that Winterhued would decide to employ her regularly?

Eudora's innards turned to water as she pondered the punishment likely to be meted out to a malefactress such as she. Ofttimes in the town marketplace she'd sniggered at people in the stocks, she'd even joined the mob once or twice to pelt the wretched creatures with stinking rubbish. But far worse, she'd sometimes seen ragged old men cringing behind their begging bowls, branded indelibly as thieves, their right hands cut off or their faces hideously marked with a hot iron. And she was quite certain that not one of those felons had ever stolen from a princess! Mayhap such a crime would be deemed treason. Eudora tried to keep such a thought from her mind, for traitors always died, and a traitor's death was too horrible to be thought of. She buried her face in her blankets and, forgetting her new gown, drew her knees up under her chin and rocked, back and forth, back and forth, in the cold and the dark.

Almost directly below Eudora, beneath the heavily vaulted roof of the hall's undercroft, stood Manicia, younger daughter of the Duke of Drumrock. All about her rose the sighs, the mutterings, the rattles and rasps of the sleeping and the sleepless nobility; they tossed as restlessly in their dreams and dreamlessness as did the common folk in the hall above. But Manicia was wide awake. She held a blanket about her shoulders, and her nut-brown tresses, still kinked from their tight plaits, hung loose down her back. Her eyes glittered in the light of her candle.

Before her lay her sleeping sister Benicia, her pretty cheeks pink again and her face peaceful. She was curled up like a child beside the massive, snoring bulk of their father; he had gone to sleep holding both of her hands within his own.

Manicia's candle trembled and she suddenly raised it to her face to snuff out its light lest someone witness the tear that traced a solitary path down her cheek.

A short distance away to the northeast, in the clammy basement of the Watchtower, King Gers lay on his back sleeping soundly. The chamber's miasmic air gurgled in and out of his open mouth; he snorted now and then, dribbled somewhat, and sometimes muttered a few words in a jovial tone. His hound lay pushed up beside him, her legs sprawling over the edge of the little bed. She occasionally sat up to scratch at her fleas and whine in a most annoying manner.

'Shh!' hissed Sir Gunford, turning aside from his tip-toe pacing of the chamber to glare threateningly at the hound. She ignored him to turn round thrice, scratch once more, and then rest her unhappy head across the king's belly.

'Hmm... molliwumma...' muttered the king blithely.

A voice from the other side of the chamber added an unintelligible somniloquy in gloomy tones, a third voice coughed weakly, and a fourth grunted disgustingly then joined the king in a horrible symphony of snoring. In three truckle beds, side by side like a row of dead crows, lay the old chancellor, the chamberlain, and the Balasorean ambassador. Before he'd fallen into a stupor some hours ago, the ambassador had drunk far too much mead and now his neat velvets were crumpled and his glossy black hair was in disarray.

Sir Gunford stared at the three lords. His stubbled face was slick with sweat and he'd developed a pronounced twitch in his left eyelid.

'Muvvelnigh champolu...' said the king, chuckling in his sleep.

'Wunnaway!' muttered the insensible ambassador, and kicked so hard that his truckle bed leapt an inch or two across the flagstones.

'God 'a mercy!' swore Sir Gunford under his breath. Behind his back he heard a stifled snort and swung around to see the young guard at the chamber door with his hand clamped across his mouth and his ears turning red. 'Fie!' hissed Gunford. 'How canst thou laugh, fool? I see naught to be merry about!' But as the four sleepers' mellifluous chorus rattled along, the guard only laughed the harder, silently, until his face had turned beetroot and his eyes were welling with tears.

'Thou art dismissed,' spat Gunford. 'Get out of my sight, thou lousy footboy. Send a sober man hither!' The guard turned as quickly as he could and staggered helplessly away up the stairs, his halberd clanging against the walls as he went.

Gunford's snarl turned into a moan and he sank down upon the stairs with his head in his hands. With a sound like a knife in the brain the hound whined again, insistently.

In the chapel built between the East Tower's massive buttresses, old Lady Ulidia dozed with her head upon the bier of her dead lord. He lay beneath a banner that the fifteen year-old Ulidia had herself embroidered for her unloved bridegroom more than two score years ago. It gleamed in the light of six tall candles; within its chequered border the black Thornliebank thorn-branch pricked a field of azure, quartered with green upon which bristled the lady's own badge of a red porcupine.

The flickering candlelight lit up the chapel; it danced upon the painted martyrs on the walls and turned the slender pillars to gold as they rose towards the pointed vaulting. Its single deeply-recessed window had been boarded up and was covered now with a hanging painted with faded sunbursts.

Young Lady Pera, her eyelids drooping, sat beside Ulidia and ran her bandaged hand across the silken stitches where the banner drooped down the side of the bier. The sudden sound of footsteps roused her and she looked up to see the Duke of Travancore enter the chapel, followed by two soldiers, one of whom held up a lantern. The duke bowed to her, a frown creasing his tired, solemn face.

'Ah...' he said, with sudden illumination. 'Lord Ladstock's daughter.' She nodded shyly. 'Ah...' he said again. His voice was soft and hoarse. 'Princess Winterhued asked me... to look in here but... ah... I have been tardy, I have had much to do.'

'I pray ye, do not apologize, Your Grace,' murmured Pera. She hardly dared look at the duke, he was so very tall. 'Ye see my lady overcome with tiredness. I have made up a bed for her in the undercroft, but... as ye see... she hath gone to sleep before I could persuade her thither.'

'We must get her to bed then,' said the duke and though he himself looked ready to drop, he walked over to the old woman and took her up in his arms. She did not wake and he carried her from the chapel as easily as though she weighed no more than a cat. At the threshold he paused and half turned to one of the soldiers. 'Stay here,' he ordered. 'Keep watch. Say a prayer for the marquess if thou knowest how. I shall send someone to relieve thee before dawn.'

Barely ten minutes later, Pera lay beneath a mound of blankets on a truckle bed in the undercroft of the King's Hall. Lady Ulidia slumbered in another bed beside her; as the duke had lain the old woman carefully down she'd woken to protest over her unbidden removal, but had drifted back to sleep in mid-sentence. The grim-faced duke had wiped her dribble from his sleeve, taken an inspectoral glance around at the lords and ladies in the undercroft and then marched himself and his lantern-bearer away on more urgent business.

The nobility now resident within the cellar had surrounded themselves with whatever luxuries their servants had managed to gather:
from hastily rigged velvet bed-curtains to furs and feather mattresses,
from cushioned chairs and footstools to silver candelabras laden
with candles. Yet these comforts seemed little aid to sound sleep,
and the great vaulted gloom was resonant still with hushed noises of
wakefulness.

Not five beds away from Ulidia, past a quietly sobbing marchioness and her consoling lady's-maid, and a snoring duke and his tossing
duchess, lay Sir Parchim, Marquess of Potrimpos. He wore a bandage
wrapped around the top of his head; falling limply from beneath it
his yellow hair gleamed in the light of a dwindling candle. He stared
wide-eyed at the vaulting above.

All of a sudden he rolled onto his side and propped himself up on
one elbow. He craned his neck to peer nervously down the hall and, to
his horror, there was Sir Criffel still, sitting rigidly on a chair in the light
of several fat candles, just staring at him as intensely as he'd been some
fifteen minutes earlier. Even as the marquess watched, he waggled an
admonishing forefinger and narrowed his glittering eyes in a frightening manner. Potrimpos flung himself back down upon his bed.

'He watches me yet,' he whimpered to a favoured old retainer who
slumbered on the floor beside the bed, one arm round a sleeping hound.

'Eh, m'lord?' muttered the fellow confusedly, waking and pushing
himself into a sitting position. The hound grunted, sighed and went
back to sleep.

'Criffel,' hissed the marquess, 'glaring horribly and wagging his
hairy finger at me. He is about to fling his gauntlet at my feet, I can
see that.'

'A duel?' rasped the man, scratching his grey head. 'Why would he
want that? He's no reputation for prowess with weapons.'

'Neither have I,' muttered Potrimpos.

'Come, my lord, what have ye to fear? The man's a puny milksop.'

'Nay, he's angry, and fortified by his anger. It's not that I'm afraid... no, never afraid. But I'm... I'm a man of peace. Hawks, horses, hounds and hunting is what I do; I don't wish to fight anyone.'

'Ye should ha' thought of that (I did warn you, sir), when ye went flirting with his bride.'

'"Twas all on her side! Besides, thou knowest that thinking is not my strong suit.'

'Oh aye... I've known you since ye were a swaddled babe and it's certain ye've never had a great deal in your head.' The old retainer chuckled. 'Thoughts nor teeth.'

'Thou'rt an insolent wretch,' growled Potrimpos, giving the fellow a kick, 'and no help to me in my need. Get back to thy snoring, dog.'

'Come m'lord, the Earl of Dunmore's naught when compared with this creature that imprisons us. If *that* allows us to survive, and if we don't in the meantime die of hunger, then when Dunmore turfs his gage at you, why... ye can always run off home. No one expects honour from the Neath family.'

The marquess looked alarmed at the mention of home. 'I'm not going home... gloomy place,' he muttered and then perked up. 'But thou art right about honour; I don't give a fig for it! "Ye have dropped your glove, sir," I shall say to him. "Take it, and your soiled bride, and leave me be. I am a north-man, moreover a Neath, sir, and I refuse to satisfy your silly southern notions of honour!"'

The old man scratched his head again. 'Ye do not want a fight, m'lord?' he asked. 'Better not mention 'soiled bride' then.'

Somewhere amongst the discontented cluster of lords and ladies in that cheerless place lay the princess's cousin Nomia, wife of Sir Auchencairn. Wide awake, she hugged her little dog close and stared numbly, unseeing, into the night. 'I am a widow,' she thought, and wondered why it was that her heart still beat within her breast.

Tip-toeing past her, Sir Criffel's man, Garston, returned to his master; the Duke of Travancore having at present no need of his inestimable skills. He sat down upon the floor and propped himself against the earl's bed, feeling hungry and cold. Why had he not thought to get his cloak back from that pretty girl? (What a cleavage she had, and how generous of her to share it with everyone!) Garston shook his head at the thought that such a wholesome lass would soon be wed to 'Mistress' Criffel... a girl married to an old woman. No, he couldn't imagine there'd be a great deal of joy in *that* union. Garston glanced up at his master (who had ignored his return). What a talent the man had for staring! He was sitting stiffly in a wooden chair gazing intently, angrily, down the hall. He appeared to be attempting to strike an adversary dead by the venom of his look. Well, it was probably his most effective weapon, Garston mused, for the man was a buffoon with a sword.

In a far corner of the undercroft, hidden behind a great wine-barrel, Deccan of Wythop sat amongst a group of his acquaintances, all of them squires to sundry knights of renown. Heads together, huddled in their cloaks and blankets, they complained of their masters.

'I thought my lord worthy! Oh, he's brave enough in the lists, I warrant you, but now that real peril is upon us, where be his flaunted valour? All fled away, and he doth naught but grumble at the inconvenience.'

'Aye, my master also; he hath slept the whole day long!'

'Yet Sir Soukar...' began Deccan.

'Pish,' interrupted the umbrageous youth Jersbek, 'we've heard enough of Soukar! He's as lily-livered as the rest.'

'Certes,' said a spotty-faced youth, 'we know now who are the most worthy: Sir Auchencairn, as well as Sir Dechmont, Sir Howth and Sir Wynford.'

'They are all perished.'

'Aye, and those left scatheless have displayed their cravenness. Quake-bottoms all!'

'When we have our gilded spurs," muttered Deccan, "we'll show them how knights should behave!'

'Shall we?' asked Jersbek. 'Go to then, Deccan. Thou needst not wait for thy spurs; why not attempt some valiant deed now? Thou hast a lance, a sword, a horse...'

Deccan made no answer, for he had none, and the youths fell sheepishly silent.

'Who *is* that?' suddenly asked Kynance, the youngest of them.

'Who?'

'That man,' he said, pointing to a noble who slept upon a camp-bed barely ten yards from their group. 'I saw him earlier talking with Travancore, but I've not seen him before today. He... he's a Callunian.'

'So?' retorted Jersbek. 'Thou sayest the name as if it were something evil.'

'Nay, I was but...'

'He is the Marquess of Carradale,' interrupted Deccan, 'a marcher lord from the north, and first son of the Duke of Arracan. He is seldom seen at court yet I have heard, from a reliable source, that he is a friend to the princess.'

'Come Kynance,' said Jersbek, 'thou hast not answered me. Dost thou have something against Callunians?'

The boy looked confused. 'The king says... and my father...'

'I know what the king says. But the king is old, and only old, foolish or ill-educated rustics think that way.'

'And thou dost love them... Callunians?'

'No more than other men, for that is what they are: men just as we.'

'They take what is ours.'

'Oh? Hast aught of thine been stolen by a Callunian? Listen, fool; they came here a generation, sometimes two or three generations back, with naught but the raiment on their backs. Whatever they have now they have earned; they deserve our admiration, not our persecution. By such ill-usage we prove ourselves no better than the tyrants that drove them from their lands. Ha! thou shakest thy dim-witted head, but what should I expect from a yokel with a narrow, mean mind?'

Kynance, red faced, clambered to his feet. 'Yokel?' he hissed. 'My family is ancient and honourable; we have been loyal for generations; unlike thee with thy treasonous talk!'

'Treason? Nay, I bear true allegiance to the throne; I am the princess's man. She is enlightened and far-seeing, and her star is in the ascendant. Sit down, dim-wit.'

'But *is* her star in the ascendant?' questioned another of the squires. 'Have ye not heard the rumours?'

'What rumours?' snapped Jersbeck.

'They say the king hath dreamed of a male heir ever since he fathered that bastard last year. They say he'll marry again.'

Jersbeck snarled. 'He wouldn't dare! He'd put Winterhued aside for some mewling brat? He'll have to fight me first.'

'I'd fight for her,' murmured the spotty-faced youth.

'Me also,' said another lad. 'I'm the princess's man through and through.'

'I was in her bedchamber today,' said Deccan. 'Ye'll not believe me, but 'tis sooth.'

'Why do we take sides?' asked the eldest of the squires, ignoring Deccan's absurd comment. 'Why rage against an unborn princeling?' He tugged at Kynance's sleeve. 'Sit down. Thou shalt wake these folk. Besides, 'tis folly that we bicker while Lawhill's aflame and people die; what valorous heroes are we!'

'Valorous starvelings more like,' muttered the spotty-faced boy. 'Methinks they're trying to feed the whole castle on half a bowl of pottage.'

Around and above the undercroft and its temporary residents, Castle Lawhill curled its great stone arms, scarred now and broken.

The huge edifice might have seemed empty of life, but now and then servants and soldiers could be descried as they scurried, like insects in a decaying body, about their endless business. And here, a splinter of light escaped from the margins of a boarded window, while there, a wisp of smoke leaked into the night from a secretive fire. Somewhere down by the Constable's Gate a few hounds set up a clamour before they were cuffed into silence, and from the southern end of the outer bailey came the soft clop and scrape of horses' hoofs as they milled about a pile of sweet hay that Travancore, following the princess's list of instructions, had had thrown out to them from a postern.

Beside the castle the town lay maimed and crumpled. Its familiar roofline was blighted with gaps where buildings had collapsed; some still smouldered, red coals aglow in the night. Those of its denizens that yet remained crouched hidden in mute and exhausted dread. But as soon as darkness had fallen, all around the town's periphery men, women and children had begun to leak out, some empty-handed, some with bundles of belongings; through the breached town walls they went, running, stooping, scuttling from blackened tree to tumbled fence, tripping over the dead, looking fearfully over their shoulders, glancing ashen-faced at the sky. From the town's broken outskirts they siphoned onto every track and road and hurried away into the night: north, south, east and west.

Good reason had those puny creatures to be fearful for far, far above, blacker than the night, a ragged blot of darkness moved noise-lessly across the sable sky. It seemed to swallow the stars as it went, and it trailed in its wake a noisome reek of death.

Brenn wriggled comfortably inside one of the princess's night-gowns. Although it was too long for her, wearing it she felt like a princess herself because it was made of the very finest white linen and embroidered exquisitely with tiny white flowers. She snuggled into the pillows and pulled the counterpane up to her chin as she waited for Winterhued.

'Art thou still wakeful?' asked the princess as she returned barefoot across the chamber. Brenn nodded, wide-eyed. 'Lo then, 'tis time for a tale!' As Winterhued climbed beneath the covers the little cat jumped onto the bed and, purring blissfully, began to knead Brenn's feet through the counterpane. Brenn laughed softly and wriggled her toes. 'This is far more warm and comfortable than that camp-bed,' murmured the princess, drawing the girl to her. As Brenn nestled her head against her cousin's shoulder she marvelled at how, in such a short space of time, the princess had been transformed from distant idol into best friend.

'Hearken, and I shall begin,' said Winterhued. She cleared her throat, but fell silent for a long moment. 'Certes, I have not told this story to anyone.' Then, with a little laugh, she launched herself into the tale's telling. 'Once upon a time, on an early morning in an old summer, a princess rode forth from a castle by a lake.'

'So the story *is* of my lady then,' interrupted Brenn.

'There are many princesses in the world, and many castles are built beside lakes,' answered Winterhued. 'Now, no more interruptions, or we shall never advance further than the castle gate.

'The princess rode with a company of courtiers, and they dazzled the young hour with their brocades and silks, their gleaming, high-bred horses, their lean hunting hounds, and with their glittering conversation. (At least, the princess, who was a little older than thee, was impressed by their chatter, but I'm afraid it must be said that she was a careless girl, with naught in her head but fripperies.)

'Riding beside their long shadows the merry company rode through a salmon-pink dawn, their horses dancing and prancing because the day was new. Beside the leap of the brook and the dart of swallows they went, as the sun climbed higher and the sky turned blue. The folk out in the fields doffed their caps and waved; the villagers on their way to market in the town by the lake stopped to bow or curtsey, and some brought flowers for the princess.

'The company's progress was but slow for, apart from all the stopping to exchange pleasantries with the people, they must match their pace with the heavy wains that rumbled behind, loaded with provender for the journey and drawn by white oxen draped with garlands. And so, with a cloud of dust at their heels, they wound their way northwards – all that day and the next, and for six more after that – up past the safe pastures and the golden harvests, past the vines on the low hills where the cloud shadows fled, up to the very edge of an old forest and the very foot of a great mountain range that stretched away into the east and into the west.

'Like a thick-woven blanket lay the forest, all draped about the shoulders of the mountains, and above it the peaks frowned their lofty brows down upon the waning day. As the shadows grew long, the company pitched its pavilions at the thicket's edge, lit its bright fires and caroused for a time, and upon the morrow's dawn rode blithely forth to hunt stag. The princess and her most trusted lady-in-waiting rode a little way with the hunt but soon, unseen amongst the crowding trees, they turned aside. Back they rode, towards the east, and presently halted in a glade where they were joined by three gentlemen... let us call them the Duke of Dumpling, Lord Leanshanks and Captain Clod-pate.'

Brenn giggled. 'Oh, I think I know who they might be.'

'Hmm... well, these three brave knights were accompanied by a dozen soldiers and huntsmen and as many eager hounds, all straining at their leashes. A map, roughly drawn upon a battered scrap of goatskin, was produced and consulted, and before long they were on their way, east for a while and then, following a tumbling stream, northwards. Up a narrowing defile they went, and through the laced branches above their heads they could see the beetling crags drawing in, until the trees vanished and bare grey rock towered up around them. How the sound of the horses' hoofs, as they slipped and stumbled, echoed from those sheer walls! The way was steep, and beside them rushed the stream, tumbling noisily down the rocks in lacy white veils.

'The princess's lady-in-waiting clutched at her pommel and moaned with fear, but the princess (though her heart beat loud in her breast) thought herself a fearless warrior and laughed aloud. (Alackaday! What an empty-head was she!)

'At last the way opened out into a fair valley, clasped like a jewel between the surrounding steeps. Here the stream ran gaily down through verdant meadows, besprinkled o'er with flowers and dappled light, and edged about with broad-girthed trees that whispered in the breeze. The soldiers and the huntsmen with their hounds spread out and melted away into the woods and the three gallant knights escorted the princess some distance up the valley. There she alighted from her pretty palfrey and her attendant embraced her tightly and moaned again.

'"Be not so silly, old thing," quoth the princess. "This is a merry adventure!" (Alas! Who was the silly one here?) Therewith, Captain Clod-pate led her horse away, Lord Leanshanks reminded her once more of what she must do, and the jovial Duke of Dumpling patted her shoulder as though she were his favourite puppy. The princess sat herself down upon the flowered meadow beneath a shimmering roof of leaves as the knights, and the old lady, took themselves from her sight.

'The breeze sighed gently, the birds sang sweetly, the bees hummed busily and all the bright faces of the flowers followed the sun as it climbed from the eastern slopes into the azure sky. The empty-headed princess spread her skirts about her and smoothed their silken embroidery, she shifted from this side to that, she leaned on her left hand, she leaned on her right, she propped herself on her elbows, she hugged her knees, she pulled the petals from flowers, she made a chain from daisies and plaited them in her hair. She sang to herself, she yawned and she nodded, she got up and she sat down... and then she dozed.

'When she awoke everything had changed. The birds still sang, the bees still hummed and the sun still shone, yet now these things were no longer peripheral to the princess's self-centred existence. They were life itself, and she was of no more importance than a passing mayfly.

'With her mind as clear as the summer sky, she turned... and lo! There he was beneath the trees at the edge of the meadow, half lost in drowsy shadow. He stepped forward into the sunlight and came towards her: a moonbeam horse with a single horn of starlight issuing from the centre of his forehead. His mane fell like a waterfall and trailed amongst the flowers, and his tail... oh! but I need not describe him to thee, my darling.' Winterhued's voice trembled.

'He was not thin though, was he?'

The princess hugged Brenn and kissed her chestnut hair. 'No, he was flawless,' she whispered, 'transcendent... he was a joy and a terror! And he went to the princess, and bent his knees before her and lay down with his perfect head upon her lap. Her heart leapt, her breath stopped and the tears started up in her eyes as fearfully, tenderly, she ran her fingertips across his silken skin.

'Yet, alack the day! Even as that single touch flung aside the shutters in her mind so that she saw before her the very truth of the world, she saw too what she had done! "Oh, arise Unicorn!" she cried. "Ye must fly from here!" But even as she pleaded, she saw the hounds unleashed and bounding from the trees, she saw the huntsmen running with their spears and net, and saw the soldiers emerge from the woods with their crossbows cranked and their swords drawn.

'She pushed at the unicorn, she hit him with her traitor's fists, gasping: "Run, run!" and at last he lifted his head from her lap. She scrambled from him; on her hands and knees she crawled and stumbled away, still gasping: "Run!" She tripped on her skirts and fell; she rolled and twisted about as a hound bounded by her, maw agape and red tongue lolling from its slavering jaws. She saw the unicorn, on his feet now (too late, oh, too late!), turn at bay as the hounds leapt at him from every side. One was lifted up on that great horn, impaled, and flung aside like a bloodied clout.

'The princess, disentangled now from her skirts, ran at the dogs, crying and shouting at them, hitting them feebly, grabbing for their spiked collars. But they were mad with the hunt and pulled her over and dragged her on the trampled earth. Bruised, winded and helpless, she saw the beautiful creature on his knees, harried and tormented; she saw bright blood running down his perfect hide.

'All of a sudden, she was grabbed from behind and dragged roughly to her feet. She cried out in pain as her arms were wrenched behind her back and an angry voice growled in her ear. It was despised Captain Clod-pate who handled her so brutishly, so she kicked him in the shins and screamed at him. "Stupid girl," he grunted, "Ye must follow the king's orders," and pushed her into the arms of her lady-in-waiting. The woman clutched at her, clucking stupidly and trying to pull the princess's face down upon her breast, but the girl twisted away, determined that she *would* see.

'And see she did… the glorious beast fallen amongst the trampled flowers, held down by a cruel net that tightened with his every struggle. The hounds – those that still lived – were restrained at last by the huntsmen, but the wounds they had inflicted bled grievously and the grass was slick with blood. The brave soldiers came forward now and stood or sat upon the unicorn, pinning him down while the Duke of Dumpling waddled forth from the safety of the trees clutching a collar of gold. He knelt to thread it through the net and, grunting and wheezing, fastened it around the creature's neck.

'The unicorn stopped struggling and became so still that the princess thought him dead. Her sobs sounded loud against the birdsong and the whispered breeze. Clod-pate turned on her with a curse, but the lady-in-waiting relinquished her hold upon the princess and stepped forward. "How dare ye, sir?" she said and hit the captain so hard with her bony little fist that he sat down abruptly with his nose spurting blood. "Ye forget yourself, caitiff! This is your princess: daughter to our sovereign lord!"

'She gripped the princess's elbow and led the weeping girl away down the meadows. She got them mounted upon their palfreys and taking the princess's rein, led her away down the rocky defile. The little woman had managed to cast aside her cravenness now that her darling was lost.

'For lost the princess was... lost with her thoughts and her terrible regrets. For three days, as the party wended its way along the homeward road, hardly a word did she speak. She rode with her head down, not daring to look at aught, for to do so was to put more into a mind already full of tumult and trouble.

'On the first day of their homeward journey the Duke of Dumpling bounced up beside her upon his huge brown horse. "Your ladyship need not grieve," quoth he in a low voice, "for the prey liveth yet."

'The princess glanced up at him in amazement. "Where is he?" she gasped. "May I see him?"

'"I crave pardon m'lady, but nay," he replied. "I will but say that it trav'leth with us in one of the covered wains. The king was not concerned whether it came to him alive or dead, yet methinks he will be pleased that it liveth. But alive or dead, this must remain a secret... or we might as well issue invitations to our neighbours to send in their armies. My lady doth understand this?"

'The princess looked at the duke with desperation in her gaze. "If it be so dangerous to possess this creature," she whispered, "why do we not take him back to the forest and release him?" But the fat man just laughed as if at a great joke, and reining his horse about, rode away chuckling.

'On the second day of the journey home Lord Leanshanks came to the princess. "Why doth my lady keep up this childish sulking?" he asked.

'"I am a wretched traitor," was her reply.

'The lean lord laughed. "The creature is but a brute beast," quoth he, "a lesser being. My lady hath helped it to fulfil its purpose, for God put such lowly kine upon this earth for no cause other than to serve mankind. My lady must put her mind at ease; she hath not *betrayed* a soulless beast."

"'Thou art wrong," was all the princess said, and she rejoiced inwardly that she *knew* this. Oh yes, she knew so much now; more than the narrow, sanctimonious lord would ever know!

'On the third day the princess half expected a visit from that blustering poltroon Clod-pate, for he owed her an apology. But of course he came not, for he was ever a whey-faced craven. So she rode with her head bowed, alone amongst the throng, for even her anxious ladies-in-waiting kept their distance. They watched, but said naught, for: "Leave me be," the princess had told them; "I need to be alone with my thoughts."

'At last, as the day ripened, the girl found that the turmoil in her mind had abated. She looked down at her palfrey's dappled shoulders, at her hoofs striking clouds of dust from the parched road, and gradually became aware that the hoofs of the horse travelling beside her had been there for most of the day. Without raising her head to look upon his rider, she looked sideways at the horse and watched him for a time. Oh, how strange were her new eyes! But three days hence she would have dismissed this creature as a worthless jade, but now... now her heart beat with love and tears spangled her view. For he was an old, old horse, tall and bigly made, bright chestnut and copper gleaming, but with grey hairs on his face and the flesh a little sunken from his big bones. He carried himself so nobly, his neck was arched and his eye so bright and proud, that she wanted to reach out and stroke him. She glanced shyly up at his rider. (Hearken to that! Shy! All her life the princess had never been shy!)'

Winterhued ceased talking and lay for a time watching the firelight flickering on the ceiling. Brenn turned her head to watch the princess's face. 'Did she fall in love?' she asked.

Winterhued laughed quietly. 'Aye,' she replied, 'upon the instant.' She lapsed back into silence.

'Was he handsome?' prompted Brenn.

The princess drew a long breath. 'He had been watching her, but as she looked up at him he glanced away. Yet not before she had seen his eyes... eyes as blue as shadows on snow.' Winterhued laughed again, softly. 'Aye, he was handsome; handsome enough to take her breath away. Tall and dark... such a smile... and eyes; wondrous fathomless eyes: surely his glory and his shame. In sooth, he was to the princess the most beautiful ornament to the world she had ever seen.

'Yet love did not blind her to the shabbiness of his garments; all neat and clean but worn, even threadbare. His tall boots too, his saddle and bridle; all polished and gleaming, but certes, they had seen better times. Only three days hence, the princess would likely have despised such a fellow (though even that empty-head could not have been untouched by his beauty). Instead, everything that she now saw only served to make her love him the more.'

'Who was he?' asked Brenn; 'and why had he suddenly appeared by her side?'

'The princess,' said Winterhued, 'had become such miserable company, that none of her friends wished to ride with her (she had, after all, done her utmost to discourage them). And he, passing by and seeing her loneliness and the tears upon her cheeks, simply stayed to provide mute companionship; gentle heart that he was.

'"My lady is sad," were his first shy words to her (after she had but gaped at him for a time, struck dumb with love). "My lady is sad," quoth he and straight away, trusting him completely, she blurted forth the great secret that she had been instructed never to divulge. "Aye," she whispered, "for I have committed a terrible crime against the world; we have captured a unicorn and it is my fault."

'Unsurprised (he never was surprised by aught), he glanced back at the covered wains and then he looked at her with his cloudless eyes and his slight smile and his generous heart. "Perhaps ye should not have told me that?" he said. It was a question to which he knew the answer, and the princess merely shook her head mutely. "I'll not tell a soul," said he, and she knew that he would not. Tears started up in her eyes once more, but these were tears of gratitude and relief, for it seemed to her that he could see all of the trouble and the truth that lay within her soul. "Do not weep," quoth he in a quiet voice; "take comfort, for ye are the princess and it lieth within your power to remedy any wrong – if not today then tomorrow, next month, next year."

'He had uttered that which the princess most needed to hear (he could always do that). Her heart lifted, and she smiled a little, then of a sudden looked away ashamedly to rub at her blotched cheeks and puffy eyes. At that he seemed to recall who she was, and began to rein his horse back and apologise for his presumption in having ridden beside her. "Oh, prithee, do not go," said she, turning in her saddle. "If thou canst bear to ride beside such a criminal as I, I would have more of thy company."

'"Criminal?" chaffed he with a smile, letting his horse walk forward to once more match step with her own.

'"Well, fool at very least," quoth she, "for I have been the most thoughtless empty-head that ever lived; not just these past few days, but all my life long."

'The knight laughed softly. "If fools were punished, my lady, there would not be a free man upon the earth. The dungeons would overflow and I for one would have swung at the gallows years hence. But not you. For ye have the face of an omniscient angel."' Winterhued laughed. 'Aye, that is what he said, and I remembered it when thou, little cousin, didst walk from the menagerie but an hour hence.'

'Me? An omni… omni…?'

'Omniscient… all-knowing. And an angel.'

'All-knowing? I do not think so; I did not even know what it meant.'

'Nevertheless, thou knowest now the world's truth, little angel. But they were his words, not mine… the words of my story-book knight.'

'Methinks he was quite bold,' said Brenn; 'a lowly knight speaking to the king's only daughter in such a familiar manner.'

'"Tis sooth he was direct in his address, but why should he not be when he, as well as she, knew at once that they had been put on this earth the one for the other? Yet he had always a quiet and modest manner. Indeed, brave as he was, 'twas clear that at first his heart quaked when in her company, for he sometimes faltered in his speech and looked discomfited. But as he grew easier with her how sweet and clever proved his converse, and how his drolleries delighted her.'

'But who was he?' asked Brenn once again, 'and why had she never noticed him?'

'Of course before that day the princess had seen him in a tourney or two, distantly and encased all in armour, but she'd felt only annoyance at seeing him knock her favourites into the mud. He had been disregarded by her circle of vain and frivolous friends, though he was not lowbred; far from it, for he was the seventh son of a great and powerful duke. But alas, the duke was out of favour with the king, his lands were poor and his coffers empty, so the seventh son possessed only the horses, raiment and gear that had been hard-used and worn-out by his brothers before him. Yet these disadvantages were as naught to the new-made knight, for he had already proven himself so deft with weapons that none could match him. Not a braggart, and ever mild in his ways, his fellows liked him well, yet through envy it was sometimes their wont to make sport of him for his lack.

'But never again, for now the princess smiled upon him... oh, how she smiled. Paying little heed to the days about her, she smiled upon him all the way home for he made her heart glad. And though her old lady-in-waiting may have clucked her tongue and waggled a disapproving finger, no one was there who could nay-say this joyous dalliance.

'And so, each with the other well content, they fared homewards through the waning days of summer; through five enchanted days. As they rode at last beneath the castle gate, the Duke of Dumpling urged his horse up close beside the princess's palfrey. "The beast liveth yet," he whispered in the girl's ear, looking askance at her blue-eyed companion. But, of course, he need not have been so secretive!

'So it was that as the sun sank upon the last day of summer, the princess, the knight and the hapless unicorn all came home to the castle by the lake.'

Winterhued lapsed into silence once more, as the little cat at her feet got up, turned about and went back to sleep.

'Is that the end of the tale? Nay, it cannot be,' said Brenn, 'for where did he go, the knight, where is he now?'

'Nay, 'tis not the end,' said the princess, rousing herself, 'and I must stop dreaming and tell the story, for dawn surely draweth nigh.

'Where was I? Ah, yes. The king now... the king was most displeased when he heard of the attachment that had formed betwixt his only child and the straitened son of a disfavoured, indeed hated, duke. He had been in the midst of arranging for his daughter an advantageous marriage with, let us call him the Prince of Balderdash, but she would have none of it and the king soon discovered that he could not force her. Stubborn and wilful she had always been, and now, all of a sudden, she had grown wise and fearless. The wrathful king knit his brow and clenched his fists; he shouted till the banners in the hall shook, all to no avail. But though he could not force his daughter to marry, he *could* forbid all communication betwixt her and the despised son of his enemy.

'In the autumn the king and his court undertook a progress of the realm. The travelling multitude included the princess and the knight; the princess circled constantly by her ladies-in-waiting who were under the king's orders not to let her out of their sights. They journeyed first to the east and whilst guests there in a lordling's moated manor-house an adventurous party rode out for the day, on a dare, into a deep, enchanted forest below a haunted mountain. Though they encountered none of its rumoured wraiths, in the tangled thickets the princess managed to magically vanish from beneath her ladies' noses and make her way to a little lake, set like a jewel within the tumbled gold of autumn. There she met the knight and, beside waters as smooth and dark as polished onyx, the two of them stood all alone. The yellow leaves fell like rain about the lovers as they stole their first kisses.'

Winterhued sighed. 'Ah, how sweet they were,' she murmured, then laughed, 'and how hurried.

'On returning to court the king and his daughter resumed their quarrel over the Balderdashean marriage. Stormy were their daily encounters until, to the princess's relief, news arrived that the irksome prince had married some other damsel. But that was not the end of it, for the king continued to rail at her about marriage: now to anyone he deemed "suitable", and she matched him with vehement complaints over the unicorn's captivity. And so they fought, all through that bleak winter.

'During that time the princess saw little of her old friends; instead, having acquired a thirst for learning, she spent many hours with her tutors and her books. In her day-to-day life, in the company of the king, of courtiers and councillors, of her teachers and ladies-in-waiting, the princess was oft seen to smile a secretive smile, but rare seemed her encounters with the young knight. When they did meet, in a passage or in the bailey or the Great Hall, she would always stop to enquire after him in a somewhat distant manner, but with just enough warmth to impress his companions. She had, however, gained an increased keenness for knightly entertainments, and during the midwinter tournament could be seen sitting in the royal gallery smiling and clapping (though her heart beat hard in her breast) as the knight carried off every prize in the joust and the mêlée.

'How splendid and terrifying was the final joust that day, as the young knight encountered that huge, doughty warrior: the King's Champion! The old red horse, caparisoned all in sable, reared up, then plunged forward down the lists. The Champion's stallion, black as coal and trapped to the ground in crimson, leapt into a gallop; how the ground trembled with the thunder of their going! They met fairly and squarely in the middle of the lists, their lances bursting into shivers, but the shock of the encounter was so great that the Champion and his horse were flung to the ground. The young knight vaulted from the saddle to kneel beside his fallen opponent, but the Champion shortly clambered to his feet and, removing his helmet, looked round at the crowds with a laugh and clapped the young knight, his own student in arms, proudly upon the back.

'But all this while, amidst the spectators' clamour, the king sat scowling, sometimes eyeing his daughter suspiciously. Then during the following winter's-end tournament, as it became clear that the knight would again be awarded the prize, the king suddenly stood up and announced that this was tedious; where were all the good knights? and that unless some worthy challengers were forthcoming, there would be no more jousting! The tourney continued to its proper end, but the king stomped off back to the castle, taking with him most of his retinue as well as his reluctant daughter.

'And so, the winter snows melted, and spring came with its blossoms, and for all of that time (couldst thou guess?) the princess and the knight, each with the other, kept sweet company almost every day. For the disobedient girl had wasted little time in showing him all the hidden ways she'd discovered within and beneath the castle walls. How many secret trysts may be kept over one winter...? Mayhap four score or more, but certainly enough for the princess's heart to be lost forever, and enough for the lovers to have plighted their troths until the end of time.

'Then, one day in mid-spring, the king stood forth in the great hall before the councillors and courtiers and loudly called for the knight. The young man stepped forward and knelt before him, and the king, with a pleasant smile, raised him up in seeming courtesy. "It hath been brought to my notice, sir," quoth he, "that thou dost crave the hand of my daughter in marriage. In good sooth, I can think of naught more desirable than such a *seemly* and *splendid* match. I find though, that I do not know thee sir, nor do I know thy worth. Granted, thou art skilled enough in the lists, but that signifies naught. Yet in my benevolence, I shall give thee a chance to prove thyself. I have set for thee a simple task: a quest, sir, a quest! And surely all true knights desire a quest!"

'The king raised his voice so that it rang the length and breadth of the hall. "Ride thou, oh knight, from this realm," quoth he; "find and slay a dragon and bring back to me the head of that dragon. Then, and only then, canst thou take my one daughter to wife! Then, and only then, canst thou return to this land with thine honour intact!" And the king smirked, and the courtiers smirked, and then they sniggered and then they laughed out loud for, as all the world knoweth, there are no dragons.'

'Oh,' murmured Brenn, 'oh no.'

"'Tis quite droll really,' said Winterhued. 'But that was not the end of it, for as the throng dispersed, the king sent unto his daughter (who had not been present) and the knight, ordering their attendance at his private chambers. Even as they entered (she: puzzled and anxious, he: stern and silent), the princess spied beside the door her old lady-in-waiting, wringing timorous hands. And the girl's heart sank, for she knew that her secret had been betrayed.

'The king, his countenance purple, stepped up to the young knight and glowered up at him. But the knight turned unflinching eyes upon his sovereign lord.

"'I know how it is," quoth the king in a wrathful voice, "betwixt thee and my daughter; I know what thou hast done, sir! If thou didst hope that that would induce me to give thee my daughter's hand, thou wert gravely mistaken. Instead, I would like naught better than to give thee a traitor's death! But I am a benevolent man so I have granted thee exile, for that is what this is, the fool's quest is but my little jest. I am not my father, but I swear: if thou dost return to this land, thou canst expect naught but death!"

'The princess cried out and cast herself at the king's feet. "Father, I beg thee," she gasped, "send him not away! 'Twas all my doing; I am to blame, not he!"

'"Get up, thou disobedient wretch of a girl," growled the king, giving her an angry nudge with his foot. "Thou hast dishonoured the memory of thy mother. How she would be ashamed of thee!"

'But the princess remained prostrate. "Do not send him away," she sobbed. "It will break my heart."

'"What if I were to bring my liege a dragon's head?" asked the knight.

'The king sneered. "Thou art a fool," quoth he. "Verily, ye both are fools; mayhap my daughter the greatest for I cannot fathom how she could stoop so low as to see aught in an ill-bred gangrel knave such as thee. And what in the devil's name did she hope to achieve by it? Did she imagine I'd ever approve of such a tainted union? Fie!"

'"My question," calmly replied the knight, "hath not been answered, liege."

'The king gave a harsh laugh. "If thou dost bring me the head of a dragon," quoth he, "of course I shall honour my word. Now leave, sir. Quit this land, and if thou dost return while I yet live, thou art a dead man."

'And so it was that on the morn of the very next day, as a bitter wind moaned about the castle walls and plucked at the rain that wept from dolorous skies, the princess stood upon the drawbridge to bid farewell to her one true love. Tears flowed down her rain-wet cheeks. "I shall die when thou art gone," said she.

'"Nay," quoth the knight, "thou art strong and resolute. Thou shalt live and prosper, and mayhap forget me in time."

'"Never," whispered she, "for thou art my very heart."

'"As thou art mine," answered he. "To thee shall I be true for the rest of my days."

'He took himself gently from her embrace to fasten about her neck a moonstone upon a silver chain, and then turned and mounted his big chestnut courser. The horse, impatient for the road, tossed his head and danced.

'"I am so afraid," said the princess, "for the world is wide. Oh my love, wheresoever thou goest, hold onto thy life, for I would see thee again." Her voice sank to a sigh. "Know thee," she whispered, "that my father cannot live for as long as my love for thee shall last."

'Twice the knight spoke her name and then, smiling slightly, backed his horse across the bridge. The steel-shod hoofs rang hollowly upon the timbers. "Methinks," quoth he, "the king shall live long, so I must perforce go hunting dragons."

'With that, he wheeled his horse about and rode away; not alone, for he was accompanied by his squire, a laden packhorse and the well-wishes of every good person in the castle.

'But the princess clutched the moonstone at her neck and sank to her knees in the rain as she watched him ride down the street and through the town gate. She stayed there long after he had gone from view. Her old lady-in-waiting came out from the gateway to beg her to come within, but the princess stayed on her knees as the rain seeped through her cloak and chilled her to the bone. Still the tears flowed from her eyes to mingle with the falling rain and join the puddles about her sodden skirts. Eventually, it was the King's Champion himself who came forth from the castle, with tears in his eyes, to lift her in his arms and carry her within.

'Oh, little Brenn, thou canst imagine the woe that followed! The world, for a time, became loathsome to the girl. So stricken was she with anguish that she might not eat nor sleep; a disconsolate ghost she became, frightening her father half out of his wits.

'But the knight had called her strong and resolute and his words proved true; before too long her tears had dried and she had determined to never again display her heart to the world. So the years ran by and the princess did not sigh away their passing but set to busying herself with the cares of her country. Then, one day, she came to the realization that her anguished heart had... had almost... learned ease.'

Winterhued's breath caught in her throat. 'Dawn must surely be nigh,' she murmured after a time.

'That is a sad tale,' whispered Brenn.

'A tale of finished times. It is as naught when compared with our present plight, for here we lie, hostages to terror, helplessly waiting for life or for death.' Winterhued stroked her cousin's hair. 'Mayhap 'twere best I give it a happy ending,' she murmured, 'and tell thee that the princess in the story lived in a land called Golp where the sunshine is pink and the trees are purple, and that it is quite certain that she wasted not a moment in grieving. For everyone knoweth that a young girl's tears vanish faster than dew in the sunshine, and it was no time at all before she had quite forgotten the knight and met another handsome and noble youth who pleased her father greatly. And so, amidst much rejoicing, they were wed and lived happily ever after.'

'Oh no... no, I'm sure she was true to him,' sighed Brenn sleepily. She was silent for a time, as the cat at their feet turned around and settled once more. 'But... but why,' she asked hesitantly, 'did the princess not release the unicorn... in secret if her father would not agree to it?'

'Be assured she thought about it,' murmured Winterhued; 'every day of her life she thought about it, planned it, mulled over ways she could take the creature past the menagerie guards, down the bailey, past the guards stationed at the castle gate, and thence along the town street and past more guards at the town gate. And if she somehow succeeded at this impossible task, she was fearful of the irreparable rift it would open between herself and the king. She could but console herself with the knowledge that one day... one day... she *would* release him...'

'If he was smaller the princess could have taken him out through a secret passage.'

Winterhued laughed. 'There is only one which leads out of the castle and it was not built with unicorns in mind.'

Brenn wriggled comfortably in the soft, warm bed and nestled her head against the princess's shoulder. 'Is there... secret passage,' she asked, her words slurring as sleep overwhelmed her, 'leading... t'this chamber?'

'Hmm? Aye... there is one that leads hither. 'Tis very secret though and may only be discovered in autumn when the leaves turn gold.'

'How...?' murmured Brenn, but sleep took her even as the word left her lips.

'Sweet dreams, omniscient angel,' whispered Winterhued, "and mayest thou find more hope in them than I can in my memories...' It was but a moment later that she followed the girl into unconsciousness. Soundly, silently, the two of them slept curled together, while Thistle purred at their feet.

Outside the chamber's shuttered window the first faint light of dawn washed the margins of the empty eastern sky.

CHAPTER 9

The gong-farmer's son scrambled on his hands and knees along the low tunnel that ran between the inner-bailey well and the well within the keep. It was still dark, but a faint infusion of dawn light seeped into the tunnel from both ends. As he always did on the rare occasions that he passed this way, Stench wondered at the madman who had had this particular passage made, for it went from nowhere to nowhere and was cut through foundation rock. It was surely as old as the keep itself and that was an edifice with an ancient and bloody history.

Shivering violently, teeth chattering, the boy reached the tunnel's mouth and, squatting at its edge, looked up at the sides of the well-shaft. The bucket and chain had been wound up to the windlass, so to climb he must use what hand and foot holds the ancient masonry provided; a nearly impossible task when his hands and feet were so cold he'd lost all feeling in them. With an effort he managed to wriggle his toes, but the movement dislodged a few pebbles and sent them over the edge. He winced as the stones hit the water with a faint splash.

While he'd been waiting in the tunnel some hours ago, he'd heard the creature leave; a sound that had set his heart hammering. The noise: a scraping, grinding and crunching on broken stone, a whining and screeching of splintered timbers, spoke of something inconceivably heavy. The beast had taken to the air amongst a rain of rubble and with such a mighty thudding of wings it was as though the very weight of it cracked the sky.

It would have been sensible to carry out his planned excursion into the keep while the creature was away, but he could go nowhere in pitch darkness. Unbuckling his purse in the hope of finding the usual bits of candle-end, he'd discovered instead a small book wrapped in oilcloth. He'd forgotten that book, and he'd also forgotten how he'd tossed everything useful from his purse when salvaging it from his parents' vacated house. Cursing himself for a sentimental fool, Stench had eventually drifted into an uneasy sleep in which he dreamed he'd fallen to the bottom of the well, and there discovered the princess showing a map of the world to his father.

He wondered now whether he would ever again see his father. He'd always tried not to feel shame for him, but he couldn't help it: he was ashamed, and for no other reason than that his father was perfectly content with his lot in life. 'Born and bred a gong-farmer,' he'd say. "Tis a useful profession and well remunerated. My neighbours may turn up their noses, but my house is bigger than theirs, my children wear shoon and they never go hungry. And look thee,' he'd conclude, 'I got me the bonniest bride in all the land.' Stench's mother was indeed a pretty and clever woman, with a smile ever upon her face, though her hands were raw from the constant washing of her husband's malodorous raiment. Yet ashamed as he may have been of them, Stench loved his parents dearly and he loved his sister, and his heart hurt when he thought he might not see them again.

In his dream Stench's father had looked at the princess's map and, pointing to the Wild Lands, told her that he was taking his family thither to grow turnips on dragon dung. The princess had protested, saying it was hardly a good plan for the dragons would eat the turnips. All of a sudden, Stench had heard a dragon coming and he'd tried to run outside to protect the turnips, but his legs refused to work... and he'd woken with a start to hear, oh, far more nightmarish than anything his unconscious mind could summon, the real dragon returning to its lair in the keep. It brought with it a heart-pounding fear and the first faint light of dawn.

Stench looked up the well-shaft once more. He'd never had trouble with this climb in the past as the pointing between the masonry had crumbled in places leaving relatively easy holds for the hands and feet. But he'd had hands and feet then. His eyes told him he still did, but all he could feel was a hurting numbness at the end of each limb. And the last time he'd eaten was when they'd given him his blanket in the King's Hall and handed him a hunk of bread. How many hours ago had that been?

Feeling hollow and weak, he looked down the shaft. He knew the water was not a great distance below him, but the dawn light had not yet reached far enough into the darkness to illumine its surface. Stench could swim, but if he fell now he knew it would be almost impossible, slippery and frozen as he'd be, to find the hand and footholds to drag himself and the weight of his wet clothes from the water.

He rubbed his hands briskly together a few times then drew in a sharp breath. 'For Winterhued,' he whispered, and swung himself out from the tunnel entrance.

A few moments later he clambered breathlessly over the rim of the well into the keep's basement, his heart pounding. He slithered to the floor and lay there for a while, listening. The room, faintly lit by its one high, barred window, was stacked to the ceiling with cobweb-draped chests: forgotten repositories of perhaps five hundred years of Manydown's history. Hearing naught, Stench got to his feet, crossed the room and eased open its iron-grilled door. As silently as he could, he climbed the newel stair almost on his hands and knees, groping ahead for each worn tread in the depthless grey gloom. A smell of charred timber and flesh grew stronger with every step.

The door into the garrison quarters on the ground floor was choked with burnt beams and rubble, so the boy kept climbing, carefully, quietly. The next door was clear, and led out into the screens passage behind the old galleried hall.

He paused to pull his cloak tighter and draw its hood over his head. Dusty dried stuff fell from its folds as he did so, but distressingly, the garment seemed to have lost much of its pungency. He shrugged, drew breath and stepped through the door. Straight away his eyes were led upwards through a clear space at the top of the partly blocked portal that led from the screens passage into the hall. Instead of a view of gloomy stone walls and smoke-blackened rafters, he realised with a shock that he looked out into a thick fog that lay heavy and grey within the walls. The keep's roof and all of its internal walls and floors must have been broken, torched and swept aside to lie as mounded rubble at the bottom of a mere shell. Stench stepped back hurriedly into the doorway through which he'd just come as he realised with what precariousness the screens passage might have been clinging to the keep's despoiled walls.

At the very same moment he became aware that another glint of light had pricked its way through the rubble obstructing the hall doorway. Something that had been blocking the light, something out there beyond the doorway, had moved. He heard the thing draw breath like a blocked drain, and at the same moment a noisome stink reached his nostrils: a stink to rival a mountain of carcasses.

The boy clamped a hand over his nose and flattened himself against the doorjamb. He stood wide-eyed; hardly breathing. Through the door he saw a raven, flying above the keep, winging its arrow-straight way through the fog.

As the moments passed and nothing rose from the hall to tear him limb from limb, Stench attempted to disengage himself from the doorjamb; a task made difficult by the broken hinge that had ridiculously skewered the back of his collar. He managed to unhook himself after a bit of wriggling and hopping, but a mood of hopelessness had settled upon him, for what chance had a clumsy wretch such as he to find Auchencairn and his men amidst such wrack? He stood directionless for a time, until he became aware of an almost inaudible sound that had crept into his senses.

The dragon's breathing went on rasping and gurgling, but beyond that was another sound: a shorter, quicker echo. Stench stopped his own breath, but the sound went on, laboured, uneven, gasping. Slowly, he turned his head to the right and peered down the shadowy passage. Barely discernable in the furthest gloom he descried two human shapes upon the floor, one stretched out prone, the other hunched over it, head bowed.

The boy left the shelter of the doorway and crept along the passage, running his fingers along the time-grimed wall. As he drew nigh, the crouched figure glanced up and uttered a stifled gasp. Stench put a finger to his lips and pointed back to the portal from whence he'd come. He could see the squatting man clearly now: solidly built, he was obviously a bowman in his jack of quilted and studded fabric over a hauberk of chain mail. He wore an iron sallet on his grey head, but seemed to have lost his longbow. The man stretched upon the floor, and from whom came the laboured breathing, was half covered by a cloak, but his fine, fluted upper-body armour made it clear that he was a knight. His head was bare, his hair shrivelled and singed, and half of his young face was a bloodied, blistered and blackened horror.

Stench indicated the door again and leant to pick up the knight's feet and the bowman, understanding at last, climbed to his feet and got a grip under the knight's arms. The young man grunted as they lifted him, but they got him as silently as they could along the passage. A tall, strongly made man, he was no light weight, and the boy staggered with the effort as they eased him in through the door and down the narrow stair. They'd barely made ten steps before he was compelled to put the fellow down and try to regain some breath. The bowman slid down the curving wall and slumped upon the worn stone treads. 'There's only one door to the keep and it's choked with wreckage,' he whispered hoarsely, staring at the boy, 'so from whence, be it hell or earth, didst thou come?'

'Not from hell,' breathed Stench. 'I came looking for Sir Auchencairn.'

The knight stirred and moaned. He tried to sit up. 'Sir Auch…' he gasped, 'slain… burned…' He opened his clenched right hand. A gold chain lay coiled within it, and from its links hung a medallion of enamelled gold. The medallion was blackened and warped, but still discernable upon its face rode a knight at full gallop.

'Lie still, Sir Dechmont,' said the bowman, 'help hath come at last.' The knight put his head back down on the stair and closed his eyes. Each rasping breath was an effort.

'Help?' Stench said despairingly, then stopped and thought. 'We cannot get him out this way… we must go back up and along.'

'Back up?' whispered the bowman. 'That thing: it'll hear us, sniff us out…' The man glanced wide-eyed up the stairwell. ''Tis a monster: it seemeth half-dead already, yet our arrows, our cross-bow bolts, bounce off its hide like paper darts. Sir Auchencairn, bravest man that ever was, all aflame like a torch, got in close and stuck a lance in its side and we saw the black blood burst forth, but the thing swatted him down like a gnat, and then, not a jot diminished, took to the air in a fury.

'The keep's but a hollow shell, and the thing carries back its prey and drops it down into its stinking larder... we'll all end up there... meat to the slaughter. There's naught we can do...'

The boy frowned at the bowman, still thinking. 'Come on,' he whispered; 'no use in talking. Take his shoulders again. Quiet as ye can.'

The bowman struggled exhaustedly to his feet. 'Whither to?'

'The south-east tower... other end of the screens passage. I... I'm the gong-farmer's son, so I know. There's access to a latrine-pit.'

'*Latrine*-pit?'

'Do not worry, sir. The latrines in the keep are seldom used and there's a way thence to a drain that empties into the lake beside the water-postern.'

The bowman nodded and knelt over the wounded lord. 'I'm sorry, Sir Dechmont,' he murmured. 'We must divest you of your armour. We have a way to go, and ye be a heavy load for a mere lad and an old man who can't remember when he last ate.'

The two of them lugged the unencumbered knight back up the steep stairs, and silently, carefully, southward along the screens passage. Beneath his armour, across his right shoulder and chest, they had found his arming doublet burnt through to raw and blackened flesh. He moaned softly as they carried him.

They had almost reached the portal when a heart-stopping clamour arose at their backs. The keep shook as though rocked by an earthquake; the timbers they walked upon bounced and groaned. A great rasping intake of breath, a roar like the suck of a giant's bellows, seemed for a moment to steal the air from their lungs.

The boy dropped one of the knight's feet and half turned. He saw the passage floorboards explode upwards in a rain of splinters and he saw broken yellow claws, each as long as his arm, burst through the gap to scrabble and wrench at the broken timbers.

'Faster!' hissed the bowman and Stench made a grab for the knight's foot and broke into a stumbling run.

The bowman was already through the door when the boy felt the floorboards disappear from beneath his feet. Still holding onto the knight, he made a desperate plunge for the doorway and half fell down the first few steps as a boiling tongue of flame licked into the stairwell above them. Stench felt the immense heat of it on the back of his head, but he kept going, tripping, jumping, three stairs at a time, tearing his garments and skinning his shoulders on the rough walls but somehow staying on his feet. Down they went as the stair spiralled into darkness, the bowman's breaths coming in sobs and poor Sir Dechmont crying out as he was jolted and bumped against the walls. Eventually the stairs ended and they all tumbled down upon a floor of flagstones and lay gasping in the gloom of the tower's basement.

But even down in the stone-muffled depths of the south-east tower, Stench heard the angry thud of the creature's wings as it climbed amongst moiling streamers of fog into the brightening dawn sky. And strangely, he felt something else. It was as if, for just a moment, the air from those wings had washed him in sadness.

It never cries out, he thought; *it hath no voice. But, oh… its heart is broken.* He could not have said how he knew this but, for that brief moment, it had seemed to him as clear as the feelings within his own heart.

Up the most north-westerly spur of Iron Crag cantered the creature the colour of moonlight. Her hoofs clattered across exposed tree-roots and lichened rocks, and splashed through puddles of melted snow. The fog-shrouded trunks thinned, and then the mist swirled aside as she burst from the trees onto the open mountainside.

The summit lay somewhere above, seeming ever to recede from her as she ascended. Snow-melt rushed and tumbled down the deep ravines to either side of the spur, and the slope before her, purple-shadowed and patched with snow, shone in the low sun. The patches grew wider and deeper as she climbed.

At last, atop a rocky outcrop that jutted from a blanket of snow, she halted and turned. She looked down upon a sea of cloud, glinting yellow in the east where the early sun had begun its climb into the clear sky. Her mountain loomed from the billowing sea like a golden island; the sun ignited its snowy flanks in sparks of light.

But an icy wind stirred in the creature's heart. She looked up the mountain and saw her future: the days, the seasons, the years, flitting by as she danced alone under the sun and stars. She looked down the mountain, towards the road that led inexorably to the land of men, where fear and death lay as thick as the clouds. And then she turned her head towards the far-distant west and saw, as she'd known she would, the wide-winged raptor gliding on air. The sun had not yet touched the lands in the west, but the winged creature flew so high above the clouds that it flashed with glints of bronze as it spiralled.

Though the morning was quiet, it seemed to the little horned creature that the gulf of air that lay between her and that vast, ancient being vibrated with its noiseless scream.

The horned one turned thrice about the rocky outcrop. Then she leapt from the high place and ran downhill, following her footprints in the snow, back towards the trees and the lifting fog.

Far below Iron Crag's sun-dazzled summit, in a clearing at the base of its cloud-wrapped flanks, the knight woke beside the ashes of his fire. He rolled onto his elbow and sat up, looking about him at the thick fog.

'Hougo,' he called softly, and the horse appeared, looming whiter than the mist, with a few strands of grass trailing from his mouth. The chestnut, his red coat frosted with droplets of vapour, was as always a step behind the grey.

'Good morrow, gentlemen,' said the knight in a quiet voice, and the horses stood together with their dark eyes upon him as he raked a hand through his hair and extricated a twig from its long strands. Shivering in the bitter chill, he pulled on his boots and climbed painfully to his feet, and then stood for a while rubbing his old aching wound and looking down at Nal. The boy was huddled into a ball beneath his blanket and, but for his snoring, lay quietly. It appeared that his dreams had ceased to trouble him.

'Poor lad,' murmured the knight. He draped his own blanket and cloak over the boy and limped through the fog down to the stream, leaving a trail of frosted breath upon the hoary air. The twisted shapes of tree-trunks loomed grey through the mist; not a twig stirred and not a bird sang. Even the voice of the stream as it rushed down from the mountain seemed muted in the vapour-laden air.

The knight, gasping at the cold, drank from his cupped hands and washed the sleep from his eyes. As he straightened, he happened to glance upon a small hoof-print lightly etched in a patch of damp earth between the rocks at the stream's edge. Frowning, he knelt again to trace its delicate shape with a finger, and then rose to gaze up at the shrouded mountain. A puzzled smile curved his lips. For a time he cast about for more tracks, but the maker of that single print must have walked very lightly upon the earth for there was naught else for a human eye to discover.

The horses had watched him all the while and now the grey came to him, rubbed his head affectionately on the man's shoulder and gave him a gentle shove. The knight laughed softly. 'Horses for emperors,' he murmured. 'If ye could but talk, eh?' He collected the brush and groomed each horse, then set to saddling them in turn: carefully, methodically and kindly. As ever, he had no need to tie them to aught as he worked, for they stood happily beside him and indeed followed him wherever he went.

By the time he had finished, faint sunlight was filtering through the fog. He walked back to the sleeping boy and gently shook him by the shoulder. 'Come on lad,' he said, 'time to rise.'

The boy groaned horribly. 'Go away,' he mumbled.

'Go away?' asked the knight. 'And leave thee here, with naught but thy blanket? For I'm taking mine.'

He lifted his blanket and cloak from the lad as Nal moaned again and snuggled himself into a tighter ball. 'Don't wanna do this no more,' he muttered.

'I'm taking the groundsheet too,' said the man as he tugged it out from beneath the boy. Nal wailed as he was rolled off the oiled sheet, but remained wrapped within his bedroll and curled tight as a woodlouse. The knight sighed as he rolled up his own bedding within the groundsheet. 'Why must we go through this every day?' he asked equably. 'Come Nal, we've no breakfast, so the sooner we're away, the sooner we'll be in Wendur and eating.'

'Why can't we stay in Wendur when we get there?' came the boy's muffled mumble. 'I want to sleep tonight in a warm room... in a feather bed.'

'Feather bed? I doubt there's such a thing in Wendur... and I doubt thou hast ever slept in one in thy life.'

'Ye'd know, o' course,' muttered Nal sulkily. His blanket parted a little to reveal one bleary eye. 'But ye can't doubt I ever slept in a warm room... wi' the fire cracklin' and an 'ot meal in me belly... roas' beef, with a big 'unk o' bread to mop up the juices.'

'After a hot bath, no doubt,' said the knight. He stood looking down at the boy, his arms crossed upon his chest, and his face expressing naught but patience and good-humour.

'Ye're always on about a bath,' grumbled Nal, withdrawing into his blanket again. 'I don' need no bath!'

'Nay, thou dost smell like a rose.' The knight gave the boy a nudge with his foot. 'Come lad, get up. Today is the first day of spring; the horses are saddled and eager to be away. All thou needst do is help me with my armour and then we'll be on our way to breakfast.'

The boy groaned again and pulled his blanket tight. ''Tis icy out there. Me 'ands'll be too cold for buckles an' points.'

'Thou shalt warm up; the fog lifteth; before long the sun shall shine.'

The boy, moaning and muttering, began at last to extricate himself from the tangled ball of his bedroll. 'Why bother wi' armour?' he whined, his teeth already starting to chatter with the cold. 'Ye won't need it choppin' wood.' The blanket fell from his shoulders as he sat up, and he shivered violently.

'Aye, that's true enough," said the knight. 'But inconveniently, and though I've little else, I retain some pride. I would like to look like a knight, and if I went about in this rusty doublet, I'd be arrested as a beggar on a stolen horse.'

'No… ye wouldn't,' said Nal, and coming from him that sounded almost like praise. The boy was upright at last, stamping his feet and hopping about like a demented scarecrow. 'Besides,' he said, 'Yer armour's not much better.' He hopped over to where it lay on the ground, wrapped in oiled cloth, and gave it a kick. 'If beggars wore armour it'd look like this.'

'Stand up, old rogue,' said the knight to his horse. The stallion had been pawing the ground so insistently that he'd dug a hole. At the knight's admonishing tone, he stopped pawing for half a moment, shook his head with a jingle of harness and snorted steam like a small dragon.

The knight knelt to unwrap his armour from the oiled cloth. 'Naught wrong with my armour, lad,' he said. 'I won this in Sardhana, three thousand leagues from here, and 'tis unlikely that even the kings of these northern realms possess its equal.'

'Looks like rusty tin to me,' muttered Nal, fumbling with the buckle of a pauldron. The armour was icy and his fingers hurt just touching it. 'And there's a big dent 'ere.'

'Aye, one amongst many. But they're easily remedied. A good smith…'

'Do smiths charge money?' interrupted the boy, and the knight laughed and made no reply.

Nal cursed through his chattering teeth as he went about his squire's task, stopping frequently to chafe his hands together or to dance about, stamping his frozen feet. 'I'm so 'ungry,' he said for the sixth time.

"Twill be but an hour or so, lad, and thou'lt be in Wendur... eating.'

The knight, clad now in his steel cuirass, pauldrons and vambraces, rolled the bedding into one bundle and attached it to the red horse's saddle. He had a little difficulty as even the placid rounsey had begun to dance about in his eagerness to be off.

'Mount up if thou canst, lad,' laughed the knight, holding the chestnut's bridle. 'Methinks our horses had a glamour cast upon them during the night, and today thou shalt ride an emperor's courser.'

Nal shook his head and scowled. ''E's barkin' mad,' he muttered under his breath. Just as he'd almost got his foot in the stirrup, with his knee up beside his ear, the horse sidestepped and the boy would have toppled onto his face had the knight not caught his arm.

'He's mettlesome today,' said the knight as Nal managed to clamber up at his second attempt, 'but leave him be; don't hang onto the reins. Thou hast no need to steer or stop him, for he'll do naught but follow Hougo.'

The boy sneered. 'I know 'ow to ride,' he muttered, trying to find the stirrup with his right foot.

'I've noticed,' said the knight. As soon as he let go of the chestnut's head, the gelding ran backwards. Nal, leaning forward to grab the reins, kicked the horse in the ribs and the horse threw up his head, whacking the boy in the forehead with his neck. Nal abandoned the reins to clutch at the pommel as the horse danced on the spot.

The knight turned away with a shake of his head, crossed to his own mount and sprang into the saddle. The old grey stallion snorted, prancing sideways, and the knight grinned. 'Let us go hunting on our princely steeds,' he said, turning the horse onto the road. He sat easily in the saddle, his reins loose.

'Huntin' what?' muttered Nal incredulously. 'Ye're barkin' mad.'

'Dragons!' said the knight with a laugh. 'I never told thee of dragons, did I?'

Hearing no answer, he glanced round to find that only the red horse followed him, empty-saddled. He halted the grey to watch Nal clamber out of a puddle and brush ineffectually at his wet raiment. 'Don' ye say nuthin',' said the boy. 'Ye give me an ill-mannered cart'orse to ride and laugh when I come unstuck, but I tell you, ye're steadfastly unstuck in the 'ead. Dragons! Ye're as mad as a bottled boggle.'

'Climb up, Nal,' said the knight, holding the fidgeting chestnut's bridle. 'Leave him alone or he'll keep putting thee on the ground. He is laughing at thee.'

'Laughin'?' sneered Nal. 'Only a madman can 'ear a horse laughin'.' He scrambled once more into the saddle, mumbling under his breath. 'Ye're mad, barkin' mad.'

'No doubt,' said the knight as he turned his horse once more. 'But who would not be when all they dream of lieth within reach, yet they must ride by?' He looked round at Nal. 'The horses want to stretch their legs, so leave the reins alone, hang on to the saddle and keep watch for low-hanging branches... and dragons,' he added.

'Oh no...' muttered the boy.

The grey plunged sideways with a clatter of weapons, was given his head and leapt forward upon the road. A rain of mud and turf flew up from his great hoofs and showered down around Nal, a large clod smiting him in the right eye and knocking him backwards. Squinting through the blinding mud, he just had time to make a grab for the pommel before the red horse, with a great clashing of accoutrements and the ominous tinkle of a loose shoe, launched himself after the stallion. 'Aaaahhh...' wailed the boy. The fog swirled and the ground shook. Soon, fading through the thinning mist, there was only the thunder of their going.

The climbing sun slanted its rays through dissipating mist. It bathed the stones of mute Castle Lawhill and brushed the tops of the lake's whispering wavelets with pale gold. Hushed lay the castle and the town, and still lay the roads and villages, the manors and farmhouses all about. From here and there, muffled by distance, came the lowing of unmilked cows, and closer to hand the stridulous croaking of seven ravens, like ragged remnants of the night, that hopped and pecked upon the lake's grisly shore. Sometimes they paused, cocked their clever heads sideways, and glanced up with eyes agleam to where, far, far above, a black and dissonant shape glided in spirals upon the breathless gulf of sky.

But within the castle only pinpricks of the luminous morn had penetrated the boarded up windows and arrow loops. In the south-east tower, in candlelight and firelight, Princess Winterhued sat before her mirror as Lady Brenn twisted her dark plaits into a lop-sided pile.

'I'm not clever at this, am I?' said Brenn. 'Lady Ulidia would be dismayed by my attempts. Mayhap my lady should have let her come.'

'Ulidia must do as she's bid and look to herself for a change. All my ladies are relieved of their duties but for thee, so we must do the best we can.'

The princess reached up to re-arrange her hair and soon, with Brenn's help, had it bound within a pearl-sewn headdress, topped by a coronet. The high-waisted gown that she wore was of simple grey-blue bombazine with a black underskirt. Winterhued contemplated her reflection in the mirror. 'Alack,' she murmured, touching the base of her neck with her fingertips, 'my moonstone would look well with this. But... never mind, I look respectable again and I thank thee, Brenn.' She rose from her seat. ''Tis thy turn now, little cousin,' she said. ''Twill be a joy to tame thine autumn tresses.'

So Brenn, her cheeks flushed, sat down in the chair and smiled with pleasure as the princess combed and plaited her hair and tried this silly style after that, and the twain were blithe for a time, forgetting the horror that waited without that fire-lit chamber.

'I have a question,' said Brenn, growing serious. 'When I touched the unicorn, and when m'lady touched him... the world changed. I felt that I saw the Truth and now am a better person... infinitely better. Could it be... what if..?' She struggled to find the words. 'If that happened for everyone, could we mend the world?'

'I have wondered that,' answered Winterhued. 'But some of the huntsmen touched the unicorn, so too did the Duke of Dumpling, and they were not changed. The king too had a desire to touch the creature, and I'm afraid I encouraged him in the hope he might become instantly wise. But the opposite befell; he became so wrathful and frightened that he could scarcely speak for days. He is sure that mankind standeth at the pinnacle of all life, with himself at the very top; he cannot contemplate that he is but part of a great web and of no more consequence to the world than a water-beetle... or a unicorn.'

'I dreamt of my unicorn,' said Brenn, suddenly remembering; 'she was standing in an oak grove watching something... watching so intently. I no longer dream of wings.'

'I dreamt too,' said Winterhued. 'A dream I have dreamt before... of a mountain-range; its heights strewn with monstrous bones that fill me with despair. There used to be wings in that dream, but now the wings are gone and there is only emptiness... and bones.'

'Dragon bones?' whispered Brenn.

'Perhaps,' murmured the princess. Brenn watched her in the mirror as she absently tidied a few strands of the girl's hair; her beautiful face looked so sad.

'The princess... in m'lady's story...' asked the girl tentatively, 'after her true love departed... did she ever *dream* of him? A *real* dream?'

Winterhued gazed back at Brenn in the glass. 'Aye, she dreamt,' she whispered, 'and just to exist had to push all thoughts of that dream from her mind. But sometimes it can still make her weep. She dreamt that he lay nigh unto death, grievously wounded, and in a fever called out her name.' Brenn stood up and put her arms about the princess, feeling the raggedness of her breath. 'I think... nay, I know,' sighed Winterhued, 'that he liveth yet, but how... and in what, perhaps diminished, circumstances...'

She was interrupted by a timid knock at the door and gently extricated herself from the girl's embrace. 'See to the door, my dear,' she said.

Brenn left her side reluctantly, walking backwards, to discover the newly promoted chambermaid at the threshold. It was Eudora's second visit that day, for she had come shortly after dawn to tend the fire. Now she had returned, following the princess's instructions, bearing a bag of Brenn's belongings and two of her gowns over one arm. Her eyes on the floor, she sidled into the chamber and bobbed a curtsey.

'I thank thee, Eudora,' said Brenn and the maid flinched. She glanced up, but not high enough to meet Brenn's eyes. As Brenn took the gowns from her, she saw how the girl's hands shook, and how pallid she was.

'Art thou ill?' she asked. 'Here, put the bag down and come sit by the fire.'

Eudora looked up, her eyes wide and as blue as the leadwort flowers that grew on the lakeshore. A salt tear had dried upon her right cheek leaving a shining track like the trail of a snail across her white skin.

'Sit thee down,' said Brenn. She draped her gowns across a corner of the princess's bed and then returned to the girl. 'Hast thou eaten? Here... we have compote and bread remaining from our breakfast.'

Winterhued passed a hand across her eyes tiredly. 'Thou art unwell, child?' she asked. 'Thou dost look wan.'

'N... nay, your highness,' stammered Eudora, 'if it please your highness... I am hale. If it please... I must go... work to do...' She backed towards the portal but Brenn had already spread preserve on a slice of bread and now put it into her hand.

'Try not to be afraid,' she murmured as the girl fumbled behind her back for the door-latch. 'She will look after us... keep us safe. And the army will come. Be not afraid.'

Eudora looked up at Brenn as more tears trickled down her face. 'I am not worthy, your ladyship,' she breathed. 'I shall never be worthy.' She got the door open, bobbed a curtsy, then turned and fled across the antechamber to the stairs.

Brenn was shutting the inner door when she heard a man's voice coming from the stairwell. She stood and listened.

'Thou dost let in the cold,' said the princess, who now sat at her writing-table.

'Someone is in the stairwell,' said Brenn, half closing the door, 'talking to Eudora.' As quick footsteps crossed the antechamber she opened it again and was surprised to find that Eudora had returned and that her tears had been wiped away.

'The Marquess of... of Carry... of Carringdale is without,' she announced in a firmer voice. 'He wisheth to speak...'

'Sir Almendral!' cried Winterhued, starting up from her table and scattering several parchments. 'Come in, sir, prithee, come in!'

A man with blue-grey eyes entered the chamber; the same man that Brenn had first seen on that fateful night (oh, it seemed weeks past, but was actually no more than a day and a half). He was of middle height and lean as a hound; he looked as though he had spent most of his life in the saddle. His straight dark hair was greying and trimmed at shoulder-length, and he was garbed in black. 'Courage, lass,' he said to Eudora as she curtsied and left. He turned to bow to the princess.

'Almendral,' said Winterhued.

'Winterhued,' said he. 'What hath my lady been at, terrifying that maid half out of her senses?'

'Me? Terrifying?'

'Aye: with too much kindness methinks. Low creatures like that want kicking and cursing, not kindness.'

'Ah... so that is how thou didst cheer her up: thou gav'st her a kick!'

'Yea, forsooth, and greatly encouraged was she to be kicked by her countryman, and to find him a marquess no less!' He suddenly transformed himself into Eudora, with her slump-shouldered stance, her dangling hands and her flinchingly hesitant glance. 'You... a... a marquess?' he said, and he'd captured the quaver in her voice so perfectly that Brenn could not help but laugh out loud.

'Oh, I shouldn't laugh,' she said, putting a hand over her mouth.

'Nay, thou shouldst not,' said Winterhued, even though she had smiled, just a little. "Tis ill-bred behaviour to make sport of a defence-less girl...'

'Alas, my mongrel breeding doth show itself again,' said Sir Almendral. 'I crave your pardon, gentle ladies... oh, and thine, little Thistle.' The princess's cat had wrapped herself around his legs, purring, and he bent to stroke her.

'I think, sir, thou hast not met my cousin,' said Winterhued, putting a hand on Brenn's shoulder. 'Lady Brenn, daughter of my cousin Lita, and of Sir Dartford of Drumalis.'

Sir Almendral turned his gaze upon Brenn before stooping to kiss her hand. 'Dartford's daughter, eh?' he said, straightening. 'What a fortunate girl!'

'Fortunate, sir?' asked Brenn doubtfully.

'Fortunate that ye look nothing like him,' said the marquess, and once more Brenn laughed out loud.

She decided that she liked Sir Almendral; he was not dull at all and now she even thought him handsome in a hawklike way. And Thistle liked him too. (Having run away from Deccan, the cat had proved herself an astute judge of men.) But of course, he was not the one, she reminded herself. *He* – the one – was somewhere unknown and far away, on a quest for a dragon...

'Can my lady spare a moment?' asked Sir Almendral and the princess wordlessly took his hand and led him to a bench beside the hearth.

'No more of "my lady",' she said. 'Thou art my friend... or hast thou forgotten?'

Brenn remained awkwardly by the door. 'Where doth my lady wish me to wait?' she asked.

'Here, come sit with us.'

The girl did as she was bid, sinking into the cushions beside the hearth and picking up a long twig to poke at the flames. She half leant against a tapestried screen upon which a yellow fox and a russet fawn peered from amongst woven flowers and foliage. Presently the cat came to curl up alongside her and her purring was as loud as a hive of bees in a sunny garden.

'Alas, Ali,' said Winterhued, from the bench at Brenn's back, 'thou hast avoided the court for so long, and now... what ill-hap to effect thy return at this time!'

"Aye,' he said laughing, 'but rather say "good-hap" for had I not come I'd have regretted missing such an ado. I worry only that my wife shall fret if I am late home...' He hesitated for a moment and then whispered (but not quietly enough for Brenn's sharp ears): 'The "secret passages"... may I mention them?'

'Of course.'

'Can I... can we not *all* get out of the castle along those passages?'

'Alas, no. Every passage doth but lead from one part of the castle to another... and the only one that doesn't hath been hopelessly flooded for many a year. Even the latrine shafts won't help us.'

'Aye, they'd only lead out to the lake or the base of the walls and there is no advantage there. My poor lass will have to wait and worry while I enjoy the diversion.'

'Rejoice that she and the children are far from this creature come to destroy us... or, so it seemeth, to entertain thee.'

'Soft, I am not such a churl; I mourn for the slain and know that we may join them yet. But verily, ye and I cannot but see how droll it is to be visited by a dragon. What sayeth your prophetic father to such a... an improbable event?'

'Prophetic?' Winterhued laughed sadly. 'Alas, my father appeareth unable to recall any words he ever said on the subject.' She was silent for a long moment. 'He rememb'reth not how he did wound me, Ali.'

'Not just you, dear heart.'

'No,' replied Winterhued softly.

There was silence for a time. Brenn poked at a glowing log until it collapsed in a shower of sparks then threw her twig into the flames. She twisted round to see that Winterhued was weeping silently against Sir

Almendral's shoulder as he held her close. Tears pricked Brenn's own eyes as she found another stick to poke at the flames.

'Enough of that,' said the marquess suddenly. 'I possess such impoverished stores of sympathy, I'd be loath to waste any.'

The princess sniffed. 'Heartless churl,' she said and laughed a little.

'That's better,' said he. 'Lady Brenn?' Brenn threw her twig into the fire and turned round. The marquess still had an arm about Winterhued's waist as she wiped away her tears, but now he leaned forward to regard Brenn with a puzzled frown. 'Tell me,' he said, 'what sort of dragon flyeth higher than a castle?'

'I do not know,' she answered, confused, even as she noticed Winterhued roll her eyes heavenwards and sigh.

The marquess's mouth curled into a lop-sided grin. 'Any sort,' said he, 'for castles cannot fly.'

Brenn laughed and the princess groaned. 'Hoyday, a jest,' said she with another sigh. 'Thou art an incorrigible fool, sir, like all of thine arrant family.'

'Arrant and errant; yet ye do love us.'

'I do. Thou didst help mend my heart, Ali; thou and dearest Fennia. But thoughtlessly ye took yourselves off to the marches where I never do see you. Oh Ali, I shall weep no more tears of self-pity, but there are times when I feel alone. Alone and fearful.'

'Fearful? But... ye be Winterhued, surrounded by people that love you...'

'I know that I am loved,' said the princess, 'and am grateful for it. But love and understanding are not the same thing.'

'Understanding?' said Almendral. 'Ye want that too? Ye're marvellous greedy, my dear.' He rose from the bench and stood, arms crossed, with his back to the fire. 'But yea, I am sorry,' he said; 'sorry for abandoning you... and for my abject cowardice. I should have come more often to court, but ye know why I stay away. In the marcher lands half of us bear Callunian blood and we live harmoniously enough. Here, anyone would think I had the pox.'

Winterhued looked up at him tenderly. 'Alas,' she sighed, 'people are so... disappointing. Yet, things shall change...'

'People will become clever when ye are queen.'

'Thou mayest laugh, but I hope, nay: *believe*, that if fate doth allow me to rule, I can make some *little* change. Thou knowest I have thought much upon this; upon whether it might be possible to make a populace clever.' Winterhued's eyes shone as she warmed to her discourse. 'One may teach every person to read and write, yet those skills are but handmaids to understanding. An education, a real education, in which one may learn all the best that man hath ever thought upon and written down, surely gives one a high point from which to view the world; a point from which to search, criticise and question... and to improve.'

'That sounds very fine, Winter, but ye know as well as I that this world will always be ruled by ignorance, superstition and bigotry. For 'tis sooth that all men and women possess the means to think critically, to search for truths, to employ reason and rationality, but how few ever take the trouble to do so? For most, even those with an education, 'tis easier to fall into an indolent habit of stupidity, easier to believe blindly in unreasoned prejudices, easier to swallow a ranting fanatic's crackbrained doctrines.'

Winterhued laughed sadly. 'Aye. And when people cannot or will not think for themselves, 'tis simple for those with the loudest voices to tell them how to.'

'I trust then ye've been practising your shouting so that ye may stand up on the battlements and bawl enlightened truths to your subjects.'

Winterhued smiled at the thought. 'When one has power,' she said, 'one can be loud without shouting. Think of King Bragdo, or my ruthless grandsire: the merest whisper in an ear could change a man's mind on the instant and have him ardent for something he had despised but a moment before. Even my father with his thoughtless blathering may utter any idiotic, even harmful, thought that comes into his head and have people eager to yeasay him just because he is the king.'

Brenn stared at the fire with round eyes and wondered if she should cover her ears.

'Hush... he is still the king, Winter,' said the marquess.

'He is an empty-headed old gander,' said Winterhued, 'and I am so angry with him.' She rose and began to pace to and fro between the hearth and the bed. 'All these years have I ruled this land in his name and still he prateth on about the need for a man to guide me. He would marry me off to any idiot...'

'*Any* idiot?' said Almendral with a laugh. 'Yet he would not allow you to marry the idiot of your choice. But Winter,' he said, growing serious, 'all of Manydown knoweth that ye *do* rule, and that ye *shall* rule. Even in my far-flung corner the people know... they know. Though the righting of grievances, the reforms, the impartial justice for all subjects come in the king's name, thanks is always given to Princess Winterhued.'

The princess turned to the marquess with a frown. 'Yet I am afraid; the king still wieldeth power, and hath powerful adherents who do not wish to see a woman upon Manydown's throne. They have been whispering in his ear...'

'Whispering what? Winter, there is no one else...'

'There was a bastard born,' interrupted Winterhued, 'last year; did ye not hear of it? A boy, born dead and the poor mother, a servant girl... too young and too small, dead also...' The princess's voice trembled. 'He cared not. He hath no compassion, no remorse. He was boastful of that dead child; it gave him and his cronies hope...'

Almendral shook his head dismissively. 'Hope!' he said. 'What hope is there in a dead bastard? Winter, there is only you. *Ye* are the rightful heir and on the day ye are crowned queen all Manydown shall rejoice! *All* Manydown, even the king's cronies if they have a morsel of sense.'

Winterhued sighed. 'And if the king doth remarry? He hath proved he is not too old to father a son.'

'Did he not swear never to take another wife? Would he break his word so blithely? Is he fool enough to bring unrest to this land and open a door to civil war? I do not like your father, but I cannot believe he is completely without sense. Nay, Winter, ye shall be crowned, and rejoicing loudest of all shall be those peasant girls who clamour for logic and rhetoric…'

Frowning, Winterhued shook her head. 'Thou dost overestimate my father's sanity, Ali. As for peasant girls, thou mayest scoff, yet if my father, if the dragon, do but grant me the chance… thou sayest that education is pointless because people are stupid, but who knoweth what may ensue if every person is educated?'

The princess resumed her restless pacing. As she turned away the marquess, still leaning beside the hearth, caught Brenn's upturned eye and flashed her a grin. 'Tush, Winter,' he said, 'ye may be the cleverest person in all of Manydown, but where is the sense in your scheme to educate peasants? What could a peasant girl do with an education?'

'I hope she'd learn to think for herself.'

'And what cause would a peasant girl ever have to think for herself? She can leave that to her father, to her husband.'

Winterhued rounded on the marquess. 'Ali!' she exclaimed, 'how many times have we discussed this? Trying to make thee see sense is as much use as arguing with a dead cockroach.'

Almendral turned to Brenn with such an exaggerated look of hurt on his face that she had to laugh. 'Verily Lady Brenn,' he said sadly, 'your cousin is not nice, for every time we converse, sooner or later she must liken me to a pile of dung or a dead cockroach.'

The princess uttered an impatient, wordless exclamation and resumed her pacing. Leaning down, the marquess cupped a hand over the side of his mouth and made a pretence of speaking confidentially in Brenn's ear. 'Have ye ever tried to trick her?' he whispered, loudly. 'No? Then ye should try it, for it is good sport; she is so easily gulled.' He straightened with a self-satisfied smile. 'For one of the reasons I was eager to see her,' he continued, 'was to inform her that Fennia and I have had built a school for poor children in Carradale; for girls as well as boys.'

Winterhued spun about. 'Ali, thou knave! This is brave news! Why, Carradale will be the cleverest place in all Manydown!' With a look of wonder on her face, she came to the marquess and took his hands within her own.

'I begin to think,' said he, 'that I must needs open a school of laughter and tomfoolery just for you, Winter; ye are become so sad and serious. Methinks ye spend too many hours closeted with dreary dotards.'

'How may I laugh when my father hath become mine enemy? How may I jape when a fell beast hath come to destroy us? When my people wait in fear and trembling...'

''Tis clear,' said Almendral, 'ye've not heard the good news. We may all escape the dragon yet, for it hath been discovered that the beast will not kill a man if he doth carry a cabbage.'

The brief look of hope that had come to Winterhued's face changed to disbelief. 'A cabbage,' she said.

The marquess nodded, his face serious. 'Yea, 'tis sooth,' he said. 'The trick is to carry the cabbage very, very fast...'

'Jackanapes!' Winterhued picked up a cushion and swung it at his head.

'...or underground if possible...' said he, ducking neatly and backing away.

'Buffoon!'

'...or better still, in Balasore or Ormsary.' He ducked again as the cushion was hurled at him, and then turned to run as the princess snatched up another and came after him. Two strides and he was at the bed; he vaulted over it but caught his foot in the hangings and fell with a crash to the floor. The little cat, startled from her dreams, leapt up from the fireside and darted away to hide in the wardrobe.

The marquess, after extricating himself from a tangle of curtain and counterpane, peered cautiously over the edge of the bed. Instantly a cushion came hurtling at him with deadly accuracy, bouncing off his head. At a glance from Winterhued, Brenn jumped to her feet and armed herself for war, and for the next few minutes every time the marquess showed any part of himself above the bed, he was pelted with a barrage of soft missiles.

With all the laughter and delighted shrieks, and the cries for mercy, it was some time before anyone noticed the banging on the chamber door. Brenn, still giggling, ran to open it as Winterhued composed herself and the marquess, kicking aside a few cushions, emerged dishevelled from behind the bed.

One of the guards from the watch-room below stood at the door. He was a narrow man garbed in a black livery jacket bearing the king's badge of a sunburst, worn over chain mail. After he'd bowed low, he stood with his narrow head ducked down between his narrow shoulders like a malnourished tortoise.

'Beggin' 'Er 'Ighness' pardon,' he mumbled, 'for any intrusion. I wot not whever I should disturb 'Er 'Ighness over such a fing.' He kept his eyes lowered as he spoke. ''Tis that boy; that boy what's always everywhere. 'E doth claim... the miscreant... that 'e's acquainted wiv 'Er 'Ighness.'

'Boy?' asked Winterhued, stepping forwards. 'Dost thou mean the gong-farmer's son?'

'Aye m'lady, beggin' 'Er 'Ighness' pardon, but that's the one.'

'Where is he? He's hale, not injured, not in trouble?'

''E's 'ale enough m'lady, though 'e doth stink. 'E's down below.' The fellow gestured at the floor with his thumb. ''E's sayin' 'e 'as news of Sir Auchencairn and that 'e's found Sir Dechmont. I wot not whever to believe 'im, m'lady.'

'Why wouldst thou not believe him?' exclaimed the princess. 'Brave boy; I dread, but must hear his news. Come Sir Clown, thou shouldst meet this gong-farmer's son.'

Brenn darted out to the antechamber to collect the princess's cloak and her own, but Winterhued shook her head. 'Nay, my dear,' said she, as the marquess draped the cloak about her shoulders, 'I would have thee remain here.'

'But why?' protested Brenn.

'Because I wish it. Here thou art warm and safe, and... and thou canst keep Thistle safe too. If the wait is irksome there are my books; I have left one upon my writing table that thou shalt like.' She did not wait for a reply, but turned and crossed the antechamber as the guard hurried to open the outer door for her. As Brenn stared after the princess with a frown, the marquess stepped up to her and bowed gallantly. He told her what an unexpected pleasure it had been to meet her, instructed her to close the door to keep the cold out, and then he was gone too.

Brenn shut the inner door, then threw her cloak to the floor. 'Warm and safe,' she muttered, stamping her foot. 'I just want to *see* something!' But she paused at a sudden thought and a wondering smile lit up her face. 'I saw something last night,' she said. She hugged herself and began a little dance across the floor; round and round she went, lost in enchanted memory, smiling and dreaming.

CHAPTER 10

The gong-farmer's son tripped on the steep, worn stairway, jumped down two steps, teetered for a heartbeat, then regained his balance and kept going... down, down, down to see the king. His hands were clammy with sweat and his knees felt weak.

'Take care, Ancaios,' came Princess Winterhued's soft voice behind him. The princess was his friend, therefore he should not be afraid of her empty-headed father: so he told himself. But that empty-head was the king, and it was not every day that a humble menial such as he got to stand before the highest man in the land.

A guard went before him with a torch, and its fitful light illuminated the curving walls of the stairwell and its eroded steps. A smell of mildew and ordure pervaded the narrow space and the boy's apprenticed nose told him that the Watchtower's latrines were in need of attention. *I shall tell Father*, thought the boy, until he remembered that his father was likely leagues away, on the road to who-knows-whither.

'Why the king doth listen to that worm, Gunford,' muttered the princess at his back, 'I know not. This must be the most wretched place in all of Lawhill.'

It will suit me then, thought Ancaios, for though he had eaten well, scrubbed his face and hands, combed his hair and put aside his stinking cloak, he was still clad in the most wretched garments in all of Lawhill.

He reached the bottom of the stairs and passed through a portal into a gloomy chamber; as Winterhued entered behind him several figures got to their feet. Ancaios could not find the boldness to raise his eyes long enough to identify his Liege Lord, but he bowed in the direction of the only figure to have remained seated.

He felt Winterhued's hand on his shoulder, pushing him forward. 'Father. My lord,' said she. Glancing back at her, he saw that tears for Sir Auchencairn still shone upon her cheeks. 'All unbidden, this courageous youth faced great danger to enter the keep. There he discovered the fate of brave Sir Auchencairn, and furthermore carried forth Sir Dechmont, nephew to your friend Drumrock. That young knight now lies in the infirmary, carefully tended but perilously close to death.'

Ancaios, humble son of a turd-shoveller, rose from another bow and looked into the face of the most powerful man in all Manydown. The king, who was sitting on a fur-draped truckle bed feeding the remains of his meal to a mournful hound, regarded the boy with little more than vague interest. He was a handsome, grey-haired old man, with an aquiline nose and straight, black brows above dark eyes, but an indolent life had trebled his chin and swollen his belly to fabric-straining corpulence.

'Poor old Auchencairn, eh?' he said.

He looked Ancaios up and down and raised an eyebrow. 'Who... *what*... is the boy?' he asked the princess, his chins wobbling. There were greasy smears around his mouth.

A sweaty man in a steel breastplate stepped up beside the king. (*Argh, no... not him,* thought Ancaios with a sinking heart.) 'I know him,' said the man with a snarl. 'Aye, I know him. This be the gong-farmer's insolent son; a rude drudge with ideas above his station.'

Winterhued rounded on him. 'I failed to hear his highness asking for thy rancorous vituperation, Gunford,' she said quietly. Although tears still marked her cheeks, she glared at him with such intensity that he backed away until he came up against the wall, and there he stood, sneering and sweating.

'Do not heed that quaking bigot,' she said to her father. 'This boy is worth twenty of him. He is clever, brave and resourceful and whatever his lineage, my lord should recall that it is an old one; good men who have served our family for generations. Indeed, our lives would be most unpleasant without their diligence. This courageous lad hath gone by ways dangerous and unknown, into the very lair of the *dragon*...' ('Dragon? Pshaw,' hissed the king) '...into the lair of the dragon, where he hath discovered the truth of Sir Auchencairn's valiant demise, and delivered Sir Dechmont and a bowman. I myself have spoken to the bowman...'

'What's *he* doing here?' interrupted the king. He jabbed an indignant finger over Ancaios' shoulder towards the door. The boy looked round and saw that Sir Almendral had entered the chamber. He bowed a little too extravagantly, then stood against a mildewed wall hanging and smirked.

'As my lord knoweth, the Marquess of Carradale is my friend,' said Winterhued, 'and I did invite him to accompany me hither.' She spoke quietly but there was a subdued anger in her voice.

'What's he doing in Lawhill?' The king's face had turned red.

'I but came here on a little business, my liege,' said the marquess politely; 'dull business that's of no interest to anyone but myself and my family.'

'Huh, thy traitorous family! Still breeding up there like verminous mongrels? And that arrogant villain, thy father; still alive is he? A doddering dotard? Senile and fat as a hog?"

The marquess's smirk turned into a smile and he looked down at the floor to hide it. 'The duke is none of those things, my liege,' he replied, 'but he is alive.'

'Must be a drivelling bag of bones then.'

'Father!' protested the princess. Her tears had dried and there were spots of angry colour upon her cheeks. 'My lord may not like the duke, but he doth forget that Arracan and his family are well nigh all that standeth betwixt Manydown and the warring hordes in Angerona.'

Sir Almendral looked up from the floor and regarded the furiously sneering king with a friendly smile. 'We have, my liege, ofttimes considered stepping aside from our self-appointed role,' said he, 'and leaving the defence of the northern borders to his highness' favourites, the Neaths. Doth my liege not agree that Potrimpos would look splendid at the head of an army? Certes, the very sight of him would strike crippling fear into the hearts of our warlike neighbours.'

'Hence, thou insolent wit-snapper!' spat the king, gesticulating towards the door. 'See thou, daughter, the company thou keepst? A galling braggart…'

'Ye do mistake him,' said Winterhued. 'He hath but reminded my lord of his family's invaluable and faithful service…'

'Faithful?' interrupted the king. 'Pah! Those rag-tag dogs do but serve their own interests. Manydown hath her army! We do not need that traitorous half-bred rabble…'

Some time ago the gong-farmer's son had surreptitiously shuffled back from the centre of the chamber and now stood with his shoulders pressed against the wall, as round-eyed and gape-jawed as a frozen haddock. He heard the princess raise her voice and call her father an envious and dim-sighted dotard, and he heard the king call Winterhued a fishwife and a bad-tempered, disobedient chit. 'Thine ill-fated mother would be ashamed of thee if she were alive!' he shouted. 'Forsooth!'

answered the princess in disgust. 'She would be far more ashamed of you!' The king's hound whimpered from her hiding place beneath the bed.

Ancaios wished he could sink through the flagstones. Then a movement behind the king's shoulder snatched his attention away from the royal tempers and, for the first time, he took a look about the chamber. One of the other occupants had sagged against the wall and appeared to have fallen asleep standing up. He was a man Ancaios had never seen before, a plump fellow with shiny black hair, wine-spills on his handsome garments and an overturned flagon by his feet. Nearby stood the chancellor, Lord Highmoor, his eyes bloodshot and his skin as pallid as candle-wax. He shook his head and frowned but hardly looked surprised. Beside him stood another black-clad councillor; it was either Sir Garthwray or Lord Ladstock (Ancaios could never tell them apart), but as there'd been talk of Garthwray's death, it must have been Ladstock. Whoever the wispy grey man was, he did not seem overly concerned as the king and the princess railed at one another, for he smirked and then he yawned, once, twice, three times.

Sooth, thought Ancaios, *they surely do this often!*

'Lords Highmoor and Ladstock, aid me,' pleaded Winterhued; 'ye do know how crucial is our dependence upon Arracan in the north!'

The chancellor coughed. 'My liege's daughter is correct, sire,' he rasped. 'To replace Arracan's forces we would need to increase our standing army fourfold and deploy it in garrisons, not just in the northeast as at present, but across the whole of the north.'

'Pah!' snorted the king, 'Let us do that then...'

'We would be forced to greatly increase our taxes, sire.'

'Taxes be hanged! I'd see Arracan's head on a stake. And the heads of every last son.' He glared at Winterhued as he spoke and she glared back at him. 'Every. Last. Son,' he repeated slowly.

Winterhued suddenly laughed. 'Good cheer, Father,' said she. 'The state of your memory is not so dire as I'd thought!'

'Pah!' spat the king again. 'Insolent chit.' He pointed across the chamber to where the marquess, looking entertained, leant against the wall. 'He's still here! I thought I'd told the verminous cur to quit my sight!'

Sir Almendral grinned crookedly and bowed. 'I am going, my liege, but before I do may I, in all humbleness, entreat my lord to curb his temper. For I am afeared it will be the death of him.'

'Death?' shouted the king, lumbering red-faced to his feet. 'Thou speakst of my death when thine own draws perilously close? My death? Knowest thou that I shall never die, and certainly not before I have cut thee and thy breed out from Manydown like a canker!' The king jabbed a furious finger towards the door. 'Now get out... out!' he bellowed.

Sir Almendral bowed low, and backed towards the door. But before he could leave Winterhued had crossed the room and taken his hand within her own. 'If thou must depart, sir,' said she, 'thou shalt depart with me. Come, Ancaios; we shall carry the news of Auchencairn to my unhappy cousin. Shall I convey a kind message from you, Father, or shall I tell her that ye are little concerned over the demise of your Constable and great Champion?'

'Great Champion?' growled the king. 'Great Disappointment more like; as Champion he should have done his job and rid me of this pestilence.'

The princess stared at her father. 'Come Ancaios,' she said again and, still holding the marquess's hand, bobbed a shallow curtsy. Almendral bowed once more and so too did Ancaios, then the three of them made a move towards the door.

'The boy can stay,' snapped the king. 'I wish to question him further.'

Winterhued put a protective hand on Ancaios' shoulder. 'He accompanies me.'

'The boy stayeth here,' said the king, his voice low and threatening. 'Oh, thou mayest act the queen all thou lik'st, daughter, but I tell thee that I... I may marry tomorrow and father half a dozen sons!'

Winterhued glared at her father and he returned her look, his face glowing like a hot coal. Sir Almendral, no longer smiling, leaned to murmur to the princess: 'Soft, my dear,' said he. 'Ye do not own the boy, and besides, to what harm can he come?'

'Go to!' said the princess impatiently. But Ancaios felt her press his shoulder then release him. 'Meseems I must then commend this youth to my lord. Grant him just quittance for his merits.' She turned and without another word, swept away up the stairs with the marquess in tow.

Ancaios felt tempted to run after her.

'"Just quittance for thy merits", eh boy?' said the king with a humourless laugh. He was still red in the face but much of his anger seemed to have dissipated upon the marquess's exit. 'What'sth'name? Hast thou eaten?'

'Ancaios, my liege. Aye, I have eaten.'

'Give him a whipping and turn him out,' growled the sweaty man from where he still stood against the wall. 'That'd be "just quittance" for his merits!'

'Did I ask thee, Gunford?' questioned the king, turning to stare at the man. 'Why dost thou not find aught better to do than cower in a smelly pit full of old dodderers? Why didst *thou* not find Auchencairn and rescue Dechmont? Get thee hence and do what thou hast been employed to do.' King Gers pointed at the door.

'That's what I *have* been doing, your highness,' said Sir Gunford, even as he scurried for the door; 'I am employed to look after my king.'

'Pah! Thou'llt be wanting to wipe my bottom next,' said the king. 'Get out.'

The armoured knight turned such a hostile gaze upon Ancaios as he made his exit that the boy flinched.

'Ha ha ha!' laughed the king as Gunford's heavy footsteps thudded away up the stairs. 'I saw that. He's jealous of thee, lad – jealous of a turd-shoveller – because th'art brave and he's a coward! Ha ha! My daughter's right about him: the man's a craven milksop! Dost thou not agree, lad?'

Ancaios stared at the floor, his heart racing. The king seemed a little mad and certainly unpredictable. Did he really want to hear a lowly menial pass judgement upon a knight of the realm? Perhaps he was but searching for an excuse to throw Ancaios into a dungeon.

'I agree,' he answered carefully, 'that her highness, Princess Winter-hued, is often right, my liege.'

The king snorted. 'Right? When she insisteth on keeping wrong company? I tell you all,' said Gers, looking around him at the assembly, 'every day do I grow more fond of my idea to remarry and beget an heir...'

'My liege!' exclaimed the chancellor. Ancaios glanced over at the old man and saw his palpable anxiety. 'I implore my liege to think again. Winterhued has the...'

'I'll do as I please,' interrupted Gers; 'I'm the king.' He glared at the chancellor for a moment and then, with a bark of laughter, turned back to Ancaios. 'Come boy,' he ordered, 'stand before me. Let's have a look at thee.' The king's hound had come out from beneath the bed to sniff Ancaios' hand and he patted her greying head. 'That's Gunda,' said the king; 'good old girl. She likes thee. So what'sth'name, boy? How old art thou?'

'Ancaios, my liege. I'm almost sixteen, m'liege.'

'And brave, eh? The fishwife said thou knowest thy way about. "Unknown ways" she said. Canst thou get thyself out of the castle?'

'Aye, my liege. I know a few ways most folk won't go... um, latrine pits and... and the like.'

'Here's thy 'just quittance' then; how wouldst thou like a change of job? Turd-shoveller to king's messenger. Eh? What sayest thou?' The king didn't wait for an answer. 'Thou'llt need a livery jacket with the royal badge, and a horse. I'll have a requisition drawn up so thou mayest get thee a horse once thou'rt clear of Lawhill.'

'I do not know how to ride, my liege.'

'Nonsense! Thou'rt a boy; all boys can ride. Highmoor! Send for a clerk so we can get these documents drawn up; offer of marriage to the fishwife, and lands and such like. Meanwhile, lad, hie thee back to the King's Hall and wait there for thy commission... and if thou seest my contrary daughter, say not a word of this to her. Ha ha! Oh... I well nigh forgot to ask... What's thy name?'

'Ancaios, my liege. Um... ah... my liege, whither am I to carry your highness' message?'

'Ha ha ha! I forgot that too. Well asked, lad, well asked! Thou art to ride south post-haste; take the road to Drumrock. Thou'llt be looking for a knight, a famous knight, riding up from Ormsary. No doubt he'll be coming through the Trongate Pass, so thou'llt find him somewhere on that road; anywhere between here and Ormsary! Ha ha ha! A trifling distance! He'll be coming for our big Dittonsday Tournament, which we might have to cancel this year, but he'll not know that. Sure to be others coming as well; when thou dost see them, thou canst give them all a hurry-up.

'But the one we want: the one to whom I shall make a generous offer, is... well, we know not his name, but they say he's the best knight in the world. Might be able to discover a bit more about him if Priwall there ever wakes up; all he's given us so far is the colour of his shield – gules – and his badge, which is a white unicorn, same as m'daughter's. If that be not an omen, I know not what is!

'So keep thine eyes peeled for a white unicorn on a red shield. Its bearer shall no doubt be accompanied by all the baggage with which knights are wont to travel; a squire or two, a couple of destriers, several spare horses and pack animals loaded with armour, pavilions, lances, spare swords and what-not. In short, he'll be hard to miss.'

Ancaios' heart had sunk into his boots. He was certain now that the king was a madman, and that he himself was about to be sent off on the biggest fool's errand of all time.

'What message am I to give this knight, my liege?' he politely asked, stroking the hound's head.

'Thou needst not give him any message, but hand him my commission and answer any questions he may put to thee. He may ask thee concerning the princess and thou mayst tell him of her beauty, but not, for heaven's sake, of her wilfulness nor her choler! Thou mayst tell him of Manydown's charms and remind him that, as well as a princedom, he may choose for himself whatever dukedom, earldom or marquisate that I have at my disposal.'

Ancaios became aware that his mouth was hanging open. He managed to close it and utter: 'And this, my liege, shall be his reward for...?'

'For ridding us of the pestilence that imprisons us. No more questions; shalt thou undertake this 'quest' for thy king? What's thy name by the way?'

'Ancaios, my liege. And, aye, I shall try with all diligence to dispatch my liege's commission.'

'Good. Then hie thee to the King's Hall and wait there.' He gave a little flick with his forefinger and Ancaios understood that he'd been dismissed. 'Highmoor, summon the chancery clerk.'

Ancaios gave the hound a last pat, bowed and shuffled backwards to the door. He fled away up the stairs, breathing hard.

Brenn sat on the princess's bed, lost in the little volume that Winterhued had left upon her writing table. It was the very book that Brenn had longed to see since she'd first spied it: the book that was bound in silver and etched with the letters 'W' and 'D' entwined. It was surely one of the most precious things that Brenn had ever seen. It contained one long poem: the tale of a knight-errant and his forlorn love for a highborn damsel, and it was filled with exquisite illuminations. Gold-leaf tendrils twined themselves about every page, and in every border flowers blossomed and bright birds took wing. Curly-tailed animals climbed, hung from or hid shyly behind capital letters. In the larger pictures the knight-errant rode his white warhorse across a luminous land of magical fountains and unicorns, of green giants, and even a little crimson dragon winging its way across a cobalt sky.

Brenn turned the last page. The magical fountain had revealed to the knight how he could win his ladylove, and the poem told of how it came to pass and how the twain were wed amidst great rejoicing. Brenn blinked back a tear and gently ran her finger across the silver binding. What a gift from a threadbare knight; a knight who wore his brothers' old armour and rode their cast-off horses! He must surely have spent all that he possessed to purchase such a gift. Oh, how glorious it would be to find a love like that!

Little Thistle lay curled up beside Brenn and she absently stroked her tabby coat, smiling dreamily. She was picturing herself in the beautiful silk from Ilala that the princess had promised her for her wedding day, and her heart was full of love and pride for her future bridegroom. She couldn't imagine what he would look like, but she knew he would have soft and shining hair, and that it would be dark. *Yes*, she thought, *I would like his hair to be dark.*

All of a sudden the cat shot out from under her hand, leapt to the floor and spat as she disappeared beneath the bed. Brenn froze. The hairs on the back of her neck prickled and her heart came into her mouth.

She hadn't heard its wings. It must have come gliding silently from the sky; it was silent still, yet she knew it was there. She knew, for this was how it had been in her dreams; the monstrous wings, unseen, above her and the paralysing fear flooding her mind. She slid off the bed onto her knees and put her hands over her head as she heard the first snuffling, wheezing breaths. It was a horrible sound; a sound of air being dragged stertorously through a half-rotted windpipe. The dragon seemed to be sniffing her out; hunting for her. She heard it collide with the top of the tower; she heard stone and slate go sliding and crashing downwards to shatter against the tower walls and smash onto the shingled beach below. She felt the tower shake as the creature

landed and she heard timbers groaning beneath its weight. She heard
talons scrabbling at beams and leading, then an ear-splitting shriek of
timber and stone as if the very tower were being torn asunder. Ash
and dust came billowing into the chamber and the floor beneath her
shook as something hugely heavy thudded into the lake. It seemed that
the whole upper section of the tower had toppled, taking the chimney
with it.

Brenn became aware that she was whimpering like a puppy. She
opened her eyes and straight away saw the little book, spine up and
splayed open upon the floor at her feet. 'Oh no,' she breathed and
carefully picked up the precious thing. One page, bordered with
gold-leaf curlicues and fluttering birds, was creased and Brenn tried to
stroke it flat with violently trembling fingers. Directly above her head
– so close! – she heard a beam groan and splinter, but she scarcely
flinched. She closed the little book and kissed its cover. '*He* would not
cower in terror, waiting to be eaten,' she whispered.

Still clutching the book, hardly breathing, she clambered to her feet.
Her heart sounded in her ears as she got herself across the bedroom
and eased the door open. The antechamber was dark and smelled of
brimstone. She crossed it noiselessly, even though she was shaking so
badly that by the time she got to the outer door she had to lean on its
frame to steady herself.

Trying not to breathe she lifted the latch. But all of a sudden the
creature's snufflings grew louder, as though they were coming from
right outside the door. *No*, she thought, *it cannot possibly fit in the
stairwell – 'tis but the sounds coming down the stairs.*

Slowly, she inched the door open. A shaft of daylight stabbed
into the chamber, swirling with dust and smoke. Broken fragments of
stonework tumbled down onto the floor and rolled, clunking across
the floorboards. Brenn stood, half blinded by the light and frozen in
dismay. The portal was blocked and the stairwell completely choked
with unmoveable chunks of masonry. Above her, where the stairs
should have wound their way up into darkness, Brenn found herself

looking through a gap in the rubble straight up to blue sky. A puff of white cloud floated in its centre.

The ragged wheezing and snuffling grew in intensity, and then the appalling stink of the creature came flooding into the chamber. Gagging, Brenn pressed a hand to her mouth and backed away, step by step and inch by inch; somehow she got herself back through the door to the bedchamber and shut it behind her. But there was no safety here; she guessed that only the ceiling – a single layer of wood – remained between her and the dragon.

Her mind flew hither and thither in desperate panic. There was no way out and nowhere to hide.

Think, think!

Brenn was certain that the creature could rip the ceiling aside in a heartbeat yet, apart from its snuffling, it had grown quite still. *It doth toy with me*, she thought.

She realised she was still holding the little book pressed to her heart. Like bright birds from its illuminations two words fluttered into her mind: 'secret passage'.

Yes… I did ask her. She said… what did she say? Oh, what did she say? Yes… yes… I remember… she said: 'It can only be found in autumn… when the leaves turneth gold.' But 'tis spring now… alas, alas, how shall I ever find it?

She turned round and round, eyes darting about the chamber. As quietly as she could, she hastened from wall hanging to wall hanging, swirling them aside but finding only blank wall beneath. She ran her hand for a little distance along the wainscoting, but gave up in despair.

The ceiling above her head creaked and groaned threateningly and she shot a terrified glance towards it. She found herself staring at golden leaves… oh! she'd forgotten about the painted leaves on the timbers between the ceiling joists. She saw now that the joists divided the chamber ceiling into quarters and that each quarter represented a season. The painted leaves changed from the pale green of spring to the

deep green of summer to golden autumn leaves and then to a pattern
of bare twigs and snow crystals.

Brenn stared wildly, stupidly, at the ceiling. *But how can a passage
be up there?* She dropped her gaze and noticed, for the first time, that
the tapestry below that quarter of the ceiling depicted an autumnal
scene. It hung beside the window-seat recess, and there was a smaller,
matching tapestry on the other side of the window. Brenn darted
towards it. Her heart hammered within her breast, but she forced
herself to look carefully about her. The cushions on the window seats
were covered in embroidered golden leaves. She tapped the seat on
the right; it felt as solid as stone. But the left seat sounded hollow. She
put the book on the floor and slid her shaking hands down the sides,
around the rim... and miraculously, there it was: a little lever recessed
near the floor.

Brenn pushed the lever in one direction and then she pushed it in
the other. Nothing happened. But then she saw that the top of the seat
had risen a little, stopped only by the bulk of the cushions. Throwing
them to the floor, she lifted the seat on its silent hinges and looked
down into a narrow, rectangular hole. The top of a ladder poked up
out of darkness. Clumsy with haste, Brenn hitched up her skirts and got
her right foot over the rim and onto the first rung of the ladder. Then
she stopped.

With a creak and a groan, one end of a ceiling beam lifted and
daylight shafted into the chamber. But Brenn, breathing in gasps,
climbed out of the hole and stepped back into the room. The hairs
prickled on the back of her neck but she dared not look up. She pushed
the precious book down the front of her bodice and then she took her
embroidery bag and shook its contents onto the floor. She got down on
her hands and knees and climbed under the bed. Grabbing the cat by
the scruff of her neck, she dragged her from under the bed and tried to
drop her into the bag. Thistle spat and raked her with needle claws, but
in sheer desperation she shoved her in and pulled the drawstring tight.

Then, still not looking up even though she knew that the ceiling was lifting above her head, she took a candlestick from the writing table and carried her wriggling burden back to the window seat. Dust and splinters showered down on her as she went. The dragon's rot-breath felt close enough to singe her hair and its stench almost knocked her down, but she looped the bag's drawstring over her shoulder and hitched up her skirts once more. As she clambered back into the dark hole she chanced a single glance up over her shoulder.

The horror and pity that filled her made her shake so violently as she fled down the ladder, that it began to bounce and sway. With one hand clutching her candlestick and the other on the rungs, she almost fell several times. But then her feet touched stone and she found herself standing at the top of the narrowest, steepest newel stair she had ever seen. With a trembling hand she held the candle down beside her feet, but she could only see the first few steps before its feeble light was swallowed by treacly blackness. The cat mewed plaintively and her claws came pricking through the bag like pins.

Knees knocking and teeth chattering, Brenn backed down the first stair then the second. Above her came a crash that shook the tower to its foundations and sent air rushing down the narrow way to snuff out the candle. The girl lost her footing and slid down four or five stairs, dropping the candlestick and grazing her shins painfully. As she fell she threw out an arm to protect the cat from being squashed against the wall, and was rewarded with more lacerations across her hand.

She sat down hard upon a stair, gasping in pain. The tower still shook, but even as the tremors died away a roar filled the stairwell and a gout of flame came rushing, bursting, blasting from above. Lurid light flared down the walls, but the last tendrils of fire died before they could reach the girl. She shrank from the heat, stumbling and falling down three more stairs, until at last she slid to a halt, gasping and sobbing. A faint red light flickered on the walls for a while as the ladder above burned, but that soon faded until there was naught but utter darkness.

The tower rocked under her when, some moments later, the dragon leapt into the sky. Brenn heard the wings this time; a great thumping that hurt her ears as the creature took flight. Trussed up in the girl's embroidery bag, the little cat mewled but Brenn could offer no comfort because she herself had begun to sob uncontrollably. Tears flowed down her cheeks to pool unseen on the stairs below.

She wept for her own terror and shock, but also for the dragon; for the desperate sadness that had washed over and through her as the creature took to the air.

After her tears were all spent, Brenn sat shivering upon the hard stair. 'I should not have been so afraid,' she whispered to the darkness. But before long an acrid smell of smoke made her get shakily to her feet. She felt carefully for the bag; Thistle cried as she picked her up, but had given up struggling. 'Sorry, little puss,' whispered Brenn, 'the tower is burning. We must go down into the dark.'

She groped for the curved wall and inched her way to the left side of the stairs where the tread was widest. Then she turned about and began to back, almost on her hands and knees, down and down, round and round, ever downwards into pitchy blackness.

Nal leaned back and gazed up at a puff of cloud that floated high in the pale blue sky. His stomach was so full of roast mutton that he thought he'd never be able to stand up again. Still, he wasn't concerned about standing up: only with finding space inside him to fit in the apple that he was carefully tossing from hand to hand. Yellow and red and a little wrinkled, the fruit seemed almost too precious to eat for it was the last of a late autumn crop and had been stored all winter long. And the innkeeper had given it to him. Nal polished it lovingly once more upon his grubby garments.

He sat on a bench outside the only inn in Wendur. There was a good fire within, but it was a mild day outside with just enough sunlight to make it tolerable. Besides, he thought he'd try to talk to a couple of the village girls who sat atop a drystone wall beside the stream on the other side of the road. Not so long ago, he'd never have been bold enough to attempt such a thing, but he was a *squire* now, and he'd seen a bit of the world.

He lowered his eyes and peeked furtively at the girls. They were whispering and giggling the way girls did, and he knew they sometimes glanced in his direction, but they wouldn't come over to talk. Trying to look nonchalant, he tossed his apple from hand to hand and stretched out his legs, but pulled them back quickly when he noticed how skinny they were.

He looked about him at the village. For a place crouched at the edge of the world it was unremarkable enough; a single row of cottages, a squat church, a tithe barn, a smithy and an inn, all built of the local pinkish grey stone. Glimpsed behind dark pines on a low hill above the village rose the buttressed walls of a small castle, and between the castle and the village lay a vineyard, an orchard and a patchwork of tilled fields. At first he'd thought it was the same village he'd glimpsed yesterday from the mountainside, but no... that castle had had a moat, and anyway, it must lie far south of here.

The fine weather had proved an excuse to bring the village women to their doors; they peered avidly towards the inn and gossiped in hushed tones. A few of them carded wool, most spun; with distaffs tucked under their arms, they dropped and caught their spindles rhythmically as they chatted. Children stared round-eyed from behind their skirts. In the still air the women had flung their shutters wide and smoke from the fires within came drifting out through the small windows.

The village looked onto a common where black-faced sheep grazed, and a collection of dirty children ran and tumbled, shouted and laughed. They were supposed to be wool-gathering: picking every scrap of fleece from the gorse bushes, but the appearance of an armoured knight in Wendur had inspired them into galloping to and fro, riding piggyback in their own rough and tumble jousting match.

Between the village street and the common rushed a thaw-swollen
stream, spanned by the single narrow stone bridge across which Nal
and the knight had first ridden into Wendur. Beyond all, beyond the
stream, the bridge and the common, loomed the great grim shape of
Iron Crag, draped in forest and capped with snow.

Nal shuddered. He was glad he'd be sleeping under a roof this
night, even though it wasn't much of a roof. For the inn had surely
seen better days. It sagged so low it was a wonder there was room to
stand up under its swayed ceiling joists. A big stone porch slouched
at skewed angles over the door and a collection of chimneys looked
ready to topple in the next gale. It was called 'The Goose's Nob'. At
least that's the name the knight had given him, and when Nal expressed
doubt he'd pointed to the sign and said: ''Tis there for all to see. Read
it thyself.' Of course he knew that Nal couldn't do any such thing, for
it was he himself who'd attempted to teach the skill to Nal, with no
success. Nal couldn't see the use in reading and the only thing he'd ever
learnt to write was his own name.

The keeper of the inn was one Mistress Mayhill, a small strong-
looking woman dressed in faded black. She was surely a widow, though
she wasn't old; indeed, she was handsome enough in a weather-beaten
way. She'd no sooner clapped eyes upon the knight than she'd given
him her best room, fed the both of them regally and then refused to
accept a single one of his copper coins. She'd sent her lad off, leading
the chestnut horse to the blacksmith's and even offered to pay for its
new shoes. Then, when she'd begged to know what else he'd like, he'd
only had to laughingly mention a bath and she'd gone scurrying about,
dragging a tin bath up the stairs, lugging buckets of water in from the
well and throwing a week's worth of fuel onto the roaring fire to get the
water heated all the sooner.

Nal yawned and scratched his head vigorously, wondering what it
was about his master that brought out the fool in so many women.

'How now?' said a sweet voice in his ear. He looked up, startled, to
find that the two girls had crossed the road and were standing beside

the bench. The one who'd spoken made his heart beat faster, for she was tall and willowy with beautiful golden locks. The other was less promising; she had woolly brown hair, but that's about all he could see of her because she was hiding behind her friend.

'Are ye really 'is squire?' asked the golden-haired girl. 'Ye don't look like a squire.'

Nal stared at her like an idiot. 'Wh... what?' he finally managed.

'I said ye don't look like a squire.'

'What does a squire look like then?'

'Someone that's going to be a knight one day.'

'And I don't?'

The tall girl turned to look at her friend and the two of them laughed. Nal scowled sullenly. He could feel his face turning red.

'What's 'is name?' the girl asked, sniggering still.

''Oo's name?'

'The knight, o' course. Who else?'

'We don't want to know *your* name,' muttered the brown-haired girl.

Nal scowled even harder. 'I don' know,' he said, ''e's never told me.'

'Ye don't know?' exclaimed the golden girl. 'How could ye not know? What sort of squire doesn't know 'is master's name?'

The woolly haired girl peered from behind her friend's shoulder. 'Where's 'e from then?' she squeaked.

'I don' know... from 'ere I think. That's what 'e said.'

'From 'ere?' snapped Woolly. ''E never is! What a dolt! Ye don't know naught!'

'Course I do!' rejoined Nal indignantly. ''E tells no one 'is name. 'E doesn' 'ave to. 'E's known far an' wide as the Knight o' the Unicorn 'cause that's what 'is badge is. 'E's a knight-errant, which means 'im an' me, we ride about lookin' for chivalrous stuff; tournaments an' battles an' the like. Sooth, we've ridden a thousand... nay, a *hundred* thousand leagues since last summer. An' everywhere we go 'e's reckoned the best. 'Best knight in the world'; I've heard 'em say so. 'E's knocked down 'undreds of other knights, maybe thousands, an' never been knocked down 'imself. 'E's led armies into battle against great odds an' 'e's...'

'What stuff!' interrupted Woolly. 'How ye do prate!'

''Tis all true. 'E's renowned far and wide. Ask anyone... ask in Ormsary, in Balasore, in... in Ilala, in Quathlamba, or Pengwern, which is where I'm from. But I'll warrant ye've never been out o' yer pocky village. Why, ye're lucky to 'ave such a great man 'ere, stayin' in yer shabby ol' Goose's Nob.'

'Goose's Nob?' gasped Gold-locks, putting a hand to her pretty mouth. 'That's wicked. *Goose's Nob!*'

The two girls simpered and sniggered. 'Methinks the whey-faced starveling is a clown,' snorted Woolly, looking almost admiringly at Nal; 'King Gers – King Goose!'

But Nal was only confused. 'If that's not its name, what is?' he asked sullenly.

'So ye weren't bein' clever? Did someone tell you it were the Goose's Nob?' The two of them laughed and laughed.

'What is it then?'

'Look at the picture on the sign, clodpole.'

Nal turned his head and peered at the inn sign, but it was so faded and peeled it was hardly a wonder he'd failed to notice whether it depicted a goose or a gadfly. ''Tis a fat old man in need o' some paint,' he said. ''E could be a goose for all I know. 'E certainly looks like one. 'Oo is 'e?'

''Ere's a clue – 'e's got a crown on 'is 'ead.'

'A crown? I thought it were a coxcomb.'

The girls started laughing again, but all of a sudden they stopped. Their eyes went wide. Then, quick as a heartbeat, Gold-locks flicked her hair back and arranged her face into a temptress's smile while Woolly dodged behind her tall friend. Nal stared at them, amazed, and then he sneered. He turned round towards the door knowing who it was he'd see there.

The knight had stepped out into the sunshine; he was clad in his rusty black arming-doublet but his hair was damp and he smelt clean even from where Nal was sitting. Mistress Mayhill must have smelled him too for she came scampering from the inn's back rooms like an eager lap dog.

'Is there aught else ye'll be wanting, sir?' she asked hopefully. 'I've some more of that treacle tart, or another stoup of wine perhaps?' She gazed with hopeful admiration at his washed hair. 'I could comb the tangles out for you, sir.'

''Tis done already.' He looked at her half frowning, half smiling. 'Ye have been too kind, mistress. I wish ye would accept my coins.'

Nal didn't hear the innkeeper's response, for he was watching Gold-locks in astonishment as she surreptitiously tugged and pushed at her bodice in an attempt to reveal some cleavage. She pinched her cheeks and bit her lips to bring colour to them and then she shook out her golden locks fetchingly. By the time the knight had turned back towards Nal and the two girls, she'd even hitched up her skirt to reveal a flash of slim ankle. All the while her companion, half hidden behind the taller girl, stared like a startled dormouse and clung to her friend's arm. 'Oh... 'e's so beautiful,' she breathed.

'Who are your friends?' asked the knight.

'They're not my friends, sir,' answered Nal sulkily. 'They're just girls. I don't know their names.'

With a toss of her head (that caused her shining tresses to swing alluringly), Gold-locks stepped forward. 'Give your worship good morrow,' she said in a breathless voice, 'I'm Zamaris, your worship, and this is my friend Tinita.'

'Nay, I'm Tamaris,' whispered the woolly-haired girl tremulously, plucking at her friend's sleeve, 'thou'rt Zinita.'

'Good morrow, Tamaris,' said the knight kindly. Tamaris just stared open-mouthed as her friend elbowed her aside. 'I'm Zinita, your worship,' said the blonde girl with a coquettish smile.

'Thou art a bold, flaunting hussy,' interrupted the landlady, 'and the twain of you can take yourselves off home this minute. Loitering about here when your mothers have chores for you!' She took them both by the elbows and hustled them out to the road.

'Good morrow, Tamaris, Zinita,' said the knight, and the two girls twisted in Mistress Mayhill's grip to gaze longingly back at him.

With a sudden exclamation, the relentless landlady reached out to pluck a muddy boy from where he'd been spying behind the wall. Another lad was too quick for her and darted over the bridge to go galloping and whooping away to join his friends on the common. The woman managed to propel her band of prisoners for no more than three steps before the boy, squirming like an eel, made his escape. But Woolly-head went quietly enough, though Goldy-locks struggled and protested all the way to her doorstep.

'Why are girls such want-wits?' muttered Nal.

'Girls want wits no more than lads,' said the knight, sitting down on the bench beside the boy, 'and like lads they can be cruel.'

'What would ye know?'

'More than thou'dst guess, perhaps.'

Nal sneered. 'A pox on 'em,' he muttered, tossing his apple from hand to hand. 'Sooth, an' ye said they wouldn't like you in this place!'

'I daresay the most exciting thing those lasses have ever seen come down from the mountain is a grimy charcoal burner or two.' The knight stretched out his long legs and leaned back against the inn wall. 'Until the morrow we have naught to do but eat and sleep,' he said, 'so make the most of it. The bath-water is still in the tub, Nal.'

'Ye'll 'ave to kill me first,' mumbled the boy.

'Thou'dst best eat that apple soon or I shall.'

Nal slid the apple into the pouch that hung upon his belt and watched the landlady as she came back up the road. She was almost at the inn when the sound of hoofbeats stopped her. She turned, as did everyone else in the village, to watch two big bay horses canter up the village street.

They halted in a spray of mud outside the inn and the men on their backs looked about expectantly. 'Where's the lad?' asked one of them.

'E's at blacksmith's, sir,' answered the innkeeper tersely. She turned on her heel and walked into the inn. The eyes of the men lighted on Nal and the boy quickly looked away. But the knight gave him a gentle shove between the shoulder blades.

'Go on, Nal,' he said quietly, 'keep these big men happy; go hold their horses.' Nal got reluctantly to his feet and slouched over to the two big bays. The men barely glanced at him as he took their reins. One of them, a stocky fellow with red hair and a fur-lined cloak, dismounted and disappeared into the inn after Mistress Mayhill. The other sat up on his high horse, probably reluctant to dismount and reveal just what a very small man he was. He had a bald, shining pate, and he was well dressed, prosperous-looking and ill mannered. For though it was plain that news of the blue-eyed visitor had spread and that the twain had come expressly to see him, the bald man uttered not a word. 'Pleasant day,' observed the knight amiably, yet the little man did but grunt, scratch his nose and stare in a hostile manner. His horse shared its master's bad manners for it shoved Nal with its nose, nearly knocking the boy off his feet. And when it had stopped shoving, it snuffled him all over and chewed his clothes.

From within the inn came the sound of a raised voice: Mistress Mayhill was angry. The knight stood up and instantly one set of reins was pulled from Nal's grasp as the little man panicked and yanked his horse out into the road. Nal smirked.

'Ye do not own me,' came the landlady's voice, 'and neither do ye own my inn. I'll do as I please, you flap-eared dolt, so get out and leave me be.' The redheaded man came stumbling backward out of the door and looked about him sheepishly, his face redder than his hair.

The knight gave him a friendly smile and sat down again. 'Good morrow, sir,' he said; 'fine weather this first day of spring.'

'Oh… ah…' said the red man, but the short fellow, deciding at last to speak, pushed his horse forward.

'I'm the bailiff of this borough,' he said, 'and this is m'lord's steward. How long will ye be staying in Wendur?'

'But the one night, Master Bailiff,' answered the knight good-humouredly. He leaned against the inn wall, as relaxed and easy as if he were talking to old friends.

'Ye came over Blackbraes?' asked the bailiff, suspicious and hostile.

'Aye.'

'Any trouble?'

''Twas quiet enough.'

'No one cometh that way now.'

'So I noticed.'

The redheaded steward heaved himself onto his horse's back and Nal let go the reins. At the same moment he noticed that the bailiff's horse, though it stood still, was chomping at the bit and foaming strangely at the mouth. Nal stared at it for a moment and then, his heart sinking, he felt for the pouch at his belt. It was empty. He turned it upside down and shook it but it was still empty.

'Ye've come from afar?' asked the steward, finding his voice.

'I have, Master Steward,' answered the knight, 'I've been on the road nigh every day since leaving Quathlamba.'

'Ahhh.' The two men nodded sagely, though it was quite possible they'd never heard of the place.

'That's a thousand leagues or more to the south,' said the knight helpfully. 'Since last spring I've journeyed through Ilala, Balasore and Ormsary. What's wrong, lad?' he added, having noticed that Nal had sat down on the road with his head in his hands.

'Poxy 'orse got my apple,' moaned Nal.

The bailiff and the steward disregarded the boy. 'Long way, very long way,' said the steward, nodding sagely. 'Ye'll be on your way to Lawhill for the Di'nsday Tourney,' surmised the bailiff.

'Nay,' replied the knight, 'I'm riding north; across the Hawksdale Pass.'

'Ye're on your way home then.'

'Home? I wish I were.'

The bailiff's thoughts scurried hither and thither. 'Well, lucky for you ye'd not planned on the tourney,' he finally said, 'for it'll be called off this year no doubt. Trouble down in Lawhill's the rumour.'

'Trouble?'

'Aye, rumour says something bad's happening in the west; flames and smoke, town's afire they say. I've heard 'tis an army from Angerona laying siege to Lawhill.'

The knight got abruptly to his feet, causing the shiny-pated bailiff to flinch and jab his horse in the mouth again. The horse tossed its head, and strings of saliva and bits of frothy, half-chewed apple flew about.

'No doubt,' said the knight, 'ye'll be gathering a company of men to ride to the succour of your king.'

The bailiff and the steward were silent for a space. ''Tis a long way to Lawhill,' the bailiff eventually said. 'We'd need more than rumours for that.'

'Aye, we'd need more than rumours,' echoed the steward, 'to go all that way.'

'Then,' said the knight, 'ye'll have dispatched one or two fast riders to investigate the verity of the rumours.'

'Ah... aye, that's what we've done,' lied the bailiff.

'Come Nal,' said the knight, 'on thy feet. We'll be leaving... as soon as thy horse is back from the blacksmith.'

'Leavin'?' squeaked Nal, trying to extricate a blob of chewed apple and saliva from his hair. 'But ye promised a bed for the night... and a warm room... and a roof over me 'ead!'

'Sorry lad, we've no time to dally. Yet be of good cheer, for we'll doing one thing thou didst want... we're riding west.'

CHAPTER 11

Many leagues west of Wendur, Castle Lawhill dozed like a wounded behemoth in the pale sunshine. Very little of that sunshine penetrated the bolted doors and boarded-up windows and the castle's inhabitants moved about in the gloom like mice beneath floorboards.

The gong-farmer's son, a little out of breath, quietly entered the King's Hall through the screens-passage. Strangely, the guard stationed there slapped him on the back in a jovial way as he passed and muttered: 'Good lad.' Even stranger, two guards he'd passed in the passage earlier had winked at him and one had made a clicking noise in his mouth as if he was a horse that wanted encouraging. Strange, because until today any guard the lad encountered would more likely have given him a boot up the rear than any sort of encouragement.

Ancaios sat himself down near the threshold to wait. Though it must have been close to midday the hall was as murky as midnight. The boy gazed about him, feeling sad and helpless and stupid. He turned his eyes towards the lofty ceiling and the knights' banners that hung limply beneath it. Somewhere in his fanciful head had always dwelt the belief that, despite his low birth, his own banner would one day hang beside them. But now he could see that that was naught but a boy's nonsensical dream. For those bright, proud banners had proved to be empty boasts, and at the far end of the hall the high dais was another lie, for its gold throne had been lugged away and hidden in a mouldy basement in the dark.

It seemed that the king and all his posturing knights, strutting in their shining armour and playing their games of war were, after all, no more to the world than woodlice in a log. And how might woodlice protect themselves from a feasting magpie but by scuttling off into any dark crevice they could find?

Ancaios put his head in his hands. He could hear the common folk; clustered in groups they talked quietly amongst themselves as they waited for who-knew-what horrible fate. 'Abandon thy dreams, fool,' he said to himself; 'thou canst not save a single one of them.' Indeed, he couldn't even try for he was being sent away on a goose's errand. As the dragon devoured these hapless folk, and as it cracked open the floor to pick out the gentry below, where would he be? Wandering hither and thither like a buffoon, searching for some useless lance-lugger who cared not a jot about the fate of Manydown's king and court... or her princess. 'I would that I could take *her* away with me,' he muttered.

'Thou'dst have to bind and gag me first, gong-boy,' said a voice in his ear and Ancaios looked up, startled. Blue-eyed Eudora bent over him with a slight smile upon her face. That smile surprised him more than her sudden appearance, because he couldn't recall ever having seen her lips curve in any direction but down. And though he could see that she'd recently been weeping, it was clear she had tidings that she could barely wait to impart.

'Still here?' she asked, gathering her skirts to sit down beside him, 'I thought thou wast running away.' She was already halfway to the floor when Ancaios suddenly jumped to his feet and withdrew three or four paces.

'Whither away?' she protested.

'Do ye not want me to move elsewhere?'

'Nay, dolt, why would I sit down beside thee if I wanted thee to move?'

'Do ye not recall? Ye made me vow never again to come nigh you.'

Eudora was silent for a moment. 'Oh... well... on this occasion I shall grant thee a dispensation,' she announced, 'though I should not talk to thee for Princess Winterhued hath named *me* her chambermaid. But thou mayest sit beside me this once,' she said, patting the floor, 'though she is like to send for me at any moment and I shall have to depart.'

'In good sooth, that is excellent news, Dora,' said Ancaios, remaining on his feet. 'Yet I think ye may still speak with me, for I too have risen in the world. The king hath made me his messenger. I have been sent on a quest.'

She stared at him for a moment and then narrowed her pale eyes. 'Thou'rt making that up. King's messenger? A dung-shoveller in a stinking cloak?'

Ancaios smiled apologetically and shrugged, holding out his hands to show that he had at least lost his cloak if not his profession. (At some point during that eventful morning, he had put his cloak down and now couldn't remember where.)

Eudora's eyes slid sideways and widened. Ancaios looked around and saw, standing at his shoulder, one of the king's guards bearing a bundle of clothing with two pairs of boots balanced on top, as well as a leather satchel and a wide black belt. The soldier was a big, broad-shouldered fellow, splendid in his black livery jacket with its sunburst badge in gold thread, yet he seemed quite happy acting as a lackey for the gong-farmer's son.

'Certes, that were a plucky job ye did, lad, out there in the keep,' said he. ''Tis the talk of Lawhill. Showed all them big knights a thing or two, eh? Here, try the boots.'

Ancaios kicked off one shabby shoe and slid his foot into a high boot of black leather. This one proved too small, but the second pair fitted reasonably well. 'To get out of here I must swim,' he told the soldier, vaguely aware that Eudora had got to her feet and was gaping like a fish, 'so all this gear will have to be wrapped in oiled cloth until I am clear of the castle. I will need a candle or two as well.'

'Right-o, brave lad,' said the guard. 'Now, here's your belt and purse; look after that purse, there's money in it. Here's your jacket (doth look a good fit to me) and a cloak; ye'll need that. Here's the commission in the satchel, sealed with the royal seal; don't be losing it! Now, stay for a bit while I fetch your oilskin and candles.'

When the fellow had gone Ancaios pulled both of the boots on and then held the black livery jacket up against his threadbare tunic. ''Tis fine, eh Dora?' he said, looking up at her with a smile. She was standing with her hands dangling at her sides and her eyes big and shiny and dismayed.

'Dora...' said the boy, bundling the livery jacket aside. 'Don't cry. I... I forgot to say how much I like your new gown; the colour matcheth your eyes exceeding well.'

''Tis a lackey's sack,' said Eudora.

'Dora... be not so sad; ye are the princess's chambermaid...'

Eudora shook her head. 'She'll shortly find me out,' she mumbled in a tiny voice, 'and I'll be hanged as a traitor.'

'Traitor? What foolish talk is that?'

''Tis not foolish, though I am a fool,' she whispered. 'That thing I gave you...'

But the soldier had returned and Eudora turned away with a tear trickling down her cheek.

'We'll get this lot bundled up,' said the big man, 'and then ye may be off. My orders are to escort you whithersoever ye would go within the castle; I hope that won't extend to sliding down a latrine shaft.'

'I don't think ye'd fit, sir,' answered Ancaios with a grin. He pulled the boots off and folded the livery jacket and the soldier parcelled them up, together with the cloak, belt, purse and satchel, inside several layers of oilcloth. As the fellow was about to tie the bundle he stopped, sat back on his heels and removed the sheathed dagger from his own belt.

'Ye might be needing this, lad,' he said and pushed it down inside the oilskin.

'But that's yours, sir,' protested Ancaios.

''Tis my humble gift to the worthiest man in the castle.'

Ancaios felt his cheeks turning red. 'Ye must have heard the wrong story, sir,' he muttered. 'I did nothing of much worth.'

The big man finished tying the parcel and stood up. 'Nay, I heard the right story,' he said. 'Now, better say farewell to your lass.'

Ancaios gave an embarrassed nod and walked over to where Eudora leant against one of the hall's immense columns. She would scarcely look at him, even when he stood right before her. 'What did ye do to be such a hero?' she asked.

'Naught, Dora. I'm not a hero.'

'He thinks ye are. Anyway, "worthiest man in the castle", ye don't want to talk to the likes of me.'

'But I do, Dora, at least to say farewell.'

'Farewell then.' Eudora had been staring fixedly at the floor, but she suddenly glanced up. 'What's your name?' she asked.

'Stench.'

'Your real name.'

'Ancaios.'

'The princess... she knew your name.'

'Aye.'

'Why would she know your name?'

'That's a secret, but 'tis a small matter now the world is turned on end. She doth know my name because I am her pupil. She taught me to read and write.' He tentatively put a hand on her arm. 'I do not know if we shall meet again,' he said, 'but I wish you well, Dora.'

'I hate you,' whispered Eudora.

As Ancaios walked away from her, the soldier gripped his shoulder and leaned in to say a few words in the boy's ear. He spoke quietly, but Eudora heard every word. 'Fine, handsome lad like you can do better than a sullen drudge like her.'

Eudora watched as the two of them made for the screens passage door. 'I am the most stupid person in the world,' she breathed and then she slid down the column until she sat in a heap at its base. She put her head in her hands and sobbed.

Brenn was lost in the dark; dark blacker than black, unending and absolute. Stooped and shuffling, she felt her way along a rough-hewn, narrow and airless passage. She'd hit her head on the roof several times and fallen twice and was bruised and grazed and frightened. *I've missed a turning or a door,* she thought, *but even so, this must go somewhere.* Gripping the cat-bag in her right hand, she crept ever forward, groping her way along the ragged walls and past slimy shoring timbers with her right shoulder and left hand.

One foot splashed into a shallow puddle. She stopped for a moment, but pressed resolutely on until the water had filled her shoes and was up to her knees. The cold made her gasp out loud. But there was nowhere to go but onwards.

She stopped again when the water was almost up to her waist. Putting a hand up to the ceiling, she groped forwards far enough to know that it sloped inexorably down towards the water. Thistle had begun to struggle again and to mew pitifully from inside the sewing bag.

Brenn turned back. Her teeth chattering violently, her heavy skirts plastered to her knocking knees, the girl sloshed her way out of the water and stood crouched and gasping in the utter darkness. She sobbed aloud twice and then she wiped the tears from her face. 'Further we cannot venture, little tabby,' she said through juddering teeth, 'and we cannot stay here, so back we must go.'

Brenn shuffled and stumbled soddenly back the way she had come. But she had barely gone a hundred paces before she tripped on her trailing skirts and fell with a cry to her bruised knees. As she was holding the cat with her right hand, she took the weight of the fall on her left, cutting her palm and wrenching her wrist. She sat for a while clutching her arm and rocking back and forth with the pain. When she stopped rocking she realised that she didn't know in which direction she faced... towards the water or away from it. The cold, the silence and the dark were absolute.

I could stumble about in this rabbit-hole, she thought despairingly, *finding the water then losing my direction, back and forth, back and forth, for the rest of my short life.*

She sniffed loudly. 'This won't do, little cat,' she muttered through her chattering teeth, 'we must get on.' She made to wipe away her tears again but stopped, astonished. Very faintly, she could *see* her fingers.

Clumsily she tried to rise and turn at the same time but, tangled in her wet skirts, came down hard on her grazed knees yet again. But she hardly noticed. A light; a tiny, flickering, yellow flame advanced towards her, illuminating the pitted walls and rubbly floor. Soon she could see the person who carried it: a young man, stooped beneath the low ceiling. His dark hair swung about his shoulders, and his face was beautiful. In his right hand he carried a candlestick with care and in his left a bundle wrapped in oilskin. He halted and stared at her with his brows raised and his eyes wide.

Brenn stared back until she recalled the tears that must still have been shining upon her cheeks. She wiped at them with her dirty fingers, suddenly conscious of her unprepossessing appearance.

'Alas, my lady is sad,' said the young man, and the cat answered him with a pitiful miaow. 'The cat, too. Yet I know not why, when they have found the finest place in the castle. Indeed, I wonder that the whole of Lawhill is not down here, the view is so agreeable...' He paused, his dark eyes gleaming in the candlelight. 'In sooth, it is from where I'm standing,' he said, then looked away apologetically. 'Begging your pardon, my lady,' he said, 'but ye be most unexpected. Whence... how... did ye come to this place?'

But Brenn had a more pressing question. 'Who are ye?' she asked shakily. She was puzzled, for though his garb was that of a lackey or a peasant, his voice was not.

'I'm no one,' he said quietly. He knelt, carefully wedged his candlestick between two rocks, and opened Brenn's restlessly wriggling embroidery bag. 'But this is someone; this is Thistle,' he said. 'I recognised her voice. Ye've come from the princess's tower then. Ye must be one of her ladies... the newest one.' He looked at her with a shy smile. 'Lady Brenn?'

'Yes,' she whispered. 'I'm glad to see you, for I was lost; I dropped my candle and in the dark came to a place where water filled the passage... I tried to go further... that's why I'm so wet.'

The young man lifted the cat from the bag and she nestled happily against his chest. 'But why are ye down here?' he asked, stroking the tabby's head.

Brenn drew a shuddering breath. 'I was all alone in the princess's chamber and the... the dragon came. It broke the tower and set everything afire. I couldn't get out by the door but I found this passage... and then I remembered the cat...'

Thistle had wrapped her paws about the boy's neck and begun to purr. But all the while he gazed only at Brenn. 'The tower broke, yet ye escaped,' he said. 'How brave ye are; braver than all our soldiers!' Whether his voice was *quite* that of a boy of gentle birth hardly mattered for it was as soft as velvet. 'May I ask... did ye know of the passage before ye found it?'

'I knew it was somewhere, but I knew not where. Thistle liketh you. I know naught of cats, except that they scratch.'

'Aye, they are bad creatures,' he said fondly, pulling the cat's ears, 'especially this one. The princess will be exceeding glad ye have rescued her.'

'How is it ye are acquainted with her cat? Do ye know her also?'

The boy hesitated, glancing down at the ground with a smile. 'The princess...' he began, 'the princess knoweth these passages well, as do I. It was inevitable that one day our paths should cross down here... in sooth, they crossed so thoroughly that she knocked me over.' He laughed at the recollection. 'Mayhap she was bored at the time and wondered, upon seeing a simpleton clambering, gape-mouthed, to his feet before her, what she could make of such mean material. Whatever her motive, she set about turning the wretch into a scholar and now I have a head as full of sundries as any lord's.' He clapped a hand to his mouth in mock dismay. 'And now I have told you our secret... certes, the princess doth say I talk too much.'

'She taught you!' laughed Brenn. 'In secret!'

'Aye, in her chamber, half buried in books, and never once had I need to get by a guard, or a lady-in-waiting, or even to pass through a chamber door.'

'Buried in books,' breathed Brenn: 'that soundeth like a sort of heaven...'

The twain knelt before each other on the floor of the passage as the candle's tiny light flickered between them and all around pressed the drowning darkness. In wonder they gazed at each other and laughed, for how full of delight seemed the world.

'What is your name?' asked Brenn. 'And who are ye?' She hugged herself and her teeth chattered. 'I pray you, say not "no one", for it is clear ye must be someone.'

'Oh, my lady, ye are cold,' said the boy. 'How stupid and slow I am! Here... I have a cloak.' He tugged at the strings tying his oilskin-clad bundle, got it open and extricated a good new cloak of black wool.

Within the oilskin wrapping Brenn caught a glimpse of clothing and boots that were not the garb of a peasant.

'Thank you,' said Brenn, gratefully wrapping the cloak around her shoulders. 'But ye've not answered my questions.'

The boy still didn't answer. He unfastened the pouch at his belt, took from it a new candle, and then one-handedly (as he still held the cat) lit it from the ruin of the old and pushed it into the melted wax in his candlestick.

At last he looked up at her with a strangely diffident smile. 'My name is Ancaios,' he said, 'and I *am* no one... certainly no one that my lady would care to know. Yet I may be of some small use to you for I can deliver you and Thistle safely up into the castle. And then I must away for I have a commission from the king to deliver, and to do it I need go through that water.' He was about to fasten shut his pouch when he stopped and withdrew from it a small, wrapped item; discarding its oilcloth he revealed a slim book, no bigger than his hand. 'I forgot I had this useless thing about me,' he said. 'It is not much, but 'tis the only book I own. Can I ask my lady to keep it for me?'

He handed the little volume to her and she held it close to the candlelight and turned a few of its pages. It was a bestiary, printed by press onto paper, and its woodblock illustrations depicted beasts of fable as well as some that the artist had surely invented.

'This is the second lovely book I have seen today,' said Brenn, suddenly aware that the princess's book, pushed down the front of her bodice, probably made her look a peculiar shape. But it had slid down too far to go fishing for it now. 'I have the princess's book down here,' she said, putting her hand on it and blushing a little.

Ancaios smiled. 'I thought it might have been a book,' he said. 'A very fortunate book... and as ye have rescued it for the princess I'm sure 'tis a more impressive volume than mine.'

'But yours is surely the future of books. The princess told me that printing shall change the world. Oh look, here is a dragon!' Brenn read aloud: 'Dragons seldom eat flesh, but when an appetite for meat ariseth

their sole taste is for humankind. It hath also been written that in times
of tribulation they are wont to feed upon their own young.'

'I know not how the author can have known such things,' said
Ancaios, 'yet it soundeth to me as though it may be sooth. Ye do like
the book?'

'Aye, 'tis lovely.'

''Tis yours then... my humble gift to my lady.'

'Nay, I cannot take your only book!'

'I would feel honoured if ye would accept it.'

Brenn turned to look at him, her eyes shining. 'Do ye always give
away your possessions to whomsoever doth like them?' she asked. 'If I
were to tell you that I like your face and hair, are ye likely to chop off
your head and give it to me?'

'Where's an axe?' answered he, foolishly looking about him. 'But
nay, ye may have it anyway, still attached. 'Tis yours... and the heart
beneath it.'

'The heart too!' breathed Brenn. Her own heart raced and leapt.
'How easily ye do give away your heart!'

Ancaios shook his head. 'I've not given it to anyone 'til now,'
said he, gazing intently, wonderingly at Brenn, 'yet it was yours the
moment I first did see you, lit like a sylph in my candlelight.' He gave a
little laugh and turned away, half hiding his face behind the fall of his
hair. 'Forgive me,' he said. 'I forget myself. I am a fool to think that a
highborn lady would want such a poor gift.'

Brenn could scarcely speak. 'How could a heart ever be a poor gift?'
she whispered.

'The heart of a low creature like me is a worthless thing; of far less
value than that book.' He got to his feet and straightened as much as he
could under the low roof. 'Come, my lady, we must go or my second
candle will burn away and leave us in the dark. I pray ye carry the candlestick, for I might need both hands for the cat if she doth struggle.'

'What of your parcel?'

'I shall leave it here. No one is like to carry it off before I return.'

He helped her to her feet, then set off almost blindly, for very little of the candlelight got past him to illuminate the passage's ragged walls. Brenn followed in a dream, stumbling along, holding the candle up with an unsteady hand as all the while her eyes drank in his lovely form. Once or twice she remembered, with astonishment, the frightened girl who had groped her way down this passage such a short while ago.

As she was holding the bestiary in her left hand she had no way to shield the tiny flame, and it was snuffed out barely fifty paces from where they had started. But Ancaios produced a flint and after some breathless laughing (and mewing) in the darkness, they shortly had the candle lit again.

So as to have her left hand free Brenn pushed the bestiary down the front of her bodice until it came up against the princess's book (which was held there by the waistband of her petticoat). Ancaios protested, saying that he could carry it once more in his purse, but Brenn insisted it stay where it was. 'I am happy to be a library,' she said. 'All I want now are some shelves, and a catalogue.'

Ancaios shifted Thistle to one shoulder. 'I would that I could turn myself into a book then,' he said softly as he set forth once more along the passage.

'Why?' asked Brenn, following behind. 'Do ye think only books shall ever lie here?'

Ancaios turned to look at her, walking backwards, and she felt her cheeks flush. Suddenly the back of his head came into sharp contact with the uneven roof. He doubled over and hopped about histrionically, clutching his pate. Adding to the pain the little cat climbed further up his shoulder, using her sharp claws for purchase. Brenn had to laugh at the performance. 'Best take care of that pretty poll, Master Book,' she admonished. 'It's mine now, remember, and I don't want my chattel broken.'

'Ye'll still have my heart intact, Lady Library,' he said, rubbing his head as he ventured forward into the treacly darkness, 'and if that's broken 'twill be nobody's fault but your own.'

With a breathless laugh, Brenn followed him. The candle's frail light flickered across the walls of the rabbit-hole along which they passed, but the girl, pink-cheeked and shiny-eyed, may as well have been dancing through a gilded hall to a fanfare of trumpets. The two of them made no hurry, but dawdled and dallied as Ancaios asked questions (about everything from Brenn's flight from the tower to her home in Drumalis) and she answered, babbling brightly, breathlessly. She questioned him too, but his answers were short and self-effacing and revealed little about himself. Yet he had a knack of adding asides to her own chatter that made her laugh, and he attended to her as though she were the most fascinating person in the world. He turned as he listened, walking sideways or backwards, and as a result knocked his head three more times on the low roof. As each knock became another occasion for tomfoolery, Brenn laughed till the tears ran down her face.

All too soon they came to a branch in the passage that Brenn had somehow missed during her terrified flight from the tower.

''Tis this way,' said Ancaios.

Brenn stopped and the laughter faded from her face. 'I wish ye would not go,' she said. 'Out there… can ye get safely away?'

'I'm not afraid of the dragon,' he answered merrily. ''Tis a poor, purblind thing.'

'It smells human fear,' whispered Brenn, with sudden cognition; 'that's how it doth hunt.'

'Ye're clever! Quicker than I am, for at first I felt sure it was our scent that attracted it. I made for myself a cloak that smelled of animals and it seemed to work, but I suspect that's because it made me less fearful. I hope so, for I've lost my cloak.' Ancaios laughed. 'Certes, 'tis simple: if I encounter the dragon again, all I need do is *not be afraid.*'

'It made me terribly afraid, said Brenn, 'and then… and then it made me feel so sad that I wept.'

Ancaios laughed again. 'I'm glad I'm not the only one. But we must move on,' he added, 'for the candle is nigh halfway gone and I do not have another.'

As the twain made their way up a steep stretch of passage and a flight of uneven stairs, Ancaios told Brenn of the daft errand on which the king had sent him and, in just a few moments, had her laughing again. They came at last to a low iron door, pitted with rust, and barely high enough to traverse on hands and knees. 'This is the way out,' said Ancaios. 'Climb through and I shall pass the cat out to you.'

'Ancaios...' said Brenn. She touched his arm. 'Come out with me – just for a moment – I would see thee in the light.'

'But... Brenn.' He spoke her un-prefixed name hesitantly. 'There's no light out there; thou'llt find thyself in a dead-ended branch of the scullion's walk betwixt the Watchtower and the East Tower... north to thy right, south to thy left.'

In the narrow passage he stood close to her, with just the cat and the candle between them. 'Oh, thy candle burneth away...' she breathed. 'Ancaios, I do promise...'

But he put his fingers gently across her mouth. 'No promises,' he whispered. She took his hand and pressed it to her lips. 'Oh Brenn,' he murmured, 'despite our talk of heads and hearts, I can but ask of thee one thing, and that is to forget me the moment I am gone. For thou art the princess's cousin and I am cousin to maggots and flies.' He withdrew his hand and knelt to open the low door. 'Prithee, Brenn... my candle dwindleth fast...'

Brenn put the candle on the floor. Its light spangled in her eyes. She got down on her hands and knees and wriggled through the door, then turned about, still on her knees to face him. 'I *shall* remember thee after thou art gone,' she said, smiling and crying, 'and I shan't break thy heart.'

Ancaios gently handed the cat through the door. She didn't want to go and clung to his garments with her claws. 'Nay, little Thistle,' he protested, 'Brenn hath saved thy life and will take thee now to thy mistress. Brenn... just hold her close... aye, like that. She won't scratch... not much, anyway.' Brenn held the cat and stroked her silky coat. A tear ran down her cheek, but just to see him there, kneeling in the low doorway with the candlelight on his face, made her smile in wonderment. 'Ancaios...' she murmured, 'return swiftly, safely... to me.'

'Brenn,' he said, 'I should have told thee the minute I first saw thee...' He looked at her with his strange reluctant smile. 'Lady, king's messenger is a low enough job, but I am not even that; the king hath employed me only because there is no one else. My father is a gong-farmer and I am his apprentice. And now I must go. Fare well, Lady Brenn; commend me to your lady.' He pulled the door shut and it closed with a thud and a click. In the gloom of the dead-ended passage, it looked like naught more than another of the wall's ashlars. Brenn reached out and touched it and then she sat for a moment, shivering in her damp skirts and hugging the warm little cat to her.

The sound of voices and hurried footsteps had her clambering to her feet. In the dim light she saw servants with stacked, empty buckets dart across the opening of the short passage in which she stood. They were heading south, towards the princess's tower. 'Oh me!' said Brenn to the cat. 'My lady shall think we've both been eaten by the dragon or burnt to cinders!'

Holding the little creature tight, she set off at a soggy-skirted run towards the servants' passage. She hardly looked like one of the princess's highborn ladies, for she was grimy, dishevelled and damp. Tears streaked her face, her hands were cut and scratched and from her shoulders flapped the plain black cloak of a king's man. Turning into the passage, she hurried south towards the princess's tower, sometimes twirling herself in a circle or pausing to kiss the cat in her arms. She smiled a faraway smile and her hazel eyes shone.

The sound of axes thudding into the ceiling timbers of the under-chamber came echoing down the stairwell. Winterhued leant exhaustedly against the wall of the guardroom below and put her head in her hands.

'Dearest Winter,' murmured Sir Almendral in a lull between axe strokes, 'do not blame yourself.'

'But it is my fault,' whispered the princess; 'she wished to accompany me and I forced her to stay.'

The axes started up again and three more servants ran by, water slopping from their wooden buckets. They crossed the torch-lit chamber and headed up the stair. It was a futile attempt to save what was left of the tower, for the water had to be carted all the way from the East Tower, and there were not enough servants to make a chain. Besides, the stairwell being choked with fallen masonry, they could but hurl water at the under-chamber's smoking ceiling.

When the news had first come to Winterhued, she had rushed up the stairs to haul frantically at the solidly wedged rubble with her bare hands, calling Brenn's name and coughing in the roiling smoke. But after Almendral had coaxed her down to the guardroom, she had seen more clearly and given the order to cut through the ceiling.

Two soldiers, coming downstairs, squeezed past the servants. They were carrying an ash-coated casket and a damp wall hanging: more rescued goods from the lower chamber. The salvaged stuff was heaped along one side of the guardroom and thrown across it was the bolt of shimmering silk from Ilala. Winterhued moaned when she saw it.

'I am a tyrant, and a hypocrite,' she said. In answer, Almendral just shook his head mutely as the axes rang out from above. ''Tis sooth,' said Winterhued, raising her voice above the noise, 'for I am full of high-minded talk about granting women the freedom to choose, yet gave my precious girl no choice.'

The axes stopped. They heard scuffling from above and, moments later, hurrying feet upon the stairs. 'Naught, your highness,' said a soot-smeared soldier. ''Tis but a charred wreck open to the sky.' His voice cracked and he paused to cough into his blackened hands. 'Pardon ma'am,' he croaked. ''Tis all burned away down to the floorboards and they'd have been consumed too but for their wet undersides. All we can do is quench what's smouldering and fetch the last of your highness' goods from the under-chamber; most of them damaged, I'm afraid, what with the water and the ash and smoke.'

The princess dismissed the man with a blank nod and he bowed and hurried back upstairs. Two more servants ran by with their buckets, but Winterhued saw them not. She stood staring at the wet flagstones.

'She hath perished then... my little cousin...'

'Your highness,' said a guard behind her, but she scarcely heard him.

'I'll tell her,' said Almendral to the guard. 'Winter...' he said, touching her arm. But Winterhued turned from him and buried her face once more in her hands.

'Winter,' repeated the marquess, 'hearken. 'Tis sooth, there's not a shadow of doubt the girl's dead and gone, but waste not a moment more in grieving for her. She was pretty and clever enough, I grant you, but ye'll find dozens just like her. Why, ye'll replace her as quick as ye can put on your shoe. As for the cat... even quicker, for already I have found for you a new one.'

The princess spun to face him, aghast and angry. Almendral flinched from her, but her fury was not enough to wipe the grin from his face. She stared at him incredulously for he was indeed holding a cat in his arms, and it was her own dear little Thistle, blinking her green eyes and opening her mouth to mewl a hungry complaint.

And then Winterhued saw the girl who stood behind Almendral, stifling her laughter behind lacerated hands. Her hair was bedraggled, her gown was damp and filthy, her face was tear-streaked and grazed, but she was the princess's own beloved little cousin.

'Brenn!' she gasped. 'How..? How didst thou..?' She took the girl in her arms, lifting her half off her feet.

'I found the secret passage,' explained Brenn breathlessly, 'I went down into the dark. I was lost. I met... I met a boy...' She whispered the last few words urgently, as if she was revealing a wondrous secret.

Winterhued held her at arms' length, laughing when she saw the girl's glowing cheeks and shining eyes.

'Ancaios,' she said.

Brenn nodded, smiling like the sun. 'He commended himself to my lady,' she said. 'He asked me to tell m'lady that he hath been sent on an errand by the king.' Her words tripped over each other in their haste to be out. 'He is to find an unnamed knight who hath a unicorn as his badge and offer him my lady's hand if he doth slay the dragon… and that he knew it was a fool's errand but he had given the king his word. He also gave the king his word that he would not tell my lady, but he thought that if he told me and I told my lady, he would not have broken his word.'

Sir Almendral snorted. 'So the king hath sent your canny lad off to find this quintessence of valour, this paragon of paladins, who will thenceforth ride hither, single-handedly slay the dragon, and win your hand in marriage!' Laughing, he put the wriggling cat down on the floor. 'Ye must be all aquiver at the prospect, my dear.'

'What folly!' exclaimed the princess, still holding Brenn close. The cat pushed herself up against her skirts and mewed. 'And what a waste. For of all those within the castle, that boy is the most likely to get where he is sent… so why, oh why, did the king not send him to hurry our army along?'

'Army?' snorted Almendral. 'Untried louts commanded by a bungling buffoon? Better to have sent the lad north to seek aid from my father.'

'The king would sooner walk into the dragon's mouth than *that*. Besides, thy father and his troops are distant and our army close. I just hope that at least one of our messengers got away and that, even now, our soldiers march to our aid. For no matter who commandeth them,' she added, 'surely a thousand bowmen may do some good against this creature.'

Nestled exhaustedly within the princess's arms, Brenn heard hardly a word of this exchange. 'The cat is hungry,' she murmured.

'And so art thou,' said Winterhued, holding the girl from her and studying her face. 'Poor Brenn. I haven't even thanked thee for saving Thistle. How brave and resourceful and... heavens, lass: what is that down thy front?'

'Books,' said Brenn, fishing out the bestiary from her bodice. 'And I have rescued your beautiful book too... but it's fallen down too far.' Gripping a handful of her gown's fabric just beneath the bodice, she shook it and the princess's book fell to the floor.

Winterhued stared at it, then knelt to take it in her hands. 'Thou hast saved the three things within my chambers that meant more to me than anything else,' she said, looking up at Brenn.

'Three, my lady? Nay... I saved but two.' Brenn's voice shook and her teeth chattered.

Winterhued rose and put an arm around the girl's shoulders. 'Come,' she said, 'we must get the both of you fed and warmed.'

'Leave the food to me,' said Sir Almendral. Promising to have a veritable feast ready in the undercroft by the time they arrived, he exited the chamber, dodging more servants as they went by with their buckets sloshing.

Brenn was already half asleep. She smiled dreamily and turned to murmur, ever so softly, into the princess's ear, 'I love him.'

'Who? Almendral?'

'Nay!' protested the girl.

Winterhued laughed as she scooped up the cat in one arm. 'Poor lovelorn lass,' she said as she pulled Brenn close with the other, 'dost thou know *what* Ancaios is?' She guided Brenn towards the door, nodding as she went to one of the guards stationed there.

'Aye, he told me,' whispered Brenn, oblivious to all around her; 'he's the gong-farmer's son... but, my lady, I care not; I would happily run away and live with him in a hovel with a dirt floor and wear homespun and eat turnips every day. I just want to see him again... so that I may tell him this.'

As they left the chamber Winterhued hugged the girl and bent to kiss the top of her head. The chosen guard, turning to follow them, grinned at his fellow stationed on the opposite side of the doorway. 'Homespun and turnips, eh?' he murmured. 'Our Stench is proving quite a lad!'

The other man frowned. 'Don't call 'im Stench,' he growled.

The knight and his squire rode along the cart track that wound its way northward from Wendur. A muddy bunch of children trailed behind them, leaping puddles, shouting and laughing, shoving, fighting and tumbling. The grey stallion swung along in a great, long-striding walk, his eyes bright, his ears pricked and his belly full of oats and sweet hay. The red gelding jogged sometimes to keep up, the nailheads of his new iron shoes punching sharp indentations into the road's surface.

Bouncing about like an ill-secured bundle of kindling, the boy on the chestnut's back grumbled incessantly under his breath. The knight turned to him good-humouredly and patted his head as if he were a favourite hound. 'Be of good cheer, Nal,' said he, 'for we have a saddlebag full of provender and the sun doth shine.'

'It won't be shinin' tonight,' muttered Nal, 'when we're sleepin' out 'ere an' that warm bed's empty.' He scowled sulkily. 'What were the name o' that inn?'

The knight glanced quizzically at the boy. 'The King's Head,' he replied.

'King's 'Ead? Then why'd ye tell me it were Goose's Nob? Ye made me look a fool in front o' them girls.'

'King's Head, Goose's Nob,' replied the knight, 'I see no difference. Not when Gers is the king in question.'

'I wouldn' be sayin' that too loudly,' muttered Nal, looking round for any lurking spies. But even the last of the children had given up the chase and turned back for Wendur. Their shouts and squeals faded on the still air.

The road crested a rise and sloped away before the riders into a wide valley. In the centre of the vale, watched over by a cluster of stone cottages, the road forked, one branch running off into the west beside the silver glint of a stream. 'That's the Otterburn,' said the knight, pointing; 'we shall follow it all the way to Lawhill.'

Beyond the cottages that huddled between dark evergreens and strips of tilled land, the northern road crossed the Otterburn via a humped bridge, then climbed the heather-clad slopes and vanished over the top into the blue hills beyond. Far, far to the north, and curving round like a great protective arm into the east, a range of snowy mountains glinted in the spring sunshine.

The two big horses jogged down the gentle descent towards the cottages. Long before they reached the first of them, half a dozen ruddy-cheeked, runny-nosed children had materialised to run beside the road, ogling wide-eyed at the strangers. Out in the narrow fields two oxen drifted to a halt as the man at the plough-handles turned to stare. Women appeared at the cottage doors, babes balanced upon their hips and spindles in their hands. 'The sele of the day to you, good folk,' said the knight in a courteous manner, but apart from two men who remembered to doff their caps respectfully, the cottagers could but gape at him as though he had just ridden down from the moon.

The knight turned west as soon as he reached the fork in the road, but Nal yanked on the reins in an attempt to stop his mount. When the horse ignored him he pulled the chestnut's head around, forcing it to circle tightly. 'Must we go that way?' he whined. 'Why can't we go north to that Anger place and get on a boat like ye said? That's what I want... to go on a boat. I've never been on a boat, but ye never do care what I want.'

With a sigh, the knight reined his horse in and turned to face the boy. ''Twas but yesterday thou hadst a great desire to go west and now we are going west.'

'Aye, 'eadlong into some great maraudin' army, what's rapin', pillagin' an' murderin'. I come from Pengwern... uncle an' cousins slaughtered. I know about armies.'

'Nal...'

'Nay, 'ear me out. What good can ye do? Ye're but one man! Why must ye always go chargin' into whatever danger 'appens along? Because this time I'm not goin' with you.'

'Nal,' said the knight, 'no indenture binds thee; thou mayest depart my service at any time. But, understand this, if thou dost choose to leave now, I can give thee little. Thou mayest have whatever coins I possess, but thou shalt walk on thine own two legs.'

'So ye want me to get off the 'orse an' then ye'll ride off, leavin' me in this backwater with no'but a few coins?'

'No, what I want is for thee to accompany me westward as my squire, knowing that thou art not bound to me. If thou dost remain set upon leaving, I'll not see thee destitute, but endeavour to provide the wherewithal for thy return to Pengwern by selling one of my swords.'

The red gelding had ambled up beside the grey and now the knight turned his horse's head to the west. The two set forth, splashing along the puddled road as, beside them, the tree-fringed Otterburn rushed and burbled over its stony course.

'I'm not goin' back to Pengwern,' muttered Nal. ''Orrible place.' He rode silently for a while, then glanced up at the knight with a sneer. 'This worthless nag,' he said, 'I wouldn' want 'im anyway. An' ye should be ashamed o' that old thing ye're sittin' on. A knight should 'ave a proud black destrier, glossy and prancin', not a bad-tempered old bag o' bones.'

'If I could purchase,' replied the knight, 'a prancing black destrier for the price of a loaf of bread I might do so, yet I'd not need him. Hougomont may not look much, but he's the finest horse I ever rode in a joust. A shift of weight turns or stops him, he runs straight and strong, and he's as brave as a lion. As for 'bad-tempered', thou art the only person he doth bite, lad. He enjoys it.'

Nal scowled fiercely. 'Y'call 'im brave?' he muttered. 'Stupid more like.'

'Thou hast witnessed his prowess thyself,' continued the knight; 'we'd not have done so well in Balasore without him. He was a bargain, too. I purchased him down in Quathlamba for a fraction of his worth...'

'What... 'alf the 'ole in a tin farthin'?' mumbled Nal.

'...for he'd been beaten and starved. The brute that sold him smirked as he took my money for he thought the horse fractious, lazy and broken down.'

'Describes 'im perfec'ly.'

'As for that poor fellow...' The knight nodded towards the chestnut rounsey. 'I found him standing in the marketplace in Pengwern with his head down, his eyes shut against the flies and his ribs staring. The butcher was eyeing him with interest.'

'So ye bought 'im for me. An 'igh opinion ye 'ad o' your new squire.'

'I could see he was a good horse: tough and sound. Thou'dst not ridden before; if I'd got thee a spirited mount that leapt and started at every shadow, I'd have seen thee on the ground more often than not.' As if to demonstrate his point, three sheep with black faces and curled horns started up from behind a clump of gorse beside the stream and ran before the horses, their heavy fleeces bouncing above quick, thin legs. The two horses barely blinked at their sudden appearance.

Standing balanced on a rock in midstream, a round eyed shepherd boy stared at the riders as most of his flock ambled away across the hillside behind him. He was half concealed by the upsweeping branches of a big alder, which stood with its roots in the stream, dropping purple and yellow catkins into the water and into the boy's hair.

'Good morrow, lad,' said the knight. He halted at the road's verge, looking down at the boy. 'Mayhap thou canst tell me: why have the birds flown away? Where are the magpie and throstle, the lark and linnet?'

The boy did naught but stare with his mouth slightly open. Another catkin fell onto his head.

'Come lad,' encouraged the knight, 'I don't bite. My squire and I have ridden across the flanks of Iron Crag and, but for the ravens, its forests are still and silent. And now we find this valley silent also. 'Tis spring; branches bud and catkins fall,' said he, with a slight smile; 'this place should be brimming with birdsong.'

The boy blinked, then shook the blossoms from his head. 'They...' he croaked, and then he sneezed, sniffed and wiped his nose on his sleeve. 'They all flew away, y'lordship,' he managed, his voice rough from infrequent use. 'They came back, follerin' winter, but all flew off again... two, three days past.' He waved his hands above his head. 'Clouds of 'em; all flyin' away as if winter were comin' back, not spring.'

'In which direction did they fly?' asked the knight. But the boy had depleted his supply of words for the day and could only gesticulate towards the east.

'I've never heard of an army that makes birds fly before it.' The knight fished a coin from his saddlebag and tossed it onto a flat-topped rock. 'That's for thy trouble, lad,' said he, turning his horse back to the westbound road.

Nal glared at him as he rode past. 'What y'give 'im that for?' he asked, but as the red horse set out after the grey, the boy's pecuniary anxieties were quickly forgotten. Nal didn't want to find out what it was that had made the birds fly away. 'Can't we go north?' he asked in a small, hopeless voice.

'I have a recollection of... was it yesterday? Thou didst complain that we perished in the wilderness when we should have been searching for adventure. Didst thou not mention ogres and dragons?'

'I never said ogres and dragons,' muttered the boy.

'And now we ride replete, with a saddlebag full of food and a chance of adventure before us and still thou dost complain.'

''Twas you said ogres and dragons,' mumbled Nal and rode on in scowling silence.

The valley stretched wide and fertile about them. It was clad in verdant, sheep-cropped turf, dotted with the enamel-bright yellow of marsh marigolds. Forest spilled down its southern slopes, the winter-bare boughs of the trees blushing pale green with burgeoning growth. There was little sign of habitation though, only the occasional shepherd's cot, sometimes circled by drystone walls, and reached by sheep tracks that muddily forded the busy rills that flowed down the valley sides to join the Otterburn. On a prominence to the north stood a ruined castle, a cluster of deserted dwellings mouldering at its bastioned feet.

'This is good land; some of the best in Manydown,' said the knight as he looked about him, 'but it lieth within the marquisate of Potrimpos. The sycophants who have held that title for over a hundred years have no interest in their lands; they merely appoint stewards to collect the taxes and, while they are about it, fill their own purses. The lords spend not a penny on the land and do naught to help its inhabitants improve their lot. 'Tis sooth that no one starves here, but neither do they prosper; they work hard only to keep their lords in velvet.'

Nal had not been listening. His mount, following the grey stallion, had broken into a baggage-clattering trot and the boy's teeth rattled in his head. 'Why must we run so fast into danger?' he juddered.

The knight glanced round at him. 'Fast?' said he. 'Good counsel, Nal.' He gave the grey his head and the stallion leapt forward eagerly. Nal groaned, abandoning his reins and grabbing hold of the saddle as the chestnut bounded after the grey.

Down the valley went the two big horses and the ground shook beneath their iron-shod hoofs. Behind them stretched a wake of broken earth; a wake that had stretched away behind the knight for many leagues and many years. Winding and turning in serpentine meander-ings, from north to south, east to west, across seas and mountains, through forests and deserts, his tracks had looped the world and now for the first time converged on this lonely road. Yet it seemed to him that but a year or two had passed since he'd journeyed, sore-hearted, along this road into exile; he'd felt angry and lost, yet somehow full of hope for he was young and the wide world lay before him.

Another horse had carried him then, carried him faithfully across many lands for a thousand leagues or more, and carried him to triumph in countless tourneys and battles; his beloved old chestnut stallion, a horse noble and strong, honest and ever anxious to please. Bred tough in the snows and icy winds of the northern marches, his bones now lay scattered far to the south, bleaching upon sands under a desert sun.

His replacement had been a fiery desert-bred horse, mahogany with gold dapples, and ears curved like scythes. Quick, clever and full of temper, for twelve years he had been a true friend and had died because of that friendship; sinking valiantly amidst the thickest press of fighting into the mud and blood of a terrible, victorious, battlefield.

Then had followed an empty time; the first since he'd worn swaddling clothes that the knight had been without a horse. Quathlamba's avaricious king, for whom the knight had ill advisedly fought, proved to be a faithless ingrate and his meanness seeped into the very hearts of his subjects. For well nigh half a year, far from home, with few friends, scant charity, and barely able to speak the local tongue, the knight had faced a wretched existence. For he had been so direfully wounded in the battle that had killed his horse that, though he had managed to cling to life, he feared his remaining years would be spent as a crippled mendicant, begging alms at a dusty roadside. Eventually, with the devoted help of his squire Lasbek, he had rallied sufficiently to feel hope again, and with the meagre funds remaining to him had purchased the old grey stallion. Looking like a parody of knighthood the two of them (accompanied by Lasbek and his bay rounsey) had shuffled away from Quathlamba. And travelling ever north, they had together made slow recoveries: the knight from his wounds and the horse from starvation and abuse.

Those days were far behind the old horse now, and he stretched himself out in an earth-pounding gallop. Before his flying hoofs the westbound road curled along the valley floor like a welcome. Above, the sky arched blue and cloud-dotted, all about lay the wide green meadows, and beside the road the Otterburn rushed sparkling along its stony course into the west... towards a wide silver lake and a great grey castle.

The knight laughed. Leaning forward in the saddle, he ran a hand down the thick crest of his stallion's neck. The horse's ears turned back attentively then flicked forward again; his tangled mane tossed like pennants in the wind.

'A pox on Gers,' swore the knight. 'At this moment, and come what may, I am home... I have come home, Winterhued.'

'Waaii...toofaashh...' wailed Nal from an ever increasing distance to the rear.

The knight eased his horse to a canter and the chestnut caught up, the boy bouncing and grunting miserably in the saddle.

'Thou'rt stiff as a post,' said the knight. 'Use thy back, lad. Move with the horse; think of polishing the saddle with thy buttocks. Relax, remember to breathe, enjoy the fine day.'

'Nnngaaah,' said Nal, who had no buttocks to speak of and could hardly have been more miserable if the heavens had opened to souse him with sleet.

They did not stop. The horses, keen and fit, cantered loose-reined and long-striding, eating up the miles. After a time they slowed to a clattering trot to pass another cluster of cottages and staring faces and for a while a few more raggle-taggle children scampered in their wake.

The valley opened out into a wide plain, with a blanket of forest lying along its far southern edges and distant blue hills to the north. The Otterburn widened, slowed and spread itself out into an expanse of marshland. Here, where the road turned southwest to skirt the marsh, the horses came at last to a walk. Lowering their heads and breathing hard, they clopped their muddy way beside sheets of still water fringed by waving sedge that whispered dryly in the wind.

Far ahead, glimpsed beyond a thicket of blackthorn and goat willow, three dark shapes appeared, moving swiftly along a loop of the road. Almost before they could be discerned as men on horseback, the sound of cantering hoofbeats came drifting on the breeze.

Nal drew breath sharply and made an attempt to rein in his horse. 'Soldiers,' he hissed; 'scouts from the invadin' army!'

'Whither art thou going, Nal?' asked the knight, amused.

'We've got to run away, 'ide somewhere. Three against one's not good odds.'

'Three against two. Use my short sword; thou dost need the practice.'

'Ye bein' funny?' said Nal angrily. 'Y'know I can't 'ardly lift it.'

'We're doomed then,' said the knight, slapping a hand to his forehead in mock dismay.

'I 'ate you,' muttered Nal, 'an' I 'ope they kill you.'

With a smile the knight reached across and rumpled the boy's hair. 'They're not soldiers, lad,' he said.

They waited in the road for the riders to reach them.

Three travel-spattered men reined in their blowing horses before the knight and his squire. One of them was a solid middle-aged man clad in the black gown of a town burgher. His face was crimson, and his wind-straggled red hair hung to his shoulders from beneath a black fur cap. The other two men were considerably younger, but they too had red faces and red hair, and were clothed in sombre respectability. Their horses had been hard ridden, but were well-bred, strong animals. The older man looked the knight up and down and sneered slightly.

'If ye're going to Lawhill for the Dittonsday Tourney,' said he, puffing almost as much as his horse, 'ye may as well turn about.'

'And a good morrow to you too, sir,' said the knight amicably. 'I *am* bound for Lawhill, though not for the tourney. I've heard rumours of trouble in the west.'

'Trouble? Ha! The very devil from hell more like! My house in Lawhill burned down two nights past. The town's ablaze. My sons and I escaped with naught but the garments on our backs. Even then we barely evaded outlaws on the road. We ride to seek refuge with my brother...'

'The steward?' interrupted the knight. He still appeared calm though his eyes betrayed the urgency of his thoughts. 'Ye're alike as peas in a pod.'

'How...?'

'I had the pleasure of his company just this morn. Give him my regards. The bailiff as well; hospitable gentlemen both. Brave too, like yourself, sir. So why did ye abandon Lawhill and not stay to extinguish the flames?'

The older man scowled and yanked at his fidgeting horse's mouth. But before he could speak one of his sons pushed forward. ''Tis not just us,' he protested in a high voice. 'Ye'll see many more on the road if ye keep going... all of them that aren't perished.'

'No, he won't,' interrupted his brother, 'for most of them are heading south on the Drumrock road.'

'It mattereth not where they're bound,' snapped their father. 'What doth matter, sir, is that no one, brave or otherwise, may stay when a creature from the very pits of hell hath come to lay the town and castle waste and prey upon humankind. And when it hath finished with Lawhill it shall go forth to wreak destruction and ruin upon all the land. 'Tis a vast and fell creature and no one tarrying may escape it...'

'What kind of creature,' asked the knight, "may raze a town?'

'They say it's a dragon.'

'A dragon.' The knight half smiled and shook his head.

'Ye do not believe me, sir. But if ye ride west ye shall discover the truth of it soon enough.'

'What of the king?'

'Methinks no one from the castle escaped. All within its walls are dead.'

'Thank you, gentlemen,' said the knight shortly. Before Nal could react, he had reached across and tugged the reins from the boy's grasp. 'Hang on to the saddle,' he said as he touched the grey stallion's flanks and the two horses sprang forward once more upon the road to Lawhill.

CHAPTER 12

Ancaios' lungs were bursting. Groping above his head with one hand, he felt at last the roof of the tunnel rise. He gave a desperate kick and broke the surface of the black water, gulping air. Three more kicks and he felt the tunnel's floor beneath his feet. Pulling his bundle behind him, he splashed through knee-deep water, feeling blindly for the rough-hewn walls.

Some time later he crawled from darkness into dappled daylight. The passage emerged from its subterranean meanderings disguised as the mouth of an overgrown culvert that emptied into the Otterburn. Access was hindered by a locked, iron-barred door, but one of the bars had rusted through at its base and by wriggling and pushing, the boy forced his way out onto the bank of the stream. Young elms grew thickly here; their interwoven branches, still bare of leaves but covered abundantly with pale green seeds, gave good cover from the air. Ancaios looked back at the castle through the trees. It was a good way downstream; the Otterburn, just before it spilled into the lake, passed narrowly between the castle gate and the town walls in a swift-flowing channel that was usually spanned by the drawbridge.

Shivering, the boy undid his parcel then dragged off his dripping, tattered old tunic. He was going to have to make do with his soggy shirt though, and there was no disguising its frayed collar and sleeves. The beautiful boots were hard to pull on over his wet stockings but fortunately they were tall enough to cover most of the patches and darns. Last and finest of all, he put on the splendid black livery jacket with the king's sunburst badge blazoned on its breast, and belted the dagger and the king's purse (full of the king's money) about his hips. The jacket had got a little damp during his underwater journey and it instantly got much wetter as soon as he put it on, but still, he felt very fine in it. So fine that, despite his shivering and teeth-chattering, he had to strut about for a bit, looking down at himself in admiration. He did miss the warm cloak, but the sudden recollection of whom he'd given it to made him skip three steps and laugh silently, joyously at the sky.

Ancaios' wet tunic lay crumpled on the ground, stuck all over with gauzy, winged elm seeds. He knelt and fumblingly tore open part of the hem stitching and extricated something from its hiding place there. Holding the object in the palm of his hand, he gazed at it… a moonstone, set in a curlicued 'W' and hanging from a thin silver chain.

'What am I to do with you?' he asked through chattering teeth, before dropping it into the satchel with the king's documents. It was not the safest place for such a tiny, slippery item, but he would think of some other hiding place when he'd warmed up a bit. He pushed the tunic and oilskins into the culvert out of sight, swung the satchel over his shoulder and set off at a jog, eastward along the Otterburn.

Using what cover he could find, he followed the stream where it flowed swiftly beside the town walls, glancing frequently behind and

above him as he ran. Smoke rose from behind the walls, curling dirtily
into the blue sky, and in an eddying pool three bloated bodies floated
face down, their hair drifting like waterweed as they whirled and
bobbed in the current. Ancaios didn't stop; he'd seen such carnage on
his last foray from the castle.

Through a last copse of young elms loomed the great round towers
of the town gates. Between them, beneath a raised portcullis, lay the
deserted road. It curled out through the gates, crossed the stream over
a stone bridge and divided, one branch heading east and the other, a
mere cart track, south. His heart thudding, Ancaios climbed up from
the stream to the road and ran, doubled over, across the bridge. With
many glances over his shoulder at the sky he took the eastbound road,
running half-crouched beside the inadequate shelter of a tumbled wall.

'Where are ye, dragon?' he muttered as he dodged around six
blackened corpses. 'Weary from the hunt, or sated and fat from
the feasting?'

The road passed a row of smouldering houses and the remains of
several shops and a smithy, and headed into open countryside. To the
south lay a deserted common, a large expanse of nettle-infested grazing
land that would normally have been dotted with sheep, goats, geese
and rowdy children. The common rose up gently towards a line of dark
trees that marked the most westerly reach of great Gostwyck Forest,
and in its midst stood a low knoll crowned with thickly growing oaks.
Ancaios had passed this way many times and had surely noticed the
knoll before, but today it looked so strange to him that he kept glancing
at it as he ran by.

The road wound its bemired way uphill, following the line of the
Otterburn as it rushed, brimming with snow-melt, down towards the
lake. The stream lay on the north side of the road; twice it was crossed
by half-drowned fords, each leading to a cluster of byres and farmsteads.
Some of the buildings were blasted and burnt, and fences broken and
trampled. Animals wandered unmilked and untended in the meadows,
or lowed plaintively from the byres; a few of the strip-fields that sloped

down to the Otterburn had recently been ploughed, yet lay unsown and bare while spring burgeoned around them.

Ancaios was breathing hard from the running. At the easterly extremity of the common the forest crept in closer to the road and the boy was tempted to seek the shelter of its branches. But he stayed on the road and kept running, jumping the ruts and puddles. At least he was warmer and his clothes had almost dried, though his beautiful boots were splashed with mud, a blister was forming on his right heel and his stomach felt hollow.

A little further on a troop of straight-trunked pines grew in a disorderly line beside the road and beneath the shelter of their branches Ancaios slowed at last to a staggering jog, then a walk. His breathing ragged, he turned and walked backwards up the hill, gazing as he went at the vista below.

At first glance it appeared that nothing was amiss. The lake lay wide and placid, its surface as blue and cloud-filled as the sky. It covered the broad valley, its scalloped edges receding in a succession of bays and headlands, each becoming paler than the last until they were finally swallowed by hazy distance. Spanning the whole of the nearest promontory, the castle crouched massively above its shimmering reflection. It looked grand and unchanged from here, until one noticed the wreckage within its bailey walls, its broken, smoke-stained towers and the besmirched and roofless shell of its keep. Protective walls ran out from the castle and looped the town, but within their embrace the once crowded dwellings and thoroughfares appeared to have been ground underfoot by a giant and lay half-obscured beneath a pall of filthy smoke.

But for the cat's-paws of wind that now and then ruffled the lake's surface, nothing stirred in all that wide vista.

Ancaios came to a halt, pushing back the strands of hair that blew across his face. Beneath drawn brows, his eyes shone with tears as he formed a wordless prayer for all of the souls trapped within those broken walls. He didn't know to whom or what he prayed, for though he sometimes used the words 'God' and 'Lord', he'd only ever set foot in a church to catch glimpses of the wealth within and to gape at the gruesome wall-paintings. But in this he was like the majority of worldly Lawhillians who, despite the railing of the priests, could seldom be coaxed through the door of a church. 'The church is corrupt,' they complained, 'and its priests greedy and sinful.' Besides, if they were to believe the priests, any effort to save their venal souls was doomed from the outset. It had thus been convenient for them to follow the lead of the king who'd vowed never again to enter a place of worship. For his beloved queen had, whilst visiting a newly constructed church, been struck by a plummeting keystone and died two days later, leaving her baby daughter motherless.

But now people were saying that this dragon had come as punishment for the town's godlessness. *That can't be right though*, thought Ancaios, *for our saintly neighbour Holkar is dead and he took his long face off to church every day and some nights as well, yet our profane and creedless king is just as cheerfully alive as he's always been. Hundreds of good church-goers have perished, yet I, who do not even know how to pray, still have life... and look how I waste it by running off like a fool to follow a fool's foolish orders.*

A shadow fell across the road and Ancaios crouched down and retreated back towards the trunk of a pine. But it was only a cloud passing across the sun. Beside his hand a spider ran across the deeply scored bark, her back covered with minute babies. The boy watched her for a moment and smiled. 'I wish I could do that, little spider,' he said; 'put all the ones I love upon my back and carry them to safety.'

He turned away and ran on up the hill without a backward glance.

The road topped the steep rise but continued to climb gradually, winding about amongst the smooth grey trunks of beeches. Brown drifts of last year's leaves lay thickly across the ground and spilled into the puddles and black mire of the road. The Otterburn could be glimpsed through the trees, sometimes sparkling over rapids, sometimes lingering in dark pools. As Ancaios climbed, it fell further and further below the road until he could only hear the stream's hiss as it rushed over rocks far below. The mud grew deeper as the road levelled and began to wind its way through a hazel coppice. Some of the trees had recently been cut and taken out by cart, and the wheels had turned the road and its margins into a slough. Ancaios made a detour into the thicket of hazels; dodging about amongst the narrow stems he tried to find a way around the quagmire while still keeping the road in sight.

The trees soon thinned and he was able to make his way down across a steep hillside to the road where it turned northeast to cross the stream over a stone bridge. But just before the bridge the road forked, and it was the other road that he would take, the road that ran south into great Gostwyck Forest, for that was the way to Drumrock. Ancaios was limping on his blistered foot and he was already weary. And on the other side of the bridge lay the village of Kelburn, and a manor house... and a horse.

For surely a manor house would be the best place in which to present the king's requisition. He'd not thought much about it, but now he smiled and patted the satchel at his side. A horse! Why, he'd feel like a lord sitting up there on the back of a horse as it cantered south. He could keep his boots clean and never have to worry about blisters. The king had said that any boy could ride, so surely it couldn't be that hard. And one thing was certain: he'd take forever getting anywhere on his own shanks.

The village of cob-built dwellings looked untouched and tranquil. Smoke from the cottages' hearths seeped through holes in their thatched roofs into the still air. Ancaios could see two children making mud pies in the roadside and as he drew closer he heard the homely clack of a loom. But then a door flew wide and a woman hurried out to grab the children; without a word she dragged them indoors, still dripping mud, and slammed the door. Ancaios walked on up the street, seeing barred windows and hearing only silence; even the loom had stopped.

The manor house was built of the same stone as the castle and glowed as yellow as honey in the sunlight. It sat foursquare above a weed-clogged moat and was reached by a drawbridge that looked as though it hadn't been raised in a hundred years. Fruit trees, clothed in spring finery, grew beside the moat and dropped white petals upon its surface, but no birds sang amongst the boughs. Loud in the surrounding silence, Ancaios' feet thudded hollowly as he crossed the drawbridge. He passed beneath a portcullis and along a dark gate-passage into a sunny courtyard. Right in the centre, growing from a cracked stone coping, an ancient yew tree cast its shadow across moss-green flagstones and the worn stairs that led up to the main door.

Ancaios took the requisition order from his satchel. He stopped limping and tried to look as important as a king's messenger should look as he crossed the courtyard and sprang up the stairs. He hammered on the studded wooden door. And waited. Very faintly, he heard what sounded like shuffled footsteps and the sound of a dog growling.

He banged on the door again. 'Open up!' he called. 'For the king's messenger!'

Still nothing. Ancaios took the dagger from his belt, reversed it, and with the round iron knob on its hilt hammered on the door. 'Open up, I say!' he shouted. 'In the king's name, I command you: open up!'

There came the sound of a bolt being drawn and the door opened a slit. "E's still alive then, old Gers?' issued a thin voice from within, barely audible over the dog's growling.

'Of course he is, but his danger increaseth with every moment ye do keep me waiting, old man. What are ye afraid of? I'm not holding the dragon on a leash. Now, open the door.'

The man wasn't as old as he sounded. He was a lean brown fellow; brown skin, brown hair and clad in brown livery, and he held a snarling brown hound by its collar. 'No need to make a racket,' he grumbled. 'What's the king want with us? He should know m'lord and his lady mother are down at the castle...'

'I have a requisition order for a horse...' began Ancaios, but the man interrupted sharply. 'We don't have no horses here...' But then he stopped and one brown eyebrow slanted up into the maze of lines on his forehead. 'Wait... aye, we do. I've just recalled; we do have one... a fine beast.' He snatched the parchment from Ancaios' hand and stuffed it into his belt. 'Follow me, sir.'

Ancaios had got barely a glimpse of the gloomy antler and weapon-hung hall before he was back in the courtyard and following the brown man under an archway into a stableyard. The man sidled cautiously along, dragging the still growling dog by its collar and peering into every shadowed nook. 'Can't be too careful, with m'lord down at the castle and the drawbridge broke and all these looters and robbers and outlaws about. Even some of them what's running away from town have come round here thieving.'

They crossed the yard and came in through a low door and Ancaios saw before him a long row of stalls with a horse in almost every one. The brown man shrugged. 'Cart horses, sir,' he lied; 'none of them broke to saddle. Eh, chatterbox! Where are ye, daft lad?' A wiry boy came from one of the stalls, cleaning moulted white hair from the brush in his hand. He turned and closed the stall door carefully.

'King's messenger,' said the brown fellow. 'Let him have the chestnut with the four white feet.'

'We don't have a chestnut with four white feet,' answered the boy.

'Yes, we do. Him in the far stall.'

'But that's...'

'Aye, him's the one... with his saddle and bridle.'

As the stable boy disappeared into the far stall, Ancaios turned to question the brown man but the fellow had already slunk off, growling dog and all. He waited, smiling as the dappled grey in the nearest stall snuffled at his hands with its soft, whiskery muzzle. The boy shortly led forth a beautiful copper-red palfrey, flaxen-maned and white stock-inged, and saddled and bridled in silver-embellished blue leather.

Ancaios was wary. 'What's wrong with him?' he asked as he followed the lad and horse from the stables.

'Naught,' said the boy brightly, patting the horse's neck. 'He's a fine young fellow, but he's not m'lord's; he belongeth to the Marquess of Potrimpos. He were bred up north and brought down for the marquess but a few days hence. But the marquess came by hunting with the king the other morn; the morn before that stinking dragon came. He left the hunt with m'lord and they came in here and fell to drinking and before long neither was fit to sit a horse, so they went back to town in m'lord's carriage.' He'd led the horse across the yard to the archway and now, still chattering, he waited for Ancaios to mount up. "Tis only fair,' he said, 'for king's orders is king's orders and I don't suppose it sayeth whether the horse has to be m'lord's or some other's. We're all of us fond of our horses here and we wouldn't want them borrowed out to just anyone. But ye'd better look after him, sir,' said the boy, grinning at Ancaios, 'or ye'll have the marquess look after you!' The horse spun in a tight circle round the boy, its hoofs ringing on the flagstones. 'Come, sir, better get up before he knocks me over.'

Ancaios hesitated as the horse danced on the spot. He'd sat on the back of his father's placid mule, but this was a *real* horse and he was about to look a fool when it was seen that he didn't even know how to mount.

'I'll give you a leg-up, sir,' said the stable boy. 'He's a big horse.'

'I'm not 'sir',' mumbled the humbled king's messenger, stepping up beside the animal. The boy grasped Ancaios' bent knee and heaved him up so energetically that he almost tipped off the other side. But managing to find his balance aboard the sidling horse, he gathered up the reins, and went looking for the stirrups.

'Too long,' said the stable boy and set to adjusting them. 'Fine saddle, this,' he said; 'real silver, and a velvet seat! Well, that looks about right, sir. Off ye go then. Mind ye keep watch for outlaws and robbers. We've heard they're rife even on the Drumrock road; come out of nowhere to prey on all them ill-starred folks running away, carrying all they yet own in this world upon their backs.' He was almost shouting by this time, for the horse, having headed off on its own accord, had already skirted the yew tree and was walking purposefully towards the gate-passage. A moment later and its hoofs were clattering over the drawbridge.

Ancaios smiled: this was easy. He pulled on the right rein once he'd crossed the drawbridge and the horse turned that way obediently. For a few happy minutes, the king's messenger rode in proud majesty along the village street. Oh, how he wished his mother could see him now, resplendent in the king's black livery, and riding such a finely bred and richly caparisoned steed. But then the horse took fright as a spotted pig trotted onto the road almost under its feet, jumped sideways, threw up its head and broke into a bouncy canter. Before they'd got halfway to the Otterburn bridge, the chestnut knew everything there was to know about Ancaios' riding skills.

A woman appeared, trudging into Kelburn with her shoulders stooped under a bundle of firewood. But as only her head and bundle showed, bobbing along above a hedge of winter-bare hawthorn, the horse mistook her for a monster and spun about instantly. Ancaios came very close to being unseated. He tried to pull on the reins, but they'd got into a tangle and anyway, he needed both hands to hang on for his feet had come out of the stirrups and the horse was plunging up and down. Then it leapt forward into a gallop, back the way it had come.

Ancaios clung helplessly to the saddle's high pommel as the manor house drew closer and closer. How droll it was that the king's messenger was about to be hurled unceremoniously to the flagstones only minutes after he'd ridden so pompously forth. 'Remember, boy: pride cometh before a fall': that was his father's favourite proverb and its words were shortly to be proven true.

But surprisingly, the horse galloped straight past the drawbridge, and soon the last cottages and fields of the village had flashed by as the animal bolted east. Ancaios hung on for dear life. It was a rough and jarring ride for the horse had constantly to be leaping over deep ruts in the road and was forced sometimes to slow down, floundering through mud. But nothing stopped it.

Miles went by. Ancaios was vaguely aware of passing startled faces on the road: farmers, villagers, perhaps a few refugees from Lawhill. Another village loomed up and was gone; a man driving oxen yelled at him and some children screamed as they scattered from his path. The road wound in and out, up and down, past cultivated land and common, through copse and wood. And always the swollen Otterburn ran somewhere to his right, sometimes out of sight, sometimes rushing and gushing along beside the road.

On one of the smoother sections of road, Ancaios had managed to find his reins and stirrups. He'd tried a tug on the reins but the horse had just thrown its head up and put on an extra burst of speed. So now he left it alone and concentrated on the road ahead so that he'd be ready for its leaps and flounderings. 'At least I look like a messenger now,' he said to himself, 'on urgent business for the king. No one could tell that I can't ride, I can't stop, and that I'm going in the wrong direction.'

At that the horse's ears flicked back and Ancaios felt it hesitate and slow a little. 'Oh, poor thing,' he said with a sudden flash of understanding. 'Bred in the north, he said, that'd be northeast: Potrimpos. Ye're going home aren't ye? Ye're only a youngster and sorely frightened.' He managed to take one hand off the pommel to stroke the horse's neck. It was slimy with sweat, but Ancaios kept stroking and he kept talking.

At last the horse slowed to a lurching trot and then a walk. It was streaked with foam and black with sweat, steaming, its sides heaving. Ancaios jumped straight off; his legs were shaking and he could barely walk. He pulled the reins over the horse's drooping head and stared helplessly at it, wondering if it was about to fall down dead. But its breathing soon slowed a little and it started to walk again, still heading east and dragging Ancaios with it.

'No,' he said, hauling it to a halt, 'I don't want to go east. We'll go west... walk for a bit till ye've cooled, then find some water.' He managed to make it turn, but no matter how hard he tugged on the reins, not one step west would the animal take.

Ancaios gave up; he turned round again and headed east. 'Ye have the better argument,' he said to the horse, "for 'tis quite likely our knight cometh this way, if he cometh any way at all. 'Tis a more direct route through the Blackbraes Pass and why would a brave knight not choose the direct path?'

The road passed through woodland carpeted with celandines, splashed yellow across last year's mouldering leaves. On the right a rocky bank dropped down to the stream where it leapt and raced along a narrow gorge. Two sleek otters cavorted across the rocks before vanishing into the shining current. But Ancaios was past caring about such things. He sank ankle deep into mud at every step, his blistered heel was becoming more and more painful and he felt weak with hunger. He looked round at the horse that walked behind him quietly, though it jumped and snorted sometimes at mere shadows. Its coat was a mess of sticky, salty curls, hardening as the sweat dried, but it had drunk from a rill some time ago and now seemed hale enough.

'I'm going to get up on your back for a while,' said Ancaios, leading the animal towards a fallen log, 'so I'd be grateful if ye'd keep to this pleasant amble.'

He clambered into the saddle, picked up the reins and turned the horse's head to the east. For perhaps seven steps the horse followed his instructions and ambled pleasantly, if nervously. But deprived of a leader, the first demon it encountered (in the form of a boulder crouched ominously amongst the trees) sent it ducking and leaping sideways.

Ancaios had had a horse beneath him but suddenly it wasn't there. His left foot was still in the stirrup and his hands were still clutching the reins, but he was toppling through thin air. The hapless horse, terrified of this falling object, leapt sideways again, snatched the reins free and took off, galloping east as hard as it could go. Ancaios' head and shoulders bounced, thumped and scraped along the ground, but his foot was wedged firmly in the stirrup. The horse's mire-caked hoofs flashed by, inches from his face; he glimpsed their iron shoes amidst the flying clods of mud. He twisted and struggled and yelled, and suddenly his foot came free.

He lay on his back gasping, staring up at budding boughs and blue sky, and listening to the horse's hoofbeats fade into the distance. After a while he sat up, extricated himself from the tangled strap of his satchel, and struggled to his feet. He was still alive, that much was certain. And he didn't seem to have any broken bones, though the horse must have trodden on his arm because it was monstrously painful and already turning purple. His hair was full of mud and his beautiful clothes were besmirched and spattered, but he was in one piece.

Ancaios brushed himself down as best he could. He stood undecided on the road for a time, looking to the east then looking back at the way he had come. Finally he slung the satchel across his shoulder once more and, nursing his sore arm, set off painfully towards the east.

Manicia had overheard someone say that it was a sunny day outside; hard to believe in the perpetual midnight of the undercroft. She stood against the blind arcade beneath the light of a torch, with a jug of wine and a goblet in her hands, watching Sir Criffel. He was lying stretched out on his couch with his eyes closed, but she didn't think he was asleep. Clad in his black raiment he looked as thin as a dagger, and the hands folded upon his breast were (beneath their thick black hairs) as white as grave-worms. His eyes came suddenly open and Manicia's heart skipped a beat. *Why am I afraid?* she thought, trying to prevent the wine from slopping over the jug's rim. *He has offered to make me Countess of Dunmore!*

As she walked towards him his eyes slid sideways to regard her, but he did not otherwise move.

'I have brought you wine, my lord.'

His dark eyes glittered and he smiled, not amiably. He was in need of a shave. 'Why, madam? Think ye I am a drunkard, craving wine all the day?'

'Nay, my lord,' said Manicia. 'It was merely an excuse to speak with you.' She could feel her cheeks flushing as she stood there like a fool, still clutching the jug and goblet for there was nowhere to put them. 'I could not help wondering… I pray you pardon my impatience… but when shall ye speak with my father?'

'What about?'

He was teasing her, surely. 'Why, that… that thing we… we discussed,' she stammered, 'but an hour hence.'

His stubbled face shone with sweat as he stared at her.

'My father is presently alone,' added Manicia.

That made a difference. 'Aye,' he said, rising abruptly and gripping her arm so roughly that the red wine sloshed down the front of her grey gown. He pulled the jug from her hand and thumped it down on the floor and the goblet went rolling and ringing away across the flag-stones. 'Let us get the thing over and done with.'

He turned and strode away in search of the Duke of Drumrock, towing Manicia behind him. Astonishingly, as he passed the Marquess of Potrimpos' vacant bed, he kicked out at it, upturning it and its pile of furs onto the floor with a clatter. If every eye in the undercroft had not been upon them before, it was now. Manicia twisted within his painful grip and wondered if he was entirely sane.

But her father just blinked up at the two of them with a sleepy smile.

'My Lord of Dunmore,' he said cheerfully, raising his goblet, 'what a pleasure. Ye'll partake, no doubt, in some of this exceptional wine? Manny dear, get the man…'

'Nay sir,' interrupted Sir Criffel in a low voice, 'I do not want wine. And neither do I want your whorish eldest daughter. But ye will be relieved to hear that, rather than putting you to the inconvenience of making entirely new arrangements, I am willing to take this one; with the same dowry, of course.' He pulled Manicia forward and dropped her arm, then gave her a little bow and a smile that could almost pass for courteous.

'Oh… ah… oh,' said the Duke, surprised. 'Is this what thou dost want, my dear?'

'Yes, it is,' said Manicia, for yes, she certainly did want to be the Countess of Dunmore.

There was a little more business to be discussed, and all of it would of course have to be worked through with a lawyer once the "dragon problem" had been resolved, but her father seemed happy to give the earl everything he required. He even threw in an extra manor house and a small forest at the western edge of the Milverton Downs. 'If I ever have a son,' he said jovially, 'I'll want it all back!' He guffawed loudly at the jest, and Manicia laughed too and even Sir Criffel managed a smile. Indeed, that gentleman's temper had improved so greatly during the course of the transactions that, at their conclusion, he accepted a cup of wine from Manicia and drank to her health. He even kissed her hand quite gallantly.

The earl bowed to the duke and took his leave, and Manicia stooped to kiss her father's rubicund cheek. 'Well, well, my dear,' said he, 'Benicia will be pleased.'

'Benicia?' snapped Manicia. 'Why should she be pleased? Is it not enough for you that I am pleased?'

'Oh my dear,' huffed the duke, 'if thou canst be happy with such a marriage, of course I am happy for thee! Why must thou be such a cross and contrary thing?'

'I'm not cross and contrary; I'm happy,' hissed Manicia, spinning on her heel and half-running to catch up with Sir Criffel. After his gallant kiss she felt safe enough to slip her arm beneath his.

But he shrugged her off. 'Do not cling,' he said quietly, turning to face her. 'If ye are to be my wife, ye must keep your place; three steps behind me at all times and do not speak unless ye be required to do so.'

He walked on, leaving Manicia with her hand still raised and her mouth open.

She dropped her hand to her side and wiped it on her gown. Her mouth closed tight. *I have grabbed at this chance,* she thought, *and I will not let it slip. Oh, I will play the meek wife for a time, but I am his equal and he shall feel my mettle soon enough.*

But it was as though she had spoken aloud, for he turned abruptly and walked back to her. 'Do not,' he said, 'allow your small woman's brain to think that ye shall change me in any way, madam. I do not particularly like you. Know ye that I *never* change my mind, just as I never forget and never forgive.' He paused and smiled a little. His lips, nestled within a black growth of beard, were as pink and plump as a woman's. 'Ye look apprehensive, my dear,' he continued, in a voice that was almost gentle. 'But ye need not be for my requirements are simple. All ye need do is remain docile and obedient. Ye shall keep house, and bear my heirs, and as long as ye show proper subservience to your husband and every diligence in performing your duties, ye shall live in comfort and want for nothing. Expect naught more than that and ye shall not be discontented.'

He turned on his heel and walked away, leaving Manicia to stare tight-lipped at his retreating back.

The road curled its way through an outflung arm of the vast Gostwyck Forest. Nal shifted uncomfortably atop the chestnut, and frowned at the trees. The trunks were split and gnarled and the inter-laced branches overhead a ghostly grey, for they had barely begun to send forth leaves. Not a bird sang from their boughs. The squire might never have noticed the lack of birds if the knight had not spoken of it, but now their absence filled him with foreboding.

Nal had no idea what kind of trees surrounded him; the knight (who knew everything) had once tried to teach him how to tell one tree from another, but Nal had no interest in accumulating useless knowledge. To him, unless it had apples growing on it, a tree was a tree. He could see though that these were ancient; some had already fallen to lie mouldering, green with moss, amongst the russet bracken, but others still stood, hollow-trunked and decayed, broken-limbed and blasted by the centuries. The protuberances and rot-holes of their hoary boles looked like grotesque faces.

'I hate these trees,' he muttered; 'they're ugly an' evil.'

The knight, who was presently walking to save his horse, glanced round at Nal with a tired frown. 'They're no doubt thinking the same about thee,' he said and returned to what he'd been doing for the past hour: striding long-legged and silent in front of his old stallion. The horse walked loose, occasionally jogging to keep up.

Some time ago Nal had surprised the knight by asking if he should get off too. 'Not unless thou dost wish to,' answered the knight. 'Thou weighest less than my armour; the horse scarcely knoweth thou'rt in the saddle.' So the boy had stayed mounted, mainly because of the effort required to get back on again.

Nal scowled at the knight's back and tried not to look at the trees. The road went on and on, curving and twisting through endless forest, and the boy dozed a little, waking just in time to save himself from falling off. No longer striding in front of his horse, the knight walked beside the animal with an arm looped over the saddle. He moved through a bar of sunlight and then back into shadow, and Nal couldn't help noticing that those shadows were lengthening. He dreaded having to spend another night in a forest, especially this one.

'Ye should get back on yer 'orse,' he said.

'I'd give him what rest I may,' replied the knight. 'We still have a way to travel.'

'But 'e's not the one what's limpin', is 'e? Get back on, sir; that's what the old jade's for.'

The knight didn't argue. Silently he gathered up the reins and mounted the grey. Watching him, Nal had to feel a reluctant admiration, because even lame, weary and clad in armour, the man could still spring into the saddle with seemingly no more effort than it took Nal to fall off.

But no sooner had he mounted than the sound of hoofbeats reached them, faint, but coming fast along the road from the west. And it wasn't the sound of one horse or even two. Nal's heart pounded, but the knight did not seem overly concerned. He calmly urged the grey forward and both animals walked, prick-eared and alert, into danger.

For Nal was certain those hoofbeats heralded danger. All he wanted to do was turn and flee, but that was impossible because the chestnut could never be persuaded to go anywhere without the grey.

Seven horses rounded the bend ahead and skidded in sprays of mud to a snorting, prancing halt. Straight away Nal knew he'd been right, for even from a distance it was clear that the men upon their backs were dangerous. That might have had something to do with the way they positioned their mounts across the road, blocking the way. Or it might have been the way they simultaneously drew their swords, battle-axes and maces.

'Seven against one,' muttered Nal in a tiny voice.

'Well counted,' said the knight. His hand rested upon the pommel of his sword, but he kept riding forward.

'Can't we turn and outrun 'em?' asked Nal, his voice sounding so high and wobbly he scarcely recognised it as his own.

'No,' said the knight, continuing inexorably onwards. The boy was forced to follow. His heart hammering, he kicked his feet from the stirrups, ready to leap off and flee into the forest.

It could be seen upon drawing closer that these outlaws were no rag-tag derelicts, but strong, well-fed, well-clad men, who'd prospered in their 'profession'. They wore steel breastplates or studded brigandines over quilted leather jacks, and they brandished well-made and costly weapons. They were dirty though; under a recent spattering of mud, everything – boots, clothing, armour, skin, hair – all was coated in a rarely disturbed patina of grease and grime. Only the blades of their weapons were clean.

The knight reined in his horse before them. 'Good morrow, masters,' he said equably. 'Will ye move aside so that my squire and I may pass?'

The ruffian who appeared to be their leader pushed his horse forward two steps. The animal pranced nervously; it was breathing hard and black with sweat. 'We'd be desirous of an equitable remuneration first,' said its rider with a rot-toothed smile. He might almost have been a handsome man if anger had not stamped his visage so indelibly. His black hair, worn in a tail longer than his horse's, was pulled back from his face to reveal, where his right ear used to be, naught more than a dirty hole and a few knobs of scarred gristle. As if to boast of his lack, a dozen rings of gold pierced the gristle. His mount was a very fine young animal, chestnut under the running sweat, with four white stockings and harnessed in costly, silver-embellished blue leather. But the horse looked spent; its eyes were glazed, its nostrils wide and red and its breathing ragged.

The knight smiled too. 'How much do ye require?' he asked in quiet voice. 'I have but little to spare.' His horse stood stock-still and four-square upon the road, as seemingly calm and unconcerned as its rider. But the outlaws, sitting atop their sweating, sidling horses, grinned and sneered. He was one and they were seven.

Almost imperceptibly those to either side of the group began to move along the verges of the road; soon they would be in a position to block any escape either into the forest or back along the eastbound road.

One-ear and two others kept their positions on the westward bend of the road. A big man to One-ear's left shifted his grip on a battleaxe and grinned. His pate was hairless and shiny and he flaunted a puckered 'T' brand on his right cheek. 'If 'e 'asn't got any pelf,' he rasped, 'we'll take 'is armour. Look at it, lads. 'Ave ye ever seen its like?'

One-ear gave a humourless laugh. 'Worshipful sir,' he said with mock servility, 'of your pity I pray you pardon these verminous varlets their covetous ways. They are doltish, unlearned clods who know not how to comport their gangrel selves whilst in the presence of a courtly paladin such as Your Lofty Eminence.'

One of the verminous varlets sniggered. He was the ugliest of them all for he was missing the tip of his nose and most of his top lip, so that his black-stump teeth were forever bared in a snarl. 'He'th got a couple o' pretty weaponth too,' he lisped. 'I thpy a ruby in the pommel of hith long-thord.'

'Courtly?' said the knight, answering One-ear. 'Not in Manydown. The moment I crossed the border I became an outlaw just like your own splendid self, sir. If Gers knew of my whereabouts, he'd string me up as soon as look at me.' He laughed softly and so did One-ear, though the ruffian looked uneasy.

'Well, well,' said he, 'Never did I imagine that the propitious day would come in which I might render our magnanimous monarch a service. Think ye he will grant me a pardon if I present him with your pulchritudinous head on a spike?'

'The 'orses aren't much,' grumbled Bald-pate, 'but they'll keep our bellies full for a few days.'

'I have heard this day that Gers is perished,' answered the knight, watching One-ear calmly, 'but yea, if he yet liveth he might grant you a pardon. But ye'll have to accomplish the deed first.'

'That old grey'll need a deal of chewing,' mumbled Lipless.

One-ear laughed again as his horse fretted and tossed its sweaty head. 'And if ye put me and my bullies to the slaughter, ha ha ha, ye'll earn for yourself a pardon instead.'

'No, I will not.'

The outlaw grunted in surprise. 'Ha! 'Tis clear, sir, that ye know not whom ye face! Do ye, in all sooth, imagine yourself to be of more worth to the king than us? Ha ha, hearken to that, lads! This pretty paladin's got such an exalted opinion of himself, ye'd think he'd debauched the king's daughter!' At that he gave a shout of laughter, though nothing resembling happiness touched his face. 'I for one would joyfully face a traitor's death for *that*.'

The ruffians had by now formed a circle about the knight and his squire, and Nal's route into the forest had been cut off. The outlaw who stood between him and any hope of escape looked to be the youngest amongst them. He was a skinny youth on a scabby, scarred bay, and he was staring round-eyed at Nal, his face white under its coating of grime. But, with a jolt of relief, Nal realised that the fellow wasn't looking at him but at the knight's shield, which was hanging from the chestnut's saddle amongst the bags of armour and cooking pots. The skinny youth made a strange whining noise and looked across at his leader. 'We should let this man pass,' he said in a thin voice. But the other ruffians didn't hear him.

'Now, what say ye, sir?' asked their one-eared leader. 'I shall detain you no longer, nor shall I enlighten our magnanimous monarch of your whereabouts, if ye will but guerdon us with your armour, weapons, horses and whatever coinage, jewellery and the like that ye happen to have about your splendid person. Otherwise, and herewith I tender my heartfelt regrets for any discomfort we may render unto Your Eminence, we must perforce take them. I think ye'll agree that I ask but a fair defrayal for your lives, and as proof of my munificence I give you my word that if ye offer no resistance I shall allow you to retain your cooking utensils.' Even as he spoke his eyes slid sideways until they fixed their dark anger upon the young man. He gave him an almost imperceptible nod.

The fellow, who was well behind the knight's line of vision, made a tiny, terrified noise in his throat and slid from the saddle like a greased pig. A bare bodkin appeared in his hand, and he dived, crouching, quick as a striking snake towards the grey's hamstrings. Nal tried to shout a warning, but he'd not got as far as opening his mouth before he saw the knight's sword flash from its sheath, burning a blue-white trail in the air. Another ruffian had leapt from his horse and was darting in from the opposite side of the road, dagger glinting. But the knight's old stallion moved almost as fast as his master's sword. From calm immobility he sprang up, spun on air and lashed out with both huge iron-shod hind hoofs. They connected with enough force to smash bone and sinew and to lift the fellow up bodily and fling him aside like a wad of rags. At the very same moment the knight twisted in the saddle, and with a flash of steel and a spray of blood, the young man's head parted company from his body. Red-gold hair trailing like flame, the head turned a circle in the air and plopped into the mud, landing face up and staring.

His eyes are blue, thought Nal, even as he leapt from the chestnut's back. He landed in thick mud and almost toppled onto his face, but he tugged his feet out of the mire and ran. At his back came a horrible metallic clash as sword collided with sword, with mace, with axe; he heard men grunting, growling and shouting wordlessly.

Nal flung himself in amongst a stand of evergreens; their needles whipped across his face as he ran. His knees were shaking and he started to stagger. A tree root tripped him up and he plunged face down in half rotted needles; he tried to get up again but his legs gave way so he stayed on his hands and knees and crawled. With a spray of broken foliage, something came catapulting through the boughs above his head. Nal recoiled backwards as a sword landed flat on its blade in front of him and slid across the needles until it fetched up against the trunk of a tree. A heartbeat later something else fell through the branches above and landed on his head. As Nal scrabbled at it in horror, it scraped limply and wetly across his face before plopping into the mulch at his knees. The boy stared at it, his gorge rising, for it was a human hand, severed at the wrist, and the warm wet stuff it had dripped onto his head was blood. Whimpering, he wiped at his face, even as he noticed that its fingers were hairy and short: it wasn't the knight's then. Besides, he didn't wear huge, heavy rings.

Nal stared at the rings. There were three of them; two had bands of yellow gold and all three flaunted large handsome-looking stones. One might have been a sapphire. Behind him the fighting sounded loud; there were shouts, grunts and groans and then, alarmingly close by, he heard someone crashing about through the trees. A horse galloped away down the road with a thunder of hooves.

Grimacing, the boy picked up the hand by the tip of one finger and clambered to his feet. He held it at arm's length before him so that it wouldn't drip blood on his boots and, creeping as quietly as he could manage on his shaking legs, headed deeper into the forest. Sounds of the battle faded. Somewhere ahead he could hear the Otterburn running, hissing and shouting over rapids.

He stopped and listened for a while, and then squatted down and carefully tried to remove a ring from one of the clammy, bloody fingers. But its knuckle was huge and the ring wouldn't budge. He tried the other two, but they were stuck even harder. Nal pulled and tugged until his own hands were slippery with blood and then, as he heard some wounded thing come floundering and groaning in his direction, he put his booted foot upon the hand. It felt squashy as he stood on it, and he felt the sinews and bones click and crunch. But knowing that he might have to run at any moment, he put his full weight upon it and tugged with both hands at the sapphire ring. The knuckle stretched and popped and the ring slid off, then a second came but the third, on the fat knobbly middle finger, wouldn't move.

Abruptly Nal realised that all sounds of fighting, even the sounds of running and groaning, had ceased. He stood wide-eyed, listening, but apart from the rush of the stream the forest was silent.

He's dead then; the fool, he thought, his heart pounding; *selfishly gone and left me in the middle o' nowhere surrounded by murderers. So what'll I do now?*

And then he heard the knight's voice. 'Nal! Come forth, lad; 'tis over.'

Suddenly he felt sick and ashamed. He stared at the hand and kicked it away. But he put the two blood-smeared rings into his purse and buckled it carefully.

When he emerged from the forest a short while later (his hands still dripping after a quick scrub in a muddy puddle), the knight was off his horse and had pulled four bodies to the side of the road. He'd even retrieved the young man's head and placed it next to its body. Three of the outlaws' horses, their reins dangling, stood quietly beside the knight's grey and the chestnut.

'Where's the rest of 'em?' asked Nal, nodding towards the line of corpses.

'One of them ran into the trees,' answered the knight tiredly; 'if he yet lives 'twill not be for long. Two fled.'

'To go an' tell the king o' your whereabouts? Why'd ye go an' tell 'em ye'd a price on yer 'ead? That were daft.' Nal scowled and wiped his hands over and over on his grubby jacket. 'Never thought to tell me neither, and I s'pose ye're not about to tell me what for.'

'Don't fret Nal; if the king yet lives, we'll reach him before they do.'

'That's supposed to make me 'appy is it?'

The knight gave no answer but walked over to the horses and gathered up their dangling reins. Nal avoided looking too hard at the corpses, but he couldn't help noticing the horse-tail of black hair that spread across the ground beside one of them. 'Ye got their leader, then.'

'Aye, and heavy hearted am I to have deprived the world of such feculent eloquence.' He'd sheathed the outlaws' weapons and buckled them together, and now threw them across the saddle of a big placid grey. The sweaty chestnut started and pulled back in fright at the clatter, and the knight calmed the poor animal with a hand on its neck and a gentle word. Its coat was matted thickly with sticky, half-dried sweat and encrusted with streaks of salt.

'This is a valuable animal,' said the knight, 'but he's been hard-ridden. He is in sore need of water; all of them are. Thou also, lad; thou'rt filthy.'

'I fell in the mud,' mumbled Nal. He jabbed a thumb over his shoulder. 'Stream's down there. I 'eard it.'

'At the bottom of a ravine. There'll be a rill crossing the road ahead.' The knight led Dunboyne forth and put the reins over his head. 'Mount up, lad,' he said.

Nal glanced at the row of corpses. 'We just goin' to leave 'em 'ere?'

'I can't bury them; we'll reach Langstone on the morrow and I'll inform the bailiff there… and deliver these horses up to him also.'

'But ye say the chestnut's worth some money, so why don't we sell 'im? Sell all of 'em?'

'Because they've been stolen.'

Nal clambered into the saddle and the knight handed him the grey's reins.

'I want to lead the chestnut as well.'

'Canst thou handle two?'

'Aye, course I can. Besides, I'm your squire so I should lead two.' The knight, bemused, handed Nal the chestnut's blue reins. But he had no time to wonder at the boy's unwonted eagerness to be a model squire, for after such a delay he was anxious to be moving. He mounted his stallion and, leading the scarred bay, set forth upon the westbound road. Once or twice, glancing round to make sure that Nal was coping, he saw that the outlaws' mounts followed the boy quietly enough.

A short time later the road forded a streamlet and they halted to water the horses. Nal, though he protested, was told to dismount and scrub his face and hands in the freezing water.

They rode on. The late afternoon sun gilded the branches where they arched overhead, and cast long shadows down the road. Nal muttered and mumbled at the knight's back: no one ever told him nothin', 'ow was it 'e'd ended up as squire to an outlaw, what was 'e supposed to do after they'd 'ung the knight, why couldn' they sell the 'orses, and what about the weapons: surely they'd be worth somethin'? The knight answered none of his questions, but eventually turned to him with half a smile and said: 'It's good to be alive, eh Nal?' The boy lapsed into sullen silence.

The horses' hoofbeats, muffled by a carpet of rotted leaves, drummed on through the waning day.

CHAPTER 13

Princess Winterhued closed her eyes as Ulidia brushed her hair. She stroked the purring cat that lay curled upon her lap and tried to clear her mind of thoughts that chased each other in circles. Ulidia worked her way from left to right, the brush sighing its way through the long skeins of hair; over and over it went, tugging at her scalp, sometimes catching on snarls. When she'd finished, the old woman started back again from right to left and this time the hair flowed beneath the bristles like water. Winterhued was glad of her skilful hands, but she heard hardly a word of Ulidia's chatter. 'He doesn't need *me* anymore,' she was saying. 'He's in the chapel vault with the kings of Manydown! We'll take him down to Thornliebank when this is all over, but for now, he couldn't be in finer company!'

With her free hand the princess pulled her cloak tighter about her shoulders. It was cold in the undercroft, though quite cheerful, for servants had partitioned off a corner for her by stringing up some bright wall hangings and the darkness was held at bay by two lamps and a candelabrum on a tall stand. One of the hangings was folded back so that she could see into the rest of the hall.

Brenn and Pera were with her also and they sat companionably on a bench, talking quietly together as they applied themselves to their embroidery. (For Pera had insisted on working even with her burnt hands.) In all the time Pera had been at court Winterhued had managed to extract from her no more than a few shy words, but Brenn, despite having little in common with the unhappy girl, had managed to keep her smiling, even laughing once or twice. Pera looked animated and grateful now as Brenn asked for help with her needlework.

It had not escaped Winterhued's notice, however, that Pera appeared to have lost some of her devotion to embroidery, for she kept glancing up from her work and peering down the hall. Then Brenn would look up as well and the two of them would put their heads together, whispering and giggling.

Ulidia grew annoyed at their behaviour. 'What dost thou look for, child?' she snapped; 'craning thy neck this way and that!'

'Naught my lady,' mumbled Pera.

'Pah! 'Tis doubtless some man; you girls are all just as silly as one other.'

But Winterhued smiled kindly at her. 'Disregard the old woman,' she said. 'Do as thou lik'st.'

Brenn stood up. 'I trust then 'twill be with my lady's leave,' she said, 'that we take ourselves elsewhere... so as to annoy Lady Ulidia no longer.' She took Pera's elbow and pulled the girl to her feet. At the princess's nod they both curtsied and then, with Brenn in the lead, ran off to another part of the hall to whisper and giggle undisturbed.

'Hmmph,' huffed Ulidia.

'Let her be, my dear,' said Winterhued; ''tis nice to see her happy for once.'

'Well, she doth waste her time ogling at men, for my Garthwray and I, and her parents, have lined up a nice match for her.'

'Oh? Ye did not think to consult me?' The princess turned to look at Ulidia and the old woman ceased her brushing. Her face turned sheepish, almost guilty.

'Oh, soothly I did think of m'lady,' she protested, 'but Garthwray, God rest his soul, said m'lady would be against the match. He told me tarry till all was finished before informing m'lady. Then, he said, m'lady would see the sense in it.' She lapsed into an uncertain silence.

'Well? Who is to be the husband?'

'Why, 'tis none less than the Duke of Drumrock!'

'Drumrock? Nay… this is a jest!'

'Whyfor, m'lady? Why is it not an excellent match?'

'Because Pera is sixteen and he is nigh sixty… and… and he is so fat!'

Ulidia huffed again. 'Certain it is,' she said, 'that no one but m'lady thinketh such things important. He is a hale man and no dotard. He hath been a widower for many years; why should he not take another wife? He hath great lands, he wanteth a male heir, he is the king's friend and one of the most important lords in all the land. What girl would not be overjoyed at such a match?'

The princess laughed incredulously. 'Doth the poor girl know of thy plans?'

'Pera is a good girl. She hath never been one for dreams or idle fancies, so why should she not be happy with such advantages?'

The princess ran a hand across her eyes. 'Certes!' she murmured. 'I wonder at Manicia's thoughts on having Pera as her stepmother.'

'Someone said the very same thing about m'lady…' said Ulidia, then put a hand over her mouth. 'Oh, I shouldn't have mentioned it… 'tis naught but gossip.'

Winterhued rounded on Ulidia. 'What gossip?' she demanded. 'What hath been said?'

Ulidia flinched and dropped the hairbrush. ''Tis but gossip, m'lady,' she said, fluttering her hands in protest. But Winterhued's gaze forced the words from her. 'A chambermaid told me but an hour ago… had it from one of Ladstock's servants… 'twas that lord himself who wondered laughingly how m'lady would like having Manicia for her stepmother.'

'Manicia?' gasped Winterhued.

'Aye, the king hath been admiring her: "quiet, obedient, and good childbearing hips", he told Ladstock. But 'tis only gossip, m'lady… heard third hand. There may be not a shred of truth in it.'

'It soundeth sooth to me,' said the princess shortly. 'Finish my hair.'

In silence Ulidia plaited and bound Winterhued's hair once more and pinned the headdress back in place. For the princess still had much to do before she could lay her head down for the night.

As the old woman finished her work, servants entered the undercroft bearing victuals to distribute amongst the lords and ladies. Winterhued had insisted she be given the simplest fare, and now she thanked the servant who, rather shamefacedly, handed her a bowl of lentil pottage, a hunk of bread and a handful of dried apple.

But she could scarcely eat a thing.

It had always been the way with King Gers that the more he was advised not to do something, the more determined he'd be to do it. He'd dropped hints enough now to indicate that he'd likely remarry. But Manicia? Winterhued had never got to know the girl well, she was too close and sly, but had frequently glimpsed her bitter unkindness. Yet it was useless to go to her father with her suspicions as to Manicia's true nature; he would only fall in love with her on the instant and make her his queen the very next day. Manicia… Queen of Manydown.

Winterhued felt sick at the thought. She wanted to weep and wail, rant and rail, but there was no time for that; no time even to *think* upon her father's nuptial plans. For there was a dragon that needed thinking about.

She had given the army seven days, of which almost two had passed. Meanwhile, she had to think of a way to evacuate seven hundred and ninety souls from the castle if the army failed to appear. But that, of course, was only if the dragon had not broken open the hall and eaten them all.

And only if they had not managed to shoot down the creature themselves; a task at which the castle bowmen had proved distressingly unsuccessful. For though presented with frequent opportunities as the dragon flew to and fro on its hunting expeditions, the men had turned to water beneath its shadow and their feebly aimed arrows had barely managed to reach it, let alone pierce its adamant hide. Not even the most skilful bowman could shoot to kill when he lay like a puddle on the roof. And since yesterday nine more men, exposed helplessly atop the towers and unable to flee, had perished by fire or talon.

Winterhued wanted – needed – to see the dragon herself. She had been horribly afraid of the beast when it came to her in her dreams, but now she felt (illogical as the notion was) that she could find the courage to face it in life.

And she wanted to have a shot at it; she was a good markswoman. *Let the men snigger,* she thought, *but on the morrow I will have my yew-wood bow brought up from the armoury.*

'Nal!' called the knight for the third time. Dunboyne stood happily beside him, reins dangling and saddle empty, and the fine chestnut and the grey were nowhere to be seen. The forest was silent. Its high branches were still bathed in rosy sunlight but between its hoary trunks dusk gathered apace.

The knight had been riding half-asleep and lost in thought when it occurred to him that he'd not heard a peep out of the boy for some time. He was somewhat surprised upon turning round to find that he'd managed to lose a squire and two horses. He'd not even noticed when five sets of hoofbeats became three.

Had the boy fallen off? Had the outlaws' horses pulled him from the saddle? Surely not, for then he would have made a noisy complaint. Had he then been struck by a branch and laid out senseless upon the road?

The knight thought such an accident unlikely. The boy had been in a terror about what lay ahead, and with the chance of making some money it was possible he'd just slipped down off the back of Dunboyne and taken himself off, with the fine chestnut and the grey and the bundle of weapons. Dunboyne had of course taken no notice; he'd just kept trotting along behind Hougomont. Most surprisingly, the outlaw's horses hadn't made a fuss at being left behind; perhaps there'd been a lush patch of spring grass beside the road that took their attention for a time.

Cursing his lapse in vigilance, the knight turned about. For he could not continue forward while there remained a possibility that the boy was lying hurt somewhere. He pushed the grey into a slow canter and, with the other two horses loping behind, retraced his tracks for two or three miles. Even in the deepening gloom he could see just three sets of hoof-prints stamped clearly into the road's muddy surface, but soon enough spied tracks indicating where two horses, and a pair of booted feet, had left the road. As he'd suspected, the horses had grazed for a while on some new grass beside the road, and then the boy had managed to drag them away up a narrow track that headed north into the forest.

'Nal!' called the knight. 'If thou'rt hiding, come forth, lad. I won't be angry. That track goeth nowhere. Thou hast seen the villages we've passed through; none big enough or wealthy enough to offer money for saddle horses. And if thou goest west to sell them, thou shalt be arrested as a horse thief.'

He listened to the forest's silence, then called out again. For a moment he considered chasing the boy along the track, but decided he'd wasted enough time. No, all he could do was inform the bailiff in Langstone that he'd mislaid a squire and two horses in the forest and ask him not to arrest the boy if he turned up.

On a thought, the knight twisted in the saddle to inspect Dunboyne's harness and discovered, as he'd half expected to, that Nal had taken the saddlebag containing their newly acquired provender. The thought of that bag of walnuts and tangy dried mulberries, and of Mistress Mayhill's treacle tart, made him realise just how hungry he was. 'I thank thee, Nal,' he muttered, 'generous lad.'

As he looked down he suddenly saw, clear amongst the tracks of his three milling horses, a print that didn't belong to any of them. And neither did it belong to the two horses led by Nal. Dismounting, he knelt upon the damp earth to examine the single print of a tiny unshod hoof. It was close to the road's verge and it was the only one – all else having been obliterated by his own horses' huge hoofs. With a puzzled shake of his head, he rose stiffly, and after tying the bay's reins to Dunboyne's saddle, mounted Hougomont and set off west again. He pushed the grey into a smart canter and Dunboyne followed, towing the bay behind him.

Through the laced branches above, the sky glowed pink, fading through turquoise to a deep cobalt blue. The first stars began to twinkle palely.

As white as a mote of moonlight and as silent as a snowflake, the horned one stepped back onto the road and followed the knight. She did not know why. It was as if the very air picked her up and hurried her along, and she had no more say in where it took her than had a fallen leaf, blown willy-nilly by the wind.

The sun had almost sunk. Ancaios wandered along, battered and bruised, following his long shadow towards the east. He felt as though he'd been walking for days. 'What am I doing?' he muttered exhaustedly as he tripped over another pothole. 'Should I turn about and try to get back to the Drumrock road? But it is already so far behind me and gets further and further with every step.'

His very next step took him into a deep rut, and he wrenched his ankle painfully. Wincing, he hopped to the side of the road and sank down upon a boulder to ease his boot off and rub his ankle. His stockings had been worn into gaping holes, but at least the holes allowed him to inspect his red-raw blisters.

He was just pulling his boot back on, having resolved to keep going east, when the sound of hoofbeats had him back on his feet and staring towards the west. Silhouetted against the last red sliver of the setting sun, came a horse and cart, rattling along at a brisk pace. As they drew nearer Ancaios saw that the horse was actually a sturdy mule, very hairy in its winter coat, and moving with surprising surefootedness along the pitted road. As soon as its driver spied Ancaios standing by the roadside he cursed and drew rein sharply; the lad couldn't see his face against the dying sun but his every movement spoke of alarm. He attempted to turn the mule about, shouting and flapping the reins, but the cart-wheels were held fast in the road's ruts.

'Fear not, good man,' called Ancaios. 'I am on the king's business! I travel east, carrying a commission that bears His Highness' seal.'

The man clicked his mule forward; fortunately there remained enough light for him to see the sunburst badge upon Ancaios' breast. 'Ye've come from Lawhill?' said he. 'On foot?'

'I made most of the journey on horseback,' answered Ancaios, 'but the poor animal took fright and threw me… which is why I am somewhat muddy.' He dusted himself down apologetically. 'But aye, I have come from the castle this very day.'

'On the king's business, ye said? So the king still breathes?'

'When I spoke to him this morn he was, in good sooth, as hale as you or I.'

'God be praised! And our princess?'

Ancaios put his hand to his heart. 'She also was in fine fettle when last I saw her,' he said, and almost laughed at the recollection. He would have liked to tell the fellow that she had called the king a dim-sighted dotard and he had called her a fishwife, but thought better of it.

'God and all his angels be praised,' exclaimed the man with great feeling, 'for rumours have spread far and wide that every last soul in Castle Lawhill hath perished. Devoured by a malevolent spirit risen on great wings from the abyss, so they say. And they've also been saying that with the king and the princess and all the dukes and earls gone, great hordes would descend upon us from Angerona with pillaging and raping and laying waste to the land...'

'Certes!' exclaimed Ancaios. 'How rumours do barge ahead like a mob of blind lunatics! But why do we stand here in the dark while your mule groweth restless and digs holes in the road? For I am sure the king would be obliged to you if ye could but carry his messenger in your cart for a while.'

'Of course, sir, of course!' cried the fellow. 'Hop up, sir. I'm bound only as far as the outskirts of Langstone, this side o' the Belford road; I hope this may be of use to you. Indeed, I only hesitated because I felt my humble cart may have been too poor a conveyance for a king's messenger.'

Ancaios scrambled up beside the driver with a grin on his face. *Poor?* he thought, *for a gong farmer?* The man clicked at the mule and the animal leaned into its collar, dragging the cartwheels from the mud into which they'd settled. Once it had got the cart moving, without needing encouragement it increased its pace until it had reached a brisk trot.

'Belford?' asked Ancaios, his teeth rattling in his head as the wheels bounced over pits and potholes, 'Isn't that where our soldiers are?'

'Aye, that's right, sir.'

'Certes, that's good news. Methinks this commission may be unde-liverable, but if I can take news to the army, my time will not have been ill-spent!' He hung on tight to his seat as the cart veered from rut to rut.

'Can your mule find his way in the dark?' he asked breathlessly, jarred in every limb.

'Aye,' answered the fellow imperturbably. Unlike Ancaios, he was stockily built with a good deal of weight to serve as an anchor. 'He knoweth this road so well I could curl asleep in the bottom o' the cart and he'd take me home just the same.'

As they bounced and rattled along the dark road, Ancaios enlightened the good man as to the true nature of that 'malevolent spirit' and the plight of Lawhill's inhabitants. The fellow was marvellously impressed. 'Ye saw it with your own eyes?' he asked several times, shaking his head and staring wonderingly at Ancaios. 'Sooth! What is the world coming to when creatures from legend become flesh?'

After passing through a small village, where candlelight gleamed through chinks in the shuttered windows, the bone-jarring road wound on invisibly and interminably. Under a star-pricked sky Ancaios' doughty companion explained what he'd been about with his cart and his good mule. 'As I always does I set off for the market in Lawhill with a bit o' me good wife's woven stuff – very fine it is too, sir – and a cartload o' turnips and suchlike. I were travelling with several others from hereabouts, all bound on the same business, but long before we'd got in sight o' the town we met some folk on the road who told us there were no market; Lawhill were razed and burning and the king were dead. So we all turned about to cart our stuff home again, as well as a barrowload o' rumours. Eh up, lad,' he said to the mule as the animal strained to haul the cart through a patch of mire.

'I've been tardy coming home,' he continued, 'for I thought to sell me edibles on the way. And as ye see, sir, I got rid o' the lot, for a song it must be said, but better than dumping 'em in a ditch. Sold some to fleeing townsfolk.'

'I think I saw some of them when I was riding my horse,' said Ancaios. 'But he was galloping so fast it was hard to see anything.'

'No doubt ye passed a few,' said the fellow, 'though there're not so many on this road. They say the road south is swarming with 'em.

With robbers and outlaws too, I've heard, preying on them poor, homeless souls.'

'Ye must be anxious then… travelling all alone.'

The fellow snorted and then he growled. 'We have our own band in these parts,' he muttered; 'ye've surely heard of 'em for they're famous enough. Devils they are, but we've an agreement: us locals pay 'em a levy each year and they mostly leave us alone, apart from thieving our livestock (which they deny) and killing anyone who crosses 'em.'

'Ye pay outlaws!'

'Aye, and they keep us poor enough,' he said bitterly.

'But the army…'

'Pah! Ravenhill's tried for years to root 'em out, but the devils hide deep in the forest and laugh at his soldiers. Leader's a wicked, clever man – Sir Adderley – used to be a landed knight before he went bad.'

'A knight!'

'Aye, an' if someone were to capture or slay 'The Adder', as the blood-monger likes to call himself…'

'The Adder! I've heard of him!'

'Everyone's 'eard of 'im, and as I was saying, if any man were to slay the devil he'd earn my undying devotion. Everyone in these parts would say the same.'

Ancaios felt weary enough to fall off the cart as the moon rose at last, gibbous and golden in the east. Its light revealed the road and its potholes; it glinted along the curved ribbon of the Otterburn and cast black shadows from every tussock and bush. As it climbed before them into the sky, they rattled past another cluster of cottages and the mule broke into a canter. 'Ye're anxious to be back in yer stable, lad!' exclaimed the man. He looked round at Ancaios with a grin. 'As ye are to be off this cart, no doubt sir; ye look done in. Won't be much longer. And if ye'll be needing lodging for the night, we've a bed ye can 'ave, and some supper. My wife'll have something cooking; there's sure to be enough for another mouth, sir, if ye'd care to partake.'

'That's very kind, good man, I thank you.'

'No thanks needed. We'd be honoured and proud to 'elp a king's man!'

Ancaios smiled to himself in the darkness. What a day it had been! No matter what happened to him hereafter, could anything ever equal this day? He had rescued two men and discovered the fate of a third, and for that his beloved princess had given him her heartfelt thanks; he had stood face to face with the king, and now wore His Highness' livery; he had fallen in love with the most beautiful and clever girl in the world and she, a highborn lady, had said that she loved him also; he had ridden the fine-bred horse of a great marquess; and now he'd been invited into the house of a good country-man and asked to share his meal as if his very presence were the greatest honour imaginable.

Ancaios, feeling every bruise as he was jolted about on the cart's seat, looked at the moonlit road as it stretched out ahead and couldn't help but grin. Just for now, he'd not allow himself to think of how he'd walked away on this foolish quest and left those he loved in desperate danger. He would, to the best of his ability, do what the king had asked of him, and he would relish the adventure. *Certes, if the dragon hadn't come,* he thought, *I might be trudging home after helping Pa, and the neighbours would be crossing the road to avoid us and holding their noses as we passed. Why, I'd still be 'Stench'!*

Lying curled beneath blankets within the soaring darkness of the King's Hall, Eudora wept in confusion and despair. She took no notice of the hall's other inhabitants as they finished a meagre evening meal and began to bed down for the night. Food had been offered to her, but she had refused it and now she felt hungry and ill.

For the drudge's fledgling hopes had been crushed. After holding herself in readiness all the day long, she'd not been sent for; it was clear that the princess had changed her mind and no longer required her services as chambermaid. *And that is as it should be,* thought Eudora, trying not to sob out loud, *for why should the princess be subjected every day to the sight of an ugly, miserable, thieving wretch such as me?*

She had failed at her one chance to rise. She had failed her family too. Eudora's grandmother had always told her to be careful in the company she kept, for in Calluna their family had lived in a fine house with servants. 'Remember that and be proud,' she'd say. 'Do not fraternise with low folk lest they drag thee down. Necessity may have handed thee scullion's work, but always know that thou art no scullion.'

But where had that advice got her? She had never managed to feel proud about anything, and her attempts at it had left her alienated from her fellows. She was alone and friendless, and a thief besides. And now she had discovered that the one person who'd tried to be her friend, Stench, lowest of the low, had been taught to read and write by the princess! Although she was always accusing him of lying, she knew he didn't lie; he never lied. And now he wore the king's livery.

He would rise and rise and she would fall back into the slough. Even if she escaped a traitor's death, she would remain in the kitchens for the rest of her dreary life, scouring pots and scrubbing floors.

Eudora curled herself up tightly beneath the blankets and buried her face in her half-frozen hands. *I am worthless*, she thought, *I left my fellow menials in the tower to burn. I could have woken them. On the morrow I shall find a door into the inner bailey. I'll walk out there and wait to be devoured.*

Pretty Lady Benicia, clad in a modest blue gown and with her hair falling loose down her back, wandered about the undercroft. She smiled sweetly at the families that she knew and stopped sometimes to exchange a few words with them. Eventually she plucked up her courage and went to see Lady Nomia to say how very sad she felt over the death of Sir Auchencairn. Tears ran down her cheeks as she handed the bereft countess a lace-edged kerchief that she had worked herself; it was the only thing she'd ever made that she was proud of. Lady Nomia embraced her and called her a sweet child, and Benicia curtsied and continued her perambulations.

At last she spied the object of her search. As she passed the gloom-shrouded door to the wall passage she happened to glance in that direction and saw the Marquess of Potrimpos peering anxiously from the doorway. She went to him, almost at a run, for she had been longing to see him ever since she'd heard the splendid news regarding Manicia and Sir Criffel.

But Sir Parchim was not himself. He barely glanced at Benicia. His eyes were red-rimmed, his beautiful hair was stringy and his peacock attire was crumpled. The bandages on his head and hand were dirty.

Benicia took his injured hand gently within both of hers. 'Alas, my lord,' she whispered, 'what is amiss? Everything will be well; the princess says so. The army will come soon and we shall be saved.'

But the marquess pulled his hand away and continued to stare distractedly into the undercroft. 'Every time I am anigh,' he muttered, 'he stareth and stareth at me, all the while fingering his dagger.'

'Sir Criffel?' asked Benicia, trying to take his hand again. 'But my lord, hast thou not heard? For hours I've been longing to tell thee! Sir Criffel careth no longer about thee or me, for he's to marry Manicia! They shall be perfect for one another! He shall still inherit half of the Drumrock lands so he's content!'

The marquess slapped peevishly at Benicia's clutching hands. 'He doth not look content!' he snapped. 'I pray ye go away, woman. I no longer wish to see you.'

'But Potty,' moaned Benicia, 'thou knowest that I love thee.'

'No ye...' began Potrimpos, but then his eyes went wide and he ducked back behind the doorway. 'Oh dear God, he hath seen me! Benicia, hie ye hence! Can ye not see how angry ye do make him? Yet 'tis me he wisheth to slay!' He turned and fled away towards the wall passage and Benicia spun about, her eyes searching for Sir Criffel. Sure enough, there he was, close enough to throw a stone at, and now he got to his feet, his hand resting upon the dagger at his hip.

Benicia rarely felt anger over anything, but she did now. She marched towards Sir Criffel with the firm intention of telling him her mind. But as she drew closer all her resolve evaporated and she walked right past him without a word. Her heart was hammering and her knees felt weak. He watched her all the way, his eyes glittering.

'Good evening, Lady Benicia,' he said softly and her skin crawled. Sitting on the bed behind him, she suddenly saw his handsome servant, his hair glimmering like spun gold in the torchlight. Garston grinned and gave her a wink, and like a little child she took to her heels and fled towards the comforting bulk of her father.

It was very late, or perhaps very early. In Winterhued's corner of the undercroft the hangings were drawn close as Ulidia, by the light of a single candle, prepared her mistress for bed. She unlaced the princess's blue-grey gown and her black underskirt, and helped her into her nightgown. She prattled and yawned in turn. 'What an honour for my Garthwray,' she said for the fourth time, 'lying with kings!' She herself was dressed for bed and showed she was ready for it by yawning yet again.

'Indeed, he must be overjoyed,' murmured the princess exhaustedly. She had just spent two long hours with the chancellor, the chamberlain, the constable, the Duke of Travancore and, because she insisted he stay, Sir Almendral, discussing what could be done about burying the piles of the dead, about destroying the dragon and about surviving.

They had agreed that the castle's populace must leave at the end of five days. The constable and the chamberlain had insisted that the only way to get everyone clear of the castle was to remove the bodies that clogged the gatehouse, bridge the stream, post lookouts to watch for the dragon's departure, and then assemble in the outer bailey and march forth like an army. But this idea filled Winterhued with foreboding, for the creature could return suddenly and she could not help but remember Travancore's report of the townsfolk trapped and dying, their corpses piling up between the dragon's flames and the broken portcullis. And even if they managed to get clear of Lawhill, surely the creature would pursue them to wreak destruction on the road.

She herself had agreed with Travancore, that it would be safer to send folk out in pairs or small groups through the breach made in the wall by the toppling of the menials' tower, for the trees growing along the ditch and stream-bank afforded good cover from the air. 'Down into the ditch through that mess of rubble?' argued Ladstock. 'Our elderly folk could never manage such a climb!'

'Our army will be here shortly,' said the chancellor, 'and then we'll have no need to go anywhere.'

'Ah yes, Ravenhill will know what to do,' said Sir Almendral. 'Or even better, the king's hero, our unknown knight, galloping to our aid at this very moment, clad in flame-proof armour.'

Winterhued thought of his sarcastic words as Ulidia loosed her tresses from their braids, and began once more to ply a hairbrush. She leant into the old woman's comforting strokes and sighed. Pera and Brenn lay asleep upon their pallets; Brenn was smiling slightly and the princess knew that beneath her blankets she clutched the boy's little book to her heart. At least the lad was likely to be well away from the castle by now and certainly safer than they. But what a fool her father was (no, she would *not* think of her father; such thoughts would only make her anxious and sick)... how foolish it was to send such a useful boy as Ancaios on such a useless errand! To look for a single knight the length and breadth of Manydown, when the man could be anywhere in the world!

The princess tried not to wonder about the unknown knight, but he would keep riding unbidden into her thoughts. She remembered that when Sir Priwall had first talked of his exploits he had mentioned that the man bore the badge of a unicorn. Her own beloved had ridden from Lawhill with a blank shield, yet it was quite possible, even probable… but no, she would not waste her time on these thoughts! There was nothing remotely possible or probable in any of them.

Yet even as she banished the knight from her mind, she felt for her reticule and withdrew from it the rescued book. 'Go to bed, dear,' she said to Ulidia, and as the sleepy old woman put aside the brush and shuffled off to her bed, she lay the little volume upon her lap.

Snuffing out the candle, she sat for a while in the dark, listening to the susurrus of restless sleep all about her. And as she sat, she took up her old, old habit of absently tracing with her finger, over and over, the embossed initial on the book's cover; the initial that lay so closely entwined within her own.

The knight rode through the night. In parts of the forest the dark lay as black as a lake of tar, but his horse's night-vision was better than his own and the animal found its way without wandering from the road. The other two followed close behind, stumbling sometimes over the ruts and holes.

At last the moon rose high enough above the trees to send shafts of moonlight slanting in through the branches. As the night wore on it climbed into the star-dusted sky until it became visible above, bright and shining as a worn coin.

With a pang, the knight thought of Nal, out in the night with his demons and not even a blanket to protect him from the cold and the dementing moonlight. But at least he had plenty to eat, thought the knight, his own stomach gnawingly empty.

The trees began to thin and suddenly the grey stallion trotted out onto a wide expanse of moonlit heathland. The slope fell away on the right side of the road down to where the Otterburn rushed along a wooded gully. The knight slowed the horses to a walk. He knew he was now more than half way to Lawhill.

Even though he'd spent two hours in Wendur, been annoy-
ingly delayed by ruffians and wasted more time searching for Nal, he'd
travelled a huge distance. He felt weary and hungry and knew that the
horses were flagging. But he was anxious to keep moving. 'Methinks
no one escaped from the castle,' the redheaded man had told him.
He wondered at his eagerness to be slaughtered, for what, in good
sooth, could he possibly do? What difference would it make whether
he got to Lawhill today or next week? His thoughts chased themselves
in exhausted circles as his horse strode on, loose-reined, down the
westward road.

Some time later he came to with a jolt, realising that he'd fallen
asleep in the saddle. He suddenly felt so tired that nothing, not even
the plight of Lawhill's inhabitants, mattered to him more than sleep. He
half slid, half fell from the grey's back, walked across to the chestnut
gelding like a somnambulist and managed to unbuckle his bed-roll
from the saddle. He threw it down in a dry ditch by the roadside and
then just lay down in his armour. Sleep took him even before he was
fully prone.

The grey stallion, reins trailing, stood over him for a while, eventually moving off the road to graze. The chestnut, with the bay gelding in
tow, followed him. To the east, above the black line of forest, the first
light of dawn came seeping into the sky, dimming the moon and slowly
snuffing out the stars.

Ancaios was up before the sun. He'd eaten well, then slept soundly
in a warm bed, and rising was not easy. So stiff was he from his ride and
sore from his fall that at first he could scarcely move. Exhaling clouds
of steam, shivering, his teeth chattering, he pulled on his clothes, dis-
covering as he did so that the turnip-farmer's wife had brushed the
mud from his jacket and cleaned his high boots. She and her husband
and two small children were nowhere to be seen when Ancaios entered
the kitchen, but she came in, her cheeks and hands red with the cold,

as he was warming himself at the fire. With a 'good morrow, sir,' she bustled about, pouring ale into a mug and putting it before him on the table with a thick slice of barley bread and a mound of fresh-picked mushrooms fried with onions.

While he ate, she prepared her loom for the day's work and went out for a time to feed her chickens. "Tis passing strange, sir,' she said on her return; 'the chickens went into their pen some days back and they won't come out. And 'ave ye noticed all the birds are flown away? Must be that old dragon. I weren't surprised, sir, when my 'usband told me of it, for I've seen it, sir; flying in the western sky at dawn. I knew it were too big for any bird.'

All the while, even as she called him 'sir' most deferentially, she flirted gently, telling him several times what a pretty boy he was. As he rose to leave she put into his satchel a few thick slices of bread spread with quince jelly, two wrinkled apples and a bag of hazelnuts, for which he paid her from the king's purse. And then, at the cottage door, she gave him a kiss. She was a buxom and a bonny woman, and as soon as he heard the door close behind her, he could not help but laugh and skip a few steps before striding out purposefully for Langstone.

Ancaios had never before been more than eight miles from Lawhill, so it was fine to be on the road seeing the world. Fed, rested, with his blisters dressed and bandaged and his stiff muscles loosening as he went, the boy felt as though he could walk a hundred leagues. He'd hardly done as the king requested but this, he reasoned, was as good a way to go as any. For every man and his dog would be on the road to Drumrock. If he had gone that way, his chances of happening upon the knight were almost naught, for news of a dragon would be old news and any sensible knight would have turned tail and fled back to Ormsary at such tidings.

The potholes and furrows of the road abruptly changed to cobble-stones as Ancaios entered Langstone. It was a large village, almost a town, with a high-steepled church, a roundhouse for prisoners, and stocks on the village green. Several large merchants' houses, stone-built with glass windows, graced the main street and down by the Otterburn the wheel of a watermill slowly turned. Though the sun had not yet risen, the village bustled as farmers went to work in the fields and herd boys drove their beasts out to common. Looms were already at work in the cottages and women everywhere, even those with buckets waiting their turn at the village well, plied their distaffs and spindles.

As Ancaios passed, men doffed their caps and women smiled, sometimes calling out a greeting. For the turnip-farmer's news had spread and everyone now knew that the king still lived and that Ancaios was about the king's business.

The lad stood for a while at the Belford turn-off. Eventually he made the decision to travel east for a little longer, mainly because the road to the east, after leaving Langstone and crossing the Otterburn on a stone bridge, climbed a long, gorse-clad slope. He set out, eager to see if he could look back towards Lawhill from its highest point.

But some way up he was regretting that decision, for the horizon kept receding and the road was steep. As he plodded on he began to imagine his meeting with the unknown knight. Almost unwittingly he based the picture in his mind on a knight he'd recently seen; a knight from Balasore who'd triumphed at last year's Dittonsday Tournament; an arrogant man with golden hair and a broken nose, and shoulders as wide as a house. Ancaios imagined looking up to see him come riding along the road, his armour flashing in the sunlight as his fiery black stallion pranced and danced. He'd be accompanied by a retinue and cartloads of baggage and have no time for Ancaios or his message. He might be mighty and strong, and sport the princess's favourite mythical creature on his shield, but this stranger was hardly about to rush to her rescue. No, he'd look down his crooked nose at Ancaios, sniff a few times (for he'd have no trouble penetrating the boy's disguise) and say: 'Tournament off? I'll be back to Ormsary then… and thou, boy, get thee to thy dung-shovel.'

Ancaios, lost in his thoughts, had reached the top of the rise. The ground levelled off and suddenly the sun rose in the east, dazzling him. He turned round to face the pink-tinged sky in the west, and the huge, purple-shadowed vista that lay spread before him, north, west and south, for as far as his astonished eyes could see. He kept walking backwards as he followed the tiny, meandering line of the Otterburn with his eyes, searching for Lake Silverhow. But no, he couldn't see it – perhaps when the sun rose higher...

'Whither away, lad?' came a voice from over his right shoulder. He spun about and found himself standing almost underneath the huge bulk of a horse, standing stock-still in the middle of the road, black against the sunrise. He jumped back, tripped and sat down in the dirt.

'Wheresoever ye go,' said the voice again, amused, 'the way lieth easier if ye do watch the road.'

Ancaios, squinting against the sun, gaped up at a man in armour sitting motionless upon a towering horse. His only retinue consisted of two more horses that stood behind him; they were attached to each other but not to the knight. One of them shifted sideways and the boy saw a shield hanging from its saddle: a white unicorn on red.

'You sir! You, here!' He scrambled to his feet. 'I was sent to find you, but I never hoped...'

'Sent to find *me*? 'Tis fortunate then I was not at the other end of the earth.'

'Aye sir. The king sent me... I have a commission...' He fumbled for the sealed papers within his leather satchel.

'The king? He liveth yet? And his daughter?'

'Aye sir, they were both hale when I saw them yestermorn...' The knight glanced away, drawing a long breath. 'But they're trapped within the castle,' continued Ancaios, 'by a... well, ye may not believe it, sir, but they're trapped by a dragon.'

'Aye, I'd heard it was a dragon.'

'The king... he requests your help.'

'My help?' The knight laughed. 'I think not. I'd be the last man Gers would wish to have help him.'

Ancaios handed him up the king's sealed letter. 'I was told to find a knight with a unicorn on his shield. Did ye win the prize at a big tournament in Balasore last year?'

'I did.'

'Ye be the man then.'

Ancaios had shifted round to the knight's side and could see him now that he was no longer silhouetted against the sun. He was not the arrogant golden haired knight of the boy's imagination, though he appeared every bit as tall and broad-shouldered. He was a handsomer man; his nose was long and straight and his hair dark, though surprisingly, the eyes with which he scanned the king's letter were blue. His smile broadened as he read the commission. 'This is wonderful indeed,' he said. 'The king doth believe he knoweth me not, yet off'reth me his daughter's hand if I slay this dragon. How generous of him to hawk her to the first stranger that may happen by, as long as he proveth handy with a lance. 'Tis no matter if he hath the face of a warthog or the brain of a slug. But yea, I'd be pleased to take up his offer, if only I had a clue as to how I could dispatch this dragon of his.'

'It's exceeding big, sir.'

'How big?'

'Bigger than a tithe-barn sir, and it breathes fire.'

'Quite hard to kill then.'

'Aye, I've seen it sir, and I can tell you that if ye had any sense ye'd turn about and ride back to Ormsary.'

The knight laughed again. He had very good white teeth. 'I've never been known for my sense,' he said. He folded the commission and slipped it into the top of his boot as his big grey stallion sidled round in a half circle. 'Shall ye return now to Lawhill?' he asked, looking appraisingly down at Ancaios. 'Ye can ride my red gelding.'

'I can't ride, sir. I had a horse yesterday, but I fell off and he galloped away.'

'Ah... it doth seem we've both been careless, for ye did lose a horse yesterday and I lost a squire; he also ran away. The gelding was his mount and doesn't require any riding. Just sit on his back and he'll follow along.'

'Thank you sir,' said Ancaios. Self-consciously he gathered up the chestnut's reins and then proceeded to make a fool of himself by putting the wrong foot in the stirrup. But after hopping about like an idiot, he managed to clamber onto the big horse's back and even ended up facing the right way. The knight watched the procedure with a quizzical smile on his face. 'Ye're an unusual messenger,' he remarked. 'Most I've encountered seem to be familiar with the use of a stirrup... and reins for that matter.'

'I'm not a messenger, sir. The king sent me because I knew how to get out of the castle. I'm really the son of a gong-farmer, and apprenticed to that trade.'

Instead of looking disgusted, the knight regarded him approvingly. 'What is your name?'

'Ancaios, sir.'

'Well Ancaios, your barrow and spade may perhaps lie idle for a time, because... well, I have lost a squire and am in need of a new one.'

'Me sir?' Ancaios looked down to hide the grin on his face. At that moment he felt so happy that he thought he might never stop smiling for the rest of his life.

The knight sat silent for a moment, gazing down over Manydown. 'Ye've not yet given me a yea or a nay, Ancaios.'

'Yea, sir! A thousand times yea!' answered the boy. Still smiling, he raised his face and looked out to the west. Straight away he saw it, just above the western horizon; a dark speck spiralling in the dawn sky, too big for a bird. As it caught the light of the rising sun it glinted like bronze.

He pointed. 'There it is, sir: the dragon.'

The knight had seen it too. 'After all these years...' he breathed.

The ride down the hill was considerably easier than the walk up. The gorse flamed yellow in the low sunlight and a jack hare, oblivious to danger, chased a female in mad circles across the road and down the slope towards the stream. On the way the knight happened to mention how hungry he was and Ancaios joyfully opened his satchel and handed across the bread, apples and hazelnuts. As the horses clattered over the bridge and into the village the boy still hadn't managed to remove the smile from his face.

The knight asked a village lad for directions to the bailiff's house and once there surprised Ancaios by handing over what the boy had thought was one of his own horses. 'This animal is most likely stolen,' he told the bailiff, 'It was ridden by one of a band of outlaws that assailed me on the east road. Four of their number now lie dead on the roadside, back some five leagues or more, and another lieth amongst the trees. Betwixt there and here I have mislaid a squire, so if a boy shows up with two of the ruffians' horses and a bundle of their weapons, I'd be grateful if ye'd not arrest him. Ye may relieve him of the horses and weapons, but I pray ye then send him along after me.'

The bailiff, a tall man with a large girth, stared at the knight. 'Four dead?' he managed at last. 'On the road?'

'Laid out in a row,' replied the knight. 'There may be bits missing if there are wolves about.'

The bailiff's mouth still hung open. 'Outlaws, ye say?'

'Led by a one-eared windbag with hair like a black horse's tail.'

'The Adder!'

The knight raised an eyebrow. 'Adder?' he asked. 'Maggot more like. A dead maggot now.'

'The Adder is dead?'

'If that name belongeth to the villain I described, then aye, he's dead.'

The bailiff looked as though he was about to fall over. Two servants who'd been listening at the doorway darted off into the village, shouting.

A short while later, when the knight and his new squire rode away from Langstone, they were surrounded by a crowd of well wishers, all of them guerdoning the knight with their undying gratitude. The chestnut's saddlebags were laden with food and both horses wore celandines and violets plaited into their manes and tails, and their necks were bedecked with daisy chains. They were followed to the turn-off and some way up the Belford road by most of Langstone's population. The men marched ahead like a guard of honour, the women ran beside the grey stallion, wanting simply to gaze upon the knight or blow him kisses, and the children shouted and squealed as they scattered petals upon the road or brought more daisy chains for the horses.

Behind them, a group of mounted men led by the bailiff galloped out from the village and took the east road; before the day was much older they planned to retrieve the Adder's corpse and hang it from a makeshift gallows on the village green.

'So we're going to Belford then,' said Ancaios after the excitement had died down and most of the throng had returned to Langstone. He'd followed the knight without question, but felt puzzled that they were now heading north instead of west.

'We are. They tell me there's been no sign of Manydown's army, so I think we must make an attempt to stir it into action. Commission or no, I have no idea how to destroy this creature, and only a halfwit like Gers could imagine that one man might accomplish such a thing.'

Ancaios' eyes went wide at such reckless talk and he glanced around to make sure they'd not been overheard. But the few children who still followed them lagged far behind. 'Ye seem to know the king, sir,' he said. 'But are ye not from far away: Balasore, or even further?'

'I'm a Manydownian born and bred,' replied the knight, 'though I've not been home for years.'

Ancaios glanced at the man curiously. This was the most he had revealed about himself but the boy was anxious not to appear impolite by asking questions. 'I've read a tale of a dragon, sir', he said; 'it was slain by one man; he shot an arrow into its eye.'

The knight raised an eyebrow. 'Ye can read?'

'Aye sir, I am a scholar in my spare time, albeit a poor one.'

'Ye're full of surprises. I believe I have read that tale, but it's not one I could hope to emulate for I'm no bowman; I would be lucky to hit the castle at ten paces. And, alas, I do not think a sword will be of much use against this creature.'

'Against its fiery breath, I think ye could not get nigh enough to do damage with a sword.'

The knight smiled wryly. 'A bucket of water,' said he, 'might do me better service.'

CHAPTER 14

Winterhued rose at dawn. Down in the undercroft there was no way of knowing that it was morning, but a servant had come as requested to tell her that the day's first light was pricking in around the edges of the castle's boarded up windows.

The cat yawned and burrowed back under the warm covers, but the princess, sleepily assisted by Lady Ulidia, dressed by candlelight. She looked pale and tired. 'I wish I knew what to do, old thing,' she said as Ulidia pinned her hair.

The old woman tutted. 'I do lament,' she sighed, 'to see my lady so weary and distressed. And to see her clad in the very same gown that she wore yesterday. Alas and alack, her beautiful gowns and jewels, all destroyed!'

'Those things matter not a whit,' said Winterhued, 'for I have yet about me all the things, bar two, that I most care for in this world.' She took Ulidia's wrinkled hand and kissed it. 'And thou art one of them, my dear.' Ulidia tut-tutted and protested, but looked as if she might swoon with pleasure. 'And here is another,' added the princess as her cousin Brenn pushed back the covers on her bed and put her feet to the cold floor.

'I have a task for thee, Brenn,' said the princess. 'As soon as thou art dressed and fed, go find Eudora. The unhappy girl may not know that my tower hath been destroyed and is wondering what hath happened to her job as chambermaid. Tell her that if ever I have a chamber again, the position is hers.'

Brenn was so busy yawning that all she could do was nod her acquiescence. 'Is it really morning?' she eventually managed.

'Aye, the sun hath risen,' said Winterhued determinedly, getting to her feet. 'This day an attempt will be made to bury the dead. A watch shall be set upon the keep and as soon as the creature doth leave, the soldiers must take up the flagstones and make a start.'

At the opposite end of the undercroft Benicia sat leaning against her father as he ate his breakfast. At the command of the king, the Duke of Drumrock had been offered a goodly array of aliments for his morning repast; his cheeks bulged as he reached with dirty fingers for another venison pasty.

Manicia wandered about them in circles, sometimes stopping to stare sullenly down the dark undercroft. 'Come hither, Manicia, m'dear,' said the duke, patting the bed beside him. 'Sit at my side and break thy fast. There's plenty for us all.'

'The princess won't have those about her consume flesh; ye do know that,' said Manicia, but she went to him anyway to cuddle up against his grimy velvet gown.

'Pah!' he exclaimed, spitting pastry flakes, and putting his arm about her in a quick hug. 'Soon thou mayest eat meat to thine heart's content, for fortune hath shone upon thee, Manny. Thou needst not be a dreary old maid after all.' His flabby sides shook as he chortled silently at his own joke. For no matter how dreary the girl might be, with her breeding and inheritance she could have entertained any number of suitors if he'd but given them leave.

'But who shalt thou marry, Bee?' he asked, turning to his other daughter. He hugged her and gave her a greasy kiss on the cheek. 'Manny here will marry for convenience; no love there, eh Manny? Only a mother could love Criffel!'

'But I thought,' said Manicia, 'that ye did like him.'

'Like him?' laughed the duke. 'Indeed, I'm pleased to have him for a son-in-law for I like his lands and his wealth exceedingly, but him? Nasty worm. I'm glad that Bee's not marrying him for now I won't have to tolerate his company so often.' He squeezed Benicia fondly. 'And now we must find a husband for thee, my dumpling! A man with breeding, eh?'

Benicia giggled. 'I like well the Marquess of Potrimpos,' she said. Manicia huffed disgustedly and pulled away from beneath her father's arm.

'So we've noticed!' said the duke. 'Certes, he's a handsome and merry fellow, though for someone bred in the north, he's a pansy. And the Neath family is old, if not... respected. They breed nice horses though; I'd take one or two in exchange for a daughter!' He wobbled again with silent laughter. 'Or what of Travancore? There's good breeding! His mother wanteth a foreign princess for him (as our own won't have him), but I think she'd be content with my blue-blooded dumpling.'

The duke leant forward to pick some meat from a duck carcass, and over the broad mound of his velvet clad back Manicia glared at Benicia through narrowed eyes. 'Do not dare,' she hissed, 'or I shall kill thee. If I cannot have him, neither shalt thou.'

'What art thou twittering on about, Manny?' asked the duke as he stuffed some smoked lamprey into his mouth after the duck. 'Ah... foolish girls! Was ever a father happier in his daughters than I?' He hugged the both of them.

'I don't want him anyway,' whispered Benicia, leaning forward to look angrily at her sister.

'Such good girls,' said the duke and bent to kiss Benicia's forehead. 'Dear Bee, dumpling, dove; thou art the image of thy mother. We must needs find thee a husband so that we may all be wed... all of us happy!'

Manicia looked at her father with narrowed eyes. 'All?' she asked.

The duke laughed again. 'Eat up, Manny,' he chortled. 'I've no more time for idle chatter for the king wisheth to see me; he would speak upon an important matter, of great advantage to me and mine, were his words.' His chins wobbled as he laughed delightedly. 'Of great advantage to me, and to you, my dears!'

Manicia rose abruptly. 'What could the king do for me?' she muttered as she stalked sulkily away.

Ancaios and the knight rode north beside their long shadows. They passed the last of Langstone's fields, sown with wheat in autumn and now rippling with green stalks, and travelled for a time beside marshy meadowland dotted with yellow kingcups.

Ancaios still hadn't stopped smiling, for surely there was nothing finer than riding high upon a noble (and compliant) steed that was all draped in a hero's garlands. Better still, to be able to call himself squire to that hero! But best of all, to discover that such a great man was neither proud nor arrogant, but ever an amiable companion. He listened attentively as Ancaios told him of the events of the last three days, asked pertinent questions and responded to the boy's tentative curiosity with laconic good humour.

'Ye appear to know the king, sir,' said the boy, 'but... do ye know his daughter?'

'She was very young when I left Manydown,' replied the knight.

'I love her...' began Ancaios, but the knight interrupted him. 'Do I have a rival?' asked he, patting the commission that was tucked into the top of his tall boot.

'Nay, sir,' protested Ancaios; 'I love her as a devoted subject, and owe her my undying allegiance. For she ruleth this land in all but name as, unlike her father,' said the boy, needlessly lowering his voice, 'she is wise and clever and strong.'

The knight smiled down at the road. 'She is surely the reason,' he said, 'that this land hath not joined Calluna as a trampled possession of Angerona.'

Ancaios turned to look at the man, his brows raised questioningly.

'When I was a boy,' explained the knight, 'this country lay poised on the brink of war. Skirmishes were fought along our northern borders and spies brought news of a vast force assembling beyond the Hawksdale Pass. But old King Caradoc, in his dotage then but still a frightening man, led an army in stealth over the mountains north of Pelliworm, swooped down upon the Angeronian troops... but ye know all this, being a reader and a scholar.'

'Aye, but I thought that battle put an end to the Angeronians' ambitions?'

The knight shook his head. 'There is no end to the warmongers' lust for land. They began raiding with renewed vigour after Caradoc's death; greatly encouraged now that a dunderhead sat upon Manydown's throne.'

At this description of his king, Ancaios smirked guiltily. He rode beside the knight through the shadows of a small, damp wood where new leaves unfurled upon bare branches and primroses pushed themselves up amongst mossy roots. A startled deer darted away between the trees.

'After I had... departed this land,' the knight continued, 'I ofttimes thought upon Manydown's precarious state; it made me sick with fear. Then, as I rode north after many years' absence, the glad day came when the chancellor of Andelana told me that Gers yet ruled in Manydown and that the land had known peace for many a year. And when I reached Balasore I heard that Gers' heir was still his unwed daughter. The king of that land thought highly of her; he said she had all the ability of her grandfather, without his fury, and that she was the reason for Manydown's peace and prosperity.'

'Surely he is right, sir,' said Ancaios enthusiastically. 'She hath put fear into the hearts of the Angeronians just as she hath put concord and charity into the hearts of Manydownians. She's the cleverest... the best person in all the world, oh... except for...'

He stopped and the knight glanced round at him curiously. When he saw the dreamy smirk upon the lad's face he grinned wryly. 'A girl?' he asked.

Ancaios looked down, embarrassed. He pushed aside the daisy garlands so that he could pat the chestnut's neck. 'Aye,' he said. 'I only met her yesterday... and she is far above me. But I would very much like to see her again.'

The knight, hearing something, returned his attention to the road ahead. 'Well met!' said he. 'Come, Ancaios; do ye wish to see Manydown's finest?' He urged his horse forward and the stallion leapt into a canter. Ancaios grabbed for the pommel of his saddle as the chestnut launched itself after the grey.

They came out of the wood where the road rose towards the crest of a hill. Even above the beat of the horses' hoofs, Ancaios could hear the noise now; a burbling murmur of voices and a great stomping as of many feet on the march. The two horses cantered to the crest and halted.

On the road below a small army came snaking southward – perhaps fifteen hundred men – their helms, breastplates and spears aglitter in the morning sun. Ancaios knew that apart from the five hundred soldiers stationed at the border garrisons in the northeast, this amounted to the whole of Manydown's standing army, for it was too costly to maintain anything larger. It made a brave enough sight however; surely enough to daunt the heart of any dragon.

In the vanguard came the mounted knights and men at arms, numbering about a hundred, their handsome steeds brightly caparisoned and their armour gleaming. Then came four hundred foot soldiers; pikemen, billmen and halberdiers, clad in mail shirts and brigandines with bright-burnished sallets on their heads. Their weapons bristled like a steel-spined hedgehog. After them came the archers; two hundred arbalesters with their powerful crossbows and eight hundred longbowmen, their tall, thick bows unstrung and slung across their backs. Above them all, brave and bright in the morning breeze, blew square banners and long, forked standards, swallow-tailed gyttons and pointed pennoncels, all blazoned with stars and sunbursts, with lions and boars, stags and bulls, roses and lilies. And behind them lumbered half a dozen wagons loaded with baggage and provisions.

A man at arms left the van and came galloping smartly up the road towards the knight and his squire. He drew rein and his big brown horse threw up its head and skidded to a halt at the top of the hill. The fellow was clad in full plate harness, unmarked and gleaming, with the visor of his sallet raised to reveal his sweating face. 'State your business, sir,' he said brusquely, but his expression was confused as he looked at the flower-draped horses and the squire who was garbed in the king's livery. And then his roving eyes lighted upon the knight's shield and went round as a fish's.

'I have a commission from the king,' replied the knight. 'Do ye march to his aid?'

'Aye, we do, sir,' said the man at arms, trying to stop his excited horse from spinning in circles.

'Ye're tardy.'

The fellow looked guilty. 'It took some time to...' he muttered. 'Our commander...'

'Who is your commander?'

'Sir Rathdown Ra...'

'Ravenhill. I remember him.' The knight smiled grimly. 'Kindly inform Sir Rathdown that I have a commission from the king that requireth my presence in Lawhill. I do not wish to tread on his toes, so tell him that though I travel with his army, I shall keep to the rearward.'

'Sir,' said the man at arms with a respectful nod. He turned his horse about and thundered away down the hill.

The knight watched him go and laughed mirthlessly. 'Aye, I remember Rathdown Ravenhill,' he said. 'When I knew him his sole talent was for playing the toad; he was one of the king's minions. And as for leading an army, I think he'd have had trouble leading a hungry horse to a hayrick. I suppose it's too much to hope aught hath changed.'

He and Ancaios moved their horses some distance from the road to watch the troops march by. Amongst the splendidly armoured knights they could not fail to see Ravenhill, riding beneath his banner of stars and ravens, and mounted upon a huge white courser. He held his pointed nose high and looked straight ahead. But every last one of the knights, men at arms and esquires that surrounded him turned to stare as they rode by the nameless knight who sat so still upon his garlanded grey stallion at the roadside. Ancaios grinned as he watched the ripple of turned heads, rumour and gossip that ran through the army as it passed.

Just before the baggage train drew level the knight urged his horse forward and he and Ancaios joined the column abreast with (but somewhat apart from) the last of the longbowmen.

Before the sun was very much higher, the army tramped into Langstone, and the village folk once more deserted their fields and houses to come running. But they almost ignored Ravenhill and his knights, converging on the rear of the marching column to flock about their hero. For though he'd been gone for less than an hour, the villagers gave him full credit for having roused the troops to action. 'Ye got old Ravenhill off his lazy backside quick smart, sir!' shouted one old man.

Soon the news that the knight had slain The Adder had spread through the whole army.

Three youths ran beside Ravenhill's knights, taunting them over their ten fruitless years of 'Adder hunting'. 'Go back to Belford, ladies, and take up spinning,' yelled one. 'Try embroidery!' laughed another. 'Ye think ye can slay a dragon?' shouted the third. 'May as well offer your services as ladies-in-waiting to the princess and leave the killing of monsters to the man that can do it single-handedly!' A man at arms left the column to ride towards them threateningly and they darted off amongst the houses, laughing and still shouting taunts. Ravenhill stared straight ahead but his looks were thunderous.

The knight knew nothing of this, yet he was uncomfortable enough with the attention and relieved when they had left Langstone behind them. As they rode past the turnip farmer's house, the fellow came running, with his wife and children at his heels, all eager to watch Manydown's troops pass by. They were surprised to find Ancaios riding with the army and even more surprised to be introduced to the man who had slain The Adder less than a day since. Indeed, the honest fellow seemed so overwhelmed that he could scarcely manage a word. 'Just think,' Ancaios exclaimed, 'even as we first spoke of him yester-eve, the villain lay stone-dead!'

The farmer managed to mumble a few words of gratitude but as the knight and Ancaios turned to go, the boy heard him mutter, 'Never thought the day'd come when I'd be offering thanks to a Callunian.' Ancaios would have liked to turn about and give the fellow a piece of his mind, but knew he could never get his mount to agree to such a thing. But as he twisted in the saddle he was pleased to see the farmer's bonny young wife give her husband a clip over the ear.

'I'm sorry, sir,' he said; 'I thought him a better man than that.'

'Sorry? Ye are responsible then for his unreason?'

'No sir... but...'

'My only surprise is that I have encountered so little of it.'

'Perhaps that, sir,' answered Ancaios, 'is because everyone doth know that the princess hath a fondness for Callunians.'

'That is good news,' said the knight with a wry smile. 'My prospects improve by the minute.'

'Sir...' said Ancaios doubtfully.

'Aye lad?' prompted the knight. His smile grew wider as he watched the boy hesitate.

'It's just that... well, sir, I think ye should not get your hopes too high... about the princess. She hath spent her life refusing suitors.'

The knight laughed. 'Have no fear, Ancaios, my hopes are not high. A dragon, bigger than a tithe barn, standeth betwixt me and Winter-hued.' That made Ancaios laugh too; low hopes hardly mattered when his spirits rode so high.

'Hello, pretty boy,' said a soft voice beside Ancaios' left knee. He looked down, startled, to find a rough looking woman, her russet skirts hitched clear of the trampled mud, walking beside his mount. She looked past him, straight across at the knight, and gave him such a brazen look that Ancaios' mouth fell open. 'To you, sir,' she said in her husky voice, 'the sele of the day.' 'And to you, mistress,' the knight answered, amused and amiable.

Since leaving the turnip farmer behind, Ancaios had scarcely noticed that they travelled now alongside the wagons in the baggage train. He looked about him, surprised to see how many women accompanied the army. Some sat in the wagons, and others walked beside the lumbering wheels, skirts hitched to their knees. Even as he watched, a few more of those on foot began to converge on the knight like pins to a magnet.

They were common women, some of them bare-footed and brown as berries, some as foul-mouthed and rough as the pikemen, some old and fat, and some young and pretty enough too. Before long Ancaios was chatting with two such as he rode. 'What do ye in the army?' he asked. 'We cook and we mend,' said a plump lass with rosy cheeks and autumn-gold hair. 'We sew standards and pennants and badges,' said a raven-haired girl. 'And we do other things,' added the autumn-haired girl with a wink and a laugh.

The knight rode for a while accompanied by several flirting women, and he was gallant and friendly with each of them. But as everyone knew, the baggage train was no place for such as he, and the women soon let him ride forward, sending after him their sighs, blown kisses and declarations of undying love. Ancaios though, slipped from his saddle and told the knight he would catch up shortly; he had some business to attend to. The knight lifted an eyebrow and looked quizzically at the boy, but let him go without asking questions.

Ancaios watched the chestnut gelding trot off after the grey and then he and the raven-haired girl, whose name was Sindia, hoisted themselves up on the nearest wagon. It was hauled through the mire by a matching pair of big, patient roans; their strawberry red coats looked as though they'd been frosted with sugar. Sitting atop the baggage in the wagon, two women busied themselves with their needles and thread, while about them lay a jumble of half-completed battle standards, gyttons and pennoncels.

'Shove over, mother,' said Sindia. 'This lovely lad's asked me to make 'im a badge.' She sat down, forcing herself into the narrow space between the two larger women, and reached for her work-bag. ''Twill be quick for I've got a shield in the right tincture finished already,' she said to Ancaios. 'I were makin' it for someone else, but 'e can wait.'

'Ye did see his shield?' asked Ancaios. 'I'd like it just like that if I may; a unicorn, rearing up, white on red.'

'Gules, white unicorn rampant,' corrected Sindia smugly. 'Don't know much about 'eraldry, do ye?'

'Nay, not much,' laughed Ancaios, clinging to the side of the wagon as it lurched and almost came to a standstill, its wheels half buried in the road's ruts. The man at the horses' heads growled and goaded, the horses leaned into their collars and the wagon-wheels slowly came free of the sucking mud.

'Ye'll 'ave to run,' said Sindia, pointing; 'army's leavin' us behind.'
Ancaios looked over his shoulder and saw that she was right: a big gap
had opened up between the last of the bowmen and the first of the
wagons. 'Don't worry, they'll stop midday, rest till we catch up and
then push on again 'ard. So we'll 'ave but a moment; just enough time
to tack your new badge over the old.'

One of the older women gasped in good-humoured astonishment.
She had flaming hair and red cheeks and her bodice was cut very
low. 'But that's the king's livery!' she exclaimed. 'Ye can't sew nothin'
over that!'

'The king only borrowed me for a time,' explained Ancaios; 'he
needed someone to deliver a letter. My new job... my *real* job, is
squire. I'm his squire... the knight that was here...'

'Ahh...' sighed the big woman, putting her hand to her heart and
pretending to swoon. 'Would ye like to swap? I'll be 'is squire an' ye can
come and sew.'

'No, thank you,' said Ancaios with a laugh, 'even though I'd always
have such nice company.'

'Sooth, but ye're lovely! Aren't 'e just lovely, Sindia, with 'is fine
manners an' 'is beautiful 'air an' 'is 'andsome, 'appy face!' Before he
could protest she'd got to her feet, scooped him into her fat arms
and kissed him on the lips. Ancaios squirmed his way from her ample
embrace, but then Sindia had to give him a kiss too, and then the third
woman, who was surely Sindia's mother. 'I thank you, ladies,' he said
laughing, and making for the edge of the wagon, 'for such a welcome.
But I think *my* lady might not have been happy to see it.'

'Ye've a lover!' exclaimed the redhead. 'Is she pretty?'

'She's the most beautiful girl in the world!' Still laughing, Ancaios
jumped down from the wagon. Leaping over the ruts and puddles, he
made for the road's verge and ran forward in search of the knight.

Brenn had spent the morning searching for Eudora. The maid wasn't in the King's Hall and no one knew where she was; few even knew whom she was. Accompanied by a lamp-bearing guard and trailed silently by Pera, Brenn went hither and thither about the hall, asking for news of the friendless girl from this servant and that. But after more than two days of fireless cold, darkness and gnawing fear, the people answered Brenn's queries sullenly, sometimes rudely. Yet Brenn remained staunch and cheerful. She even smiled sometimes as she went for she had her love's cloak about her shoulders and it seemed proof against any amount of gloom.

Several times was she told the tale of a servant who had gone out early that morning through a door into the Inner Bailey. 'Stood there, she did, just stood there by the door, dumb and crying, till a fellow put his hand out and hauled her back in.' Then, by and by she spoke to a lady's maid who told her that she'd heard from a chambermaid that the girl who'd gone out into the bailey was a Callunian. 'I'm sorry, m'lady, but if she's the one ye're after, I never heard where she went after that.'

At last, she spoke to two women who knew Eudora. One of them suggested she look in the infirmary, where a few servants had gone to attend the wounded. 'In good sooth, I wouldn't bother,' said her companion sourly; 'the girl's such a misery. I doubt she'd want to minister to another's woes when she's so many of her own.' Brenn thought the second woman was probably right, but she'd looked everywhere else.

Still accompanied by the guard and followed by Pera, she made for the East Tower which was but a short distance away along a trail of water-spills and wet footprints. (For all of the castle's water was being fetched in buckets from the well in the East Tower's basement.) The trail splashed its way down a newel stair, but Brenn went in the opposite direction and climbed past the door to the chapel and up to the tower's first floor. She hesitated in the doorway, frowning and a little daunted, and Pera fearfully took hold of her arm.

'I'll go ask, if m'lady wisheth,' said the guard.

'No need," replied Brenn; 'I shall go. Wait for me here. Thou also, Pera.'

'I want to come with thee,' whispered Pera, and so the two of them ventured into the room, the older girl still clinging to the younger's arm.

Though the East Tower was a substantial edifice, its walls were so massively thick that the round chamber within them was not large. Three arrow slits, a quarter as deep as the chamber's width, pierced its walls, but they had been boarded over and let in no more daylight than would a keyhole. Between the slits, three torches flared from wall brackets, casting a trembling light over the wounded who lay so close together that it was difficult to find room enough to walk amongst them.

Five women moved quietly about the chamber administering to the patients, and Brenn had no need to ask for Eudora for she recognised her slump-shouldered form straight away. Drawing nigh, she spoke the girl's name softly and Eudora glanced round, startled. She looked different somehow, though it was hard to see why as her face appeared just as sad and wan as Brenn remembered it.

'M'lady,' she said huskily, 'I... I thought I'd try to help... to make up in some way.'

'Make up for what?'

'For being bad and selfish and craven... and everything wicked ye may think of.'

'That cannot be true,' said Brenn, 'for the princess thinketh well of thee. I was sent to tell thee that her tower is burned, but when she hath a chamber again she would like thee as her chambermaid. Indeed, she told me that thou hast promise.'

'I know not why she would think that,' whispered Eudora, tears welling in her blue eyes.

Tears came to Brenn's eyes too as she looked about her at the wounded, and heard their moans and cries and laboured breathing. Pera gripped her arm and whimpered. 'What can be done for them?' asked Brenn.

'Naught,' replied Eudora. 'The surgeon saith he can do naught for burns. Some of them are burnt so deep they do not even hurt. The surgeon purges and bleeds them and we apply emollients to their wounds, but many will die. Look, look,' she suddenly said and turning from Brenn, walked five paces to the side of the last bed in the row, pushed up against the wall.

A young man lay upon it; he seemed unconscious and his breath came in shallow gasps. His dark hair was singed and one side of his face was raw, blistered and blackened. ''Tis Sir Dechmont,' whispered Eudora, 'he that were delivered from the dragon's den by... by...'

'By Ancaios,' murmured Brenn.

'Aye... by him.' Eudora cast a puzzled glance at Brenn and then turned back to Sir Dechmont. 'How beautiful he is and how brave,' she whispered. 'But he shall die, the surgeon sayeth.'

Brenn put her hands to her face. 'No,' she breathed, 'mayhap he need not. Mayhap none of them need die. I must speak with the princess...' She turned to go and then stopped, looking back at Eudora. 'How many souls lieth within this chamber?'

'Two-score and three, m'lady,' replied the girl.

'I thank thee, Eudora," said Brenn. She took Pera by the hand and hastened from the chamber. Urgent thoughts tumbled about her head as she made her way down the spiralled stair: *I cannot take from him, but I can ask... for forty-three... nay, too many... twenty... mayhap a dozen will suffice. But how shall I? I would sooner fall dead than ask such a thing... but I must... I must... for that poor knight... for each one of those suffering souls...*

She emerged from the stairwell at a run and almost collided with four guards who were making their way along the wall passage. 'Ladies!' exclaimed their leader, throwing out his arms to block the way. Brenn looked impatiently up into his face to discover that he was no guard, but the Duke of Travancore himself. He was very tall, with a countenance as long and doleful as a donkey's. Standing with his arms wide, he cast a cursory glance over bashful Pera and then stared at Brenn as though he'd never seen her before. She stood poised to run, holding the skirts of her blue-green gown above her amber petticoat. Her chestnut hair fell across her shoulders in tangled curls, and her hazel eyes sparked. The duke struggled to find breath. 'Ye are... ah... the princess's cousin, are ye not?' he managed in his hoarse voice. 'Lady... ah... Brenn?'

Brenn's patience had evaporated. 'From the way ye're inspecting me, sir,' she said, 'I might be a brood-mare at a horse-fair. But I'm not for sale and I am in haste, so stand aside.' She pushed past him and the guards at his back and set out along the passage. Pera scurried after her, and her own guard ran to catch up. 'Alas Pera,' she said, turning to give the girl a sympathetic look, 'surely he cannot be the object of thine affections?'

Pera looked stunned. 'Why ever not?' she gasped. 'Is he not seemly? Is he not tall and lean? I do not like fat men... but... but he would never have me because he is a blue-blooded duke and my family are nothing...'

'A fig for his blue-blood,' said Brenn. 'Better to wed a merry gong-farmer than a dreary duke with a face like a funeral.'

'A gong-farmer? Thou dost not mean that.'

'But I do... I do!' Brenn broke into a run, hugging her secret to herself as she went.

They reached the portal, marked by two torches, that led to the undercroft of the King's Hall. "Stay here," Brenn said to Pera. 'The princess hath gone to the Constable's Gate and I must get myself thither as fast as I may.' Pera opened her mouth to protest, but then nodded like an acquiescent child and turned away.

As she disappeared through the door, a servant coming from the undercroft moved aside to let her pass and then stepped out into the passage. She was carrying two empty buckets, and ducked a half-curtsy as she scurried by. Brenn gazed at her in surprise.

'Mashona?' she inquired and the girl spun about.

'Oh!' gasped she, staring like a startled rabbit. 'I didn't recognise your ladyship.' It was indeed the maid who had come with Brenn from Drumalis.

'Don't be daft,' answered Brenn; ''tis but three days since thou last saw me.'

'But ye've changed, your ladyship! Ye do seem so old.'

'Old? Hath my hair turned grey?'

'Nay, m'lady, I meant... I meant that ye're not a girl anymore.'

'No? Am I then a boy, or a cow... or a botfly?'

'Nay, m'lady... ye're a woman.'

'Certes, that's a relief,' said Brenn with a smile. 'Keep thee safe, Mashona.'

She turned away, nodded to her escorting guard, and the two of them set out for the northern end of the castle and the Constable's Gate.

Manydown's army marched hard for some three leagues, following the westward flow of the Otterburn. Ancaios, perched comfortably upon the broad back of the placid rounsey, looked about him at the spring-burgeoning meadows and enjoyed the bright day. They passed through two sunny villages and the boy remembered seeing their candle-lit windows when he'd rattled by in a mule cart little more than twelve hours ago. Then, he'd gone unnoticed; today, he was cheered as a conquering hero!

Riding with the knight at the tail end of the army, Ancaios could but wonder at the swift and steady stride of the soldiers that marched before him. Having walked some of that road himself, he marvelled that they could maintain such a pace over its pits and potholes. 'How long can they keep this up?' he asked the knight.

'All day by the looks of them,' came his answer. 'Ravenhill hath certainly trained his troops to march. Yet they'll need to go harder than this if we're to reach Lawhill before nightfall.'

'Before nightfall? Is that his plan?'

'So the women told me, and they often know these things before the soldiers do.'

'Doth he have any plans beyond that?'

'I think not. Ravenhill was not a canny man when I knew him, and neither would he take advice.'

'So he shall just march in, pitch his tents and light his fires on the common, and then wait for the dragon to swoop down and slaughter his soldiers?'

'Ye know him well,' said the knight. Ancaios glanced across at him. Though he appeared relaxed and good-humoured, there was an urgency, an intensity, about him that grew as the hours went by.

'I've never met him, sir,' said the boy needlessly, 'but... I suppose that he feeleth invulnerable surrounded by his thousand bowmen."

'No doubt... though he might be wondering how sure is their aim in the dark.'

A man and a woman and their five tousle-haired children stood by the boggy roadside, watching the soldiers march by. They carried a few possessions upon their backs and looked hungry and mud-splashed, but their faces were full of hope as they cheered the army onwards.

'Kill that stinkin' ol' dragon!' yelled the tallest of the boys. 'Fill 'im full of arrows and cut 'im up in a fousand bits!' He set off running beside the longbowmen and with excited cries and laughter the other children followed him.

"Tis a brave show ye make, sir,' called their father to the knight.

'Be Lawhill's saviours!' cried the woman with her hand on her heart. She ran, splashing through mud, across to the knight and gripped his stirrup. 'Deliver us from the dread beast and give us back our homes!'

The knight looked down into her grimy face. "Tis certain that Manydown's troops will do their utmost, goodwife,' said he kindly, but she suddenly hissed at him, let go of his stirrup and made a stupid sign in the air, as though she warded off evil. The horses jogged away from her and left her standing ankle-deep in the mire.

The knight shook his head and smiled wryly. 'Splendid it is to be hated for no reason,' said he.

'I do know a little about that, sir,' murmured Ancaios.

The knight glanced round at him. 'Yes, of course,' he said.

'I once loved a Callunian scullery maid – at least, I thought I did – but she looked upon me with scorn and called me a lowly worm and a dung-fly maggot.' Ancaios grinned and the knight laughed.

'I'd have thought,' said he, 'a Callunian kitchen drudge would be the lowliest creature in all of Manydown, but no.' He reached out and gripped Ancaios' shoulder. 'Here he is: the lowest of the low; my new squire.'

Ancaios laughed too. The breeze lifted his hair and tousled the red-gold mane of his fine mount. The sun shone upon him; it sparkled on the water that lay across the marshy meadows all about and gleamed on the yellow petals of ten thousand buttercups. Ahead of him the bright standards and pennoncels of the marching army floated and curled upon the air and beside him rode the man who had but yesterday slain the dreaded 'Adder'. Ancaios felt nothing like a lowly worm.

He looked over his shoulder and saw that the grimy woman and her family had changed direction and, like all the other refugees they'd passed that morning, were following the army confidently back towards Lawhill. And like all of the others, they were being rapidly left behind.

'She'll rue the day she hissed at you,' said Ancaios happily, 'after ye've slain the dragon and married the princess.'

The knight half smiled at the boy's jest, but his mind was already elsewhere.

Ancaios watched him for a moment. 'Do ye wish to ride past the army and gallop all the way to Lawhill?' he asked.

'Ye read me like a book,' said the knight. 'Aye, I do… but what would I achieve? I'd kill my horse and then be slain myself, for I have no more plan than Ravenhill… probably less.' His horse jogged sideways for a few steps and he ran a hand down its arched neck. 'Nay, methinks that woman will have little cause to remember our encounter, let alone rue it.'

With perhaps an hour to go before midday, a halt was called beside a rill that flowed in from the north through a meadow. Beyond the meadow the road entered a stretch of woodland, while to its south the Otterburn rushed down over rapids into a narrow defile.

The foot soldiers filled their water bottles at the rill, upstream from where it had already been muddied by trampling horses, and then they sat or lay down by the roadside, munching on the victuals they had carried with them. A small, brightly-coloured tent, transported in pieces on the backs of a few soldiers, was quickly erected so that Sir Rathdown Ravenhill need not sit outside to take his rest and repast.

Resplendent and uneasy in his gleaming armour, the commander perched upon a stool at his fold-up table, eating an almond cake and taking sips of wine from a silver goblet. He was a vain, handsome man who, though of middle years, still possessed a fine mane of tawny-blonde curls. But he'd become rather corpulent of late and his flushed face glistened with sweat. The nails at the end of his plump fingers were bitten to the quick.

He looked up, dabbing at his mouth with a napkin, as his sergeant entered to inform him that the 'unknown knight, slayer of the Adder' stood without, requesting an audience with his lordship. Ravenhill frowned. He scratched his ear and then he scratched his pointed nose. He stared at the floor and made a growling noise in his throat. 'Sir, ye must needs see him sooner or later,' said the sergeant with a narrow smile; 'he beareth a commission from the king.' Scarcely waiting for his commander's reluctantly nodded assent, the sergeant opened wide the tent flap and ushered the newcomer in.

Ravenhill didn't look up straight away; he'd snatched up an armoury list from his table and pretended now to study it intently. When he did look up, the height and easy presence of the man who stood before him, his unwavering gaze and his slight, amused smile, made the blood pound in Ravenhill's temples. With an attempt at nonchalance, he leaned an arm upon the table and the sight of his pristine blue steel – the finest armour in all Manydown – calmed him a little. He looked back at the knight; looked him up and down, stared at his blue eyes and the specks of rust on his battered armour (my! that armour, he'd never seen its like) and his mouth turned down in a sneer.

'They tell me ye have a commission from the king,' he said, then coughed for his voice had emerged higher than expected. The knight's direct gaze and slight smile were unchanged. He handed Ravenhill a folded parchment and in interested silence watched him read. After perusing the first two lines, the commander's sneer changed to a look of confusion. 'But this... this says "dragon",' he muttered.

'Is that not the reason ye're marching to the aid of your king?' asked the knight.

'The messenger was ranting. We could not believe...'

'Thus, despite your liege lord's urgent request ye waste two days disbelieving. What of the words of the villagers we have passed, and the refugees by the roadside?'

'Fool-compounded rumour!' snapped Ravenhill. 'Dragons are no more than flimflam and vaporous claptrap.'

'Your king sayeth otherwise.'

Angrily, Ravenhill stared at the commission, and then he snorted. 'He wants you to kill this thing by yourself? If the messenger is to be believed, the beast is the size of a town!' The commander laughed ill humouredly as sweat trickled down his face. 'Do yourself a service, sir: turn about and hie ye back to wherever it was ye came from. Ye're not about to win the princess's hand; even if she'd have you, which she won't!' He laughed again, then suddenly stopped, looked up from the parchment and stared at the knight. "S'blood!' he swore. 'Do I not know you?'

The knight smiled. 'Not as well as I know you, Rathdown,' said he.

'I could arrest you.'

'Not while I have this.' The knight took the commission from the table and tucked it back into the top of his boot. 'Meanwhile,' said he, 'I'd stay and give what help I can. As ye have made clear, only an arrant fool could imagine that one man might accomplish this task. I have no plans to attempt it and unless a useful course of action presents itself to me I shall but stand aside and watch the army do its work. Ye may arrest me after ye've dispatched Lawhill's tormentor.' He turned to leave and then stopped. 'Sir,' said he over his shoulder, 'ye could do worse than speak with the lad who rideth with me. He hath seen the creature.'

But mention of the boy only served to make Ravenhill angrier; his face turned red and the veins stood out on his forehead. He got to his feet, leaning hard on the table. 'After my years of loyal devotion,' he said, 'why did he not send to me with offers of earldoms or marquis-ates? Why did he not offer me the princess's hand? All he hath ever done is toss me the crumbs. I've a mind to turn about and march back to Belford, leaving the damned dragon to you, just as His Highness doth desire.'

'I pray ye do not, sir! For when *ye* have accomplished the deed and delivered the king, 'tis likely all these rewards will be yours. I think ye should speak with the boy.'

But Ravenhill thumped his hand on the table. 'Go to hell,' he spat. 'I long only for the day when I shall see you hang!'

'Hang?' asked the knight as he lifted the tent flap and ducked out beneath the low opening. 'Gers will want something more protracted than a hanging.'

'Hold the horses,' the knight had said, but that was easier said than done. Hougomont wanted only to follow the man and he carted Ancaios round in circles, walking beneath the chestnut's neck until the reins were in a tangle. The boy let go of Dunboyne – he was unlikely to go anywhere – and the gelding put down his head to graze, trod on the trailing reins and then got them caught round his forelegs. When Ancaios turned his back on the stallion in an attempt to free the gelding, the stallion bit him on the arm. Though it was more of an experimental nip than a bite, it was on the arm that had been badly bruised the day before, and it hurt. Ancaios spun round and growled at the horse; Hougomont nuzzled him apologetically and then nipped him again. 'Ow!' gasped Ancaios.

'Give him a smack, lad,' said a voice at his back; 'that's plain bad manners.'

Ancaios turned to discover that a man at arms, very fine in his polished armour, had come to the rescue by untangling Dunboyne's reins. 'Looks like your horses could do with a good feed,' he said, producing two nosebags full of oats.

He was a lean man with thinning hair and a sharp but kindly face. 'Our fat horses are all eating,' said he, slipping the strap of the nosebag over the grey's ears, 'and I thought they wouldn't mind sharing with these twain.'

'Thank you, sir,' said Ancaios, fumblingly attempting to get the other nosebag onto the chestnut's head. The long shanks of the horse's bit didn't help, and neither did the horse's eagerness. 'They've come a long way,' he explained; 'thousands of leagues... halfway around the world.'

'No wonder they're hungry then,' laughed the man at arms. 'But they're nice horses, the both of them; strong and well-made. I like this grey; I've had my eye on him ever since I saw you standing by the roadside back before Langstone. He'd be a fine fellow with a bit more flesh on his bones.'

'You like horses, sir.'

'I do... more than people most days.'

'I like horses too, especially this one,' said Ancaios, proudly stroking the chestnut's neck. 'He's the nicest horse I ever rode.'

'What of you and him... the knight? Do ye need feeding as well?'

'Nay, sir, thank you.' Ancaios pointed to his full saddlebag. 'They gave us plenty in Langstone. I'm just waiting for him, my master, to return.'

'There are rumours flying about concerning your master,' said the man at arms mysteriously as he took his leave.

Ancaios walked around the horses as they munched happily, pulling the last of the wilted flowers from their manes and tails and thinking of his shortcomings as a squire. What sort of squire, he wondered, couldn't even hold two horses without help? He was sure that as soon as the knight's *real* squire showed up he'd be out of a job, for the man had several times expressed concern for the lad and was obviously fond of him; clearly he'd been an excellent attendant.

So Ancaios was somewhat surprised when the knight returned. 'Well done,' said he. 'If I'd left Nal holding the horses, they'd have had their heads in Ravenhill's tent almost as soon as I got there myself.'

The two of them shared some of the Langstone provender, and then Ancaios, with a good deal of instruction, helped the knight on with his leg armour. After several mirth-inducing attempts to put things on back-to-front or upside-down, and much fumbling with laces, buckles and pin-catches, the knight was eventually clad in his sabatons, greaves, poleyns and cuisses.

As Ancaios buckled the shield-shaped tassets to the skirts of the knight's cuirass, the man looked down at him with a wry smile. 'Now ye know how vain I am, Ancaios,' said he. 'I have put you to this futile task merely so that I may vaunt myself as we strut and swagger down to Lawhill. Still, we needn't make things easy for the beast; after it's roasted me in here it shall have a hard time picking out its meat. Like Gers with a boiled crab.'

'Sir! Do not say such things,' said Ancaios, fastening the buckle of the left side-tasset. 'Wearing armour is not a vanity but a right and an honour, which ye have earned. More so than most of these peacocks we ride with.' Ancaios turned red and shut his mouth as he suddenly saw the absurdity of a gong farmer instructing a great knight on the subject of honour.

'Would ye like to be a knight?'

'I'm a gong farmer,' answered Ancaios quietly.

'Really? I thought ye were my squire.'

'For the time being, but... is that not an impermanent arrangement?'

'Why should it be? Are ye so eager to return to your barrow and spade?'

'No!'

'If I am slain by the dragon... or indeed by the king, ye may have need to take up your old profession, but if not I'd be pleased if ye'd stay with me until ye've earned your own spurs.'

Ancaios picked up the right side-tasset but his hands had begun to shake. 'Spurs?' he asked, struggling with the buckle. 'I'd be a knight?'

'Why not?' asked the knight, as casually as if gong farmers were knighted every day of the week.

All the time Ancaios had been about his task, soldiers had been traipsing past, singly or in groups. They pretended to be on their way to the rill to fill their flasks, or to be about some other task, but it was clear that their purpose was to ogle the renowned warrior who'd unexpectedly come amongst them. It was also clear that he provided them with their main topic of conversation. Ancaios felt like a monkey in a menagerie yet the knight scarcely seemed to notice; perhaps he was accustomed to it.

But now, just as Ancaios finished with the last buckle, three men in armour stepped up to the knight. Ancaios straightened and turned anxiously, but he saw that their faces were friendly, indeed, the eldest of them wore a broad grin.

'I couldn't hope to go anonymously for long amongst old friends,' said the knight, 'Lord Rosebery, Sir Lynton... and...'

'Hollinwood,' said the third man.

'Of course. It hath been a long time.'

'Too long,' said Lord Rosebery, and he took the knight's hand in a firm grip. 'Be assured, sir, that if ye desire to remain unknown we will be mute, yet we wished you to know that we are glad to see you, as are many more amongst us. Welcome back, sir.'

Ancaios noticed that all about the meadow soldiers were climbing to their feet, and at the same time he heard the rumble of wagon wheels. The knight, who could surely read his mind, looked at the boy quizzically and tilted his head in the direction of the approaching baggage train. Ancaios grinned, nodded and set off at a run. He passed the soldiers as they trooped up to the leading wagon to collect parcels of food to sustain them on the next hard march. This also was a last chance to have blisters dressed, to collect extra arrows and crossbow bolts, and to have nails knocked through loose horseshoes, for from here on the baggage train was to be left to its own pace while the army made all speed.

By the time Ancaios got to the third wagon the women had already climbed down. Several had gone forward to talk to the soldiers, the rest sat about on crates and baskets, still at their sewing. He looked around for dark-haired Sindia and spotted her flirting amongst a group of pikemen. But she'd not forgotten him for when she saw him she smiled and waved his badge above her head. She had a needle threaded and ready in her hand, and as soon as she'd got away from the soldiers, darted up to him and without a word, slapped the badge over the king's sunburst and began stitching. He looked down at it and saw, upside down, a rearing white unicorn on a red shield. 'It's beautiful… perfect,' he said; 'ye're clever, Sindia.' She glanced up at him, pink-cheeked and shiny-eyed, and went on with her work.

A joy had been building inside Ancaios and now it welled up until he felt like leaping and shouting. But he just said quietly: 'I'm going to be a knight.'

'Of course ye are, Sir Ancaios,' said Sindia, 'but stand still, or I shall sew this to you instead of your jacket.'

Around them the other women plied their needles and their gossip. 'But I've heard he's a Callunian,' said a pale girl with freckles.

'But 'ave ye seen 'im?' asked the big redheaded woman. She turned to Ancaios. 'Where is 'e, lovely?'

'Over by Ravenhill's tent,' answered Ancaios; 'talking to Lord somebody and two other knights.'

The big woman took the girl's sewing from her and gave her an encouraging shove. 'Quick, ye'd best 'urry.'

'Come on, Lota,' said the freckled girl. She grabbed the arm of a curly-headed lass and the two of them scampered off amongst the soldiers, giggling.

The flame-haired woman laughed. 'Ye'll not care where 'e comes from when ye see 'im,' she called after them, 'for 'e's the prettiest sight ye'll see in a month of 'olidays!'

'Did 'e truly slay the Adder?' asked Sindia.

'He did,' replied Ancaios; 'only yesterday.'

'They're saying 'e's far-famed,' said Sindia; 'renowned through all the world.'

'That's why the king sent for him.'

'Ooh, I need another look,' said the redhead, putting down the livery jacket she was working on and hastening off after the two girls.

The army was beginning to form ranks.

'But they're also saying,' said Sindia, dropping her voice as if she were about to tell a secret, ''e tells no one 'is name because... well... a pikeman just told me that Sir Pinmore told 'im that Sir Rathdown knows who 'e is... for Sir Pinmore said 'e heard Sir Rathdown say 'e could arrest 'im. Sir Pinmore says...' she lowered her voice to a whisper, ''e says... 'e used to be the princess's secret lover, and for that the king doth want 'im dead.'

Ancaios stared at her. 'That's nonsense,' he said; 'he doesn't know her.'

'Ach... pay no heed to Pinmore,' said Sindia's mother, who'd been listening; 'the man's a snake.'

For a moment Ancaios stood wrapt in thought. Sindia had finished with his badge, the army was beginning to march away and the women were returning to the baggage wagons, giggling and breathless. Then he shrugged, looked about him and patted the new badge on his jacket. 'Thank you, Sindia,' he said. 'I hope I may be in a position to repay you some day.'

'One more of these will suffice,' said she, and before he could react, she took his face between her hands and kissed him on the lips. 'Beautiful man...' she murmured, letting him slip from her grasp.

With a laugh he was gone, and Sindia stood watching him as he sped away past the marching soldiers, his dark hair flying. Blazoned proudly upon his breast was the shield she had made: gules, with a white unicorn rampant.

The knight had moved the horses to the road's verge and was already mounted when Ancaios came hurtling up. He grabbed the reins and flung himself into the saddle so fast that he almost ended up on the ground. For he'd forgotten that the knight had loosened the horse's girth when they'd dismounted almost an hour ago, and now only the breastplate and crupper, and Dunboyne's high wither prevented the saddle from sliding round beneath the horse's stomach.

Red-faced, he slid back to the ground, straightened the heavy saddle and pulled tight the girth. 'Do ye still want me as your squire?' he asked, looking up at the knight shamefacedly.

''Tis the best way to learn,' said the knight. 'And that splendid badge would go sadly to waste if I were to send you packing now.'

Ancaios mounted Dunboyne more carefully and turned the horse about. His heart, already high, soared like a kite, for right before him one hundred mounted knights rode down the westward road and the earth shook with their passing. Their big horses champed at the bit, they tossed their heads, pranced and sidled. The sun shone on bright coats of chestnut and bay, of grey, mahogany and black; manes and tails floated silkily on the breeze, bits jingled and stirrups clashed. Some of the horses wore long damask caparisons embroidered with heraldic shields, others sported brightly coloured reins, breastplates and cruppers that were dagged or patterned, or hung with shining bells, fringes or tassels of gold. Filling the air above them the gaudy heraldry of standards and banners cracked and curled upon the breeze, and upon their backs, atop the high-cantled war saddles, rode the noble knights and men at arms all agleam in their splendid armour.

Ancaios could not help his heart swelling with pride as many of the knights looked towards his master and saluted or bowed their heads as they passed. He stole a look then at the silent man beside him and the contrast made him smile with a fierce joy. For the knight sat, lean and weary upon his thin, patient old stallion; his armour was beautiful, but notched and scored in places, and finely pitted with rust, and his horse's undecorated harness of dull, dark leather was worn smooth, its rings and buckles tarnished. Yet Ancaios felt sure that if he were an enemy, he would much rather face the bright, untried one hundred than that single battered, battle-hardened warrior.

Ancaios looked proudly down at the unicorn badge that was sewn against his heart. 'If I am slain or arrested, lad,' said the knight, 'promise me ye shall tear that from your breast and wear again the king's livery.'

'Nay sir,' answered Ancaios; 'I cannot make such a promise. Though the vow of a gong farmer is of little worth, I would rather promise to serve you faithfully unto death.'

The knight looked keenly at Ancaios for a moment, but whatever reply he may have made remained unspoken for he was interrupted by the pounding of approaching hoofs. Sir Rathdown Ravenhill, preoccupied by peevish thoughts, had been left behind at his army's departure and rode now near the tail end of the vanguard. Upon spying by the wayside the cause of those thoughts, he yanked his white destrier aside and spurred the animal across to the knight. The huge horse came plunging across the sward, clods of mud flying up from its hoofs. It was caparisoned to the ground in billowing green damask powdered all over with embroidered ravens and fringed with black silk; along the arched crest of its neck was a crinet of overlapping steel plates, and on its head was a shining steel shanfron with a horn rising from its centre.

Ravenhill dragged the stallion to a halt in front of the knight and the distressed animal danced on the spot, anxious to avoid its rider's foot-long, sharp-rowelled spurs. But the great commander appeared to have forgotten what he wanted to say for he did naught but snarl at the knight like a mettlesome lapdog.

The knight looked back at him levelly. 'I have been told, sir,' said he, 'that ye plan to march hard, reaching Lawhill before dusk. That is all of five leagues.'

Ravenhill drew breath through his teeth. 'Five leagues,' he rasped, 'are as naught to well trained men.'

'Five leagues of mud and pot-holes will tire any man. And are they aware of what they must face at the end of it? I still recommend ye speak with this young man,' said the knight, putting a hand upon Ancaios' shoulder, 'for he hath seen the creature. And he is the only man here who knoweth how stand things in Lawhill, for he was there just yester-morn.'

Ravenhill sneered. 'Why would I wish to ask aught of a snivelling turncoat brat? They tell me he wore the king's livery until five minutes ago; how foolhardy of him to vaunt now the badge of a traitor. Or have ye not told him that ye are marked for the gallows?' The commander's face was turning purple; an unpleasant match beside his tawny locks. 'I came,' he spat, 'not to ask advice of a traitor or a turncoat, but to warn you to keep your long nose out of my business. This army is mine and it followeth my orders.'

The knight bowed his head. 'Sir Rathdown,' said he, 'the army *is* yours and would, I am sure, follow you into perdition. As I told you, I have no intention of meddling in your affairs.'

'That is well,' said Ravenhill, raising his voice so that his passing troops might hear, 'for we do not need your meddling. I think fifteen hundred highly trained soldiers may kill a dumb beast without trouble!'

He laughed mirthlessly. 'This is but a jaunt to show the people of Lawhill the splendour of their army.'

Ancaios suppressed an incredulous snort. 'Hardly any remain in Lawhill to admire such splendour,' he muttered, 'and if he rusheth in without plan or strategy, there won't be a great deal of splendour left either.'

Ravenhill heard little of this but he glared angrily at Ancaios then, without another word, spun his horse and spurred it into an earth-churning gallop. With his nose high and his tawny curls bouncing, the commander thundered past the vanguard, spattering them with mud as he passed. His standard-bearer, heraldic raven and stars flapping above his head, rode hard to catch him up, and the two of them resumed their accustomed place near the head of the army.

The last of the van had ridden by, and now Ancaios and the knight watched the foot soldiers pass: the pikemen, billmen and halberdiers, the arbalesters and the longbowmen; fourteen hundred men already marching hard in a rhythmic, ground-covering stride. Yet a number of them so craned their necks towards the side of the road that they tripped and stumbled, and had to hop and skip to find their rhythm once more.

As the troops left the meadow and entered the dappled light of the wood, the knight and his squire took up a position some distance behind the last of the soldiers. The old grey and the chestnut, after their feed of oats, stepped out through the damp, flower-dotted wood as keenly as yearlings. On the riders' left, well down below the road, the Otterburn rushed hissing and shouting through a narrow gorge. The knight looked round at Ancaios. 'Do ye ever stop smiling?' he asked.

'I've been told I have a happy disposition, sir,' answered Ancaios. 'You smile quite often yourself.'

'How can I not when every time I turn around I see your ear-to-ear grin?'

'I can't help it, sir. Come what may, the world is grand.'

'It is,' answered the knight quietly. He rode through a band of sunlight and all of a sudden brought his stallion to a halt and reined him back two or three strides, looking down at the road as he went. Halting again in the sunlight, he dismounted and knelt in the dirt. The chestnut horse had, of course, stopped also and Ancaios watched in puzzlement as the knight reached into a rut in the road and withdrew from it something that gleamed like mercury as it slithered across the palm of his hand. The knight stood up, staring with a look of disbelief at the object in his hand.

Ancaios' heart jumped. That was why he recognised this place! It was here that he had fallen off Potrimpos' horse and been dragged. With all the wonders that had happened to him since leaving Lawhill, he had completely forgotten about the princess's moonstone necklace, but it must have slithered from his satchel during the fall. He opened his mouth to tell the knight that he had dropped the necklace, but then shut it again. 'What is it, sir?' he asked instead. He pushed the horse closer and looked down at the moonstone with half a smile on his face. 'That's pretty,' he said, 'I wonder if it was dropped by a soldier? Or perhaps a squire.'

The knight just stared at it. 'I've seen it before,' he finally said.

So ye do know her, thought Ancaios, grinning again. 'Mayhap 'tis an omen, sir,' he said; 'it might bring you luck... after all, many men have marched right over it, but it was you who found it. Ye should wear it, sir.'

'Wear it,' echoed the knight, still staring confusedly at it.

'Round your neck. Here, turn around, sir, and I'll fasten it for you.'

Ancaios leaned from the saddle and fumblingly fastened the catch while the knight scooped his hair out of the way. 'It cannot have been a soldier...' said the man, pushing the lucent stone down inside his collar of mail.

'A lady may have dropped it, sir.'

'Only one lady could have dropped this, yet by your account she was still at Lawhill yesterday.' Frowning, the knight mounted his horse and set out westward once more. The marching soldiers had got well away by now and there was no sign of them on the long curve of tree-shadowed road ahead. Within the wood Ancaios spied a red squirrel scurrying through dappled light up the trunk of an oak.

'My road hath lately become bemired with puzzles,' murmured the knight, barely audible above the roar of the Otterburn as it rushed along its narrow way, 'and now I have another hanging about my neck.'

CHAPTER 15

Winterhued tilted her head so that the sunlight fell across her face. After more than two days of darkness, she felt like dancing. Sir Almendral took her hand and she turned to him with a smile. 'I feel like a bear emerged from her winter sleep.'
Almendral laughed. 'I've not often seen a bear attired in a comely grey gown,' said he, 'or armed with a longbow like a huntress from legend.'

For indeed, Winterhued had her self bow of gleaming yellow yew slung across her back, as well as a silver-embossed quiver of arrows: ash-shafted and fletched with grey goose feathers. And laced to her left forearm she wore a bracer of etched silver.

'Thou dost mock me,' she said, looking at Almendral narrowly.

The two of them stood atop the Constable's Gate at the northern end of the castle. Its parapet was broken in places and through the gaps it looked a long way down to the flagstones of the outer bailey. Behind them lay the town and before them the castle, sprawled massively across the peninsula that jutted into the lake's eastern reaches. A breeze ruffled the silver waters and soughed through the wreckage in the bailey, sending plumes of ash eddying and swirling.

'I do not mock you,' said Almendral, 'and if any of these churls do, it is because they do not know ye have a draw equal to the most puissant amongst them and an aim equal to none.'

Winterhued withdrew her hand from his. 'I claim naught more than competency though I have trained with a bow all my life.' She gave the marquess a withering look. 'Unlike thee and thy kind: knights too high and mighty to use a common man's weapon. I should like to see how fare your swords and lances against this flying beast.'

Three ravens rose up with the swirling ash and settled beside the four of their kind that already perched in a line atop the ruin of the Garrison Hall. The wind stood their blue-black feathers on end as they cocked their clever heads and gazed bright-eyed across the bailey towards the south.

There, beyond the King's Gate and the wall that separated the two baileys, rose the keep, befouled and grim. But the dragon's lair was empty at present, for the guards on duty had seen its occupant fly out, or at least, faces down and quaking, they'd heard its wing-beats pass overhead and sweep away to the west. Now they waited and watched, and thought with pity of the shore-dwellers along the lake who would this day see the dragon came stooping from the sky to burn their villages and feast upon human flesh.

From every standing tower within the castle, the watchers' fearful eyes scanned the horizon and the sky. And listening anxiously for the first warning shout, two score of townsfolk passed sloshing buckets in a line up from the lake to quench the last of the town fires. Within the castle a pit was being dug in the outer bailey; an expanse of flagstones had been lifted and now a dozen guards and as many servants worked with picks and shovels, with wooden stakes and broken hinges, with rusty swords and old kettle helmets: anything they could find that might shift earth. The corpses, some burnt to almost nothing, were being carried from the gatehouse and elsewhere in sheets. So that they might one day be reburied by their families with due ceremony, Winterhued had enjoined the guards to collect and label whatever belongings each soul had had about them, to have descriptions made of the remains and, as the dead were laid in the pit and covered over, to record their locations.

Almendral took her hand again. 'I but use raillery,' said he, 'to disguise my fear, for I am afraid that ye shall put yourself in harm's way with that bow.'

'I shall endeavour not to,' replied the princess shortly. She watched the faraway figures of the soldiers as they bent over the corpses, poking and prodding, and she saw that the clerks at their backs, working with their scribe's tools, would gag sometimes and turn away. But they kept bravely on with their tasks, though they often glanced skywards.

Winterhued's eyes moved to the breach in the wall where the menials' tower had toppled; built of solid stone, it had been thrown down as easily as a child's castle made of sand. Piles of rubble had fallen into the ditch below the walls, but she could see that there *was* a route of sorts there, out of the castle. 'I should have begun to send folk out through that gap two days ago,' she said to Almendral, pointing.

'Should?' asked Almendral gently. 'But that is a path naked to the sky, and so steep and treacherous that not even the horses wish to use it. Thankfully, after the gate is cleared there will be no need for it.'

Winterhued cast a fruitless glance towards the east. 'Whatever route we use, if our army doth not come to our aid we *must* leave.' She looked towards the roof of the King's Hall where it rose above the wall between the baileys. 'See how laughably flimsy is our present shelter. There never was refuge there; the creature doth toy with us.'

'Winter...' said Almendral hesitantly, 'a fear preyeth upon my mind almost as much as this beast: fear of your father's threat to remarry. Is it real or is it bluster?'

Winterhued gazed towards the far end of the bailey where the loose horses milled hungrily about, the dominant animals biting and bullying as they searched for remnants of the hay that had been thrown out for them hours ago.

'Winter?'

'It is not bluster. It began as an idle threat, brought forth whenever we bickered, but the notion hath grown ever more attractive to him.'

'Ye must stop bickering then,' said the marquess urgently. 'Do not create opportunities for such a notion to take hold!'

'Dost thou wish me to give way and never again raise my voice against bigotry and nonsense?'

'Of course not... but Winter, this is dangerous. I thought not at first 'til ye told me of his dead bastard... If the king doth beget a legitimate son, then dieth, leaving a child on the throne and a widowed queen, there will be squabbles over the protectorship, perhaps civil war... as all the while Angerona watcheth like a hungry wolf in the north. Or the king may live another score of years to watch his son grow, under his tutelage, into an idiot like his father or a tyrant like his grandfather. Ah, Winter! All your hopes for the realm may come to naught...'

'I believe they already have. I have heard, and I think it more than rumour, that my father hath chosen his new queen.'

Almendral stared at her in dismay. 'Who?'

'Drumrock's youngest daughter,' said Winterhued. Her face was sad as she gazed, unseeing, across the bailey.

'I know her not. What is she...?'

'She is... oh, unfortunate girl! I have attempted to find good in her, but discovered only spite and envy. She is sly, secretive and she hath never liked me.'

'Alas, Winter... this could hardly be worse. The hopes of my family... of the north... indeed, of the whole realm, lie with you. Ye *must* be queen. I see war brewing...'

'War?' The princess laughed. 'I see a castle, a town, a realm held under siege by a dragon. Do not fret over a nonexistent war; we must survive our present peril first.'

'Aye, we must... and while we are at it, let us pray that the dragon chooseth this Drumrock daughter as his next meal and chokes on her overcooked bones.'

Winterhued flashed him a look but, to her disquiet, could not prevent a smile from turning up the corners of her mouth. She looked back towards the bailey and absently searched, as she had many times already, for her dear black mare amongst the milling horses. There were two or three that might have been her, but the animals were far away and bunched too closely to make out any distinguishing markings. At least, after the Constable's Gate was cleared and planks laid down over the gap where the drawbridge had burned, the guards could drive the horses out and they need not starve.

She had thought too about the animals in the menagerie; she could not leave them to perish in their cells from hunger and thirst. Before abandoning Lawhill, without consulting her father, she would order all of the birds to be released, but as to the beasts, if she could find no way to save them, she feared she'd have to have each and every one dispatched with a merciful arrow.

But for one. She had made him a promise, though she had no idea how that promise was to be kept.

'My lady,' said a voice behind her. She turned and found her little cousin at her elbow, breathless and blinking in the sunlight. Her auburn tresses flew about in the breeze and her cheeks glowed after her hurried journey. 'Brenn!' exclaimed the princess. 'What dost thou here?'

Brenn bobbed a curtsey, then looked round at the bowmen atop the gatehouse, at the guard who had accompanied her hither, and at

Sir Almendral. She stepped forward and, standing on tiptoe, whispered into Winterhued's ear.

'Sir Almendral knoweth of our captive,' said the princess quietly. She drew the marquess and Brenn towards the parapet, far from listening ears. 'My cousin proposes that we beg some hairs from the unicorn,' she said to Almendral, 'and discover for ourselves whether the books speak truth.'

'There are so many who lie in the infirmary, grievously hurt,' whispered Brenn urgently. 'I know he is not to be used... but he is generous... and they are in terrible distress...'

But Almendral laughed softly, distractedly. 'How lax ye are, my dear,' said he to the princess. 'For two days now, (or is it three?), ye have failed to save those who can walk and now it seemeth ye have forgotten to try magic on those who cannot.'

'In sooth, I did not forget; how could I forget? This morning I made a request to my father... I put aside my qualms and asked him for some hairs for the wounded. I wished to take naught from the unicorn, but the king hath his own miser's hoard locked in a casket. He refused. He said that the books lied, for he had experimented, to no effect whatsoever. But can I trust him?'

'Astonishing as it may seem, I do trust the king on this matter,' said Almendral. 'He hath saved you from disappointment. Think on it: ye *know* that there is no truth in the myth, else why would sickness and death be rife yet in Lawhill? And why else would ye have gone all these years without seeking to test the myth yourself?'

'As to the first, I have told thee; the king doth keep the hairs to himself, and always have the keepers been diligent and careful. As to the second...' Winterhued frowned. 'I do know; have always known, that the unicorn is not on this earth for our use, and besides... thou knowest I have rarely seen and never touched him since... since that first year.'

Brenn huffed impatiently. 'But my lady *hath* seen and touched him... she cannot have forgotten!' she exclaimed. She looked with disdain at the marquess. '*He* is just a man, a flesh-eating man; he hath not seen the unicorn nor felt his vast power! Besides, sir, I do not see why ye should scoff at 'magic' when a mind-reading dragon hath lately come amongst us.'

'Mind-reading?' questioned Almendral, but Winterhued wrapped her arms about Brenn and kissed the top of her head. 'I could never forget,' she sighed, 'but it is a long time since I first beheld him and felt the world change.' She straightened and turned again to the marquess. 'Brenn is right; this must be tried.'

Almendral shrugged. 'What would I know? I am just a man. Though, like all of Winterhued's friends,' said he, looking at Brenn, 'I am no flesh eater.'

The princess gazed down across the bailey towards the solid bulk of the menagerie. It stood right beside the breach in the castle walls. Brenn too looked down and her heart jolted as she recognised the barred skylight in its roof. The memory it stirred brought tears pricking to her eyes.

'I have no access now from my tower,' said the princess, 'so I think we must wait for nightfall as we shall have to approach from the bailey.' She gripped Brenn's shoulder. 'Bring scissors; they must be of silver; ask Lady Ulidia for hers. Come to me at dusk and... bring Eudora with thee also. I have a separate task for Eudora.'

'Silver scissors and Eudora,' repeated Brenn. 'Whither am I to come?'

'Meet me at dusk,' replied Winterhued, 'in the guardroom in the east tower of the King's Gate.'

'Is that your mare?' asked Almendral. The princess spun about to look down into the bailey again. As she turned, the seven ravens flew up with a clap of their ragged wings, glided over the western battlements and disappeared one by one down to the lakeshore. A horse, almost the same colour as the ravens, had detached itself from the mob and was trotting across the bailey, white feet flashing. 'Thank the stars... 'tis her,' breathed the princess, smiling at the mare's floating trot and her pricked ears. It was clear that in her familiar, friendly manner, she was bent on visiting the humans she could see digging in the bailey. But then a big grey came out after the mare, teeth bared and ears flattened, turned her and drove her back to the herd.

'If she's hale come next spring,' said Almendral, 'she'll have a youngling at her heels, a grey colt I'll wager.'

Winterhued laughed wonderingly. 'Waste not thy wager,' she said; 'it will be an ebon filly, with four white feet and a crooked blaze.' She turned to Brenn. 'I had forgotten, but I dreamt of such a filly... so vividly...'

'Were there folk in my lady's dream?' asked Brenn. 'Were we still alive?'

'Alas, I know not... I saw only horses...'

Ancaios and the knight went on foot through the village of Kelburn. They'd dismounted to stretch their legs and rest the horses, and the animals jogged along behind them, reins looped over the pommels of their saddles. As they passed the manor house above its moat, the boy could not help smiling when he thought of how far away seemed yesterday. He'd never even sat a horse when he stepped over that draw-bridge, and now a fine big chestnut followed him amiably, for all the world as though they'd been friends for years.

And now, instead of hiding behind barred doors, the inhabitants of Kelburn stood beside their cottages full of hope, waving as the last of the longbowmen crossed the bridge over the Otterburn, passed the Drumrock turnoff and marched away up the miry road. A few of the villagers called out greetings to the knight and his squire as they strode by, and for a while two small girls tagged along behind the horses, sometimes hanging onto their tails.

Somewhat distractedly, the knight questioned Ancaios about the nobles and knights at court he'd once been acquainted with. Told of Sir

Auchencairn's fate, he looked down at the road and walked in silence for a space.

'You knew him well, sir?' asked Ancaios.

'He was my friend and teacher,' answered the knight and lapsed again into silence.

They had passed the branch in the road and were halfway up the hill when the knight, seeing the soldiers in front of them floundering through mud, took up his horse's reins and mounted. Ancaios followed, this time managing almost as well as his master. He felt quite proud of himself as he landed nimbly in the saddle. They rode on once more without speaking, for it seemed that the knight wished to converse less and less as the day wore on. It was a companionable silence, but it was silence nonetheless, and Ancaios needed to talk.

For the sun was subsiding, the shadows were lengthening and Lawhill lay beyond the next ridge. The boy's stomach churned at the thought of what might transpire before nightfall.

Besides, the knight had earlier talked a little about the lands he had seen and, though Ancaios was anxious not to annoy his new master, his head buzzed with questions. 'Sir...' he said tentatively as the horses squelched their way into a hazel wood. The knight looked round at him, frowning. 'Before... ye said the people who'd made your armour had brown skin...'

'Aye,' answered the knight, though his mind was clearly elsewhere; 'they dwell far south of here... a people curious and erudite of mind. They know how the world doth turn and have even measured the distance to the sun. I myself looked through their lenses of glass and saw the blasted surface of the moon and great rings around the planets.'

Ancaios' eyes were wide. 'I wish I might one day see such wondrous things.'

'Ye do not have to travel far to see wonders; even this wood we ride through is a wonder.'

'This wood? It's just a lot of mud and hazels.'

'Aye, hazels: trees that rarely live as long as a hundred years. But when they are coppiced as these are, they can live for a thousand years.'

'Ye know everything.'

The knight shook his head. 'I wish I did. Then I'd know how to slay this "wonder" that we are soon to encounter.'

The horses ploughed their way through the mire. The hiss of the Otterburn as it tumbled over rapids far below the road sounded clear through the birdless wood, but Ancaios could only hear the beating of his heart. His hollow stomach churned.

'Ancaios,' said the knight suddenly, 'ye may find this hard to credit, but I have spent half my life searching for dragons. Unhappily though, I did not believe in their existence so rather than discover how to dispatch them, I squandered the years and now am found unready.' He laughed exasperatedly. 'Even if I had hidden beneath my lady's bed all that time I could scarcely be less ready.'

Ancaios stared at the knight. 'Ye were searching for dragons? Why?'

'"Twas King Gers' jest,' replied the knight; 'his fool's quest. He told me that if I returned to Manydown without a dragon's head I could expect naught but a traitor's death.'

'Ye must kill this dragon then!'

The knight looked round at Ancaios with a half-smile. 'We shall shortly arrive,' said he, 'at the gates of Lawhill accompanied by fifteen hundred soldiers. If the dragon is slain, it will not be by me.'

'Ye should ride away then! Leave Manydown! Ye are a knight of renown... anywhere else ye could live in great honour.'

'But I don't wish to. In the past I tried, but always grew restless, for how can I live elsewhere when my heart is here?'

Ancaios frowned confusedly. 'Ye would sooner go to the gallows,' said he, 'than live elsewhere in honour? What of Balasore? It is nigh and I've heard 'tis a goodly place.'

'Would ye have me now run away... leaving the souls in Lawhill in peril without knowing their fate? How could I live anywhere with honour after that?'

'Stay for a little then. See the dragon slain and then gallop back to the border. I will come with you!'

'And kill our good old horses? They are bone-weary already.'

'Get some other horses! Sir, Gers is old; he will die soon. Ye can return to Manydown when he is in his grave.'

'Gers may live to a hundred, and I too will be old by then. Ancaios, I shan't run anywhere. If I survive the dragon I must hope my friends have power enough to save me from the gallows. If not... I shall die in Manydown. Oft-times, when I was thousands of leagues from here, I wished only for that.'

Ancaios shook his head and fell silent. The road sloped downhill now, wending its way through a leaf-littered forest of beeches; they had at last begun the final descent to the lakeshore and the castle. The boy's thoughts tumbled about in his head; desperate, confused, and treasonous, for he hoped and prayed that the dragon had eaten King Gers while he'd been away.

'Ye've stopped smiling, lad,' said the knight gently. 'Is the world no longer grand?'

'I'm frightened, sir. Not for myself, but for what may happen.'

'I also, Ancaios.' The knight put his hand on Ancaios' shoulder and they rode in silence until the trees began to thin and the low sun came slanting and dazzling in through the straight trunks. Far below they caught a first glimpse of the lake, lying placid and silvery-mauve in the early evening light.

'This dragon,' said the knight; 'ye've told me much... is there aught more I could know?'

Ancaios hesitated. 'Ye may think me a madman,' said he.

'We shall make a matching pair then.'

The boy managed a small smile. He wished he didn't feel so sick. 'Ye could think this naught but fancy,' said he, 'but... the dragon is no dumb beast; it is cognisant and canny. I have felt it in my head... it casteth fear into folks' minds, more than they'd otherwise feel, and they become so afraid that they cannot look upon it but fall down in a terror. And it doth hunt fear. But if ye force yourself to look… a little of the fear doth go, and the creature looketh elsewhere. That was why I got a good look at it, sir.'

'Ye did say it seemed half-dead… full of wounds.'

'Aye… and Sir Auchencairn, before he died, found a gap in its scaly armour and put another wound, a gaping wound, in its left… I suppose you could call it an armpit.'

The knight nodded, thoughtful and frowning. They had come out of the trees and the horses were half jogging down the steepest section of the hill.

'One more thing, sir,' said Ancaios, trying to quell the tremor in his voice; 'as I said, after I had looked, even though the creature was a terrible thing, I was not so afraid. It was still in my mind, but instead of fear I felt… its sorrow. A great sorrow; it made me want to cry. But… that is not useful to you…'

'Useful enough,' said the knight; 'a weapon is sure to be more effective when wielded by a sad man than by a man lying face down in the mud.' He gave a dispirited laugh. 'But perhaps I should just lie down in the mud, for what use are these weapons against a canny behemoth that glideth on air and blasteth forth fire?' He looked at the boy with half a smile, but Ancaios felt hope desert him as he saw the sadness and weariness in the man's eyes.

'Sir… sir…' he stammered, 'we… we need not go further. We could halt here and watch.' After all his talk of facing the dragon without fear, he was more frightened than he'd ever been. *Because*, he thought, *this is the last chance; all our hopes rest with the army, and they go strutting in unready and unsuspecting*. Ancaios' heart raced and jumped. *And*, he thought, *I want this man to live*.

The knight ignored his suggestion and rode on, but soon, beside an untidy line of pines he reined in his horse and with eyes narrowed against the low sun, gazed down over the broad vale. Snaking away from him in a long line down the road marched the army, sunlight sparking from its helms and weapons and blazing upon the bright colours of its streaming heraldry.

Before them all, cupped by the verdant hills, lay the great, shining, sun-gilded lake, its scalloped bays receding into purple distance. And upon the closest promontory, jutting into the waters, rose the castle. It was black against the sun but limned with golden light, and it cast a dark and ragged shadow across the lake and onto the eastern shore.

The knight drew a long breath. 'I have seen the world, Ancaios,' he said, his voice low and a little husky, 'and I can tell thee that there is naught finer in all of it than this broad vale.' He looked round at the boy again, and this time his smile was real. 'I'm glad to be home.'

'I never imagined I'd ride down here with the army,' said the boy, plucking up a little courage; 'all its banners flying, and me a squire and mounted on a fine horse.' Ancaios leaned forward to wrap his arms around the gelding's neck.

'Ye like him?' asked the knight.

'Aye. But I would I knew what hath happened to the poor horse I rode yesterday… the Marquess of Potrimpos will have my hide if he ever heareth that I lost him.'

'Potrimpos!' exclaimed the knight as he urged his stallion forward once more upon the road.

'Ye know him, sir?'

'Not, I think, the present marquess, but if he's a Neath, he's bound to be a fool, a fop and an utter disgrace.' Ancaios half grinned at this rather accurate description of the present incumbent, but his stomach still churned and his heart still hammered as the chestnut set out after the grey. The two horses broke into a trot and then a slow canter as they followed the army down the road to Lawhill.

In the west the low sun dipped towards the horizon, igniting a fiery path across the lake. And along that path, hardly more than a ragged pinprick of night in the cloth-of-gold evening, something ancient and terrible came a-flying.

The foolish, foppish and disgraceful Potrimpos had been missing all day. Though Benicia would hardly have agreed with that description, she was beginning to wonder as to his courage. Sir Criffel might be odious, but he was not a murderer, so why had her sweetheart run off after she'd told him the news of her sister's betrothal?

Neither hide nor hair of him had been seen for hours, so she decided he must have taken refuge in his own apartments (for no one had told her that those apartments had become a smoking ruin). She was confident now as to their location, and sure that her father wouldn't miss her as he'd answered a summons from the king hours ago and the two of them, for all she knew, had drunk themselves under the table. Plying her charms to get past the guards at the door, she set out for the Bellhouse Tower.

She got as far as the guardroom in the King's Gate and there discovered she need go no further. For sitting alone in a corner in the cold and semi-dark like a sulking child was her beloved. He was dishevelled and grey-faced and he would hardly look at her.

Benicia stared at him in dismay. 'Potty, how have I offended thee?' she pleaded, 'I thought thou didst love me. My father is willing to give his blessing to our union; he says it would be an advantageous match for thee.'

The marquess's eyes slid sideways at that and he peered up at her. He ran his hands across his face and scratched at the dirty bandage on his head. 'Don't call me Potty,' he whispered hoarsely. 'Don't like it... never have.'

'Parchim then,' said Benicia. 'Parchim, please speak to me.'

The marquess put his head in his hands and cleared his throat with a harsh cough. 'Benicia... Bee...' he moaned, 'mayhap when this is over...'

'But it may be over!' cried Benicia, sinking to her knees beside him. 'People are saying that the dragon hath been gone for so long this day that haply it hath gone forever!'

'When Criffel too is gone from Lawhill… little Bee…' He stroked her cheek gently with the back of his hand, but suddenly plucked it away as though he'd been stung. His eyes went wide as he heard the scuff of booted feet in the passage outside and he scrambled to rise. 'He followed you!' he hissed, staring wide-eyed over her shoulder.

Benicia turned to see Sir Criffel stride in through the doorway. He stopped abruptly and his mouth twisted when he saw the two of them together. Benicia jumped in fright and stepped back until she stood next to Potrimpos with her back to the wall. But it was the sight of Criffel's handsome servant Garston sauntering into the guardroom behind his master and giving her an encouraging wink, that jolted her to her senses. 'Stand up to him, sir,' she hissed at Potrimpos, 'he's but a man, not a monster.'

The frightened marquess emitted a strangled sob and reached for his dagger.

'Stab me shall ye, coward?' sneered Criffel. 'Nay, let us do this meetly : here is my gage!' He pulled a glove from his belt and flung it to the ground. 'At dawn on the morrow we shall duel with short swords here, in the gate passage beneath the portcullis.'

'Ye cannot do that!' gasped Benicia.

'Sir, that is inadvisable,' said Garston, looking alarmed.

'I shall fetch the princess,' cried Benicia, starting for the door; 'she'll not allow it!' She dodged past Criffel and darted away down the passage.

For a long moment the marquess stared at the earl, his eyes wide, his mouth agape. Then he leant forward, plucked Criffel's glove from the floor and threw it back in his face. 'I don't care for that,' he squeaked, 'and I don't care for thee, thou hairy ape. I shan't fight thee, on the morrow or any day.'

'Thou shalt fight, thou toothless yellow pansy!' With a gleam of steel in the dark, Criffel drew his dagger and lunged at Potrimpos.

'Sir, no!' cried Garston, stepping forwards in an attempt to stop his master.

When two guards, alerted by Benicia, dashed moments later into the guardroom, Garston was staring helplessly at the struggling men and clutching his arm as blood soaked into his livery jacket and dripped onto his boots. 'He's mad ye know,' he gasped; 'his mother died stark raving mad, and his grandmother.' Even as he spoke, one of the daggers went spinning, kicked out of reach by a desperate foot, and then the other; and the two noblemen went for each other tooth and nail, grunting and groaning, crashing from one side of the guardroom to the other. The guards lunged at them, but the assailants were too fast and furious. They hurtled by, thudding into a low door which burst open, spilling them into the gate passage. Locked together they rolled down the passage, Criffel tearing at Potrimpos' hair as the marquess raked his opponent's face and wailed like a baby.

Even as the combatants rolled in one direction, men came running from the other; they dashed in from the outer bailey carrying picks and shovels, parchment and quills. 'Dragon!' they cried.

But the fighting men heard them not as they tumbled out into the bailey, rolling and scrambling. Potrimpos struggled, desperate to get away, but the hairy man sat on him and held him to the ground with a strangling grip, hitting and punching at his face and bashing his bandaged head upon the flagstones.

Benicia returned, running before the princess, sobbing and breathless. She found the guardroom crowded with workers and their tools; several were gathered around the open door. Pushing past them, she dashed out into the gate passage and almost collided with Garston who clutched his arm and bled profusely. He stared into the bailey and Benicia gasped when she saw what he was looking at. 'Stop him…' she sobbed, and then she ran from the shelter of the gate passage, beneath the portcullis and straight out into the open reaches of the outer bailey.

Behind her Winterhued, armed like a huntress, stepped through the low door. 'He's gone mad, your highness,' said Garston, bowing and bleeding.

'Have that seen to,' said the princess; 'go to the infirmary.' Garston bowed again, but he didn't go, for there was Benicia running into the bailey, there were the two men scrabbling on the ground and, above them came the dragon, swooping down until its vast bulk blocked out the sky.

Garston crashed to his knees and fell onto his face with a terrified moan but Winterhued strode forward along the gate passage. Fear flooded through her like a tide but she waded into it, pushed it aside, and raised her eyes to look full upon her adversary. 'I know you, old, clever thing,' she whispered, 'for ye have filled my dreams. And I have had enough of fear.'

Beneath the fangs of the portcullis she halted and with one swift, practised movement she braced her longbow against her instep, bent the tapered yew-wood and slipped the bowstring into its polished horn nock. Though her heart raced, her hands were steady as she plucked an arrow from the quiver at her back and stepped out into the bailey.

Before her the two men were still fighting; she saw Criffel's snarling mouth and his maddened eyes as he hit and scratched and punched, and she saw Potrimpos go limp as he suddenly spied the horror beyond Criffel's shoulder. Benicia ran towards them, faltering, stumbling and falling at last to her knees.

Filling the sky behind the three tiny human figures came the dragon, gliding on nothing. Its great jaws gaped wide, strings of steaming drool hanging from its rows of scythe-like teeth, and as it dropped down into the bailey Winterhued saw the fire in its throat, banked like flaming coals in an infernal oven. *Too far,* she thought as she nocked her arrow. The creature came straight on and she aimed for its eye: her heart pounded as she drew the bowstring back to her jaw... an inch more... and loosed. The arrow flew high: she lost sight of it as it dropped, but it surely hit close to the mark for the creature snatched its head sideways as though it had been stung by an insect. It came on inexorably though, dropping down until its talons struck sparks from the flagstones; lowering its huge head to scoop the still struggling earl and marquess into its maw. They hung for a moment skewered, kicking and shrieking, upon its curved and bloodied teeth, then with a toss of its head it threw them up, they turned in the air like a juggler's balls and fell, flip, flop, down into its fiery throat.

Benicia screamed a terrible scream and fell onto her face. Walking as if in a dream, Winterhued reached her at last and stood over the senseless girl. *I have just thrown my life away*, she thought as she raised her eyes to look up at the dragon.

Its horned and bony head was as big as a slaughterhouse and it reeked like a hundred rotten carcasses. One of its eyes was but a torn and empty socket, the other was the colour of clotted blood. To look into it was to glimpse damnation.

'Why do ye not leave us be?' whispered the princess, and the creature cocked its head. It seemed to be trying to see her through its one failing eye. With a despairing laugh, Winterhued nocked a second arrow. *I do not want to hurt you*, she thought hopelessly; *I wish only to live without hurting anyone.*

Shocking her, the dragon's voice entered her mind like wind soughing through ash heaps. *Thy kind do hurt the earth by living*, was the creature's soundless reply. *Ye believe ye stand above all life, but ye are naught but a plague, a pestilence, that must be burned away to save the host.* The dragon's torn wings filled the bailey; one rested heavily upon the charred remains of the bakehouse. Her forelimbs, bent grotesquely under her weight, were armoured in steely scales and weaponed with talons, stained and splintered. *To be rid of thee and thy kind*, came her voice again, *I would sear the earth to her bare bones.*

Belching black smoke, the dragon opened her jaws to suck air into the roaring furnace of her throat. Her exhalation would be Winterhued's death.

Winterhued drew back her bowstring until her sinews twanged
with pain. She felt the goose-feathers cut her cheek as the arrow flew,
she saw the ash shaft burn with a bright flame as it sped between the
dragon's teeth, but the short-bodkinned arrowhead spun on to bury
itself with such force in the flesh of the creature's throat that the huge
head jerked upwards and back. Winterhued dropped, crouching over
Benicia's prone form, as a ragged tongue of flame rushed above her
head. She scrambled to her feet, reaching for the quiver at her back.
But even as she nocked her third arrow the dragon, shaking her head
and spraying blood, sprang clumsily into the air. Her huge wings, the
colour of iron streaked with rust, pumped the air once, twice, and the
gale that filled the bailey almost knocked Winterhued backwards. She
reeled from the stench: saw, too late, the creature's massive barbed tail
swing towards her. It hit the flagstones with a splintering crash, sending
shards of stone flying, then thudded into her right shoulder with the
force of a battering ram. The barb, jagged as a broken knife, skimmed
by within an inch of her temple as she was flung aside. Even as she fell,
she saw her bow, snapped in half, fly up into the air and spin, its yellow
wood catching the sun before it dropped back down into blue shadow
and clattered uselessly to the ground.

Winterhued sat up, gasping and clutching her arm, wondering if
its bones were broken. Across the flagstones at her feet fell a black
rain: dark drops spattered in an arc across the bailey as the creature
swung her head. Winterhued heard the fire in the dragon's throat roar
as she drew breath and, looking up, saw her hanging impossibly in the
air, black and vast across the glory of the evening sky. Just above her
yawned the furnace of the beast's gaping maw; the heat of it seared her
skin and burnt all hope from her heart.

There was naught to be done; Winterhued disentangled her skirts
and got to her knees. She glanced over at Benicia; the girl was still
unconscious so at least she would know nothing when her death came.

In the centre of the bailey the princess knelt like a defiant sacrifice.
A soft breeze fanned her fire-reddened cheeks and a few dark tendrils

of hair escaped to flutter about her face. Her eyes were raised so that she saw the dragon suddenly swing her head away. Flapping her wings with a mighty thud, almost knocking Winterhued down again, she lifted higher into the air and launched herself clumsily to the east.

Shakily, still clutching her arm, Winterhued climbed to her feet to watch the dragon fly out over the castle walls, trailing blood. As she went her tail smashed through the battlements, crumpling the stone merlons. Barely audible above the thump of wings and the crash of tumbling masonry, a voice cried out from atop the Watchtower: 'The army cometh! Our soldiers are here! They march in upon the East Road!'

Ancaios stood upon the road holding Dunboyne. The gelding ran in circles and neighed for his grey companion loudly and continuously. For the new-made squire had been told to stay behind and all he could do now was watch and wait.

When the dragon had come swooping silently in from the west, growing more monstrously vast with every wing-beat, the army had halted in disarray. The men swore oaths and cried out in alarm, and some of the foot soldiers sank to their knees on the road. But the creature's attention was not upon them; as it glided in towards the castle, black and terrible against the sun, it seemed unaware of their presence. And thus most of the men were able to stand, dismayed and trembling but upright, and watch as the dragon canted its diabolical wings and dropped down within the castle walls.

The knight though, had halted his horse and gazed at the creature in awe. Ancaios thought that he seemed unafraid. 'Auchencairn wounded this thing?' he asked, softly, wonderingly. 'There never was a more courageous man.'

The army had waited nervously as Ravenhill shared a few panicked words with his officers. Finally an order must have reached the bowmen for they were seen to string their longbows and crank their crossbows.

'About time. Surely they should have…' began Ancaios, but then shut his mouth because his voice sounded too high and wobbly.

'Ancaios,' said the knight apologetically, 'I would have thee stay behind. Lead thy horse back to the pines and wait there; be ready to flee up into the forest if the need ariseth.'

'No!' protested Ancaios, 'Please sir…'

'Hast thou trained with weapons, lad?'

'No, but…' said Ancaios.

'Do as I bid,' said the knight gently. 'When we have all been slaughtered thou canst tell the world our tale. And I want thee to let Winterhued know that I came back for her.'

Ancaios stared at him dumbly for a moment. 'Who am I to tell her came back? I do not know your name, sir.'

The knight smiled a little. 'She will know who I am,' he said.

Ancaios got the reluctant gelding moving. Walking backwards, tugging at the reins, he saw that the soldiers had spread out over the common to the left of the road, with the bowmen to the fore. Their bright banners and pennons were nowhere to be seen. *They shall all be slaughtered,* he thought; *they shall fall on their faces in the nettles and die without loosing a single arrow.* At least the knight kept himself apart, staying watchfully at the rear while his horse turned anxious circles.

Squinting into the low sun, Ancaios looked past the soldiers at the castle and town, and the molten gold waters of Lake Silverhow. The scene looked peaceful and almost normal but for the horrible shape, like a sagging black tent, that poked up above the castle's eastern wall.

The boy had barely taken five steps of his backward journey when the shape moved and split asunder and then, with a flailing of wings, the dragon rose up from the castle, jagged and ghastly as a creature from nightmares. It hung in the air for a moment then turned its head and flew, tail scraping over the battlements; with four more thumps of its wings it lifted into the sky, before dropping in a long glide towards the army.

At a shouted order the longbowmen nocked their arrows and the arbalesters raised their crossbows. For a moment they stood their ground, but behind them the knights and foot soldiers, in dismay and disarray, broke ranks and many of the men turned and ran. The horses, maddened by fear, reared, spun about and collided with each other and their riders could do naught but flop about or tumble to the ground, for they too were stricken stupid by terror. Riderless horses came careering back up the hill, stirrups and reins flying; one of them was a great white destrier, galloping flat out with its green damask trappings billowing.

As the dragon swooped low, flame dribbling from its mouth, a few arrows left their bows, but they were badly aimed; they pattered as harmlessly against the creature's scaly sides as raindrops in a spring shower. Even the lethal crossbow bolts did naught but bounce off its armoured hide and fall to the earth. The feeble assault petered out as the bowmen flung themselves onto their faces or fled as fast as their shaking legs could carry them, hurling away their weapons as they ran.

On its first low pass, the dragon had done nothing more than knock a few soldiers to the ground with its trailing tail. But now, tearing the air with the thudding of its wings, it rose high in the golden sky, twisted on the breeze and stooped like a hawk upon the fleeing men. The soldiers had scattered in all directions but the largest number of them, perhaps five hundred, headed southeast across the common; running, staggering, falling, gasping and weeping, they made for the cover of the forest. But roaring a great gout of red flame, the dragon came amongst them with its scything talons and its wide-sweeping barbed tail, and it cut a ruinous swath through their midst.

Ancaios had stopped on the road, transfixed and horrified. But as three more riderless horses galloped past him, his attentions were taken by Dunboyne who began to plunge about in a panic. By the time he'd regained some control, calmed the big horse and turned to look once more down the hill, there was no army. The soldiers lay dead or wounded, or they had scattered to every point of the compass, running for their lives.

All but one man: a lone knight in glinting armour who cantered his brave old stallion across the gentle slope of the commons. Accompanied by a long shadow and blazoned by the evening sun, he leant down from the saddle as he went and plucked up a lance that had been abandoned by a fleeing knight. His head was bare and his dark hair flew out as he twisted in the saddle to watch the dragon's murderous flight.

He turned and halted his horse, and then sat waiting, balancing the long lance in his right hand. Ancaios saw him laugh and shake his head at his own foolhardiness. He may as well have been a mouse taunting an eagle.

With a flap of its wings the dragon turned. Trailing smoke, flames and blood, it cast about until its failing eye spied the long shadow and sunlit shape of a horseman. The fire died as its mouth curved into something that resembled a smile.

When he saw that smile, Ancaios yelled wordlessly. He leapt scrambling into the saddle even as the red gelding began to trot down the hill, neighing. His heart knocking against his ribs, he kicked, flapped the reins and shouted, and the horse lumbered into a canter then a gallop.

'Don't ye dare!' he yelled, stupidly. 'Leave him alone, ye vile, craven worm!'

Shouting a stream of nonsensical insults, weaponless, knowing only that he had to distract the dragon, draw it away somehow, the boy hauled his horse off the road and hurtled down across the commons.

The knight tossed his lance into the air and caught it as his horse sidled, snorting. 'Good old lad,' he said quietly; 'best horse in all the world. How came this day, eh? It had a morn like any other, but I think we shall not see the sun set.'

The dragon floated on the air, impossibly vast. Its ragged wings seemed as wide as the sky. It was plated in iron scales that gleamed dully beneath encrusted, rust-coloured streaks. Horny excrescences sprouted from its head, down its neck, its spine, and its sinuous tail terminated in a serrated barb. Its talons were broken, splintered, sharp as knives, stained with slaughter. It was as bitter as an ocean of tears, and it was dying. Riddled with seeping wounds and trailing a slow spattering of black blood, it turned its one hellish eye upon the knight and smiled its malignant smile. Fiery death glowed in its throat.

Ah, thought the knight, *there is the place for a lance; there is Auchencairn's wound.* Just as the boy had said, a long black wound, opening wetly at every wingbeat, gaped and oozed between the creature's breast and armpit. *But to get anywhere near it my horse must grow wings.*

The dragon came on, a tongue of flame licking from its grinning maw. Hissing, boiling blood dribbled from the corners of its mouth and splashed down its iron flanks. The old horse blew air from his lungs like a leviathan and danced sideways, but not a single step back did he take.

With a bemused frown the knight stood in the stirrups and raised his lance, balancing it in his hand. 'Fool,' he said. All he could do was hurl the puny weapon, and after that the best he could hope for was a swift death. 'I'm sorry, old man,' he murmured to his horse. But with a gusty thump of its wings the dragon rose and climbed into the air, too high for the lance. The knight spun his stallion to watch the creature bank and turn as lithely as an eagle after prey; its wings thudded twice and then it dropped again towards him, talons outstretched.

But it left the knight alone, hurtling high above his head and swooping down upon a boy on a red horse who came galloping across the commons, eyes wide and mouth open in a shout.

The dragon picked up horse and rider, carrying them back up the slope and raising its head to the sky as it went to cough out a tongue of flame. It dropped them onto the hillside and turned again, one wingtip hitting the ground so hard it gouged out a swath of turf and spurted gouts of earth into the air.

The knight was not looking at the dragon; he watched the hillside and saw the red horse scramble unsteadily to his feet.

But the boy lay still.

The knight moaned, a mingled sound of sadness and anger. Then he looked up at the dragon gliding towards him down the breeze, and within his mind he could feel her blind rage and her bleak and terrible pain. 'Beldame from hell,' he cried as his horse pranced beneath him, 'come slay me if thou canst!'

Ancaios tried to rise. He felt as though he'd been trodden into the earth like a squashed insect. He moved his head and saw the sad rent in his beautiful livery jacket. It ran from his neck to his waist and the fabric all about it was damp and dark. Strangely, the white unicorn newly stitched to the breast had turned red. He looked at it for a moment and then noticed a pool of dark liquid on the ground beside him. Even as he watched, the pool grew wider. *I am dead,* he thought. It puzzled him that such a thing had happened, but it didn't seem to matter very much.

He tilted back his head and saw Dunboyne; the reins were trailing on the ground only inches from his head. The big gelding was standing up but Ancaios saw him upside down. He could have reached up to touch his soft, whiskered muzzle. The horse snorted and stared; he seemed ready to spin and run, but stood his ground. He was watching something down the hill and Ancaios knew that it was important he watch too. He got an elbow beneath him and half rolled; the rent in his jacket overflowed with blood.

Ancaios tilted his head and looked away down the hillside, squinting into the sun. Ah yes, there was a dragon; that was what had put this hole in him. He wondered idly if the hole went right through and came out the other side.

The dragon hung in the bright evening sky even though she was surely far too heavy to fly. Her serpent tail hung down, the barb on its end bouncing and scraping across the turf. Ancaios could feel the thud it made every time it hit the earth. She looked like a creature made of broken black iron and rust; she was horrible and sad like a loathsome old widow who'd lived all alone for years in rags and squalor. The stink of her rotting flesh came wafting on the breeze.

And there was the knight whose name Ancaios didn't know. *I am still his squire*, he thought and that made him feel happy and proud, for he was surely the bravest knight in all the world. But Ancaios also felt sad because, though the knight's heart was huge, he himself appeared hopelessly small as the dragon glided towards him with her death-dealing talons outstretched and fire licking from between her terrible teeth. The lance he held looked as insignificant as a darning needle.

I wasn't much of a squire, thought Ancaios. *I disobeyed orders and now there is no one to tell Winterhued that he came back and died for her.*

Turning her near-blind head from side to side, and trailing from her mouth a thin stream of blood, the dragon came on. The knight hurled his lance; even as he did so, he touched a heel to his horse's flank so that the grey twisted into the air and leapt sideways mightily. For a moment horse and rider disappeared beneath the creature's wing as the dragon hit the earth in an explosion of mud and flame. Pieces of the shattered lance spun in the air and fell amongst a rain of dirt and torn nettles. The dragon scrabbled, flapped her wings and rose once more into the air, leaving behind her a welt of black and smouldering earth.

But the old horse was still on his feet, galloping up the hillside as the knight leant from the saddle to snatch up another abandoned lance.

The dragon shook her head, spraying blood. She pumped her ragged wings and rose higher; she flew over the knight but suddenly seemed to lose interest in him. Her tail flicked the air as she passed and strands of the man's hair lifted like dark fire.

Flying in a wide circle, the dragon glided toward Ancaios where he lay on the hillside and landed heavily near a stand of oak trees growing atop a low knoll. Clumsy and graceless on the ground, she stretched out her neck and peered towards the thick-growing trees like a nervous horse ready to run.

But then a rain of arrows came hurtling through the air to bounce off her adamant hide, and she turned ponderously on her grotesque limbs. Ancaios twisted his head and was vaguely surprised to see that a few bowmen had returned; they crouched a good way off by the roadside and fired another badly aimed volley. Several of the knights had also crept back on foot as well as a number of halberdiers, but they huddled aimless and orderless behind the bowmen.

Ignoring the arrows, the dragon fixed her dim and awful eye once again upon the mounted knight who had followed her up the hill; the man couched his second lance and sat easily upon his sidling stallion. 'Come ancient hag,' said he, and he had no need to raise his voice in the silent evening; 'try again.'

Ancaios was having trouble seeing. All colour had leached out of the world and it was getting so dark, even though the sun still shone low in the sky. But he saw the dragon's bloody jaws gape and he heard the fire in her throat roar like bellows on a giant's furnace. She raised her wings and in their vast shadow the world became as black as death.

Oh yes, Ancaios knew he had died, for suddenly, into that dark, dark space beneath the dragon's wing, stepped a little white horse that shone like the moon. And from its forehead rose a horn that glimmered like a chain of stars in the night sky.

The dragon turned her huge warty head. She looked upon the unicorn and the fire died in her throat.

In an instant the knight had touched the grey with his heels. With a huge leap the greathearted stallion lunged forward, flinging wads of turf up from his iron-shod hoofs. At an earth-pounding gallop the knight came up the rise, full-tilt into the dragon. Tardily, the dragon swung her head and huffed out a surprised cloud of steam. But she had no time to do aught but half rear and make a blind lunge before the knight had driven the lance deep into the wound beside her left breast, and deep into her tenacious heart.

The horse crashed into the dragon and half fell, but sheer momentum kept him moving, scraping and bouncing along the creature's scaly flank. Putting his weight in the offside stirrup the knight ducked low, and the horse smashed under the dragon's wing to emerge, cantering head high upon the bright hillside. The knight turned and reined his horse in and the two of them stood in the rosy evening sunlight on the slope above Lawhill, and the horse's mane and tail, and the knight's dark hair, flew behind them in the clear breeze.

The unicorn stood at the edge of the trees transfixed by the dragon's fading eye.

'Old one, light of the stars,' came the dragon's ash-dry voice in her mind, 'I thought your kind were all gone from the world.'

'Ancient one... firedrake,' answered she, 'why did ye leave your fiery uplands? For there ye were free from earth's scourge: mankind.'

The dragon sighed as blood ran like a river from her breast. 'I flew from my mountains in bitterness and envy,' she answered, 'thinking to purge the earth of that disease. For there was naught else left to do. My mountains are dead, their fires extinguished. All the high land lieth tired and still, and upon those cold heights my kind went mad. We fought and perished, one by one. We fought until there were but two.'

The dragon's wings sagged. Slowly her huge bulk subsided until it lay upon the sodden ground where her blood ran and pooled. 'In madness I slew my daughter,' she whispered, 'and wept as I devoured her. I am the last.' Her hoary chin sank down until it rested on the drowned earth. Her terrible eye, dim and sightless, sank from view as she turned her great head and laid it carefully down in the dark lake of her blood.

When her voice came once more into the unicorn's mind, it seemed no more than a breath of wind in an eternity of sky. 'Remember the world in her youth,' she sighed, 'when she flung up mountains and sang to the heavens in tongues of flame. Remember the dragons flying, wide-winged across a fiery sky...'

The great red ball of the sun touched at last the shimmering waters of the lake.

'I too am old,' said the unicorn, though she knew there was no longer anyone to heed her, 'though not so old as you. I remember a world clothed in a mantle green. I remember the breeze shivering the grass, trembling the leaf as another unicorn danced in sunlight and shadow. But I too am the last.'

Ancaios tried to blink the darkness from his eyes. Still propped on one elbow he saw the dragon's wings sag like a dismantled tent as her ebbing blood spread in a wide black pool.

But though he peered and peered into the gathering gloom, Ancaios could no longer see the unicorn. *It will come when I am dead*, he thought.

The dragon's head tilted forwards into the pool as if it wished to slake a thirst. It drooped sideways until only its empty socket stared at the sky.

Ancaios shifted his gaze to the knight and the old grey stallion who, even in his dwindling sight, stood so bright in sunlight upon the hillside. *I am squire to a Dragonslayer*, he thought and his weary heart beat with pride.

At last he laid his head back in the grass and looked up at the darkening sky. For a moment before the world turned black, a whiskery muzzle filled his view and the boy felt Dunboyne's warm breath snuffling at his face. He smiled and sighed.

CHAPTER 16

Winterhued flew down the spiral stair from the top of the King's Gate. She could barely see her way in the twilit darkness and should have fallen several times on the steep, uneven steps, but it seemed as though her feet had grown wings. Twice she brushed the wall with her bruised shoulder and arm, and gasped with the pain but kept on. By the time she ran out into the ground-level guardroom the three or four guards that followed her had been left far behind. She discovered the chamber empty, for upon hearing of the army's arrival every soul in the castle had ascended to whatever vantage point could be found.

'My lady!' cried a voice and the princess, startled, saw she'd been mistaken, for Lady Brenn and Eudora stood forlornly in a corner, almost swallowed by the gloom. Winterhued had forgotten their arranged meeting at dusk.

'The dragon is destroyed!' said she, breathless after her swift descent.

'Destroyed!' gasped Brenn. 'We heard shouting; they said the army had come, but I thought we should wait. I would we'd seen them slay the dragon.'

'But *they* didn't slay it,' said Winterhued. 'Come, I'll tell you as we go.' She took Brenn's hand in her left and would have taken Eudora's if her right arm had not been so painful. 'Follow us, Eudora,' said the princess as she pulled Brenn towards the door into the gate passage. 'We must not tarry... for we go to the town gates, to welcome the Dragonslayer!'

'Slayer? Was it not the arrows of many...?'

The princess uttered a wondering laugh. 'Nay,' she said as the three women hurried from the passage into the bailey, ''twas one man alone; the beast just lay down before him and made hardly a protest as he ran her through with his lance.'

'One man? But what of the army?'

'The army gave up before it had begun; in terror it melted away. Many of the soldiers were slaughtered as they fled, and we, watching from the battlements, cried out and wept for it seemed all hope of salvation had fled also. But he did not flee.'

'Who was he then... this slayer? Was he not part of the army?'

'He held himself apart.'

'Is he then the knight the king sent for?' Brenn did not mention the king's messenger, but thoughts of him filled her mind.

'Perhaps he is!' The princess laughed and so did Brenn, for above them was the glorious sky, rose-gold in the sunset, and it seemed a marvel to be running beneath it unafraid.

'Could he be... the knight from m'lady's tale?' asked Brenn, pulling back on Winterhued's hand in an attempt to slow her a little. The princess's legs were much longer than her own.

Winterhued looked round at her. 'There are,' she said, "thousands of knights in the world.'

'Then why do we go so swiftly?' puffed Brenn.

'Because I must speak with this man before my father doth!' answered Winterhued, kicking aside a broken end of tapered yew-wood as she passed. 'There is my poor bow.'

Brenn turned her head to stare at it. 'My lady's bow?' she asked confusedly. 'Why is it here?'

'I shot the dragon,' said Winterhued as the two of them began to skirt the raised flagstones and the partially-filled trench in the centre of the bailey.

The princess looked round for Eudora but the girl had dropped behind; her shoes did not fit well enough to allow for much running. The guards and servants that were now pouring out of the castle had already caught and passed her, yet all of them stayed behind Winterhued, following her like an arrowhead of migrating birds.

Brenn gazed wide-eyed at the princess. 'M'lady shot...?'

"Twas a mere pinprick, yet it brought blood. The beast knocked me down with her tail before I could try again; if she had been surer in her aim she would have squashed me like a gnat.' Winterhued laughed. 'I shall be royally purple with bruises.'

Brenn still stared in astonishment. 'My lady's cheek bleeds,' was all she could say, 'and her gown is torn at the shoulder. Her headdress is awry.'

Winterhued took her hand from Brenn's to reach up and pluck the coronet from atop her headress. She tossed it away and it sparkled in the sunlight before clinking to the flagstones and rolling away into the bailey's twilit shadows.

Brenn hitched up her skirts so that she could keep pace with her tall cousin's swift stride. The princess, unfastening the headdress, tossed it after the coronet and shook out her ebon locks as she went. 'What a bitter and pitiless old being she was,' said she. 'I am sorry that she came here and sorry that she is destroyed, yet glad to have witnessed her puissant splendour. We may count ourselves fortunate to have seen her...'

'I had but a glimpse...'

'But thou didst glimpse her alive. Many now shall look upon her cold carcass, but we saw her breathing fire! She was magnificent; ancient and canny, rancorous and heartbroken... and the last of her kind.'

'I shan't forget her sorrow,' murmured Brenn.

The two cousins, hand in hand again, hurried towards the Constable's gate. They were alike and yet so unalike. One tall, dark-eyed, pale-skinned, with hair that floated like skeins of black silk in the breeze. Clad in a gown of grey-blue with a grey cloak about her shoulders, she strode as lithely as a deer. The other half-ran to keep up. Her cheeks were flushed pink, her hazel eyes shone, and her hair fell past her shoulders in a tumble of chestnut curls. Her gown was of blue-green trimmed with amber and she wore a plain black cloak, like that of a soldier or a king's messenger.

Together they entered the passage of the gatehouse, finding it scorched but cleared of the dead. Running beneath the murdering portcullis, they came out of the castle at last and crossed the planks that had been laid across the gap once spanned by the drawbridge. Beneath them the swollen Otterburn rushed hissing through a narrow race to spill itself out into the lake. Along the course of the stream, beyond the wide expanse of Lake Silverhow, the sun melted into the waves, setting the lake and sky on fire.

Winterhued and Brenn turned east and hurried up the charred and ruined street towards the town gates. Folk stood at the roadside, more arriving as the welcome tidings spread; relief and hope were written upon their weary faces. They greeted the princess with love, glad beyond measure to see her hale, then followed respectfully behind her.

But Brenn was thinking of her dear love; was this 'dragon-slayer' the knight Ancaios had been sent to find and if so, had he delivered the king's commission and returned with the man? And if not, surely he would soon hear that the dragon had been slain and hasten back to

Lawhill. She smiled to herself, for she knew she would shortly see him again. Pulling the black cloak about her with her free hand, she skipped for a stride or two as she ran along beside the princess.

Winterhued hardly knew why she hurried, or why she felt happy. For even though she had kept her life, surely too many had died and too much lay in ruin for present joy. And she did not wish to think of hopes and dreams.

All she was certain of was that if, by some extraordinary chance, this turned out to be the knight her father had sent for, she would express her gratitude but politely decline his hand before her father arrived. But then she laughed to herself; this was all nonsense, for why should this stranger want her anyway? She suddenly remembered the arrogant blonde, broken-nosed knight who'd been the victor at last year's Dittonsday tourney. He'd been ten years her junior and husband to a wealthy Balasorean duchess. *Aye, 'tis likely him*, thought Winterhued. Which was odd for she'd seen as clear as day that the Dragonslayer had hair as dark as night.

The Dragonslayer's dark hair drifted in the evening breeze as he rode slowly across the hillside towards his dead squire. Even in the fading light he could see the pool of blood in which the boy lay. He ran his eyes across the chestnut horse, a little surprised that he stood yet beside the boy and had not come running to join his old companion. The gelding was gouged in three places and blood trickled from the wounds, but they were not deep and would heal well enough. The saddle though was torn and broken and it was clear that by stopping the dragon's talons it had saved the animal's life.

As the knight wearily dismounted, a group of soldiers approached him: the same brave knights, bowmen and halberdiers who, returning earlier, had made an attempt upon the dragon's life. 'Noblest and best of warriors,' said their leader, humbly bowing his head, 'though ye be deserving of a more illustrious guard, we have come to offer our poor services to escort you, in honour, to...'

But the knight raised his hand to silence the man. 'I thank you,' said he, 'but my squire lieth dead and I would have time with him. Go ye to the castle; I require no escort and shall follow when I am ready.'

'We could bear him for you, sir,' said a bowman hopefully.

The knight shook his head. 'I shall do that myself,' said he quietly. He would honour the boy by carrying him home; it seemed the least he could do.

And so the remnant of Manydown's army put hands to hearts, turned and marched away across the common towards Lawhill.

The knight stood before the sprawled figure of his day-old squire. His armour, his grey horse and the hillside were stained blood red by the sunset sky; twilight came on apace, blue and shadowy as sorrow. He knew that many souls had perished that day, but that did not prevent his heart from twisting painfully as he gazed down at this lad, for he'd been young and full of promise, and bright and brave and happy and in love with the world. And in an extraordinary act of generosity he had given up his life in an attempt to save a man he hardly knew: a man whose name he'd not even known. The knight bowed his head and buried his face in his hands.

He stood thus for a time, and then he squatted down in the bloodied grass to smooth Ancaios' tousled hair from his face. To his surprise the lad still felt warm though the evening had grown chill, so he ran his hand down past the boy's chin and pushed two fingers against his neck. He tried here, there, and then he smiled slightly. 'Stout lad,' he murmured.

He got to his feet, frowning, and cast about the hillside. But he'd sent away his only means of help. Most of his belongings had been torn from the chestnut horse's saddle, but his bedroll was still there. Working swiftly, he folded the blanket into a wad to staunch the blood and, using the dagger at his hip, tore the canvas into strips to bind the wound. 'Hold on, lad,' he murmured over and over, and yet he knew this was a hopeless task, for he'd spent a good deal of his life upon battlefields and had never seen a man survive such a wound.

Finishing, he turned and looked across the common towards the dead dragon beside the wooded knoll, and then he unbuckled the steel couters and vambraces from his arms. 'I'm sorry, Ancaios, if I hurt thee,' he said, though the boy could not hear him, 'but if I leave thee here thou shalt die. If I bear thee elsewhere thou mayst die also, but I must make the attempt.' As carefully as he could, he got his arms beneath the boy and lifted him, staggering as he got to his feet. He was weary and Ancaios was not the lightest load. The boy's garments were wet with blood.

He crossed the hillside and his horses followed patiently behind, the grey stallion well-nigh spent and the red gelding lame. The way was furrowed and rank with weeds and though he took every care, time and again he jolted his hapless burden. By the time he arrived at the oak-covered knoll, he was breathing hard and felt like crying in despair, but astonishingly, Ancaios still clung to life.

The dragon lay close by, gaunt and terrible in the dying light. But the knight spared hardly a glance for the broken creature; instead he stood before the knoll and gazed into its tangled thicket. Spring here had barely begun, but the trees' leafless branches were swathed in ivy, and between their vine-shrouded trunks shadows gathered deep and watchful.

'Lady Unicorn,' said the knight quietly. His horses had raised their tired heads and, beside him, stared prick-eared into the umbrous gloom.

The man waited, hearing only silence. 'I have been aware of your presence these last few days,' said he; 'you have followed me, I know not why. And now ye have helped me, perhaps unwittingly.' He paused, looking down at Ancaios and making an attempt to ease the weight in his aching arms. The boy's blood felt viscid and warm in his hands. 'Some years ago,' he said, his eyes still lowered, 'there was, kept captive in yon castle, something that... belongs to you. If it remaineth there, I mean to return it to you.'

Not a sound did he hear, but when he looked up the unicorn was there. She stood deep within the trees, half-glimpsed and spectral; luminescent in the twilight. Her dark eyes were upon him and he could do naught but cast his own to the ground and sink to his knees. 'O, Unicorn,' said he, holding Ancaios before him, 'ye who have lived ten thousand years, behold this young man who hath barely begun his short span on this earth.' His voice was hoarse and low; little more than a whisper. 'Yea, he is a man, but he is also generous, compassionate and loving of all life. And now he is in dire need of succour; I pray you... a single hair from your mane...'

But when he glanced up again, the unicorn had gone; melted silently into the deep-shadowed trees. His chief hope blighted, the knight got back to his feet. 'Tarry here, Unicorn,' said he to the shadows, 'for I mean to return that which is yours. Wait – if not until dawn, at least until midnight.'

Despairing, he glanced at the boy bleeding in his arms and then at the distant castle. But his gaze returned to the boy, for Ancaios was changed. It may have been no more than his imagination, yet the lad's face seemed less deathly pale and his breathing less shallow. And he himself felt not as bone-weary as he had; it was certain that his troublesome old wound had for the moment ceased to give him pain. His horses too appeared brighter and he suddenly recalled their magical transformation of two nights ago.

He looked back at the trees with a slight, bemused smile, and then he carefully set forth across the dusky common towards the castle. The two horses stayed close behind him, the grey at his elbow and the still-limping chestnut a little further back. He had to watch his path for the way was strewn with corpses, and discarded weapons and cast-down pennants lay tangled amongst the nettles and gorse.

Before him, spread along the purple vale for as far as the eye could see, lay the lake, shimmering damask-pink under an incarnadine sky. The sun had gone but high above its roseate afterglow, where the sky faded through azure to deepest sapphire, the first stars had begun to shine.

Princess Winterhued and Lady Brenn walked out through the great gates of the town and halted. Before them the road crossed the Otterburn over a stone bridge and curled away to the east; passing a row of burnt-out shops and dwellings, it climbed beside the common towards the dark line of forest that rimmed the horizon to the west and southwest. A dozen foot soldiers and a handful of unmounted knights came traipsing in from the common and marched up the road towards the gates.

Their leader, a stocky knight of middle years, looked mortified as he made obeisance before his princess. 'We are shamed, your highness,' said he, 'that Manydown's army hath been unmanned and disgraced. 'Tis a stranger that hath slain the dragon, though some say he is no stranger to Lawhill.'

'A stranger yet no stranger?' questioned Winterhued. Her heart would not be quiet though she told herself, *it cannot be, it cannot be!*

'I know no more than that,' said the stocky knight, 'and that was but rumour.'

'Where is he then, our brave Dragonslayer?' she asked, unable to suppress the tremor in her voice. 'We have come to do him homage and to offer him our gratitude.'

The fellow pointed back up across the common. 'His squire was slain, highness,' said he. 'We offered to escort him hither but, grieving, he sent us away. He will come shortly.'

Winterhued raised her eyes once more to the dusky hillside. In the gathering gloom she could see the great mound of the dragon's carcass beside the wooded knoll, but no sign of any living thing. 'What of your fellows?' she asked. 'Not all perished. Where is the remainder of our army? Where is Sir Rathdown?'

The man looked down at the road to hide his face. 'Methinks the knights ran after their horses… and they all galloped east for Belford. Our baggage train is on its way hither; 'tis likely that the survivors will go to meet it for they will be ashamed to show their craven faces here; Sir Rathdown most of all.'

The fellow looked chastened and broken-spirited. When they had first met the princess, his companions had gone down on their knees in the road and there they remained, their faces downcast. Winterhued put a hand now upon their leader's armour-clad shoulder. 'Thou and these other brave men returned,' she said gently. 'Very few have faced the dragon so ye, of all the army, have no cause to kneel in the mud; indeed ye may stand tall and hold up your heads.'

Anxious that her father would arrive before the Dragonslayer, she glanced over the man's shoulder up to the common... and suddenly saw him: a dark shape moving, small and far away, down over the twilit common. And then she had naught else to say to anyone.

Unaware of the soldiers rising to their feet, or of the murmuring crowd of town and castle dwellers growing ever larger at her back, she watched the approach of the unknown hero. Leading two horses and cradling his dead squire in his arms, he wended his slow and careful way downhill; as he drew closer Winterhued saw his armour gleam crimson in the gloaming and saw his long hair lift upon the breeze.

Thoughts chased themselves round her mind.

Why so anxious? I am a fool; these thoughts can only lead to disappointment. (Of course it is not he... it cannot be!) I must find something to say to him... this stranger; it will not do to stand in the road gaping at him. (Oh, there is that about him... yet it cannot be!) What shall I say to Lawhill's saviour? Of course I must offer him our thanks; offer him... not myself or the kingdom, but a dukedom, marquisate or earldom as my father promised? But they are hardly to be plucked from thin air. The keys to Lawhill? It is burnt and ruined. Welcome him with a great feast? But we have no kitchens and little provender. Provide a grand burial for his squire? When we have so many of our own dead? (But there is something about him! But nay, it is not he; it cannot be...)

She had not even noticed Brenn taking her hand and leaning companionably against her. 'I can feel m'lady's heart beating,' murmured the girl. Winterhued responded with a dismissive laugh. 'That is because I am a fool,' she said, enclosing the girl's hand within both of her own.

But when the approaching knight changed direction for a space to skirt a clump of bushes, a gasp escaped her, for she saw then that he did not lead his horses; that they followed him with the reins looped over their saddles. And she had once known a man whose horse shadowed him like a faithful hound.

He reached the road at last. The sun's light lingered still in a wash of crimson along the western horizon, but behind Winterhued people were bringing torches that cast her shadow along the road towards him as he came to her over the bridge. Her hair blew out sideways and she took her hands from Brenn's so that she could push it back from her face.

And then he stood before her, tall and strong and so beautiful that there was naught in the world she wanted to do besides look at him. 'Dalgonar,' she said. It was little more than a whisper, but it was the first time she had spoken his name aloud for more than ten years.

'Winterhued,' said he, and it was the first time she had heard her name spoken in that dark, entrancing voice for many more years than ten.

But beside her Brenn gave a despairing sob. 'Ancaios!' she cried, darting forward. Winterhued, momentarily confused, watched her stop before the knight and the lad he carried in his arms. It *was* Ancaios; his face marble-white, his head lolled back, his limbs hanging limply and blood seeping around crude bandages that bound his wound. Brenn put her hands over her mouth and gasped in distress.

'He liveth yet,' said Winterhued's love, in a voice so soft that none could have heard his words but she and Brenn. 'Winter, my own; dost thy father's captive still languish within?' Winterhued nodded, realizing what it was he asked. 'It must be tried; 'tis the lad's only hope,' he said. 'And then the captive *must* be freed...'

The princess understood and she put a hand to the girl's shoulder. But Brenn had not heard a word. 'Why is he with you?' she asked, crying. 'He departed only yesterday and he was but a messenger… why hath he been killed?'

'Brenn,' said the princess, pulling the girl to her. 'He is not dead, my love. There is no time for questions.' But Brenn still sobbed in distress, so Winterhued gripped her by the shoulders, and half-knelt to look into her face. 'Brenn, hearken, she said; 'mayhap thou canst save Ancaios' life. Remember our dusk mission? Hast thou the silver scissors?'

Brenn suddenly understood. 'Oh yes, yes,' she said breathlessly.

Winterhued took a signet ring from her right hand. 'If anyone doth attempt to stop thee,' she explained, dropping it into Brenn's palm, 'show them this and tell them thou art about my business. Where is Eudora?'

The princess looked around at the hushed crowd. There were hundreds of people standing beneath the town gates, upon the road and on the slopes below the gates; the guard's torches splashed yellow light upon their watching faces as the night pressed in. They had been expecting a jubilant speech from their princess; indeed they had come to give their saviour a hero's welcome and laud him to the skies. And there he stood, tall and puissant, the greatest knight in all the world ran the rumour, but he cradled his dead squire so sadly, before him a lady wept in distress, and Princess Winterhued stood solemn and so sorrowful that they could do naught but watch in silence.

Hearing her name, Eudora shouldered her way through the crowd and stepped forward. When two guards moved to push the servant girl back, the princess stopped them and with a word sent them running towards the gates. The people moved aside to let them pass. Winterhued took the girl's hand, and drawing her away from the crowd, handed her a bundle of keys and knelt to whisper to her urgently.

Eudora nodded and nodded, though she looked confused and half terrified. 'I shall forget your highness' instructions,' she said.

'Thou shalt remember,' replied Winterhued; 'trust me, Eudora. Go thee with Lady Brenn now; make haste.'

Brenn, with a last wild look towards Ancaios, grabbed Eudora's hand and tugged her towards the road. Winterhued raised her voice. 'I pray ye, good people, make way,' she cried; 'this lady's mission is urgent!'

The murmuring crowd dutifully opened up a gap along the road to the gates, and the high-born lady hitched up her skirts and ran through it as fast as she could, towing the bewildered serving girl by the hand. Beneath the gate one of the servant's shoes flew off but she kept going, hobbling along on her stockinged foot. The gap closed but then had to open again as the two guards returned from the gatehouse carrying a litter.

The two stared at their new hero with awestruck curiosity as the knight laid Ancaios upon the litter and Winterhued covered the lad with her cloak.

'This gong-farmer's son hath chosen his friends well,' said the hero in a puzzled tone.

'And in the short space since leaving here,' replied the princess, 'he hath done so again, with surprising swiftness.'

'This time to his cost.'

Winterhued looked up at the knight across the prone form of his squire. Her eyes shone with unshed tears. 'Can he survive?' she asked.

The knight held up his bloodied hands. He wore no armour below his shoulders, and the sleeves of his arming doublet were steeped in blood. 'He hath lost too much of this to live,' said he, 'but... with some help...'

'I am fearful he'll get the wrong kind if the surgeon reacheth him before Brenn.'

The knight looked down at his squire. 'Hold on, Ancaios,' he murmured. He smoothed some hair back from the boy's forehead, then looked up. 'Guards,' he said, 'carry my squire, with every care, to the infirmary. Tell the surgeon to look to the lad's comfort, but not to touch him otherwise; to keep his hands and his leeches, his knife and his quicksilver, to himself.'

The chestnut horse neighed as the stretcher bearers, at a measured pace, departed. As the crowd made way, those closest gazed down upon the white face and the tumbled dark hair of the mortally wounded squire, and though one or two thought they recognised him, straight away did they change their minds, for was this not the brave squire of the Dragonslayer, the most feared and famed knight in all the world?

Winterhued watched the knight make his way down the bank beside the bridge and kneel to plunge his arms into the swirling waters of the Otterburn. When most of the boy's blood had been washed away he climbed back to where she waited in the flickering torchlight beside his patient horses, and halted before her.

They stood all alone before hundreds, and at last there was naught to hinder Winterhued from looking long upon the face of her love and marvelling at the beautiful changes that time had wrought there.

'Thou hast been tardy in thy homecoming,' said she softly, her eyes shining.

'Oh? I thought my timing admirable,' objected he with the slight, wry smile that had been the elusive subject of her daydreams for so many years. He glanced over her shoulder at the murmuring crowd. 'Thy people await a laudation from their princess,' said he; 'mayhap thou couldst mention the king's commission and my promised reward. Which doth remind me... where is thy father?'

'On his way to a rude surprise,' smiled Winterhued. The way he looked at her with such tender solicitude made her heart hurt with joy. 'As to thy reward,' she said, 'the king had that document drawn up without my consent. If I had known of it, I'd have told him he could throw whatever rewards he liketh at whomsoever he pleaseth, but that he must leave me out of the bargain.'

'Insolent daughter,' said the knight; 'wilful as ever. So I have not won thy hand after all?'

'I but wish thee to know,' said Winterhued, 'that I won't be handed out, willy-nilly, like some prize at a fair. Yet that doth not mean thou canst not ask me for it.'

'But I asked thee eighteen years ago,' said he with a sigh, 'and now thou wouldst put me to the trouble all over again.' Gazing upon her face he sank to his knees before her, undistracted even when his horse stretched out its neck to snuffle into his hair.

Winterhued laughed. 'Get up, sir,' said she.

But he stayed on his knees and looked up at her with his slight smile. 'Winter,' said he, tilting his head quizzically to one side, 'dost thou yet have the gift I gave thee when we parted?'

Winterhued's smile faded as the knight's grew broader. 'Come closer, my love,' said he gently; 'my hands are wet… feel about my neck… thou shalt find a narrow chain beneath my collar.'

Puzzled and almost shyly she leaned forwards and reached beneath the dark fall of his hair. She touched his neck; softly, she slid her fingertips beneath his mail collar until she found the thin chain lying there, and felt his pulse beating as hard and strong as her own.

'I have found the chain,' she breathed.

'Something hangs from it,' said he. She slipped her fingers down into the hollow of his throat, discovered the pendant lying there and eased it free of his collar.

'How…?' she gasped, staring wide-eyed at her moonstone. 'I lost this, two or three days past!'

'So thou dost not know how it came to be lying in the muddy road halfway to Langstone?'

'No… that is a mystery,' she whispered and then looked up at his amused, tender, perplexed face. 'Thou didst not think I had discarded it because I no longer cared for thee?'

'But I did,' he replied, 'yet consoled myself with the thought that thou must have grown big, fat and brawny to have hurled it from the battlements five leagues along the east road.'

Winterhued flicked the pendant at him and gave him a little push. 'Tomfool,' said she with quiet joy; 'off thy knees now; I have a proclamation to make.' She straightened and turned to face the murmuring crowd.

'Hearken, good people,' spake she, scarcely needing to raise her voice as her audience fell instantly silent. She paused, gathering her thoughts. The evening had grown cold; without her cloak she had begun to shiver, and the cloud of her breath shone gold in the torchlight. Her night-dark hair and the skirts of her gown drifted sideways in the chill breeze.

'Before you standeth the man...' said she, sweeping her arm out towards him even as she noticed that he was yet on his knees, watching her as if she were the only thing in the world worth watching. Her eyes sparkled with laughter. 'Here, before you,' she continued, her voice shaking a little with the cold, '*kneeleth* the man who hath brought us salvation and life. He was already a knight of renown, indeed his fame had spread o'er the wide world, and so it was to him that the king sent for succour during our days of peril. And by this day's generous and courageous deed hath he proved to us, beyond doubt, his inestimable worth.'

As Winterhued spoke, the knight got to his feet and fetched his rolled cloak from behind the grey's saddle. He fastened it about her shoulders, and though it was an old garment, threadbare and flecked with white horse hairs, it was more lovely to the princess than the costliest robe.

The crowd had begun to cheer and whistle, but she held up a hand to silence them. 'Sir,' said she, looking into the eyes of her love, 'we rejoice in your coming and offer our heartfelt thanks for your services. Besides winning the honour, love and respect of all Manydown, the king, in his gratitude, shall assuredly guerdon you with lands and title.

As well, he hath offered unto you the hand of his only daughter in marriage.' Winterhued stepped closer to her beloved and took both of his hands in hers. 'And though I know I am scant reward for such courage and prowess, I say yea... with all my heart I shall be your wife.'

For a moment there was only stunned silence, but then an exultant shout went up to the starry heavens. Surely what followed; the yelling, the whooping and the whistling, the tossing of caps, the embracing, the leaping and the dancing, had not been seen nor heard in Lawhill for many a long year.

King Gers muttered and grumbled as he skirted the burial pit in the outer bailey. Two guards went before him bearing torches, at his feet trotted his faithful hound, and behind him scurried the Lords Highmoor and Ladstock and, puffing and blowing, his friend the Duke of Drumrock. Bringing up the rear came Sir Gunford, the sweaty captain having oiled his way back into the king's affections by being the first to wake him with news of the dragon's demise.

Gers and Drumrock had spent that afternoon drinking to the king's impending marriage with the duke's youngest daughter, the Lady Manicia. 'He he he,' Drumrock had chuckled, red cheeked and inebriated, 'Criffel'll be none too pleased, but he'll step aside for his sov'reign or have his nasty head cut off... eh, m'lord?' The two befuddled friends had eventually nodded off to sleep and King Gers, though he seldom dreamt, had suffered such a nonsensical dream that he snarled now at the very memory of it. He had been about to wed, not the Duke of Drumrock's daughter, but the Duke of Drumrock himself, and he and the duke, and everyone else in Manydown, had been joyfully excited at the prospect. And because of such arrant nonsense he had snored and mumbled his way through all of the real excitement. It didn't help that Highmoor and Ladstock had also nodded off (and probably the guard at the door).

Thus, while everyone else had rushed up to the battlements to watch the knight: the knight *he'd* had the foresight to send for (he wondered what his daughter would have to say about *that*), fight the greatest battle ever seen, he'd been trying on a wretched wedding gown. In white brocade! White? Pah! Couldn't it have at least been royal purple?

Gers puffed and wheezed; it was a long way to the town gates when he didn't have a horse beneath him. 'Why didst thou not wake me in better time?' he snapped over his shoulder at Gunford.

'I did try, my liege,' said the captain, 'but m'lord was exceeding difficult to wake... exceeding difficult. He seemed in the midst of a wondrous pleasant dream...'

'Stuff and nonsense!' spat the king angrily. 'I never dream!'

They were almost at the Constable's Gate when two girls, a young lady and a servant, came darting out from beneath the gate passage. Gers wasn't familiar with the lady, but was taken aback when she didn't even glance at him as she sped by; at least the servant, who was wearing only one shoe, sketched a hurried curtsey before running on.

'Is everyone going mad around here?' growled Gers as he puffed his way through the gate and over the bouncing planks that spanned the Otterburn. He was angry, not only at having missed seeing the dragon slain, but also because his daughter must surely have got to the knight before he had. And Winterhued was always rude to men, seldom finding a word of praise for any of them. Moreover, despite her supposed cleverness, she was no match for him on occasions such as this. Ah yes, he'd always had a talent for speech-making and he was determined to use that skill now, no matter what his daughter might have said to the conquering hero.

'Of course, she hath refused him already,' he muttered, 'but no matter, no matter... I have my own plans. A sweet wife to care for me... a son and heir... two sons, maybe three...'

The king hurried along the main street behind the torch-bearing guards; he moved swiftly for an old man with a big belly. The lords had been left behind, teetering windmill-armed on the planks, and as Gunford had reluctantly stayed to help them, the king had only his old hound on which to practise his grandiloquence.

'Celebrated, far-famed, glorious sir,' he muttered; 'in a blaze of glory thou hast come... nay, nay, too many glories. O renowned sir; thy noble deeds, thy peerless valour, thy glorious fame have travelled before thee; even here we had heard of the great esteem... blah, blah.' Gers' voice grew louder and he began to wave his arms about as he went. 'And now, oh great and noble sir, beyond all hope... in our direst need... thou hast come to succour us and deliver us from... blah, blah... Since great deeds must be duly guerdoned, we have offered... nay, I *give* thee now my only daughter – she that is possessed of every virtue and ranks among the world's fairest ladies...'

The king's speech petered out and he frowned fiercely. 'Aye, feast thine eyes upon her, brave sir,' he muttered; 'the ever-contrary, all-too-clever, bad-tempered fish-wife that she is... just the sort of consort any Dragonslayer might dream of.'

Gers came to a halt. He was barely halfway to the town gates, but he was out of breath and had a painful stitch. As he stood panting and clutching his side, two guards came in the opposite direction carrying a wounded man on a litter. They ducked their heads reverently as they passed and the king stared at the pallid young man under the grey cloak, quite sure he'd never seen him before.

By the time he'd got his breath back and the pain in his side had subsided, Gunford, Drumrock and the two lords had caught him up. Old Highmoor was wheezing and coughing as though he were about to drop dead in the road. 'Hear me Highmoor, Ladstock; thou also, Drumrock,' said Gers with a scowl; 'this is how it shall be: my final word. If my daughter agreeth to wed this knight...'

'If he desireth it and is not wedded already,' interrupted Lord Highmoor.

'Obviously: I'm not an idiot!' growled the king. 'If she'll marry him, I'll *consider* putting aside my own plans for a male heir, but if she doth refuse him I shall straight away disinherit her and marry as soon as I may, and not another word from any of you.' Gers spun about and set off again, hound at his heels, towards the gates.

The royal party soon came in amongst crowds of folk on the road, their eager faces lit by torchlight, all of them wishing to get out through the gates to ogle the Dragonslayer. 'Make way for the king!' cried the guards and as Gers passed through the gap that opened for him, he heard snatches of gossip: 'They say 'e's ever so 'andsome.' 'She's 'appy; just smiles and smiles.' ''E's on his knees to 'er!' 'Has he kissed her yet?' There was a smattering of laughter at this, but the king only scowled. 'Some hope,' he muttered.

Gers paused as he came up to the gates; he'd heard his daughter. But she hadn't raised her voice enough. 'Weak woman's voice,' he sneered; 'useless before a crowd. Wait for me and I'll show thee how it's done.' But he was only as far as the gate passage when a joyous shout went up; a mighty hooting and a whistling and a yelling. A felt cap hit him hard above the eye and then another one knocked his own hat off. Waving his arms about as though he were warding off attacking birds, Gers strode out of the gate, halted and looked down through the leaping, prancing crowd towards the bridge over the Otterburn.

The first thing he saw was a chestnut horse, a large rangy animal that was bleeding from several wounds. Hanging from its broken saddle was a shield: gules, white unicorn rampant. He felt a surge of triumph at that, for this was indisputably the man that he, farseeing King Gers, had sent for. The horse was looking prick-eared at the crowd, but another animal, a big, gaunt grey, was watching something else intently.

The king turned his head... and there they were: the great Dragon-slayer and his contrary daughter, standing hand in hand and face to face amidst a rain of falling hats. He was a tall man, almost a head taller than tall Winterhued, bigly made and impressive, and surely well-favoured enough even for her finical tastes. Rather strangely, he was wearing no armour below his shoulders and his sleeves looked sodden. But no matter: he had Winterhued's hands in his and that was a surprising turn of affairs.

The cavorting crowd was noisy, but Gers had confidence in the power of his voice. He drew a deep breath and opened his mouth, ready to quiet the masses and boom out his under-rehearsed welcome.

But his lungs remained inflated and his mouth gaped as he watched his daughter take her hands from the knight's, thread them through his hair, and kiss him on the lips. A hush fell upon the crowd. And as though he and the princess were all alone under the stars, the knight returned her kiss, so tenderly that Gers heard the foolish women all about him sigh and swoon. And then he kissed her again…

'That was quick work,' said Gers in confusion. 'She'll surely marry the fellow after that!' And he supposed he'd have to be content with that, for this was clearly a man who could rule his headstrong daughter; the sort of son-in-law he'd dreamt of for years.

Lord Ladstock had come up beside him to stare in horror. 'Such behaviour should be reserved for the bedchamber!' said he, tut-tutting like an old woman. 'Before the whole court, all these townsfolk…!'

But what cared the townsfolk at such a time? They clapped and whistled, they found their hats, or anybody's hats, and tossed them once more into the air; some of them pushed past the guards and ran down to circle the lovers, surrounding them with exuberant goodwill.

Lord Highmoor had stepped up beside the king's other shoulder. ''Tis Arracan's youngest,' said he quietly, unable to hide his happiness.

Gers almost sat down on the road. 'No,' he said, then, 'no,' again. He staggered forwards two steps and then staggered back one, treading hard on his hound's paw. The animal yelped and whimpered. "No, no, no, no, no,' moaned Gers.

'My liege lord!' exclaimed Ladstock.

'What can I do?' groaned the king. 'Is there a way out of this?'

'I think not, highness,' replied Highmoor serenely. 'My liege gave his word to the lad, eighteen years ago, and just yester-morn verified his verbal promise on parchment; it hath been witnessed, signed and sealed, my liege. And the hand of the princess is but part of the agreement; there is also the matter of lands and title.'

Gers put his hands over his face and wailed. But no one took much notice of him for the guards had lost control of the crowd and folk poured out through the gates, dividing around the king's party like water around a rock. For a short time he lost sight of his daughter and the hated son of his enemy, but then the guards managed to open up a path again and Winterhued, looking straight up through the gap, met his eyes.

The king's face turned hot as she smiled at him: triumphantly he thought. And his blood boiled as the son of his enemy took his eyes from her face and looked upon the countenance of the man who was to be (and it seemed there was no escaping this) his father-in-law. They walked towards him, the two horses following of their own accord, and Gers' anger rose like bile.

But then someone, without a by-your-leave, stepped in front of him. It was another son of his enemy: that insolent dog, Carradale. 'Little brother,' said he, though his brother was a good deal taller than he was.

'Almendral,' said the knight quietly, and there was such affection in his voice that Gers sneered.

'Arracan's damned mongrels,' he spat as the brothers embraced.

'My liege!' begged Highmoor. 'He is a hero to the people: our saviour. I implore m'leige, do not...'

'Don't tell me what not to do!' snapped Gers; 'I'm the king! I do as I please and all my subjects will do as I please. Drumrock!' He looked round at his fat, panting friend. 'Is your daughter here? Bring her to me.'

Highmoor opened his mouth again to protest, but then the great knight had stepped away from the princess and his brother and was walking towards the king. Gers swore inwardly when he saw the parchment, dignified with his royal seal, in the man's hand.

The knight halted and bowed before him; it was a plain, seemingly respectful bow and nothing like his brother's insolent flourish. The grey horse, who had followed the knight as if he too wished for a royal audience, peered politely over his shoulder. And when the man straightened, there was no triumph or arrogance in his face; he looked serious, gaunt and tired. King Gers sneered at him. The envy and loathing that filled him made the veins on his forehead bulge. His hands shook with anger.

'Highness,' said the son of his enemy, 'I have, unarguably, fulfilled all that was asked of me in this, Your Highness' commission. As to the reward Your Highness promised: Winterhued hath agreed to be my wife; now there is but the matter of lands and a title.'

Gers made a noise in his throat that might have been words but sounded more like the snarl of a dog. At that, the knight's horse flattened its ears and showed its teeth, and the knight half turned to push it back a step or two. Positioning himself between the horse's teeth and the king's flesh, he looked back at Gers with half a smile. 'For Winterhued's sake,' said he, 'we should try to find a way to get on.'

'Get on?' hissed Gers. 'I cannot get on with any of thy brood, and I won't speak with thee. Daughter! Here!' he shouted, pointing to the ground at his feet.

Winterhued stepped up beside the knight and took his hand. 'Father,' she said quietly, 'we should not quarrel in this place. M'lord doth but display dishonour and unreason to his subjects.'

'Unreason?' spluttered the king. 'Hear then reason; hear fairness! Aye, this... this *man*... may claim his reward: he can have thee. I'll give him an obscure baronetcy and he can cart thee thither so I need never see either of you. And I shall marry and get a male heir and all thy prospects, daughter, all thine intent as queen of this land shall come to naught.' Gers leant forward and jabbed a forefinger at Winterhued. ''Tis thy choice, daughter. Marry this man and lose thine inheritance, or reject him, and straightway marry a man of my choosing, and I shall forsake my own marriage plans and retain thee as my heir.' Gers smiled. ''Tis surely an easy choice.'

Winterhued answered him in the same quiet voice. 'My lord's sense of what is right and honourable should inform him that there is *no* choice,' said she. 'I have been twice promised to this man; I am his by right. It is not my future that is at stake here, but your reputation; do you think that you can retain the respect of your people when you dishonour pledges, refuse to remunerate their saviour and betray your daughter?'

The king stared at her, his face purplish. Sediments of white scum had collected at the corners of his mouth. 'So,' he said slowly, 'thou hast made thy choice. Where shall I send ye? Landed titles do not grow on trees, but mayhap I can find something small, out of the way, unimportant...'

'Winter,' said the knight, gazing at her with both love and dismay, 'let me go...'

'Wheresoever thou goest, I go,' replied Winterhued. She moved closer and stood, serene and proud, at his side. 'Doth my lord know,' she asked her father, 'that this very eve an earl and a marquess were eaten by the dragon?'

Gers gaped. 'What?' he spluttered. 'Who was eaten?'

'Dunmore and Potrimpos, my lord, and both of them departed this world leaving no issue.'

'He's not having Dunmore,' spat the king; 'never Dunmore! Besides, there's a brother...'

'Aye, Criffel had three brothers. But Parchim did not. And neither did he have a sister, or a nephew or a niece.'

'Potrimpos...' growled Gers. 'Loathsome hole... aye, he may have Potrimpos.' His daughter looked up at the knight and he looked back at her; it was a very slight communication but it made the king feel sick with anger. 'Satisfied, sir?' he snarled, half shouting. ''Tis far more than I wished to give, so hie thee hence as quick as thou mayest before I take it back!' He jabbed a finger towards the northeast.

Sir Gunford, standing at Gers' back, stepped close to the king's ear. 'But your highness...' he protested quietly, 'the whole of the north... the whole of the north, my lord... will now be controlled by the Carigernes. Is that wise...?'

'The north?' shouted Gers, rounding on Gunford so that the man flinched and backed away. 'What care I for the north? All rocks, sleet and snow, and mongrel-curs on both sides of the border.'

He turned, ready to storm off through the gates. The crowds of rejoicers had long since collected their hats and now stood about uneasily, murmuring and confused. Held at a distance from the royal party by a ring of guards, they had little idea of what was happening and rumour was rife. 'The king is mad,' was the common thread; 'been going that way for years and now he's completely barmy.'

Forcing his bulk through their midst came the Duke of Drumrock, his two daughters in tow, and the king headed towards him, angrily waving his arms at the folk before him as if they were a swarm of insects.

Benicia clung to her father's arm to keep herself upright; her face was tear-streaked and blanched white from terror and the shock of seeing her sweetheart eaten alive. Her sister though was angry; angry at fate, the dragon, everyone in the castle, for conspiring against her. She hadn't shed a single tear over the violent death of her betrothed, but she had *so* wanted to be Countess of Dunmore.

The two girls had been lagging at the tail end of the crowd when their father had found them; Manicia goading and almost dragging her older sister towards the town gate. Their father, who stank of wine, was so out of breath that he could hardly get a word out. Excitedly, he grabbed their hands to speed them onwards. 'The king wisheth...' he gasped, 'to see thee...'

'Which one of us?' asked Manicia.

'Thou... thou, Manicia!'

And now the king rushed towards them, waving his arms about. He stopped when he saw Drumrock. 'Ha!' he barked, jabbing a finger towards Manicia. 'Come hither, girl. What's-yer-name... in the grey.'

'My daughter's name is Manicia, my liege,' said Drumrock.

Manicia took a step forward and curtseyed clumsily. She was feeling flustered before so many onlookers and bewildered as to why the king should wish to see her at such a momentous time.

As she rose she caught sight of the famous knight; he appeared to be pleading with Winterhued and she was shaking her head, yet smiling. He was tall and beautiful, but she had no time to gaze, for the king had walked forward and grabbed her arm. His face was purplish and there were wine dribbles on his velvet gown.

'Maneeta,' he said, forgetting her name already. Gripping her so hard that it hurt, he turned to face the crowd. 'Good people,' said he in an angry voice, 'Winterhued hath informed you that she will wed that man, and she may do so with my yea-say. But she is no longer my heir; I renounce her. This,' he said holding up Manicia's arm, 'this, is your new queen! Queen Maneeta, daughter of the Duke of Drumrock: well bred and ready to breed. I shall marry her as soon as may be.' He suddenly poked at her hips with his fat fingers. 'Better make plenty of boys in there, Queen Whatsername,' he muttered. Manicia flinched away from the angry old man but he tightened his grip on her wrist and strutted forwards. 'Come, people,' he barked, glowering round at the bewildered, deflated crowd, 'why do ye not acclaim your new queen?' At that, several subjects dutifully clapped and one or two even cried: 'Queen Maneeta!' Then her father's voice boomed out behind her: 'Long live Queen Manicia!' and that shout was taken up by Sir Gunford, Lord Ladstock and a collection of the king's cronies. The king lifted her hand to his lips and an acceptable portion of the crowd responded with clapping, cheering and even a solitary whistle. Manicia tilted up her chin and a small smile crept across her face. She turned to look at her father who smiled delightedly back at her, his eyes twinkling and his head nodding. Suddenly, Manicia thought she might die of happiness, and she laughed out loud when she saw the look of astonished dismay on her sister's tear-stained face.

Her future husband put a fat arm about her waist, but he was not looking at her. He was glaring at Winterhued and the Dragonslayer, who faced him hand-in-hand. Seeing them, Manicia's laughter died for they looked as proud and beautiful as deities from legend. She noticed that many of the courtiers, Lord Highmoor amongst them, had moved to stand behind the princess, and saw with a jolt that Sir Audny, Duke of Travancore, was there too. He was looking at her. *Aye, thou dost see me now,* she thought, *for I shall be Queen and Winterhued naught. She shall remain thus, for the king is a dotard and he'll do my bidding. I shall see thee also brought low, fool… and my sister too.* Manicia glanced round at Benicia and she laughed again.

Hearing her, Gers stopped scowling at Winterhued and the traitorous courtiers. He turned to examine Manicia's face and gave a snort of surprised laughter. 'Daughter,' he said, looking back at Winterhued and chortling, 'how dost thou like thy new mother?'

His anger still seething beneath the laughter, he spun on his heel, nearly tripping over his hound. He pushed the animal away with his foot. 'Come, my queen,' said he, slapping Manicia's buttocks so hard that she gasped and jumped, 'let us eat!' He grabbed her hand, leered round at his followers, then set off through the gate passage and along the crowded road to the castle. The guards hurried to clear a way for him, and the light from their torches flickered and flared, trailing smoke and long shadows, and glinting golden on their weapons of war.

CHAPTER 17

Ye cannot see him, my lady,' said the surgeon to Brenn. He was holding a jar of black leeches and it looked as though they'd been feeding on his face, it was so red and blotchy. 'The young man is dying,' he said, 'torn from gullet to gut, and there's naught to be done for him.'

'Then I shall sit beside him as he doth die,' said Brenn, out of breath from her long, desperate run.

'Whyfor? Ye cannot know him; he is the Dragonslayer's squire and haleth from some far land.'

'Yet I *will* see him,' said Brenn. 'I am cousin to Her Highness.' The surgeon gave in with a shrug, bowed his head, and stepped aside to let her pass. 'Where is he?' asked Brenn and this time the tremor in her voice betrayed her fear. The man pointed to a bed not far from the infirmary door.

In trepidation, the girl made her way to the bed and looked down upon Ancaios' prone form. She saw that they'd not moved him from the litter, but propped its ends on two chests to make a bed and draped a blanket over the cloak that already covered him. They'd put a pillow beneath his head, and a jug and cup on the floor beside him showed that they'd attempted to give him water.

But his face was as white and bloodless as old bone and he looked so dead that Brenn could not prevent a cry of dismay from escaping her lips. She knelt by his side, took up his cold hand and searched, heart in mouth, for a pulse. At first she could find nothing but then, pressing hard, there it was: slow, sluggish, but struggling on.

Brenn looked over her shoulder to see if she was observed, but the surgeon had gone and the sole woman present was busy with another patient. Feeling like a village witch, she sat down on the floor, pulled the black cloak secretively about her, and took a pouch from the purse at her belt. As she carefully withdrew its contents any doubt she may have had evaporated, for there *was* magic in the world and she held a piece of it in her hand. It shone like the moon.

In the end she hadn't counted each hair. The unicorn, at her stammered request, had moved his beautiful head close until he had almost touched the terrible iron bars of his cage. Her hands shaking and tears blurring her vision, she'd separated a small strand from his forelock and snipped it off with her silver scissors, feeling like the worst desecrator.

Brenn took three of the shining hairs from the strand. 'A few hairs' the princess had said; surely three was a few? The strand looked so slim with three gone from it and there were so many souls lying desperately ill within the chamber. But then she looked at her love who, every moment, drew closer to death; she saw his long, dark lashes lying so still upon his white cheeks, and she took one more hair from the strand.

And then she had to do something that she'd avoided thinking of till now. Shuddering, she stood up and leant over Ancaios so that her cloak fell about the both of them; she folded back the blanket and the grey cloak and with the silver scissors cut through three of the canvas strips that bound the wound. It was a difficult job for the strips were tough and blood-soaked and her scissors were small.

Holding her breath, she eased her shaking hand into the sticky mess of blood beneath the blanket wadding. She found the wound in Ancaios' chest – indeed it was so wide that her hand slipped easily down between torn, pulpy tissue and the jagged edges of broken ribs – and pushed the four unicorn hairs deep into the wound. Gasping, she withdrew her bloodied hand and replaced the cloak and blanket. And then she could do nothing but sink down onto the cold floor, curl up beneath her cloak and cry.

Eudora stood beside the iron-clad door in the menagerie, peering down the dimly lit corridors and listening. There had been no guards present when she and Lady Brenn had first arrived at this place, and none had since returned; indeed, it seemed as if she were the only person left in the castle.

The princess had told her to wait. She did not mind waiting; she could wait forever, for she felt as though her mind had been swept clean with a broom. All of her restless, stupid thoughts had gone, replaced by a calmness that was as bright and clear as a cloudless sunrise.

'Wait and watch,' Winterhued had said. 'Wait until we are back inside the castle. There shall likely be a feast for all in the King's Hall and the bailey deserted... wait until midnight or later if need be. Get rid of the guards... send them to me... thou hast my ring.'

Wait, she'd said. But all of a sudden, Eudora knew she could not wait. *Now,* said a voice inside her head; *it must be now.*

The girl removed her one remaining shoe and walked barefooted, back across the two chambers to the barred door. She took down a golden chain that hung from a hook beside the door and wiped its coating of dust off on her apron. Her hands shook a little as she searched for the right key. She found the one the princess had shown her; it turned smoothly in the lock and with a soft click the door opened.

She walked to the unicorn, past his murderous horn and his eternally forgiving eye; she touched the gleaming satin of his breast and felt, once again, all the world in his heartbeat. For just a moment, with her head bowed and her eyes closed, she stood touching him… and felt her heart beat in time with his, in time with the earth, the sky, the sun and the stars.

Then she clipped the gold chain to his gold collar and led him out through the iron door.

There were two more doors, and two more keys to turn two more locks, and each had then to be closed and locked so that no trace would be left of their passing. And all the while, as the unicorn waited at her shoulder with the zephyr of his breath on her arm, the voice in her head insisted: *hurry – it must be now!*

Following the princess's instructions, she led the unicorn along the north-slanting corridor. It was lined on both sides with cages and, as they passed, each and every occupant moved closer to the bars or turned its head or woke, wide-eyed, from slumber. Eyes sad and dark, or fierce and unblinking, eyes bright or dim, black or yellow, eyes clouded and half-blind; all followed the unicorn as he passed them by. In silence and sadness they gazed, and Eudora hung her head in shame and watched her bare feet on the flagstones, step after step.

She came at last to the end of the cages and, turning into a short corridor, saw with a jolt that she'd been careless: there was a guard! He was asleep in an alcove, slumped forwards and dribbling. Eudora watched him for a moment, uncertain, her heart beating hard. He seemed very deeply asleep; she wondered if he even knew that the dragon had been slain. She stepped forwards, for there was no going back now and the voice in her head was insistent.

The guard's halberd blocked the way; Eudora had to prise it one-handed from his flaccid grasp and lay it carefully down upon the flagstones. Her heart sounded like a drum in her ears, and at her back she could feel the unicorn's fear too, and his loathing. But while she held the golden chain he would do naught but follow her.

The iron-studded door at the end of the corridor had three locks, seldom used. She had to hold the chain in her mouth and use both hands. When the door eventually came open it whined a complaint as she pushed at it and her heart came into her mouth.

Outside, it was a black, moonless night. Eudora peered from the portal out into the bailey. On the far side of the partially-filled pit in which lay Lawhill's dead she saw several folk moving towards the town carrying torches and lanterns. Beyond them the loose horses milled restlessly, their hides flickering black and yellow in the torchlight; the rest of the bailey was empty. But Eudora knew that outside the Constable's Gate a crowd congregated, and it was only a matter of time before most of those people came crowding back into the castle.

Now! insisted the voice in her head.

The blue-eyed maid gripped the golden chain and walked forwards; she heard the light tread of the unicorn as he crossed the threshold behind her and stepped out under the open sky. A soft breeze blew from the east and tendrils of his mane brushed across her cheek. Above, a million stars turned in the heavens.

Brenn lay on the cold floor, curled beneath her cloak. Her eyes were wide open; she stared at naught and she thought of naught, though the tears still ran sideways across her face and onto the floorboards. She heard voices, quiet but excited, and breathless laughter as two or three women returned to the infirmary. After a time soft footsteps came towards her and a gentle voice asked her if she was alright. "'Tis a cold hard place to be layin', m'lady,' said the voice.

Brenn, without looking up, pulled her cloak tight and told the woman to please go away. She could not hide the quaver in her voice, nor the involuntary sob that escaped her after the last word, for Ancaios was surely dead by now. His wound had been so deep and so horrible that nothing could heal it. Magic was only a tale for children.

'Ye know the young man's not dead?' asked the woman. 'Surgeon told us to leave this one alone, but... certes, I've seen 'em look a lot worse than this and pull through... so come, m'lady, don't cry. The dragon is slain and they say our princess is to marry the bravest man in all the world... and look now, I'm certain I can even see a little colour in the young man's cheeks.'

King Gers strode up the street towards the castle, scowling like thunder. His hound and his bride trotted to keep up, and so did Lord Highmoor, his black robes flapping and his face crimson. The guards went before them, their torches lighting up the smoke-stained shops and dwellings that had been saved, and between them, mounds of wreckage drowned in ash. All along the way stood the people of Lawhill with their lanterns and candles. None of them cheered. They had been more than ready to forget their sorrows for a time and celebrate the Dragonslayer's victory but now they only looked tired and confused.

'Reconsider, I beg m'liege,' pleaded Highmoor, his breath coming in wheezing gasps; 'the people love... love Winterhued. There... there shall be... dreadful... unrest in the realm...'

'Damn the people!' spat the king. 'And I'll be damned if ever I see Winterhued sit upon the throne! She can sit and rot in Potrimpos instead; see how she liketh her life on that cold dunghill with no say in the affairs of state. I shall rule Manydown, I alone! I did it before she stuck her nose in and I shall do it again!'

'My liege doth... invite civil war,' panted Highmoor in desperation, 'and when our... our backs are turned, m'liege, the Angeronians...'

Gers spun in his tracks and jabbed a finger at the old man's chest. 'I shan't be needing thee anymore, Highmoor, so thou canst totter off to Potrimpos with thy mistress and die there.' He turned on his heel and strode away with his hound towards the planks over the Otterburn and the Constable's Gate.

Briefly, before following the king, Lady Manicia smirked at Highmoor and then she laughed. The old chancellor bowed his head. 'My lady,' said he courteously, though his heart shrank at that laugh. And just as soon as Manicia had tossed her head imperiously and swept off after her new bridegroom, Highmoor was once again at their heels, desperate and dogged.

Under the starry skies, Eudora gripped the golden chain and led the unicorn across the short distance to the breach in the castle wall. She had not looked at the creature since clipping the chain to his collar, but now, halting at the edge of the breach, she turned to face him.

He stood refulgent, potent with life, his breath cloudy in the cold night air. Though there was no moon, a faint light washed his form in silver. His eye was an unfathomed mystery; it was deepest night, adorned with a single star.

Eudora lifted up her arms and threaded her fingers through the silken skeins of his mane. She pressed her face against his neck and closed her eyes, wanting only to stand like this forever... to stand at the centre of the universe and feel it turn about her.

'This is all there is,' she whispered; 'truth and love... life's sum and substance.'

But she stepped back from the touch, and fumbled for the small gold key amongst the bunch Winterhued had given her.

'Ye must find a path down through the tumbled stones,' she whispered. 'Skirt the castle and the town; keep away from men.' A tear ran down her cheek as she turned the key in the gold lock.

Even as she took the collar from the unicorn's neck and glimpsed the terrible raw mark it had made there, Eudora saw his horn flash past her face swifter than a sword and she saw his eye upon her, full of darkness. But then he had turned so quickly it was as though he had never been there.

The maid lost her balance and fell, dropping the collar. Gasping, she watched the unicorn spring weightlessly away, leaving a trail of light like a comet's tail behind him. But he did not go down over the tumble of rock and rubble.

'No!' gasped Eudora.

For the unicorn had cantered out into the centre of the bailey. Gleaming like moonshine, he skirted the grave-ditch and ran towards the Constable's Gate. And with a great clatter and a ringing of iron on stone, a spinning, a slipping and a scrambling, all the loose horses in the bailey leapt to follow him.

Night deepened around the gutted town as the princess and her troth-plight lord walked up the street hand in hand, the brave old horses following. They had fallen some distance behind Gers and his syco-phants for their progress was hindered by the townsfolk who, repelled and bewildered by the king's fury, were glad to find their princess as gracious and solicitous as ever. And as the knight's eyes looked as black as anyone else's in the torchlight, all found him wondrously handsome, good-humoured, humble and kind, and thought him the most perfect hero in the world. After such a short acquaintance, he was remarkably devoted to their princess.

He put a hand to her arm and stopped her in the street where a torch in an iron bracket cast a bright glow. Ignoring the crowds, he turned her to face him and tenderly ran his fingers across the deep scratch on her cheek. 'Thou hast loosed an arrow this day with some force,' said he. 'Whereto?'

Winterhued shook her head. 'I cannot say for certain where it went.'

'Into the dragon's maw? Come, concede: thou didst not need me; I could have stayed in my bed, or at least, in my ditch, all the day.'

'Ditch?'

'That is where I slept last night; four hours in a ditch. Thy father would say it is where I belong.'

As if in affirmation, they heard Gers raise his voice in a furious shout. Though they could not hear what he said, the words 'decrepit dog' and 'traitor' were clear enough. 'Highmoor,' said the princess, taking the knight's hand and hurrying forwards. The crowd made way and they saw before them, all lit by the garish light of the torches, the Constable's Gate and the planks that had been laid down over the Otterburn where it sluiced through a narrow channel on its way to the lake. Right in the centre of the planks, perched above the rushing torrent, sat old Lord Highmoor. The furious king, his way blocked, stood on the bouncing planks gripping the arm of his teetering bride while his hound cowered on the bank, her tail between her legs.

'I am no traitor,' pleaded Highmoor, his voice just audible above the race of the stream, 'but Your Highness' oldest councillor; for two score years and ten have I served the crown loyally...'

'Loyally?' yelled Gers. 'Get out of my way, thy perfidious old buffoon, or I'll knock thee into the lake!' Letting go of Manicia, the king leant forwards and grabbed the old man by the collar. 'And when we've fished thee out,' he shouted, shaking Highmoor until the planks bounced, 'we'll do what's done to all traitors: we'll cut thee into quarters and I'll give the bits to my daughter as a wedding gift!' Manicia, staring down at the torrent, wobbled precariously and gave a fearful little scream.

But her cry was not heard for suddenly the ground rumbled and shook and a huge sound came issuing from the gateway. It rang, iron on stone; the sound of galloping hoofs, thundering, rolling and rever-berating along the gate passage. The king released his grip on the chancellor's neck, took a step backwards and knocked Manicia off balance so that she tumbled, wailing, into the rushing waters below.

But not a glance did he spare for her, for out of the gate, bursting forth from a thralldom of stone and iron, came a creature of dreams.

Swift he came, shining like the stars, and in his wake a mob of horses – wide-eyed and wide-nostrilled, slipping, colliding, scrambling – hurtled headlong through the passage. The creature of dreams passed beneath the portcullis' iron teeth, found his path blocked, and leapt.

Clothed in light, mane and tail streaming, the unicorn rose into the air. For an eternity, or just a heartbeat, he rose. Below him yawned the chasm and its tumultuous waters, above him stretched the glory of the boundless sky. He was free, unfettered; durance fell from him like darkness at dawn.

The nobles, courtiers and townsfolk – all who had open hearts and minds, and un-blinded eyes – stood immobile and entranced. For that soaring moment only the creature of dreams was real to them and all of their fears, falsehoods and doubts flew away. Hearts brimmed with love.

But not the king's heart. Gers saw only that the thing he prized above all else was escaping him. Perhaps he had forgotten about that sword-sharp horn for as the unicorn began his descent; as he stretched out his neck, reaching for the far bank, the king jumped up, arms raised and fingers clutching. His voice was almost unintelligible in its fury. 'Thou'rt mine!' he bellowed. Desperation and anger gave him strength; his leap was extraordinarily agile for an old, fat man, and his hands grabbed at the unicorn's head and neck and gripped hard onto a hank of mane.

Encumbered with so much weight, the unicorn came down too soon, landed on the end of a plank and kicked off desperately. The plank bounced, flipped into the air and, turning a circle, plummeted into the torrent below. Scrambling at the bank, horribly weighed down, the unicorn's flailing hind legs found purchase on a charred strut of the destroyed drawbridge and with an almighty push he sprang up onto the roadway.

Staggering and spinning, the unicorn lowered his head and the king slid away from him at last, down the long horn, one hand tenaciously clutching a fistful of mane. He fell onto his feet, a benevolent and mildly surprised look upon his face, and then he toppled backwards, over the bank's edge and down into the surging stream. Like a loose sack of millet he fell, and the blood spurting from his body left a black swath down the channel wall.

The unicorn, trailing light, spun about and leapt forwards upon the road. His eyes were black, his nostrils red, his horn stained, and his moon-white coat was splashed with blood. The crowds scattered before him.

Behind him came a crash of iron-shod hoofs as a big grey stallion landed after jumping clean across the channel. Four more horses cleared the huge gap, two tried and failed, falling back into the stream, and three more on the opposite side scrambled frantically to stop but slid over the edge. Several more got across on the remaining, bouncing, teetering plank and the grey stallion led them all in a flying gallop down the street towards the town gates. But the unicorn had left them far behind; fleet as a winter's wind, unstoppable as a gale at sea, he fled through the gates and was gone.

Courtiers and townsfolk alike, nobles, knights, guards and servants, all stood for a moment frozen in place – stunned, entranced, aghast – but Winterhued ran to the channel's edge and looked wild eyed down into the swift torrent of snow-melt. Dalgonar, calling for torches, followed behind her and took her arm as though he feared she might jump in. At the very lip of the channel the king's hound trembled, staring down into the churning black water and crying; below, several fallen horses struggled against the current that swept them towards the lake.

'There,' gasped Winterhued, pointing downstream, 'he liveth yet... I saw him struggling.' She pulled away from the knight, tugging the cloak from her shoulders.

'Nay, Winter,' he said urgently, 'thou canst do naught. The stream is too swift... too cold. He shall be swept into the lake where the water is calm... we can find a boat...'

'But he is hurt and old and he cannot swim... he will drown before the lake.' Kicking off her shoes, she took a step towards the channel's edge. 'He is my father; I must try.'

The knight put out a desperate hand to stop her. 'Do not risk all for a father so unkind,' he pleaded as she twisted away from him. 'Winter, he's already dead!'

But she was gone.

Looking down into the current, he saw her rise to the surface, gasping at the bitter cold. Her gown, still full of air, buoyed her up and with a flick of her wet hair she struck out, swimming strongly. He heard a scrabble of claws beside him, and saw the king's old hound leap out into the air, legs flailing, and hit the water with a splash. The knight, scarcely aware of what he was doing, made a move to follow but was stopped by a hand gripping his wrist. 'Don't be a fool,' said Almendral at his shoulder, 'thou'rt in armour.'

'Get it off me then.' But glancing round at his brother, the knight saw something else and cursed softly. 'Go Ali,' he said, pulling away; 'follow her... along the bank; try to fish her out; don't let her out of thy sight. I'll be with thee as soon as I may.'

Almendral sprang away. 'Travancore,' he said to the tall young man in armour who stared down at the stream in frozen dismay, 'Come with me. Call for torches, men who can swim, ropes, blankets.'

Travancore, despite his surprise at being thus addressed by a man of lesser rank and breeding, set off downstream after the marquess, shouting for his men.

Dalgonar went in the opposite direction and in two strides reached the single plank that still spanned the channel. For he had seen that out in its centre, hanging upside down like a fruitbat and almost invisible in the dark, forgotten Lord Highmoor still miraculously clung. One hand was crushed and bloody from having been stepped on by a horse, but he'd managed to wrap his legs round the plank and he was helped greatly by a large splinter that pinned the hem of his gown to the wood. It was no easy business rescuing the chancellor, for the old man was in agonies of pain and terror and clung like a limpet. 'Trust me, my lord,' coaxed the knight, balancing on the narrow beam as he tried to pry Highmoor from the plank, 'ye're safe now... I won't drop you.'

By the time he had carried the old man to safety and left him in the care of speechless, ashen-faced Ladstock, Winterhued had vanished in the night-shrouded waters and his brother was nowhere to be seen amongst the crowd that thronged the bank.

Dalgonar, his horses loping behind him, ran down the path that led between the channel and the back-walls of a dozen houses to a postern in the town walls and the lake shore beyond. Courtiers and townspeople crowded the way, finding nothing more useful to do than gaze in shock and bewilderment at the rushing waters, or run to and fro with torches and lanterns.

The knight dodged and shouldered his way through the throng. Amongst them, Lady Benicia wailed her sister's name and wept, while beside her, her father the duke stood like a rock in a river, gazing at naught.

At the base of the town wall the knight came upon Almendral, Travancore and four of his men scanning the stream. The water ran like a mill-race, black as pitch in the cold night. Below them three of the fallen horses had been swept into a recess in the bank and scrabbled exhaustedly at the steep sides; one found its footing on an underwater stair and lunged up onto dry land, streaming water and breathing like a forge bellows.

'We tried,' puffed Almendral, out of breath. 'So dark... the water so swift... we thought we had sight of her...'

'She's... ah... surely out in the lake by now, sir,' said Travancore uncertainly. 'We need a boat that's not been burned.' Two of his men had got the postern gate open and Dalgonar ducked through the low opening, halted and stared out at the lake. The others came through behind him and a torch was held aloft, but its light scarcely scratched the darkness.

The moon had not yet risen and the stars cast no light. From the knight's left came the tumultuous hiss of the Otterburn as it rushed into the lake, from before him naught but the whisper of wavelets on the shingle. He could see nothing in the pitch-drowned night.

He turned to his brother, his brows drawn and his face sharp-shadowed in the torchlight. 'I cannot have lost her,' he said.

Manicia was drowning. Seconds after the king had knocked her into the water, a plank of wood had come plummeting down almost on top of her, catching her skirts and dragging her under into turmoil and terror. Yet when it bobbed to the surface up she came too, choking and gasping, struggling to draw breathe in the crushing cold. She'd grabbed hold of the plank as it was swept downstream, bucking and spinning in the torrent.

Hardly knowing up from down or air from water, her hands numb, she lost her grip and went under, thrashing and flailing. Water filled her mouth and nostrils and ran down into her lungs, but the thought that filled her mind was that she would not be Queen of Manydown.

'Hold on,' gasped a voice, a female voice. She felt hands beneath her arms, raising her, pushing her back to the plank; she gripped onto it as though it were the shining crown.

For an eternity she clung, retching and coughing; each time her hands slipped she felt those other hands holding her up. 'Don't let go,' came the breathless voice. The beam of wood thumped and scraped along the side of the channel and, through the veil of hair that hung streaming across her face, she saw a flaring of orange light in the dark.

'Here... we're here,' called the voice beside her, shaking with cold and exhaustion.

The plank hit the bank and turned sideways. Manicia lost her grip again and went under; drowning, she kicked out desperately. Her feet connected with something soft and yielding and she kicked again.

And then she was breathing air instead of water. She could not feel the hand that gripped her numbed wrist but knew she was being lifted; it was he who had slain the dragon who hauled her, streaming water like a dishrag, up onto the bank. He set her down, calling over his shoulder for blankets. 'It's not her,' said another voice as Manicia flopped into a coughing heap.

'Clearly,' said the Dragonslayer. He gripped her shoulders and turned her to look at him. 'I heard her voice,' he said. 'Was she with you?'

'Who?' asked Manicia through shuddering jaws. She could do nothing but shake and cough and he dropped her again and strode away, calling for more light. Booted feet ran by her, torches flared and voices shouted; someone put a blanket round her shoulders. 'Come lady,' said a voice, 'we must get you to a fire. Can ye stand?' Manicia turned her head and through her sodden hair saw Sir Almendral looking down at her disdainfully. She shook so much that her teeth clattered in her head, but wretched as she was, she felt her anger rise. 'Lady?' she croaked. 'I am to be thy Queen!'

Almendral's expression didn't change. 'The king is dead, lady,' said he, 'and so, perhaps, is Winterhued. I would have thrown you back in.' He stared at her. 'Can ye stand?' he repeated.

Manicia shook her head as slowly, dully, it dawned on her that it was the princess who had saved her life.

Winterhued, tumbling through gelid darkness, felt the urgent torrent of the stream slow as it swept out into the lake. But she could not get back to the surface and no longer knew if she faced up or down.

She'd been sure of staying alive when she dived in because she was a good swimmer, but the current had been relentless, the cold pitiless, and her waterlogged gown had fettered and dragged her down. Even so she had managed to find, not her father but Manicia, and while clinging to her own life, had done her best to preserve the girl's. But on the

verge of rescue, Manicia had kicked her away, kicked her so hard that
the remaining breath was knocked from her body, and the rushing
stream had engulfed and overwhelmed her.

She had no strength to fight now, and her lungs burned. In the
black lake, without sight, without direction, without air, there was
naught left to do. In her mind she spoke the name of the one she loved,
and then she opened her mouth and breathed.

Brenn must have slept for a space for when she returned to con-
sciousness her hip and shoulder were hurting from the floorboards,
and for a confused moment she had no idea where she was. Remembering, she scrambled to her feet and turned towards Ancaios.

He was looking at her.

'Did the dragon kill thee too?' he asked huskily.

'Why? Do I look dead?' said Brenn, suddenly aware that she was
a mess.

'Thou lookst like an angel,' said Ancaios, 'so I must be in heaven.'

'Thou hast low expectations then,' said Brenn, even as the tears
began to run down her face again.

Ancaios smiled. 'I could drink a well dry,' he whispered, and Brenn,
her mind in disarray, hurried across to the buckets beside the door.
Splashing water onto the floor, she managed to get some of it into a
basin to wash the blood from her shaking hands. It was only as she
carried a jug and cup back to her love that she remembered there was
already a jug beside his bed.

Ancaios drank greedily, but though she knelt beside him to prop
his head up, much of the water was spilt. Eventually he sighed, thanked
her, and laid his head back upon the wet pillow.

'Where is this?' he whispered, his eyes wandering about the ceiling
and upper walls of the chamber. 'I thought I was slain.'

Brenn put down the cup. 'The East Tower,' she said shakily. 'Thou rememb'rest a dragon... dost thou remember a knight?'

'Aye,' said Ancaios with a smile; 'he that slew the dragon.'

'He called thee his squire.'

'And so I am... since this morn... if it's still the same day. He said he shall make me a knight... but I know not how I yet live.' Ancaios frowned. 'I have a big hole in me but it doesn't hurt; methinks 'tis magic.'

'It *is* magic,' whispered Brenn, taking his hand in hers and kissing it. 'Sir Ancaios: that soundeth very fine.'

'For a gong farmer's son.' He still looked pale and ill, but he smiled and his dark eyes shone as he gazed at her. 'Why is thy face so wet, Lady Library? Thou shalt stick the pages of thy books together.'

Brenn laughed, and wiped at her tears with the back of a hand. 'Never fear, Sir Book,' said she; 'While the roof doth leak I have taken the volumes from my shelves.' She stroked his hand. 'How dost thou feel?'

'As quick as a squashed snail,' he murmured.

'I've never wanted to kiss a squashed snail before.' Before he could speak she leaned across him so that the wealth of her autumn hair fell around his face, and kissed his lips.

'Again,' said Ancaios and so she kissed him again, and then three more times.

'I wouldn't mind if I were to die now,' he whispered.

'But thou shalt not die.'

'No, not now...' He lay for a while watching the torchlight flickering across the ceiling timbers then turned his head to look at her again. 'Brenn,' he breathed, 'I saw something on the common... beside the wooded knoll.'

'A knight slaying a dragon.'

'That too... but I saw something else.' Ancaios' voice was so soft that Brenn could scarcely make out his words. 'I saw a unicorn, Brenn... and some of its magic got inside me. I can feel it there...'

'A unicorn? On the common? That is not possible.'

'I know that, and yet I saw it.'

Brenn shook her head wonderingly. 'If that is so then unicorns must be becoming as plentiful as kisses.' And she leaned over and kissed him again.

He was with her, the one she loved, gently pushing strands of wet hair back from her face. 'I thought I had lost thee,' said he in his deep, quiet voice.

Waves sighed upon the shingle and torchlight spangled in Winterhued's eyes. 'How didst thou find me?' she whispered, and coughed again, though it seemed she had already coughed up half the lake. She knelt upon the shore, wrapped in blankets and surrounded by folk holding torches and lanterns and more blankets, but she saw only Dalgonar.

'It was the king's old hound,' said he. 'She jumped in after Gers but found thee instead. I saw her dragging thee shorewards and waded out to help.' He laughed quietly. 'When I lifted thee from the water she growled and might have bitten me if her jaws had not been full of gown.'

'Gunda... where is she?'

'Here,' said the knight with a sideways glance. Winterhued turned her head and saw that the hound, swathed in blankets, sat only inches away and watched her anxiously. She reached out her hand and Gunda licked it, whimpering softly and trembling with cold. 'I thank thee, brave girl,' whispered Winterhued. 'Thy master hath gone.' She looked back at Dalgonar and his eyes, lucent in the lamplight, held her. 'He *hath* gone... my father?'

'Aye Winter,' said he gently; 'thou knowest he was lifeless when he went into the water. The guards search along the shore; I think they will not find him in the dark.' He stroked her cheek. 'Come, we must get thee and Gunda to a fire.' He went to lift her, all sodden and blanket-wrapped as she was, but she protested. 'I can walk,' she said, and so she did, though her feet were numb and her wet gown clung to her shaking legs. 'Lioness,' said Dalgonar. He kept his arms about her as they crunched their slow way up the shingle, the shivering hound at their heels.

'Nay, I am a fool,' said she. 'Do not protest; 'twas a rash thing that I did. Yet he was my father... and I had come to hate where I should have loved.'

'Thou dost feel guilt?' asked the knight. 'I think he felt none as he disinherited thee.'

'His last words to me were full of hate,' whispered Winterhued. 'When I leapt into the stream all my desire was to change those words for, a long time ago, he was my beloved papa.'

'His *thoughts* changed,' said the knight. 'Saw thou his face?'

'Aye... the unicorn took away his life and his anger. He looked... kind.' Winterhued wiped at her eyes with a half-frozen hand. 'How is the girl?' she asked suddenly. 'She was rescued?'

'Aye, she'll live.'

'Queen Manicia,' she said. 'I am glad my ill-considered swim served some purpose.' They had come up to the portal in the town walls and the Duke of Travancore and two of his men ducked through it before them. 'The poor girl hath lost two husbands in less than two hours,' said Winterhued: 'one eaten by a dragon, the other slain by a unicorn.'

'And then she was rescued by a queen,' added the knight with a smile. 'Who will ever believe her?'

All of a sudden they heard a babble of voices down where the Otterburn spilled into the lake and turned to see a young man emerge out of the dark, running towards them with his feet crunching on the shingle and his lantern swinging. 'We've found him stuck on an abutment,' he called excitedly. 'The king!'

The knight stepped forward. 'Alive?'

'Dead as a boiled frog!' called the lad, and then, noticing who it was that stood behind the knight, fell onto his knees. But he was forgotten as Travancore came darting back out through the gate, issuing orders over his shoulder for a litter, a royal standard, and a guard of honour. He bowed solemnly to Winterhued before striding away down to the water's edge.

In silence, Dalgonar took Winterhued's hand and led her through the gate in the town walls.

The knight's two horses stood beyond the portal; they neighed when they saw their master appear and, as if at a rallying call, the anxious crowds came flocking. Dalgonar held up a hand and the hubbub fell. 'The king is dead,' said he, and knelt before his queen. 'Long live Queen Winterhued.'

All of those about her, courtiers and townsfolk alike, dropped to their knees. 'Long live the Queen.' They did not shout, but their voices were jubilant. Outward spread the murmur: 'The king is dead; long live the queen.' It grew and rose like a hymn to the night: 'Long live our queen; long live Queen Winterhued.'

Winterhued stood before them, the old hound shivering at her feet. She clutched a blanket about her shoulders, her skin was bluish with cold and her hair hung wet and halfway to the ground. She wore no jewellery but a moonstone on a silver chain, and a smile that was surely the very wonder of the world.

It wasn't much of a feast: there was beer, ale and cider, some mulled wine, heated over the fires, and a gallimaufry of pickled and salted stuff to share. But though the townsfolk would have liked more, though their homes were destroyed and they'd lost neighbours, friends and loved ones, they had, for now, done with weeping. For the dragon was dead, their own lives had been spared and beloved Winterhued lived. And she would shortly be crowned Queen of Manydown and, to the surprise of all, would wed the mighty Dragonslayer.

No one returned to the castle, for the single plank across the Otterburn had been removed while a group of soldiers worked to construct a more solid bridge. Even the king's corse, after being borne up from the water's edge, was laid temporarily in a town church where it formed a widening puddle on the flagstones.

Beside a bonfire, blazing high in the ruined market-place, townsfolk mingled with courtiers and castle servants. A juggler juggled, three tumblers tumbled and a band of musicians set a solemn pace for a score of dancers on shawm, sackbut and tambour. Thus it was that after three silent and fearful days, as the stars twinkled in an empty and unthreatening sky, sounds of music and merriment rose up from the town beside the lake.

Far from the subdued celebrations in Lawhill, in the village of Langstone on the east road, another bonfire blazed on the green. The villagers had of course no knowledge of the dragon's death or their princess's impending coronation, but they celebrated the demise of their own monster in rowdy triumph. The guest of honour was the Adder himself, who swung cold, stiff and blood-caked from the gallows, ghoulishly lit by the fire's leaping flames. The long horse-tail of his hair lifted in the breeze as he turned slowly on the end of a rope.

But a second guest was enjoyed the feasting rather more than the Adder. He was a skinny lad who'd been found wandering in the forest that day by the bailiff and his men. Despite having no horses about him (they'd run off, he said), he matched the knight's description, and so Nal of Pengwern, squire of the great knight who had slain their enemy, was conveyed back to Langstone in honour.

Sitting at the boards like a king, lauded by one and all, he had consumed enough roast beef for two men and rather too much ale. His voice slurred, he'd regaled the villagers with a tale of the Adder's slaying, though he didn't tell them he hadn't actually seen the event because he'd been hiding in the forest at the time. He finished his tale by describing, in gory detail, how he'd hacked off the sword hand of the toughest and meanest of the outlaws... after the Adder of course. Then, befuddled with ale and confused by the skirling and thudding of pipes and drums, he fell off his chair.

The moon rose in the east as they carried him from the green. 'Think I'll stay 'ere,' he muttered as they tucked him into a comfortable bed. 'Ye needin' a baker? I make ex... exel... excellen' bread...'

Eudora had been sitting in the cold and the dark for she knew not how long. So much filled her mind that she would have to spend the rest of her life thinking of it... but not here. She got up. Pins and needles pricked her, yet she was well... very well; the person she had been that morning was a stranger to her and now she felt clear-headed and strong.

The unicorn and the horses were long gone, and she'd seen not a soul since they'd disappeared through the Constable's Gate. *He must have got away*, she thought, and somehow knew this to be true.

Faint sounds of music drifted up from the town, indicating a celebration of some sort; that must be why no one had come back to the castle. Eudora looked out across the broken wall to the east where spots of torchlight moved along the east road and up over the common; perhaps the lights of sightseers going to ogle the fallen dragon, or soldiers searching for dead comrades. A few campfires burned too, up where the road came out of the forest; surely the army's baggage train had set up camp there to wait for its surviving soldiers to straggle in.

So many, thought Eudora. *But the unicorn will avoid them; he will know where to go.*

Walking to the menagerie door, she shut and locked it. Her bare feet were not cold, in fact she wasn't cold at all; surely the unicorn's magic lingered. That thought made her recall Sir Dechmont and those others so sorely injured and she knew she had a job to do; she must return to the infirmary to help Lady Brenn.

She stooped to pick up the gold collar and chain, and straightening, saw that the moon had risen, huge and low in the east.

All of a sudden she heard song.

Though it did not seem to be her ears that received it she heard it nonetheless, for it resonated in every part of her being. It was song that could make the stars dance and weep, it was joyful and sorrowful and so beautiful that the world surely stopped turning just to listen.

Eudora stood beside the broken wall at the top of the ditch and gazed with shining eyes into the night. The east wind blew her skirts out behind her and the golden collar dangled forgotten from her hand. She knew from whence came that song.

For it was the song of two unicorns, voicing their exultation to the world as they ran together, fearless and sorrowless, swift as the wind, keepers of all the mysteries of heaven and earth.

Eastward they ran – silver gleams in night's shadows – up across the common, through the forest, beneath the wide sky, under the moon and the stars, towards the sunrise. Eastward they ran, ever eastward, away and away from the world of men.

Winterhued and Dalgonar heard the unicorns' song as they walked in moonlight upon the lakeshore. Winterhued was dry again, dressed in a borrowed gown that was too short for her. She halted to listen, leaning back against her love, and he wrapped his cloak around the both of them. A spring-scented wind blew across the water, shivering the lake's moon-silvered surface, and lifting and entwining the lovers' dark hair. Along the castle walls behind them, a line of swallowtail pennants drifted, their sinuous lengths curling and unfolding along the breeze.

The song of the unicorns rose, fell and faded until only the wind was heard, sighing and whispering around Lawhill's time-eroded battlements.

'Gone forever,' breathed Winterhued.

The knight was silent. He rocked her gently in his arms and kissed her hair.

She looked round at him. 'Together, my lord,' she said, very softly, 'together we shall rule Manydown and turn it into a paradise for all.'

Dalgonar kissed her again. 'It is already a paradise,' said he.

Winterhued turned in his arms and looked up at his face with its slight, wry smile. 'O, renowned, unvanquished knight,' she murmured, smiling too, 'after all that thou hast seen in the world... all that thou hast done... shalt thou not soon grow weary of this dull place?'

'Never,' he answered. 'Every road I ever travelled eventually led me back to this land of wonders.'

Winterhued laughed softly. 'Manydown?' she said. 'A land of wonders?'

'Only in Manydown,' answered he, 'have I seen a dragon flying, black against the sun, and only in Manydown have I seen unicorns, and heard their voiceless song.' He took her face gently within his hands. 'And only in Manydown...' For a moment he gazed at her as though he wished never to look elsewhere, then bent to kiss her lips, and after that there was no more need for words.

The night was hushed, the breeze had died and only the wavelets sighed as they ran ever and ever up the shingled shore of Lake Silverhow. But somewhere close by a bird, returned from its brief exile, sang a soft piping song to the moon.

THE END

About the author:

E. H. Alger grew up in Melbourne, Australia. After graduating in art and design she went on to a career as an artist and freelance book illustrator, also writing and illustrating an acclaimed children's book, 'Bertie at the Horse Show' (Penguin).

With a passion for history and adventure, she has travelled widely and voyaged the world's oceans aboard seven sailing ships including the great Russian four-masted barques, Kruzenshtern and Sedov.

A horsewoman, animal lover and animal-rights campaigner, she lives in rural Victoria surrounded with rescued animals, including ex-battery hens, roosters, cats, dogs, six horses and a Brahman bull.

www.ingramcontent.com/pod-product-compliance
Lightning Source LLC
Chambersburg PA
CBHW032031120726
47901CB00001BA/87